THE ANNALS
OF THE
HEECHEE

By Frederik Pohl
Published by Ballantine Books

THE HEECHEE SAGA
Gateway
Beyond the Blue Event Horizon
Heechee Rendezvous
The Annals of the Heechee

BLACK STAR RISING

THE COOL WAR

STARBURST

THE WAY THE FUTURE WAS

BIPOHL

POHLSTARS

With Jack Williamson
UNDERSEA CITY
UNDERSEA QUEST
UNDERSEA FLEET
WALL AROUND A STAR
THE FARTHEST STAR

PREFERRED RISK *(with Lester del Rey)*

THE BEST OF FREDERIK POHL
(edited by Lester del Rey)

THE BEST OF C.M. KORNBLUTH
(edited by Frederik Pohl)

THE ANNALS
OF THE
HEECHEE

Frederik Pohl

DEL
REY

A Del Rey Book

BALLANTINE BOOKS · NEW YORK

Copyright © 1987 by Frederik Pohl

Library of Congress Cataloging-in-Publication Data

Pohl, Frederik,
  The annals of the Heechee.

  "A Del Rey book."
  I. Title.
PS3566.036A79   1987   813'.54   86-26584
ISBN 0-345-32565-6

First Edition: March 1987

10 9 8 7 6 5 4 3 2

CONTENTS

CHAPTER

1	On Wrinkle Rock	1
2	On the Wheel	20
3	Albert Speaks	60
4	Some Parties at the Party	70
5	The Tide at Its Crest	79
6	Loves	93
7	Out of the Core	112
8	Up in Central Park	128
9	On Moorea	142
10	In Deep Time	158
11	Heimat	191
12	JAWS	211
13	Kids in Captivity	225
14	Stowaways	250
15	Scared Rats Running	269
16	The Long Voyage	272
17	At the Throne	296
18	Journey's End	313
19	The Last Spaceflight	319
20	Back Home	322
21	Endings	324
22	And Not Endings	332

THE ANNALS
OF THE
HEECHEE

1

On Wrinkle Rock

It isn't easy to begin. I thought of a whole bunch of different ways to do it, like cute:

> You don't know about me without you have read some books that was made by Mr. Fred Pohl. He told the truth, mainly. There was things which he stretched, but mainly he told the truth.

—but my friendly data-retrieval program, Albert Einstein, says I'm too prone to obscure literary references anyway, so the *Huckleberry Finn* gambit was out. And I thought of starting with a searing expression of the soul-searching, cosmic angst that's always (as Albert also reminds me) so much a part of my normal conversation:

To be immortal and yet dead; to be almost omniscient and nearly omnipotent, and yet no more real than the phosphor flicker on a screen—that's how I exist. When people ask what I do with my time (so *much* time! so much of it crammed into each second, and with an eternity of seconds), I give them an honest answer. I tell them that I study, I play, I plan, I work. Indeed, that is all true. I do all these things. But during and between them I do one other thing. I *hurt*.

Or I could just start with a typical day. Like they do in the PV interviews. "A candid look at one moment in the life of the celebrated Robinette Broadhead, titan of finance, political powerhouse, maker and shaker of events on all the myriad worlds." Maybe including a glimpse of me wheeling and dealing—for example, a table-pounding conference with the brass hats at the Joint Assassin Watch or, better still, a session at the Robinette Broadhead Institute for Extra-Solar Research:

I stepped up to the podium in a storm of serious applause. Smiling, I raised my arms to quell it. "Ladies and gentlemen," I said, "I thank each of you for making time in your busy schedules to join us here. You are a distinguished group of astrophysicists and cosmologists, famed theorists and Nobel laureates, and I welcome you to the Institute. I declare this workshop on the fine physical structure of the early universe to be in session."

I really do say that kind of thing, or at least I send down a doppel to do it and my doppel does. I have to. It's expected of me. I'm not a scientist, but through my Institute I supply the cash that pays the bills that lets science get done. So they want me to show up to greet them at the opening sessions. Then they want me to go away so they can work, and I do.

Anyway, I could not decide which of those tracks to begin on, and so I won't use any of them. They're all characteristic enough, though. I admit it. Sometimes I'm a little too cute. Sometimes, maybe even often, I am unattractively burdened with my own interior pain, which never seems to go away.

Often I'm just a touch pompous; but at the same time, honestly, I am frequently quite effective in ways that matter a lot.

The place where I'm actually going to start is with the party on Wrinkle Rock. Please bear with me. You have to put up with me only for a little while, and I have to do it always.

I would go almost anywhere for a really good party. Why not? It's easy enough for me, and some parties happen only once. I even flew my own spaceship there; that was easy, too, and didn't really take any time from the eighteen or twenty other things I was doing at the time.

Even before we got there I could feel the beginning of that nice party tingle, because they had the old asteroid dressed up for the occasion. Left to itself, Wrinkle Rock wasn't much to look at. It was patchy black, spotted with blue, ten kilometers long. It was shaped more or less like a badly planned pear that the birds had been pecking at. Of course, those pockmarks weren't from pecking birds. They were landing sockets for ships like ours. And, just for the party, the Rock had been prettied up with big, twinkly starburst letters—

> Our Galaxy
> The First 100 Years Are the Hardest

—revolving around the rock like a belt of trained fireflies. The first part of what it said wasn't diplomatic. The second part wasn't true. But it was pretty to look at, anyway.

I said as much to my dear portable wife, and she grunted comfortably, settling herself in my arm, "Is garish. Real lights! Could have used holograms."

"Essie," I said, turning my head to nibble her ear, "you have the soul of a cybernetician."

"Ho!" she said, twisting around to nibble back—only she nibbled a lot harder—"Am nothing *but* soul of cybernetician, as are you, dear Robin, and kindly pay attention to controls of ship instead of fooling around."

That was just a joke, naturally. We were right on course, sliding into a dock with that agonizing slowness of all material objects; I had hundreds of milliseconds to spare when I gave the *True Love* its final nudge. So I gave Essie a kiss . . .

Well, I didn't exactly give her a kiss, but let me leave it that way for now, all right?

. . . and she added, "Are making a big deal of this, you agree?"

"It is a big deal," I told her, and kissed her a little harder, and, since we had plenty of time, she kissed me back.

We spent the long quarter of a second or so while *True Love* drifted through the intangible glitter of the party sign in as pleasant and leisurely a fashion as one could wish. That's to say, we made love.

Since I am no longer "real" (but neither is my Essie)—since neither of us is still really *meat*—one may ask, "How do you *do* that?" I have an answer for that question. The answer is, "Beautifully." Also "lavishly," "lovingly," and, above all, "expeditiously." I don't mean we shirk our work. I just mean that it doesn't take long to do it; and so, after we had pleased each other powerfully, and lounged around for a while afterwards languidly, and even showered sharingly (a wholly unnecessary ritual that, like most of our rituals, we do just for fun), we still had plenty of time out of that quarter of a second to study the other docking sockets on the Rock.

We had some interesting company ahead of us. I noted that one of the ships docked ahead of us was a big old original-Heechee vessel, the kind that we would have called a "Twenty" if we'd known that so huge a ship existed, back in the old days. We didn't just spend that time rubbernecking. We're shared-time programs, you know. We can easily do a dozen things at once. So I also kept in touch with Albert, to check on whether there were any new transmissions from the core, and make sure there was nothing from the Wheel, and keep in touch with a dozen other interests of one kind or another; while Essie ran her own search-and-merge scans. So by the time our locking ring mated with one of those bird-pecked holes that were actually the berthing ports for the asteroid, we were both in a pretty good mood and ready to party.

One of the (many) advantages of being what dear Portable-

Essie and I are is that we didn't have to unfasten seat belts and check seals and open locks. We don't have to do anything much. We don't have to move our storage fans around—they stay right where they are, and we go where we like through the electrical circuits of whatever kind of place we happen to be plugged into. (Usually that's the *True Love* when we're traveling, which we usually are.) If we want to go farther than that, we can go by radio, but then we're up against that tiresome lag in round-trip communications.

So we docked. We plugged in to Wrinkle Rock's systems. We were there.

Specifically, we were on Level Tango, Bay Forty-something of the tired old asteroid, and we were not by any means alone. The party had begun. The joint was jumping. There were a dozen people gathered to greet us—people like us, I mean—wearing party hats or holding party drinks, singing, laughing. (There were even a couple of meat people in sight, but they wouldn't even discern that we had arrived for many milliseconds yet.) "Janie!" I shouted at one, hugging her; and "Sergei, *golubka!*" Essie cried, hugging another; and right then, while we were in the first moment of greeting and hugging and being happy, a nasty new voice snapped, "Hey, Broadhead."

I knew the voice.

I even knew what would come next. What bad manners! Flicker, flash, pop, and there was General Julio Cassata, looking at me with the (barely) controlled sneer of soldier-to-civilian contempt, across a broad, bare desktop that hadn't been there a moment before. "I want to talk to you," he said.

I said, "Oh, shit."

I didn't like General Julio Cassata. I never had, though we kept running into each other's lives.

That wasn't because I wanted it that way. Cassata was always bad news. He didn't like civilians (like me) messing in what he still called "military affairs," and he didn't much like machine-stored people of any kind. Cassata was not only a soldier, he was still meat.

Only this time he wasn't meat. He was a doppel.

That was an interesting fact in itself, because meat people don't make doppels of themselves lightly.

I would have pursued that odd fact farther, except that I was too busy thinking about all the things I didn't like about Julio Cassata. His manners are lousy. He had just demonstrated that. There is an etiquette to the gigabit space that we machine-stored people inhabit. Polite machine-stored people don't just dump themselves on each other without warning. They approach politely when they want to talk to you. Maybe they even "knock" on a "door" and wait outside politely until you say, "Come in." And they certainly do not impose their private surrounds on each other. That's the kind of behavior that Essie calls *nekulturny*, meaning it stinks. Just what I would expect from Julio Cassata: He'd overridden the physical bay we were in and the gigabit-space simulation of it that we were jointly occupying. There he was with his desk and his medals and his cigars and all; and that was just plain rude.

Of course, I could have pushed all that out and got back to my own surround. Guys do that sort of thing when they're stubborn. It's like two secretaries one-upping each other about whose boss gets put on the PV-phone first. I didn't choose to do that. It wasn't because I have any hang-up about being rude to rude people. It was something else.

I had finally got around to wondering why the real, or meat, Cassata had made a machine duplicate of himself.

What was before us was a machine simulation in gigabit space, just as my own beloved Portable-Essie was a doppel of my also beloved (but, these days, beloved only at second hand) real-Essie. The original meat-Cassata was no doubt chomping a real cigar several hundred thousand kilometers away, on the JAWS satellite.

When I figured out the implications of that, I actually almost felt sorry for the doppel. So I suppressed all the instinctive words that suggested themselves. I only said, "What the hell do you want from me?"

Bullies respond well to being bullied. He let a little of the fire go out of the steely-eyed glare. He even smiled—I think he meant it to be friendly. His eyes slid from my face over to

Essie, who had popped herself into Cassata's surround to see what was going on, and said, in what could have been intended as a light tone, "Now, now, Mrs. Broadhead, is that any way for old friends to talk to each other?"

"Is very poor way for old friends to talk," she said noncommittally.

I pressed: "What are you doing here, Cassata?"

"I came to the party." He smiled—oily smile, fake smile; he had very little to smile about, considering. "When we came off maneuvers, most of the old ex-prospectors got leave to come here for the reunion. I hitched a ride. I mean," he explained, as though, of all people, Essie and I needed explaining to, "I doppeled myself and put the store on the ship that was coming here."

"Maneuvers!" Essie sniffed. "Maneuvers against what? When Foe come out, are going to pull out six-shooters and fill skunks with holes like Swiss cheese, blam-blam-blam?"

"We have better than six-shooters on our cruisers these days, Mrs. Broadhead," Cassata said genially; but I had had enough small talk.

I asked again, "What do you want?"

Cassata abandoned the smile and got back to his natural state of nasty. "Nothing," said Cassata. "By that I mean *nothing*, Broadhead. I want you to butt out." He wasn't even trying to be genial anymore.

I kept my temper. "I'm not even butting in."

"Wrong! You're butting in right now in your damn Institute. You've got workshops going on. One in New Jersey, one in Des Moines. One on Assassin signatures. One on early cosmology."

Since those statements were perfectly true, I only said, "The Broadhead Institute is in business to do that kind of thing. That's our charter. It's what we founded it for, and it's why JAWS gives me ex-officio status so I have a right to sit in on JAWS planning sessions."

"Well, old buddy," Cassata said happily, "see, you're wrong about that, too. You don't have a *right*. You have that privilege. *Sometimes*. A privilege isn't a right, and I'm warning you not to put it on the line. We don't want you getting in the way."

I really hate those guys sometimes. "Now, look, Cassata," I began, but Essie stopped me before I'd even picked up speed. "Boys, boys! Cannot save this for another time? Came here to party, not to fight."

Cassata hesitated, looking belligerent. Then he nodded slowly, looking thoughtful. "Well, Mrs. Broadhead," he said, "that's not a bad idea. It can keep a while; after all, I don't have to report back for five or six meat hours yet." Then he turned to me. "Don't leave the Rock," he ordered. And vanished.

Essie and I looked at each other. *"Nekulturny,"* she said, wrinkling up her nose as though she still smelled his cigar.

What I said was worse than that, and Essie put her arm around me. "Robin? Is pig, that man. Forget him, okay? Aren't going to let him make you all gloopy and sour again, please?"

"Not a chance!" I said bravely. "Party time! I'll race you to the Blue Hell!"

It was, actually, one hell of a fine party.

I hadn't taken Essie seriously when she asked if I thought the party was too much of a big deal. I knew she didn't mean it. Essie had never been a prospector herself, but every human being alive knew what this party was.

It was to celebrate nothing less than the centennial of the finding of the Gateway asteroid, and if there was ever a bigger deal in the history of the human race, I don't know what it could have been.

There were two reasons why Wrinkle Rock was chosen for the site of the hundredth anniversary party. One was that, basically, the asteroid had been converted into an old folks' home. It was perfect for the geriatric cases. When the treatment for atherosclerosis made the osteoporosis worse, and the antitumor phages brought on Ménière's syndrome or Alzheimer's, Wrinkle Rock was the place to be. Old hearts didn't have to pump so hard. Old limbs didn't have to struggle to keep a hundred kilos of meat and bone erect. The maximum gravity anywhere was about one percent of Earth-normal. Totterers could trot and skip; they could turn cartwheels if they wanted to. They couldn't be caught by slow, uncertain reflexes in front of a speeding car; there weren't any cars. Oh, they could die, of course. But that didn't have to be fatal, because Wrinkle Rock had the very best (and most heavily used) personality-storage facilities in the universe. When the old meat carcass passed the point of repair, the ancient put himself in the hands of the Here After people, and the next thing he knew he was seeing the world with unflawed vision, hearing the tiniest sound, forgetting nothing, learning fast. He was bloody well reborn!—only without the mess and nastiness of the first time. Life—maybe I should say "life"—as a machine-stored intelligence was not the same as being in your own body. But it wasn't bad. In some ways it was better.

So say I, and I ought to know.

You never saw a happier bunch of machine-stored citizens than the folks who lived on Wrinkle Rock. It really was a rock. It was a lumpy old asteroid, a few kilometers through, more or less, just like the million others that circle the Sun between Jupiter and Mars or some other place. Well—not *just* like. This particular asteroid was pierced and drilled with tunnels from crust to crust. No human being had drilled them. We found it that way; and that was the other reason why it was the best place to have the celebration for the hundredth anniversary of human interstellar flight.

Wrinkle Rock, you see, was quite an unusual asteroid, even a unique one. Originally it circled the Sun in an orbit at right angles to the ecliptic. That was the merely unusual part. The unique part was that when it was found, it had been stuffed full of ancient Heechee spaceships. Not just one or two, but *lots* of them—nine hundred and twenty-four, in fact! Ships that still worked!—well, that worked most of the time, anyway, especially if you didn't care where you were going. We never knew where that would be, at first. We got in the ship, and we fired 'er up, and leaned back, and waited, and prayed. Sometimes we hit lucky.

More often, we died. Most of the ones of us still around for the party were the ones who had been lucky.

But every successful voyage in a Heechee ship taught us something, and by and by we could go anywhere in the Galaxy, and even be pretty sure of arriving alive. We even improved on the Heechee technology in a few ways. They used rockets to get from dirtside to low orbit; we used Lofstrom loops. Then the asteroid wasn't necessary anymore to the people running the space-exploration program.

So they moved it into Earth orbit.

First they were going to turn it into a museum. Then they decided to make it a home for survivors of the Heechee trips. That's when we began to call it Wrinkle Rock. Before that its name had been Gateway.

Now, here we are going to come up against another communication problem, because how do I say what Essie and I did next?

The easy way is just to say we partied.

Well, we did that, all right. That's what you do at parties. We flitted around in our disembodied way to greet and hug and trade catch-up stories with our disembodied friends—not that all our friends on the Rock were disembodied, but we didn't bother with the meat ones right away. (I don't want to give the impression we don't love our meat friends. They are just as dear to us as the machine-stored ones, but, my God, they're tediously *slow*.)

So for the next tens of thousands of milliseconds it was just one long succession of, "Marty! Long time no see!" and, "Oh, Robin, *look* how young Janie Yee-xing has made self!" and, "Remember the way this place used to *smell*?" It went on for a long time, because after all this was a pretty big party. Well, I'll give you the numbers. After about the first fifty big hugs and glad lies I took a moment to call up my faithful data-retrieval program, Albert Einstein. "Albert," I said when he ambled in, blinking at me amiably, "how *many*?"

He sucked his pipe a moment, then pointed the stem at me. "Quite a lot, I'm afraid. There were, all in all, thirteen thousand eight hundred forty-two Gateway prospectors, first to last. Some are, of course, irretrievably dead. A number of others have chosen not to come, or couldn't, or perhaps are not here yet. But my present count is that three thousand seven hundred twenty-six are present, about half of whom are machine-stored. There are also, to be sure, a number of guests of former prospectors, as in the case of Mrs. Broadhead, not to mention a number of patients here for medical reasons unconnected with exploration."

"Thank you," I said; and then, as he started to leave, "One more thing, Albert. Julio Cassata. It has been bugging me to try to figure out just why he is getting nasty about the Institute workshops, and especially why he is here at all. I'd appreciate it if you could look into the matter."

"But I already am doing that, Robin." Albert smiled. "I'll report to you when I think I have some information. Meanwhile, have a nice time."

"I already am," I said, satisfied. An Albert Einstein is a handy gadget to have around; he takes care of things when I'm having fun. So I went back to partying with an easy mind.

We didn't know all of the 3,726 reuniting veterans. But we knew an awful lot of them; and that's what makes it a little hard to tell you exactly what we were doing, because who wants to hear how many times one of us shrieked to one of them, or one of them cried to one of us, "What a surprise! How wonderful you look!"

We zoomed through gigabit space all up and down and through the riddled quadrants and levels and tunnels of the old rock, greeting this one and that one of our colleagues and machine-stored peers. We had drinks with Sergei Borbosnoy in the Spindle—Sergei had been Essie's classmate in Leningrad before taking off for Gateway and, eventually, a mean, lingering death from radiation exposure. We spent a long time at a cocktail party in the Gateway museum, wandering with glasses in hand around the exhibits of artifacts from Venus and Peggys Planet, and bits and pieces of tools and fire pearls and prayer-fan datastores from all over the galaxy. We ran into Janie Yee-xing, who had been going with our friend Audee

Walthers III before he took off to visit the Heechee in the core. Probably she'd wanted to marry him, I thought, but the question no longer was relevant, because Janie had got herself killed trying to land a chopper in the middle of a winter-weather hurricane on a planet called Persephone. "Of all dumb things," I said, grinning at her. "An *aircraft* accident!" And then I had to apologize, because nobody likes to hear that their death was dumb.

Those were the stored souls like us, the ones we could talk to easily and without intermediaries. Of course, there were a lot of meat people we wanted to greet, too.

But that was a whole other problem.

Being a disembodied mind in gigabit space is not easily described.

In a way, it's like sex.

That is, it's something that you can't easily say what it's like to someone who hasn't tried it. I know this about sex, because I've tried to describe the joys of making love to some rather odd people—well, not exactly *people* but intelligences—never mind who they were just yet—and it takes a lot of work. After many milliseconds of listening to my attempts at description and discussion and metaphor—and a lot of incomprehension—what they've said was something like, "Oh, yeah, now I get it! It's like that other thing you do— *sneezing*—right? When you know you have to, and you can't do it, only you *have* to? And it gets to be more and more of an itch until you can't stand it if you don't sneeze, and then you do, and it feels good? Is that right?"

And I say, "No, that's wrong," and give up.

It's just as hard to tell what it's like in gigabit space. I can describe some of the sorts of things I do there, though. For instance, when we were drinking with Sergei Borbosnoy in the Spindle, we weren't "really" in the Spindle. A Spindle did, actually, exist; it was the central hollow in the Gateway asteroid. At one time the bar it contained—it was called the Blue Hell—had been every prospector's favorite place for drinking and gambling and trying to get up enough courage to sign on for one of those terrifying, often fatal and one-way rides in a Heechee ship. But the "real" Spindle wasn't used for drinking anymore. It had been converted into a sunlamped solarium for the feeblest cases among the geriatric inhabitants of Wrinkle Rock.

Did that cause us any problems? Not a bit! We just created our own simulated Spindle, complete with Blue Hell gambling casino, and we sat there with Sergei, swilling down icy vodka and nibbling pretzels and smoked fish. The simulation had tables, bartenders, pretty serving waitresses, a three-piece band playing hits of half a century ago, and a noisy, celebrating, party crowd.

It had, in fact, everything you would expect in a happy little gin mill except one thing. "Reality." None of it was "real."

The whole scene, including some of the partying people, was nothing but a collection of simulations taken out of machine storage. Just as I am, just as Essie is in her portable form—just as Sergei was.

You see, we didn't have to be in the Spindle, real or otherwise. When we sat down to have a drink, we could have created any setting we liked. We often did, Essie and I. "Where want to dine?" Essie would ask, and I'd say, "Oh, I don't know, Lutece? La Tour d'Argent? Or, no, I know, I've got a taste for fried chicken. How about a picnic in front of the Taj Mahal?"

And then our support systems would dutifully access the files marked "Taj Mahal" and "Chicken, fried," and there we would be.

Of course, neither the background nor the food and drinks would be "real"—but neither were we. Essie was a machine-stored analog of my dear wife, who was still alive somewhere or other—and still my wife, too. I was the stored remainder of me, what was left after I died on the exciting occasion when we first met a living Heechee. Sergei was stored Sergei, because he'd died, too. And Albert Einstein—

Well, Albert was something else entirely; but we kept him with us, because he was a hell of a lot of fun at a party.

And none of that made any difference! The drinks hit just

as hard, the smoked fish was just as fat and salty, the little bits of raw *crudités* were just as crisp and tasty. And we never gained weight, and we never had hangovers.

While meat people—

Well, meat people were a whole other thing.

There were plenty of meat people among the 3,726 Gateway veterans gathered to celebrate the Rock's hundredth anniversary. A lot of them were good friends. A lot of the others were people I would have loved to have for friends, because all us old prospectors have a lot in common.

The difficulty with meat people is trying to carry on a conversation with them. I'm fast—I operate in gigabit time. They're *slow*.

Fortunately, there's a way of dealing with the situation, because otherwise trying to talk to one of those torpid, tardy, flesh and blood people would drive me right out of my mind.

When I was a kid in Wyoming, I used to admire the chess masters who hung around the parks, pushing their greasy pieces over the oil-smeared boards. Some of them could play twenty games at once, moving from board to board. I marveled. How could they keep track of twenty positions at once, remembering every move, when I could barely keep one in my head?

Then I caught on. They didn't remember anything at all.

They simply came to a board, took in the position, saw a strategy, made a move, and went on to the next. They didn't have to remember anything. Their chess-playing minds were so quick that any one of them could take the whole picture in while his opponent was scratching his ear.

See, that's the way it is with me and meat people. I could not stand to carry on a conversation with a living person without doing at least three or four other things at the same time. They stood like statues! When I saw my old buddy Frankie Hereira, he was licking his lips as he watched some other ancient codger struggling to open a bottle of champagne. Sam Struthers was just coming out of the men's room, his mouth opening to shout a greeting to some other live person in the hall. I didn't speak to either. I didn't even try. I just set up an image of myself and started it in motion, one for each of them. Then I "went away."

I don't mean I actually went anywhere; I just paid attention to other things. I didn't have to stay around, because the subroutines in my programs were perfectly capable of walking one of my doppels toward Frankie and one toward Sam, and smiling, and opening "my" mouth to speak when they noticed "me." By the time I had to make a decision on what it was I wanted to say, I would be back there.

But that was the meat people. Fortunately for my boredom threshold, there were lots of machine-stored people (or not exactly all of them *people*) as well. Some were very old friends. Some were people I knew because everybody knew them. There was Detweiler, who had discovered the Voodoo Pigs, and Liao Xiechen, who was a terrorist until the Heechee appeared and he changed sides. He was the one who had exposed the entire gang of murderers and bomb-throwers in the American space program. There was even Harriman, who had actually seen a supernova explode, and coasted long enough on the expanding wavefront to win a five-million-dollar science award in the old days. There was Mangrove, who wound up in a Heechee station orbiting a neutron star and found out that the queer, tiny, maneuverable globes moored to the station were actually sample collectors and could be made to go down to the star's surface and bring back some eleven tons—a chunk almost as large as a fingernail—of neutronium. Mangrove ultimately died of the radiation dose he got bringing it home, but that didn't keep him from joining us on Wrinkle Rock.

So I raced along the conduits of Gateway, quick as the lightning in the serried sky, and greeted a hundred old friends and new. Sometimes Portable-Essie was with me. Sometimes she was off on her own excursions of greeting. Faithful Albert was never out of call, but he never joined in the hugs and embraces, either. Fact was, he never showed himself except to me, or when invited to. Nobody in that giggly, steamy, high-school-reunion, New-Year's-Eve, wedding-reception atmosphere wanted to bother with a mere data-retrieval system, even though he was about the very best friend I had ever had.

So when we were back in the Spindle, back drinking with Sergei Borbosnoy, and things got a little tedious for me, I whispered, "Albert?"

Essie gave me a look. She knew what I was doing. (After all, she wrote his program, not to mention my own.) She didn't mind; she just went on rattling along in Russian to Sergei. There wasn't anything wrong in that, because of course I understand Russian—speak it fluently, along with a bunch of other languages, because, after all, I've had plenty of time to learn. What was wrong was that they were talking about people I didn't know and didn't care about.

"You called, O Master?" Albert murmured in my ear.

I said, "Don't be cute. Have you figured out what's going on with Cassata?"

"Not entirely, Robin," he said, "because if I had I would of course have sought you out to report. However, I have drawn some interesting inferences."

"Infer ahead," I whispered, smiling at Sergei as he poured another freezing shot of vodka into my glass without even looking at me.

"I perceive three discrete questions," said Albert comfortably, settling himself down to a nice, long tutorial. "The question of the relevance of the Institute seminars to JAWS, the question of the maneuvers, and the question of the presence of General Cassata himself here. These could be further subdivided into—"

"No," I whispered, "they could not. Quick and simple, Albert."

"Very well. The seminars are, of course, directly related to the central question of the Foe: How they could be recognized through their signatures, and why they wish to alter the evolution of the universe. The only real puzzle is why JAWS should now express concern about the Institute's seminars, since there have been many similar conferences, without objection, from JAWS. I believe that that is related to the question of the maneuvers. For this belief I can adduce a datum:

Since the maneuvers began, all communications from both the JAWS satellite and the Watch Wheel have been embargoed."

"Em*what*?"

"Embargoed, yes, Robin. Cut off. Censored. Prohibited. No communication of any sort with either is allowed. I infer that, first, these events are related, and both are related to the maneuvers. As you know, there was a false alarm on the Watch Wheel some weeks ago. Perhaps it was not a false alarm—"

"Albert! What are you saying?" I wasn't speaking out loud, but Essie gave me a puzzled look. I smiled reassuringly, or tried to, though there was nothing reassuring about the thought.

"No, Robin," said Albert soothingly, "I have no reason to believe the alarm was other than false. But perhaps JAWS is more concerned than I; this would account for the sudden maneuvers, which appear to have included testing some new weapons—"

"Weapons!"

Another look from Essie. Out loud I said cheerily, *"Na zhdrovya,"* and raised my glass.

"Exactly, Robin," said Albert gloomily. "That leaves only the presence of General Cassata to account for. I believe that is quite simply explained. He is keeping an eye on you."

"He isn't doing a very good job of it."

"That's not exactly true, Robin. It is a fact that the general seems to be quite involved in his own affairs just now, yes. He is in fact closeted with a young lady, and has been for some time. But before retiring with the young person he ordered that no spacecraft may leave for the next thirty minutes, organic time. I think it quite probable that he will check up on you before that time has expired, and meanwhile you cannot leave the asteroid."

"Wonderful," I said.

"I think not," Albert corrected me deferentially.

"He can't do that!"

Albert pursed his lips. "In the long run, that is so," he agreed. "Certainly you will sooner or later be able to get higher authority to overrule General Cassata, since there is still some degree of civilian control of the Joint Assassin Watch Service. However, for the moment I am afraid he has the asteroid sealed."

"*Bastard!*"

"Probably he is." Albert smiled. "I've taken the liberty of notifying the Institute of this development, and undoubtedly they will respond—unfortunately, that will be at organic speeds, I'm afraid." He paused. "Is there anything else? Or should I go on with my investigations?"

"Go, damn it!"

I stewed around in gigabit space for a while, trying to cool off. When I thought I was at least marginally fit to talk to again, I rejoined Essie and Sergei Borbosnoy in their simulation of the Blue Hell drinking parlor. Essie glanced up amiably in the middle of a long anecdote, then fixed her eyes on me. "Ho," she said. "Something is upsetting you once more, Robin."

I told her what Albert had told me. "Bastard," she said, concurring with my own diagnosis, and Sergei chimed in, "*Nekulturny*, that one." Then Essie took my hand fondly. "After all, dear Robin," she said, "is not important at this time, you agree? Had no intention of leaving party for quite some considerable time, even meat time."

"Yes, but, damn his soul—"

"That soul is well damned already, dear Robin. Drink a little. Will cheer you up."

So I gave it a try.

It didn't work very well. Nor was I having a lot of fun listening to Essie and Sergei talk.

Understand that I liked Sergei. Not because he was handsome. He wasn't. Sergei Borbosnoy was tall, cadaverous, balding. He had soulful Russian eyes and a sincere, systematic Russian way of swallowing vast quantities of ice-cold vodka, a tumblerful at a time. Since he, too, was dead, he could keep that up indefinitely without getting any drunker than he wanted to be. However, according to Essie, he had had the same capacity when they were students together in Leningrad and both were still meat. That kind of thing is a lot of fun, sure, if you're

a student—especially if you're Russian. It wasn't that much
fun for me.

"So how's it going?" I said genially, when I noticed that
they had stopped talking and were gazing at me.

Essie reached over, smoothed my hair affectionately, and
said, "Hey, old Robin. Is not so interesting for you, all this
old-times stuff, right? Why not go look around?"

"I'm fine," I said untruthfully, and she just sighed and said,
"Go." So I went. I had some private thinking to do, anyway.

It isn't easy for me to say just what I needed to think about
because, no offense, meat people can't quite take in the large
number of assorted topics a shared-time, machine-stored personality like me can keep in my head—that is, my "head"—
all at once.

Which leads me to realize that I've already made a mistake.

Meat people can't juggle that many thoughts. Meat people
are hardly any good at all at parallel processing. Meat people
are linear. What I have to keep in mind is that when communicating with meat people I must make allowances for these
lacks.

So, having tried three times to figure out how to start, I now
perceive that I should have started in a fourth and wholly different way.

I should have started by telling about the kids who lived on
the Watch Wheel.

2
On the Wheel

So now we have to go back a little bit in time. Not very far, actually. At least, it isn't far in meat terms; not *nearly* as far as we'll have to go for some other things, I'm afraid. Just a few months.

I have to tell about Sneezy.

Sneezy was eight years old—in his personal counting of time, which was not the same as any other time we've been talking about. His real name was Sternutator. That was a Heechee name, which is not surprising, because he was a Heechee child. He was unfortunate (or fortunate) enough to be the son of two Heechee specialists in useful disciplines who happened to be on standby when the Heechee found out that they

20

couldn't go on hiding from the universe anymore. There were a whole lot of Heechee personnel waiting for just that emergency. The massed minds of the Heechee Ancient Ancestors recognized the need, and so the standby crews were dispatched at once to the outside galaxy. Little Sternutator went with them.

"Sternutator" was not a fortunate name for a kid in school, at least not when most of his classmates were human beings. In the Heechee language the word meant a kind of particle accelerator, vaguely akin to a laser, in which particles were "tickled" (or, more accurately, stimulated) until they were emitted in one huge, high-powered burst. The boy made the mistake of translating his name literally for his classmates, and naturally they called him Sneezy after that.

Or most of them did. Harold, the smart-ass human nine-year-old who sat behind him in Concepts, said he was one of the Seven Dwarfs, all right, but his parents had picked the wrong dwarf to name him after: "You're too dumb to be Sneezy," said Harold during recess in the play pit after young Sternutator had beaten him out in a pattern-recognition bee. "What you really are is Dopey." And he bounced across the trampoline and gave Sneezy a push that sent him flying into the tai-chi instructor robot. Which was fortunate for both of them. The gamesthing reacted instantly, catching the Heechee boy in its padded arms safely. Sneezy didn't get hurt, and Harold didn't lose his recess time.

The schoolthing at the far end of the pit didn't even see what had happened. So the tai-chi robot dusted Sneezy off and politely adjusted the pod that hung between his legs, and then whispered in his ear—in Heechee—"He's only a child, Sternutator. When he's older he'll be sorry."

"But I don't want them to call me Dopey!" he sobbed.

"They won't. Nobody will. Except Harold, and he'll apologize for it some day." And, as a matter of fact, that part of what the gamesthing said was true. Or almost true. Few of the other eleven children in the class liked Harold. None followed his example except five-year-old Soft-Stick, and that only briefly. Soft-Stick was also a Heechee, and a very young one.

Usually she tried her very best to be accepted by the human children. When she found out that they didn't follow Harold's lead she reversed herself.

So no harm came to young Sneezy, except that when he told his parents about it that night they were, respectively, angry and amused.

The angry one was his father, Bremsstrahlung, who took his skeletal son on his bony knee and hissed, "This is sickening! I am going to request a work order on the schoolthing for letting this fat-bodied bully hurt our son!"

The amused one was Sneezy's mother. "Worse happened to me in school, Bremmy," she said, "and that was back Home. Let the boy fight his own battles."

"Heechee do not *fight*, Femtowave."

"Human beings do, Bremmy, and I speculate that we will have to learn this from them—oh, in a nondamaging way, to be sure." She put down the shiny, light-emitting instrument she had been studying because she had brought some work home from the office. She stepped—it was a motion more like skating than walking, because of the light gravity on the Wheel—across the room to lift Sneezy from his father's lap. "Feed the boy, my dear," she said good-humoredly, "and he will forget the whole matter. You are taking it more seriously than he."

So Femtowave scored fifty percent on that exchange. She was quite right in that her mate was far more upset than their son. (In fact, Bremsstrahlung was reprimanded the next day in his Dream Seat, because he was still irritated. That caused him to allow his mind to drift toward the smart-ass human kid when it should have been kept vacant. That was a no-no. It meant Bremsstrahlung was broadcasting more remanent irritation than he should be letting himself feel—after all, the very purpose of Dream-Seat specialists like himself was to feel nothing, but only be wholly receptive to whatever sensations might come through the Seat.)

However, Femtowave was wrong in her other assertion. Sneezy never forgot it.

Perhaps he did not remember it properly. What stuck with

him was not just that human beings did indeed fight sometimes, but that their fighting did not take place only with those grossly bulging fists or grossly swollen feet. They could hurt someone simply by calling a name.

Did I do it wrong again? Should I have started by explaining the purpose of the Watch Wheel?

Well, better late than never. Let's back up again to get the loose ends reraveled.

When the first Heechee who could not control his own destiny (his name was Captain) met the first human being who could (his name was Robinette Broadhead, because he was me), the Heechee child named Sternutator was on that standby ship in the core with his parents. He was homesick. "Home" was a cozy little city of eight or ten million on a planet of an orangey-yellow little star inside the great black hole that was the core of the Galaxy. Even at three, Sneezy knew what that meant. He knew that the reason his family was on the ship was that there might come a time when they would all have to drop everything and plunge through the Schwarzschild barrier, and rejoin the outside stars.

He didn't expect it to happen to him, of course. No one ever does. Then, when he and his family were assigned to the Watch Wheel, Sneezy found out what *real* homesickness was.

The purpose of the Wheel was simple.

It was a place to put Dream Seats.

The Dream Seats were a Heechee invention that we'd come across before we ever met a living Heechee. What the Heechee used them for (among other things) was to keep tabs on planets where intelligent life might someday evolve but hadn't yet— like our own planet, a few hundred thousand years ago, when the Heechee last came to Earth.

The "dream" signals weren't dreams. Basically, they were emotions. A Heechee (or a human being), encased in the Dream-Seat web of glittering antenna-metal, could feel what others were feeling—even when the others were far away. "Far away" in planetary terms, at least. They didn't work in any useful way in galactic terms. This was because the Dream-

Seat signals unfortunately came by simple EMF. They were limited by the speed of light and obeyed the law of inverse squares, so the effective range of the Dream Seats was only in the billions of kilometers, not the trillions of trillions that separated star from star.

The job of Bremsstrahlung and the other Dream-Seat operators, both human and Heechee, was to be the eyes and ears of the Wheel. Their assignment was to monitor the most important object in either Heechee or human cosmology, the kugelblitz that hung outside the galactic halo. There wasn't any point in the galaxy itself close enough for the purpose. So the Wheel had been built and flown to a position only six AU from the kugelblitz, in its lonely position in near-intergalactic space.

That was, everyone agreed, a reasonable way to do it. It was true that in the event that something at last did transpire around the kugelblitz, and the watchers did finally receive the signals they feared, it would be some forty-odd minutes after the actual event, because that was how long it would take light-speed signals to cross six times the distance of the Earth from the Sun (which is what 6 AU means, dummy).

There was also just a *tiny* bit of uncertainty over whether the Dream Seats would catch anything at all in that event.

After all, some argued, the model of the Dream Seat the Heechee had originally used did not have any sensitivity for, say, machine-stored intelligences like my very own Albert Einstein; it was only after people like Essie tinkered with them that they could handle that chore. What reason was there to believe it would be able to detect the wholly unknown signatures of the basically theoretical Assassins?

But there wasn't anything they could do about the second problem.

And as to the first, as nothing had happened around the kugelblitz for, almost certainly, some millions of years, it did not seem that three quarters of an hour one way or another would make any difference.

The next morning Sneezy was awakened by the voice of the housething in the wall, saying in the Heechee language, "Drill

Day, Sternutator. Drill Day. Wake up now for Drill Day!" It
kept repeating its message until Sneezy had slid out of the
warm hug of his pouchy hammock, and then it relented: "Drill
Day, Sternutator—but it is only a Class Two Drill. There will
be no school."

That was a case of bad news turned good for Sneezy! He
slung his pod between his skinny thighs and pulled on the rest
of his clothes and put a call through to Harold—for they did
not always fight—while he oiled his teeth. "Shall we watch
the ship come in?" Sneezy proposed, and Harold, rubbing
sleep out of his eyes, yawned and said, "You bet your tiny
ass, Dopey. Meet you in ten minutes at the schoolhall corner."

Since it was a Drill Day, even a Class Two Drill, both
Sneezy's parents were already gone to their posts, but the
housething parented for both of them. It pleaded with Sneezy
to eat some breakfast (not this morning! but he let it make
him a sandwich to eat on the run) and urged him to take an airbath (but he'd had one the night before, and even his father
was not that strict about hygiene). Sneezy closed the apartment
door on the housething's entreaties and hurried through the
quiet Drill-Day passages of the Wheel toward the schoolhall.

When Harold was not being overbearing, and Sneezy not
sullenly resentful, they were friends.

That hadn't happened right away. Harold was nearly the first
human being Sneezy ever saw, and Sneezy was definitely Harold's first Heechee. The looks of each appalled the other. To
Sneezy, Harold looked fat, bloated, grossly swollen—about
like a corpse that's been in the water for a week, maybe. To
Harold, Sneezy looked worse than that.

The thing a Heechee looks most like is a human being who
has died in the desert and dried out to rope and leather. Sneezy
had arms and legs like a person, but he didn't have any flesh
to speak of on them. And, of course, he had that funny *pod*.
Not to mention that faint ammonia smell that hovers around
all Heechee all the time.

So friendship wasn't instinctive at first. On the other hand,
they didn't have much choice. There were fewer than fifty
children on the whole Watch Wheel, and two-thirds of those

were in the other schools spaced around the rim. So their choice of peers was limited. The babies, six-year-olds and younger, of course didn't count. The near-adult teenagers counted a lot, to be sure—either Sneezy or Harold would have been thrilled to be allowed to hang out with any of them—but they also, of course, didn't want to be bothered with *kids*.

They could have gone to one of the other sectors. Even eight-year-old Sneezy had done it many times, alone or with classmates. But there was nothing in either of the other sectors that was not duplicated in their own, and the children there were strangers.

There was no rule against Sneezy going almost anywhere he liked, in fact, with companions or without—at least, if you didn't count the forbidden cubicles on the outer perimeter where the Dream Seats were constantly manned. Sneezy wasn't forbidden to play in dangerous areas. There weren't any dangerous areas. In the huge Watch Wheel there were certainly places where truly dangerous amounts of energy were deployed without warning—for signal bursts, for spin regulation, for mass shifting—but there was no employment of energy anywhere on the Wheel that was not constantly monitored by unflagging machine intelligences, and often enough by stored dead human or Heechee intelligences as well. And of course there was no danger from *people*. There were no kidnapers or rapists on the Wheel. There were no uncapped wells to fall into or forests to get lost in. There were groves of trees here and there, sure, but none that even an eight-year-old could not see his way out of from its very center. If any child got lost even for a moment, he had but to ask the nearest workthing for directions and be set at once on his way. That is, a human child would do that. A Heechee child like Sneezy didn't even need to find a workthing, because he could simply inquire of the Ancient Ancestors in his pod.

The Watch Wheel was so safe, in fact, that most of the children, and even some of the grown-ups that served it, sometimes forgot what supreme danger they were watching for.

So they had to be reminded. Even for the children there were the frequent Drills—especially for the children, because when and if the watchers in the Dream Seats ever found what they were watching for, as some day they surely would, the children would have to take care of themselves. No adult would then be able to take care of them. Even the workthings would be busy, their programs instantly switched to analysis and communication and data storage. The children would have to find an approved place to hide—to stay out of the way, really—and cower in it until they were told they could come out again.

There were precedents for this sort of thing. In the middle of the twentieth century, schoolkids in America and the Soviet Union had had to learn to leap under their desks, lie prone, clasp their hands over the backs of their necks, and sweat with fear—if they failed in any of this, their teachers told them, the nuclear bombs would French-fry them. For the children on the Watch Wheel the stakes were higher. It was not only their own lives that might be lost. If they caused trouble, what might be lost was, perhaps, everything.

So when there was a Drill they, too, sweated with fear.

At least, they usually did. But now and then there was a Class Two Drill.

"Class Two" meant only that routine precautions were to be taken because a supply ship was coming in. Class Two Drills were not scary at all—at least, they were not if you didn't think the thing through. (If you did, it was frightening to realize that the Watch Wheel had to shut down all its normal activities, while even the off-duty Watchers hurried into the extra Dream Seats, to make sure that some undesired thing was not showing up under cover of that very desired thing, a supply ship.)

There was no school on the days when a supply ship came in. There was no work done anywhere on the Wheel (always excepting the Dream Seats), because everybody would be too busy with the ship docking. Those families who had served their time and were ready to be rotated would be packing, and gathering at the dock to get their first sight of the ship that would take them back to the warmly inviting huddle of stars that was the Galaxy. And everybody else would be getting

ready to oversee offloading the supplies and the new
personnel.

By the time Sneezy got to the schoolhall corner he had already eaten his sandwich, and Harold was waiting. "You're
late, Dopey!" the human boy snapped.

"They didn't sound the sighting signal yet," Sneezy pointed
out, "so we aren't late for anything."

"Don't argue! That's a baby thing to do. Come on."

Harold led the way. He assumed that was his right. He was
not only older than Sneezy (at least in personal time, though
actually, in terms of the great, ever-expanding clock of the
universe, Sneezy had been born several weeks before Harold's
great-great-grandfather), but he outmassed Sneezy three to
one, forty kilograms of Harold to not much more than fifteen
for the youthful, skeletally skinny Heechee boy. Harold Wroczek was a tall child with pale hair and blueberry-colored eyes.
But he was not much taller than Sneezy, whose people were
all emaciated and elongated by human standards.

To Harold's annoyance, the other thing he was not more of
than Sneezy was strong. Under that dry, leathery Heechee skin
were powerful tendons and muscles. Though Harold tried to
climb the handholds to the docking levels faster than Sneezy,
the Heechee boy kept up easily. He was off the top of the
ladder before Harold was, so Harold panted up to him: "You
watch it, Dopey! Don't get in the way of the workthings!"

Sneezy didn't bother to answer. Not even a two-year-old on
the Wheel would have been stupid enough to get in the way
on such an occasion. The ships came only four or five times
in a standard year. They didn't linger. They didn't dare to, and
no one dared delay them.

So as soon as the boys were in the huge spindle-shaped space
of Bay 2, they retreated as close to a wall as they could, well
away from the scurrying carrythings and the grown-ups arriving to watch the ship come in.

All the landing docks, Bay 2 included, were on the inside of
the Wheel. Its external shell was transparent at that point, but
there wasn't anything to be seen through it yet except the inside

curve of the Wheel itself, with the other two landing docks, identical to the one they were in but empty, peering in at them.

"I can't see the ship," Harold complained.

Sneezy didn't answer. The only answer was to say that of course Harold could not, since the ship was still approaching faster than the speed of light, but Harold had explained often enough to Sneezy that he didn't enjoy the dumb Heechee habit of giving answers everybody knew to questions that weren't really meant to be answered.

Traffic to the Wheel was almost all one-way, except for people. The human and Heechee complement were sent back when their tours of duty were over, usually roughly the equivalent of three standard Earth years. Then they went back to the Galaxy and their homes, wherever those might be. Most went to Earth, quite a few to Peggys Planet, others to one of the habitats. (Even the Heechee usually went to some human planet or place rather than back to their real homes in the core, because of time dilation and mostly because there was too much need for Heechee in one capacity or another outside it.) But supplies never went back. Machinery, instruments, parts, recreational materials, medical outfits, food—they stayed. When the items were consumed or broken or outmoded (or when the food supplies passed through the bodies of Wheel inhabitants to become excrement), they were recycled or simply retained as extra mass for the Wheel. Extra mass was a good thing. The more mass the Watch Wheel had, the less it would be affected by movements inside it, and so the less energy would have to be expended to keep it spinning straight and true.

So the cargo-handling carrythings had little to do while the ship was coming in, only to stack the personal possessions of returning personnel. There wasn't much of that; there were only eight families to be rotated.

A mellow note sounded; the ship was in normal space.

The dockmaster stood over his screens and boards, checked the readings, and called, "Lights!" It wasn't an order. It was a courtesy for the audience, just to let them know what was happening; the actual extinguishing of the lights, like almost everything else that happened, was controlled by the sensors and the docking programs.

The lights in Bay 2 went out. So, in the same moment, did all the lights on the rest of the Wheel visible through the shell.

And then Sneezy could see the sky.

There was not much to see. There weren't any stars. The only stars bright enough to be seen from the Watch Wheel were those from their own galaxy, and their eyes didn't happen to be pointed that way. There were other galaxies by the hundreds of millions in their line of sight, but only a few dozen of them were naked-eye objects, and those only pale, tiny smudges of firefly light.

Then, as the Wheel slowly spun through its endless round, the westernmost of the smudges dipped out of sight, and the onlookers murmured.

A pale colorless flicker of light, hard to see, painful to the eyes when seen . . . and then, abruptly, like a slide projected without warning on a screen, there was the ship.

The supply ship was immense, itself a spindle 800 meters long. The shape meant that this time it was an original-Heechee ship, not one of the new human-built ones. Sneezy felt a special glow. He didn't have anything against the human ships, which were usually either torpedo-shaped or simple cylinders. As everybody knew, the shape made no difference at all in interstellar travel. They could just as easily have been spheres or cubes or chrysanthemums; the shape was only a matter of the whims of the designers. Most of the supply ships that visited the Watch Wheel were human-made and human-crewed—and generally loaded with human recruits, too, so that that minor fraction of the Wheel's complement that was Heechee was still further outnumbered.

A Heechee ship might mean more Heechee to redress the balance! So thought Sneezy . . .

But not this time.

The great spindle settled inside the embrace of the Wheel. Its approach course was a corkscrew turn, beginning to twirl to match the Wheel's own slow spin, so that by the time its teat was touching the hatch of Bay 2 they were synchronized.

Rings meshed. Seals locked. From the aft quarters of the ship, cables spun out to the capstans at Bays 1 and 3, securing themselves and tightening to make the ship an integral part of the structure of the Wheel. The mass shifters in the utility conduits shuddered and chugged, adjusting the balance of the Wheel to match the new increments. Harold stumbled, off balance, as the floor twitched beneath them. Sneezy caught him, and Harold shoved him away. "You take care of yourself, Dopey," he instructed.

But then the ship was securely locked in, and its wonders began to pour out.

The carrythings were the first to spring into action, hurrying into the cargo hatches and emerging with crates and bales and articles of furnishings and machines. Most could not be identified by sight, but the cargo bay was suddenly brightened with lovely smells as the handlers offloaded crates of fresh fruit, peaches and oranges and berries. "Wow! Gosh! Look at those bananas!" cried Harold as a handler came off the ramp with all four limbs upraised, each one holding a stalk of unripe fruit. "I wish I had one right now!"

"You aren't supposed to eat them until they turn yellow," Sneezy pointed out with pride in his knowledge of strange human foods. He got a withering glare from Harold.

"I know *that*. I mean I wish I had one *ripe* one now. Or some of those what-do-you-call-them berries."

Sneezy bent to whisper to his pod for help, then straightened up. "They are strawberries," he stated. "I wish I had some, too."

"Strawberries," Harold whispered. It had been a long time since he had seen a strawberry. The Wheel grew or manufactured most of its own food, but no one had yet got around to a berry patch. It was easy enough to make food with strawberry *flavor*—or any other flavor imaginable for that matter; CHON-food was endlessly variable. But the crispness, the texture, the smell—no, there was always a difference between CHON-food and the real stuff, and the difference was that the real stuff was *wonderful*. The boys slid carefully closer to the stacked crates of fruit, inhaling deeply. There was space between the crates and the wall of the bay, out of the way of the carrythings, and the boys fit into that space as no adult could. "I think those are raspberries," said Harold, peering across stacks of lettuce and carrots and scarlet-ripe tomatoes. "And look, cherries!"

"I would like to have some strawberries best," said Sneezy wistfully, and a carrything, gently setting down a box marked *"Instruments—Fragile,"* paused as though listening. It was. It heard. Two of its long handling arms extended themselves to the crates of strawberries, opened one of the crates, extricated a little basket of fruit, resealed the end of the crate, and reached over the other crates to hand the basket to Sneezy. "Why, thank you!" said Sneezy, surprised but polite.

"You are welcome, Sternutator," said the carrything in Heechee. Sneezy jumped.

"Oh! Do I know you?"

"I was your tai-chi teacher," the carrything announced. "Give some to Harold." Then it turned and raced off for the next load.

Harold looked resentful for a moment, then dismissed the emotion as unworthy—who would be jealous of the attentions of a low-grade machine intelligence? The two boys divided the fruit, nipping each berry between fingertips by its short green stem and nibbling it away. The strawberries were perfect. Fully ripe, sugar-sweet, taste fulfilling all the promise of look and smell.

"The people will be out in a minute," Harold announced, chewing blissfully—and was surprised to see Sneezy suddenly stop eating. The Heechee boy's eyes were staring at the ship.

Following the direction of Sneezy's eyes, Harold saw the first of the passengers at last emerging. There were fifteen or twenty of them, adults and children.

That was always interesting, of course. It was the biggest reason the boys were there, to see what new companions or rivals the ship might be bringing them. But the expression on Sneezy's face was not just curiosity. It was either anger or fear—astonishment, at least, Harold decided, annoyed as he always was because Heechee expressions were hard for a human to read. The newcomers looked human enough to Harold, though there was something about the way they walked, hard to see at this distance, that was odd.

Harold looked again, and saw something else.

The Wheel had turned a bit farther.

Now, just past the bulk of the ship, out in the emptiness of intergalactic space, was the cluster of patches of dirty-yellow light the Wheel was there to watch.

The light was not really yellow to begin with, of course. Spectroscopy showed that far more than ninety percent of the radiation from the kugelblitz was in the violet end of the optical spectrum and beyond; but those frequencies were bad for human or Heechee eyes. The transparent shell had been doped to exclude them. Only the yellow came through.

Harold grinned in satisfaction. "What's the matter, Dopey?" he said patronizingly. "You suddenly scared about the kugelblitz?"

Sneezy blinked those great, pink, odd-looking Heechee eyes at him. "Scared of the kugelblitz? No. What are you talking about?"

"You look so funny," Harold explained.

"I'm not *funny*. I'm *mad*. Look at that!" Sneezy waved a skinny arm at the dock. "That's a Heechee ship! And the people are all wearing Ancestor pods! But every one of those people is *human*."

If Harold had been a Heechee boy instead of a very human one, he wouldn't have laughed about the kugelblitz.

The kugelblitz was not a laughing matter. The kugelblitz was where the Foe lived—the beings the Heechee called "the Assassins." The Heechee had not given them that name as a jest. To the Heechee there was nothing jestable about the Foe. Heechee didn't laugh at dangerous things. They ran away from them.

That was another significant difference between Sneezy and Harold. And then there was Oniko, who was different still.

Oniko Bakin was one of the new arrivals. Her contingent of replacements included twenty-two humans and no Heechee at all. Four of them were children, and the one who turned up in Sneezy's school was Oniko. When she appeared for classes on her first day, the other children clustered around her. "But you're human," one said. "So why do you wear a Heechee pod?"

"We always have," she explained. Then she courteously shushed them to pay attention to the teacherthing.

Oniko was indeed human. She was also female, and just about Sneezy's age. Her skin was pale olive. Her eyes were black and hooded with an epicanthic fold. Her hair was straight and black, and Sneezy was proud to be able to identify her by these signs as one of that subgenre of human beings called "Oriental." She spoke colloquial English, though. To Sneezy's surprise, she spoke colloquial Heechee, too. Lots of humans spoke a little Heechee, more or less, but Oniko was the first in Sneezy's experience who was equally at home in both the language of Do and the language of Feel.

That did not lessen his astonishment at seeing a human child wearing a pod.

In eurhythmics, that first day she was in school with him, Oniko became his partner for stretch-and-bend movements. Sneezy got a close-up look at her. Although he still thought that her flesh was distressingly flabby and her mass worrisomely large, he liked the sweet smell of her breath and the gentle way she spoke his name—not "Dopey," not even "Sneezy," but "Sternutator," in the Heechee tongue. He was disappointed when their housething called early to take her out of school for some formality with her parents, because he wanted to know her better.

At home that night he tried asking his father why a human being should wear a pod. "Very simple, Sterny," Bremsstrahlung said wearily. "They were a lost catch."

The reason Bremsstrahlung was tired was that he had been doing double duty. All the watchers had. The times when a ship was docked at the Wheel were thought to be specially vulnerable, since a certain amount of confusion was inevitable. At such times every Dream Seat was manned and all the watchers kept on duty until the ship had departed and the

Wheel was secure once more. It had been a very long shift for
Bremsstrahlung. "A lost catch," he explained, "is a group of
human beings who flew one of our ships to a one-way destination. As to this one, ask your mother; she talked to the ship's
crew."

"Only for a moment," Femtowave protested. "I was hoping
for news from Home."

Bremsstrahlung patted her fondly. "What news could there
be when they left only—what was it, three or four hours after
we did?"

Femtowave acknowledged the correctness of his observation with a flexion of her throat. She said in amusement, "The
poor crew still was in shock. They were all Heechee. They left
the core with specialists and materials to go to Earth, stopped
there, were loaded with supplies for us, stopped on the way
to pick up the new people from the lost catch—oh, how confusing it all must be for them!"

"Exactly," said Bremsstrahlung. "Anyway, once the original humans reached the artifact, they couldn't leave. So then
they were stuck there forever."

"If it were forever—" Femtowave smiled "—they would
not be here now, Bremmy." She did not smile in the human
way, since Heechee musculature is not the same. What happened was that a knot of muscle gathered below her cheek-
bones. The taut flesh itself did not move.

"You know what I mean," her husband said. "Anyway,
Sternutator, this little group of less than one hundred humans
turned out to be very rich in sensitives." He said it demurely.
To be a sensitive meant that one was particularly good at using
the Dream Seat to "listen" for signs of external intelligence,
and of course Bremsstrahlung himself was among the most
sensitive beings ever found. That was why he was on the
Wheel.

"Will Oniko work in the Dream Seat?" Sneezy asked.

"Of course not! At least, not until she grows up. You know
that it is not only important to be able to receive any impres-
sions that may come. A particularly gifted child might be able

to do that, but it is just as important to be able to refrain from broadcasting one's own feelings.''

"More important," Femtowave corrected. There was no smiley knot of muscle on her cheek now. That was nothing to smile about.

"More important, I agree," said her husband. "As to whether this child is a sensitive or not, well, there's no way for me to know that. She will be tested. Probably she already has been, as you were, since surely one of her own parents must be a sensitive, and there is quite a strong genetic component involved."

"Does that mean that I will work in the Dream Seat when I grow up?" Sneezy asked eagerly.

"We don't know that yet," his father said. He thought for a moment, and then added somberly, "For that matter, we don't know if the Wheel will still be here—"

"Bremsstrahlung!" his wife cried. "That is nothing to joke about!"

Bremsstrahlung nodded but didn't say anything. He was really quite tired. Perhaps, he told himself, that was why he hadn't been joking.

Actually, Sneezy's best witness about the human girl was Oniko herself. She was assigned to his schoolhall, and of course the schoolthing introduced her at once to the other students. "Oniko," it said, "was born on a Food Factory, and hasn't had much chance to know much about the world. So please help her when you can."

Sneezy was willing. The chances didn't come very often, though. He was not the only child curious about the newcomer, and most of the others, being human, were far more forward than he.

Sneezy's school was almost like the storied one-room red schoolhouse of American antiquity. There really was only one room. It was different from the antique, though, in that it didn't have just one teacher, or not exactly. Each student got quite individual instruction, with his or her own custom-tailored battery of learning programs. The schoolthing was a mobile unit.

It cruised around the room as needed, mostly to keep discipline and to see that none of the students was still eating his lunch when he should have been parsing sentences. It did not teach. For that purpose each student had his own carrel.

When the schoolthing had finished counting heads and checking on the reasons for any absences, it bustled around, making sure of clean hands and freedom from symptoms of illness—and, in the case of the youngest pupils, fastening the seat belts that kept them in their carrels. Not to mention escorting them to the toilet as needed, not to mention all the other functions required for children who, a few of them, were still quite tiny.

For all of this the schoolthing was quite adequate. It even looked reassuring. It had a face. When it was wearing its normal schoolthing equipage, it appeared to be a little old woman in a shapeless gown. The gown was cosmetic, of course. So was the smiling face. So were all of its physical attributes, for when school was not in session the schoolthing did quite other jobs and wore quite other appearances. And, of course, when more help was needed—when the children needed more supervision at exercise time or if any special problem should arise—the schoolthing coopted as many other artificial intelligences as needed from the Wheel pool.

Sneezy noticed subconsciously that the schoolthing was hovering around Oniko much of the time, but he was too busy trying to prove to the satisfaction of his number-theory program that 53 was congruent to 1421 to the base 6 to pay much attention. It wasn't that number theory was difficult for Sneezy. Far from it. Like all Heechee children, he had absorbed most of its principles at about the same time he learned to read. What made mathematics challenging for Sneezy was the silly human system of counting—to the base 10, imagine! With positional notation, so that if you got two digits in the wrong order, the number was hopelessly wrong!

Then, "Exercise time!" the schoolthing chirped cheerily, and Sneezy found out why the schoolthing was paying particular attention to Oniko Bakin.

All the individual teaching programs logged off. The restraining straps slid away from the small ones. The children stood up and stretched and, laughing and shoving, trooped out to the safe area outside the schoolhall. Except Oniko. She remained behind.

Sneezy didn't notice that at first, because he was busy, as all the children were busy, with the vigorous muscle-against-muscle tuggings and shovings and bendings and pressings that all of them had to perform twenty times a day. That was mandatory all over the Wheel, and not just for children. The light pull of the Watch Wheel was enervating. It didn't encourage children to develop strong muscles, or adults to keep them. In any practical sense, as long as they stayed on the Wheel, that wouldn't matter, because what did a human or Heechee need muscles for there?

But no one would stay on the Wheel forever, and once they got back to normal gravity, they would regret the flab accumulated on the Wheel.

Sneezy, being Heechee, was more methodical and purposeful in his exercising than most of the human students. He finished early and looked around. When he saw that Oniko wasn't in the play pit, he peered into the schoolhall. There she was. The girl was strapped into a sort of jointed metal casing that followed the shape of her body. An exoskeleton! And the contraption was writhing and twisting and bending with the girl inside it.

"Oh," said Sneezy, understanding at once. "You're being acclimated to gravity."

Oniko opened her eyes and looked at him levelly without answering. She was gasping for breath. Heechee are no better at reading human expressions than humans are with those of the Heechee, but Sneezy could see the strain lines on her face and the sweat on her brow.

"It's good that you're doing that," he said. Then it occurred to him to be tactful. "Do you mind my being here?" he asked, because the girl was certainly being twisted and shaped into some rather extraordinary positions.

"No," she panted.

Sneezy tarried indecisively. As he looked more closely he

could see that it was not only exercise she was given. A stinger needle was in the vein of her arm, gently seeping some sort of fluid into her bloodstream. She saw his eye and managed to say, "I'm being recalcified. To make my bones stronger."

"Yes, of course," Sneezy said encouragingly. "I guess your habitat didn't have much surface gravity? But this will help, I'm sure." He thought for a moment, and then said in charity, "I guess you can't do the real exercises yet, Oniko."

She took a deep breath. "Not yet," she said. "But I will!"

When the next half-holiday came around, Sneezy and Harold planned to visit the coconut grove. Oniko was just outside the schoolhall door as they left, and on impulse Sneezy said to her, "We're going to get some coconuts. Do you want to come along?"

Harold grunted annoyance from behind him, but Sneezy paid no attention. Oniko pursed her lips, considering the invitation. Her poise and manner were very nearly adult as she said, "Yes, thank you very much. I would enjoy that."

"Sure," Harold put in, "but what about lunch? I only brought enough for myself."

"I already have my lunch," said the girl, patting her school bag, "since I was planning to explore the Wheel today, anyhow. It's quite interesting, I think."

Harold was indignant. "Interesting! Look, kid, it's not just *interesting*. It's the most important thing in the whole universe. It's the only thing that keeps the whole human race safe!— Heechee too," he added as an afterthought. "I mean, if we weren't on guard every minute who knows what would happen?"

"Of course," Oniko said politely. "I know that it is our task to monitor the kugelblitz. That is why we are all here, certainly." The look she gave Harold was almost maternal. "Both my parents are watchers," she said, with that self-deprecatory tone that announces great pride, "and my uncle Tashi as well. Nearly everyone where I come from is good at that sort of thing. Probably when I grow up I will be too."

If there was one thing Harold couldn't stand when he was

condescending to someone, it was to be condescended to. He glowered. "Are we going to get some coconuts," he demanded, "or are we going to stand around talking all day? Let's get going!"

He turned, leading the way. His expression said that he personally had had no part in inviting this funny new human kid with the pod, and expected nothing good to come of it.

In a moment it seemed he was right.

The coconut grove was not far from the schoolhall in the curved geometry of the Wheel. In fact, it was directly "above" the school. There was a lift chain just a few dozen meters away, at the intersection of two main corridors, but in the light gravity of the Wheel active children seldom bothered with such things. Harold pushed a door open to reveal the vertical shaft with handholds just next to the schoolhall. He scuttled up out of sight; Sneezy nodded encouragingly to the girl; she hesitated.

"I don't think I can manage that yet," she said.

"Naturally," sneered Harold from above.

"No problem," said Sneezy at once, embarrassed at his lack of thoughtfulness. "We'll take the lift," he called up the shaft, and didn't wait to listen for Harold's answer.

They got it, all the same, when they stepped carefully off the lift chain and found Harold waiting. "Oh, *God*," he said, "if she can't handle the ladders, how's she going to climb a tree?"

"I'll climb for her," Sneezy said. "You go ahead."

Ungraciously Harold turned away to pick the best tree for himself.

He went up, hands and feet, like a monkey. The coconut trees were a dozen meters tall before you got to the crown, but they were no trouble for an agile child to climb with only Wheel weight. Harold, vain of the muscles he religiously cultivated, had naturally chosen the tallest and richest-laden, and Oniko looked up at him with some fear.

"Just stand clear," Sneezy encouraged, "in case he drops one."

"I won't damn well drop one!" snapped Harold from above, sawing away at one of the husks.

"It probably wouldn't hurt even if he did," said Sneezy, "but all the same—"

"All the same you think I'll break," said Oniko with dignity. "Don't worry about me. Climb a tree. I'll watch."

Sneezy glanced around and chose a shorter tree with fewer fruits, but, he thought, larger ones. "We're only allowed two each," he explained, "or else the guardthing will report us. I'll be right back."

And he swarmed up his tree even faster than Harold and made his choice among the triangular green fruits. He carefully tossed three good ones to the ground a few meters away from Oniko, and when he was down again she was studying them in surprise. "But these aren't coconuts!" she exclaimed. "I've seen pictures of coconuts. They're brown and hairy and hard."

"Those are inside the green stuff," Sneezy explained. "Take that big one. Tap it with your knuckles to make sure it's ripe—"

But she didn't know how to do that, either. Sneezy did it for her and handed the nut back to her. Oniko took it in her hand and hefted it thoughtfully.

Although it weighed nothing much on the Wheel, its mass was the same as it would have been anywhere else in the universe, and it looked formidably hard to penetrate.

"How do we get the green stuff off?" she asked.

"Tell her to give it to me, Dopey," Harold ordered from behind them, his own coconuts already on the ground. He snatched it, and with two quick strokes of his knife he had the stem end open and handed it back to her. "Drink it," he commanded. "It's good."

The girl looked at it suspiciously, then at Sneezy. He nodded encouragement. Hesitatingly she lifted it to her lips. Tasted. Made a face. Rummaged around the inside of her mouth with her tongue, exploring the flavor of the coconut juice. Tried a larger sip—and reported in surprise, "Why, yes, it is good!"

"We'll open them up and get the meat later," Sneezy said, working on his own coconut. "Maybe we should eat our lunches now; the juice is good to drink with the sandwiches."

But though Sneezy's family had adopted the human habit of sandwiches, Oniko's had not. What she pulled out of her bag was a collection of lumpy little objects in gaily colored paper. In the red, a pickled plum. In the golden, a hard, brown piece of something she said was fish, although neither Sneezy nor Harold was willing to taste it to find out. Nor was Oniko interested in Harold's extra deviled egg, nor in the ham sandwiches Sneezy had persuaded his father to let him take. Ham was enough of an adventure for Sneezy; he had only in the last year begun to accept human food—or as close to real human food as the Wheel's synthesizers created.

"But you should try these," Oniko scolded.

"Thank you, no," said Sneezy. Harold was less diplomatic; he made throwing-up noises.

"But I try your food," Oniko pointed out. "These coconuts, for instance, are quite good." She took another deep sip, found the nut empty. Silently Sneezy opened another and passed it over to her. "I think," she said judiciously, "that when I grow up and return to Earth I will buy an island where these grow, and then I too will be able to climb the trees."

Both boys stared at her. They were almost equally astonished, though for different reasons. Harold because he was deeply impressed at the girl's casual assumption of such wealth—buy an island? Return to earth? One must be very rich to contemplate either! And Sneezy was simply baffled by the entire concept of owning land at all. "I have been told of such nice islands," Oniko went on. "There is one called Tahiti, which is said to be very pretty. Or perhaps one nearer the islands of Japan, so I can visit my relatives whom I have never met."

"You have relatives in Japan, Earth?" asked Harold, suddenly respectful. His own family were descendants of early settlers on Peggys Planet. Earth was not much more than a myth to him. "But I thought you were born on a Heechee artifact."

"I was, and my parents before me," Oniko said, taking another sip of the coconut milk and settling down to repeat once again an often-told story. "But my father's father, Aritsune Bakin, married in the great temple at Nara. Then he took his bride to Gateway and sought their fortune. *His* father's father had himself been a Gateway prospector, but was badly injured and confined to the asteroid. He had some money. When he died, that money paid for my father's father's trip, with his wife along. They took only one trip. The first time out they found their destination was the artifact. There were eighteen large Heechee ships there, none of which could be made to fly by them, and their own ship would no longer respond to the controls."

"That was so that the information from the artifact would be kept secret until the proper time," Sneezy put in in some embarrassment. He had already heard a fair amount of criticism of Heechee practices with their abandoned ships and stations.

"Yes, of course," said Oniko forgivingly. "Six other Gateway ships arrived at the same destination and were all, of course, marooned there. There were four Threes, a One, and another Five, like my grandfather's, so in all there were twenty-three original prospectors. Fortunately, eight of them were women of childbearing age, so the colony survived. When finally we were—" For the first time, she hesitated.

"When you were rescued?" Harold offered.

"We were not *rescued*. We were never lost, merely detained. So when finally we were *visited again*, just four years ago, the population of the artifact was eighty-five. I was just a small child then, of course. Some of us went directly to Earth or other places, but because I was little my parents remained so that I could begin to be prepared for these horrible heavy places."

"You think this is heavy!" Harold snickered. "Wow. Wait'll you try Peggys Planet! Or Earth!"

"I shall," Oniko said firmly.

"Sure you will," Harold said skeptically. "What about the money?"

"Of course, original Gateway rules applied," Oniko explained. "There were earned bonuses and royalties for the prospectors and their descendants. According to the rules, the value of the artifact and its contents was estimated at two billion eight hundred million and some odd dollars, divided by the number of prospectors who reached there alive, twenty-three."

"Wow!" said Harold, goggle-eyed as he did arithmetic in his head.

"Of course," Oniko added apologetically, "my parents are the only descendants of four out of the original twenty-three, so I will inherit all four shares—about one-sixth of the total—if they die without having any other children—I hope they will not," she finished.

"Wow." Harold was speechless. Even Sneezy was impressed, though not with the money this child possessed—avarice was not a Heechee vice. But he admired her for the lucid, cogent way she told her story.

"Really," she said, "it was quite nice there when the new people came. Many new experiences! Much to talk about! Not that it wasn't very nice before—oh, what is happening?" she finished in distress, gazing around.

It was getting dark. The overhead light dimmed swiftly, replaced by a much fainter red glow. In a moment it was as dark as it ever got in the coconut grove—dark enough so that the palms, evolved to thrive in the circadian rhythm of the Earth's tropical climates, had their period of rest before the lights came on again and photosynthesis resumed. "It's so the trees won't get sick," Sneezy explained. "But they'll leave the red lights on so we can see; the trees don't mind that."

Sneezy didn't mind that either, as Harold well knew. The older boy chortled, "Dopey's afraid of the dark, you know."

Sneezy looked away. It was untrue, but it was not wholly false. In the densely packed star cluster at the Heechee core there was seldom a time on the surface of any planet without one degree or another of sunlight. Darkness was not exactly frightening, but it was at least discomfiting. He said, "You were telling us about where you came from?"

"Oh, yes, Sternutator. It was so nice! Even the original prospectors came to love it, I think, though of course they wished they could see their families again. But there was plenty of food and water, and much to do. We had a great many Heechee books, and more than one hundred Heechee Ancient Ancestors stored there to talk to. They taught us how to use the pods," she said proudly, patting hers.

Sneezy reached out a finger to touch hers and felt the warm stirrings of the presence within. "Your Ancestor seems very nice," he told her.

"Thank you," she said gravely.

"Your pod is much smaller than mine, though," he offered.

"Oh, yes. We don't need the microwave, you see. We only have them for the Ancestors. My father says we had much to learn from the Heechee—once we learned the language, of course."

"Thank you," said Sneezy in return. He wasn't sure what he was thanking her for, but it seemed polite.

Harold was not in a polite mood. "What we had to learn from the Heechee," he said, "was how to be cowards. And we just wouldn't learn that!"

Sneezy felt the knots of muscles at his shoulders gather. Heechee emotions aren't the same as human emotions, but even the Heechee can feel annoyance. He said unsteadily, "I do not want you to call me a coward, Harold."

Doggedly, Harold said, "Oh, I'm not talking about you personally, Dopey, but you know as well as I do what the Heechee did. They just ran away and hid."

"I do not want you to call me Dopey, either, anymore."

Harold jumped to his feet. "And what are you going to do about it?" he sneered.

Sneezy rose more slowly, wondering at himself. He was ill at ease in the gloomy palm grove, but he was also beginning to shake for other reasons. "I am going to tell you that it is wrong for you to call me that. No one else does."

"No one else knows you as well as I do," Harold said stubbornly. Sneezy perceived that the human boy's feelings had been hurt in some way—it did not occur to Sneezy to use the word "jealousy." Harold's forearms were raised, his fists were clenching; why, Sneezy marveled, it looked as though he wanted to *fight*.

Perhaps he would have. Perhaps Sneezy would have fought him back. Heechee did not usually practice violence on each other, but Sneezy was a very young Heechee, not as civilized as he would be in another decade or so.

What stopped them had nothing to do with civilization. It was Oniko. She made a gagging sound, glared at the coconut in her hand in revulsion, then suddenly flung it away.

"Oh, my *God*," she said in strangled tones, and began to vomit profusely.

When the two boys got her down to the classroom, the schoolthing, which possessed paramedical skills among all its others, reproached them bitterly for letting the poor child drink so much of an unfamiliar juice. As penance they had to escort her to her apartment and stay there with her until a parent returned.

So both Harold and Sneezy were late for dinner. "Hurry it up, can't you?" Harold complained, just behind him in the downshaft. "I'm going to get smacked!"

Sneezy was already hurrying as much as he could, swinging down from one handhold to another on the descending cable. He was not afraid of being smacked. Neither of his parents would strike a child, but he was impatient to see them. There were questions he wanted to ask. As they hurried down the long passageway to the crossway where both their homes were, Sneezy right, Harold left, he was framing the questions in his mind.

And then they stopped short. Sneezy hissed in surprise. Harold groaned, "Aw, *shit*."

They both heard the piercing metallic-electronic squeal that seemed to go right through bone into brain. To make sure they noticed, the ceiling lights flashed on and off three measured times. And all the voices of all the workthings awoke at once: "Drill!" the nearest ones called to the boys. "Take rest positions at once! Empty your minds! Lie still! This is a *Drill*!"

I wish I had a better way of talking to meat people.

I wish it were possible for me to tell about Sneezy and Oniko and the Wheel as I experienced them. I don't mean that I experienced them directly. I didn't; I wasn't there. But I just as well might have been, because everything that happened on the Wheel, like everything that happened anywhere in the Galaxy, was recorded somewhere in gigabit space, and thus available to those who had been vastened. Like me.

So, in a certain sense, I *was* there. (Or "was" there.) But while I was accessing that particular store I was also doing forty-eleven other things, some of them interesting, some of them important, some of them just a lot more of that poking around among the yearnings and sorrows inside my head that I seem to keep on doing all the time. I don't know how to convey all that.

I don't mean that I wasn't paying attention to the story of the kids. I was. They touched me. There is something infinitely heart-melting, for me anyway, about the courage of kids.

I don't mean the physical, fistfight and name-calling kind of courage, like when Sneezy stood up to Harold, though that was very brave (if not actually sociopathic) behavior for a Heechee boy to exhibit. I mean the way a child can stand up to a real danger, maybe even an irresistible and undefeatable danger. It's futile and hopeless and heartbreaking, like a two-week kitten mewing defiance to an escaped pit bull. It melts me.

Albert isn't always tolerant of the way I feel about kids. He tells me sometimes that Essie and I probably should have had children of our own, and then maybe I wouldn't idealize them the way I do. Maybe so. But regardless of whatever I maybe should have done or possibly wouldn't be, I do have this sudden rush of liquefaction around the region of the heart (well, the analog, at least, of the physical heart I once had but don't have anymore) when I see kids doing what they must do in the face of the overwhelming fear.

Actually, neither Harold nor Sneezy was that frightened at first. A Drill was a Drill. They'd had plenty of Drills before. They flopped where they were. They closed their eyes. They waited.

This was no Class Two Drill, like the landing of a ship. It was an all-out alert, the kind that happened at random times and had to be carried out perfectly. As soon as the warning whistle quieted down, the rest of the Wheel did, too. The workthings that had no duties turned themselves to standby and stood frozen. The lights dimmed themselves to murk, just enough to make things out. The inertial sensors that monitored the spin of the Wheel gave their mass shifters one more pat into place and shut down; so did the vertical lift cables; so did all the other nonessential inorganic (or no longer organic) machines and intelligences of the Wheel.

Sneezy and Harold were shut down too, or as close to it as active children can get. Among the required courses for every child in the Wheel's schoolhalls was practice in what some people used to call "satori," the blanking of the mind. They were quite good at it. Lying curled like a fetus next to the equally curled Harold, Sneezy's mind was emptied of everything but the gray-gold, not-warm-not-cold, not-bright-not-dark haze of abandonment of self.

Or almost.

Of course, you could never achieve perfection at satori. An attempt to be perfect was itself an imperfection. There were thoughts stirring in Sneezy's fog. Questions. Questions about Oniko that Sneezy still wanted very much to ask his parents. Questions about whether—by some terrible chance—this Drill might just possibly be no Drill at all but reality.

The deck of the Wheel felt dead under his cheek. No buzz of air pumps or whine of cable motors. No voices. No rustle or footstep of anyone moving. No irregular, satisfying thump and rumble as the mass shifters worked to keep the Wheel turning true.

Sneezy waited. As the questions tried to form themselves in his mind, he separated himself from them, letting them dwindle away half formed. Until one question began to recur insistently:

Why was this particular Drill lasting so long?

In fact, it was over an hour before the nearest cleanerthing suddenly jerked itself erect again. It pointed its sensor toward the two boys and said, "The Drill is over. You can get up now."

They didn't need to be told, of course. Even before the

cleanerthing's words were spoken the Wheel began to come back to life. Lights sprang up. Distant whines and thumps and shudders said that all the caretaking machinery was turning itself on again. Harold jumped up, grinning. "I guess my dad had to go on duty," he cried happily; the translation of that remark was, *So he won't remember I was late.*

"Mine too," said Sneezy; then, struck by a thought: "And probably both of Oniko's parents had to go on, so probably—"

"So probably they had to leave her alone anyway." Harold nodded. "So what was the use of making us stay there? Dumb things!" he said, kicking the cleanerthing as they passed. "See you tomorrow."

"Of course," Sneezy said politely, and hurried home.

As expected, neither parent was there. The housething told him that his father had been called to the Dream Seats and his mother had been caught by the Drill far into the third sector of the Wheel. Both were on their way home.

His father arrived first, looking again tired. "Where's your mother?" he asked. It was the housething that answered for Sneezy:

"Femtowave has been delayed by a slight problem; one of the maintenance circuits was sluggish in coming back on line after the Drill. Shall I prepare dinner?"

"Of course," Bremsstrahlung grumbled, tired and irritable. "Why is this, Sternutator? Why haven't you told the cookthing to start already? And besides," he said, remembering, "why weren't you here two hours ago?"

"Oniko was sick," Sneezy explained.

Bremsstrahlung paused, his memory pouch half unslung, on his way to the airbath. "And is that now something that you must worry about? Are you now a medicthing?"

Sneezy explained about the coconut juice. "We had to take her home. I wanted to leave, Father," he protested, "but her housethings told us to stay with her, and her Ancestor agreed."

Ironically, Bremsstrahlung repeated, "*Her* ancestor?"

"No, of course I mean not really hers, Father, but she carries the Ancestor in her pod. Her name is Ophiolite, the Ancestor, I mean."

"For a human," Bremsstrahlung said approvingly, "this Oniko shows considerable intelligence. I have wondered why more humans don't carry memory pouches. Of course, they don't require the radiation as we do, but still, the pods are so convenient in other ways."

"Yes, but she has an Ancestor in hers."

Weary as he was, Bremsstrahlung was a good father. He sank down on a forkrest, his pod loose beneath him, to explain things to his son. "You must remember, Sternutator, that if a group of Ancestors were inadvertently left behind during the Removal, it must have been very lonely for them. Of course, they would have formed attachments to the first intelligent beings who appeared there, even if they were human."

"Yes, but," said Sneezy, "I don't have an Ancestor in my pod yet."

"Children don't have Ancestors in their pods," Bremsstrahlung explained. "Even many adults do not, because the Ancestors are very busy with important work, but when you grow up—"

"Yes, but," said Sneezy, "*she* does."

Bremsstrahlung groaned and stood up. Neatly hanging his memory pouch beside the bath door, he begged, "Later, son, please! I'm really tired."

It wasn't just intellectual curiosity with Sneezy. It wasn't even the jealousy of one kid toward another with a better toy. There were almost moral questions involved, perhaps almost religious ones.

Both Heechee and humans had learned how to supplement their own brains with machine-stored intelligences, but they went by different routes. Human beings had gone the way of calculators and computers and servo-mechanisms, all the way to the supple and enormous gigabit webs that nurtured such Artificial Intelligences as Albert Einstein. (And, for that matter, me.) The Heechee had never developed A.I. They hadn't had to. They had learned early on how to store the minds of their dead in machine form. Few Heechee truly, permanently died. They wound up as Ancient Ancestors.

A human astronomer who desired to calculate the orbital elements of the planets of a double-star system would as a matter of course turn the problem over to a computation facility. A Heechee would employ a battery of dead Ancestors. As a practical matter, one system worked as well as another.

But it was not entirely a practical matter. Humans didn't revere their computers. Heechee Ancient Ancestors, on the other hand, deserved—and demanded—a kind of respect.

Sneezy's mother came in while his father was still bathing. She listened to his questions and said, rubbing the back of his neck, "After dinner, Sterny, all right? It takes a lot out of your father when he's on extra shifts in the Dream Seat. And, then, of course, he's worried."

Sneezy gaped. Worried? Fatigued, yes; Sneezy expected that. That was the price a watcher paid, sitting in the Dream Seat for hours on end, trying to sense some alien presence, always fearing that he might some day succeed—as some day, surely, someone would, with consequences no one could guess.

But *worried*?

When at last the cookthing had dinner on the table and his parents were restored and almost relaxed, Bremsstrahlung said heavily, "It was not a planned Drill, Sternutator. Two shift watchers thought they detected something, so the emergency was called." He writhed his forearms, like a shrug. "What they felt is very uncertain. It was not clear, not strong—but they are good watchers. Of course there had to be a shutdown."

Sneezy stopped eating, knife halfway to his mouth. His father said quickly, "But I felt nothing at all when I came on. I am sure of that. No one else did then, either."

"There have been false alarms before," Femtowave said hopefully.

"To be sure. That's why there are so many of us: to make sure such alarms are false. It may be a million years before the Assassins come out, you know. Who can tell?" Bremsstrahlung finished his meal quickly, then sat back on his pouch.

"Now, Sternutator, what are your questions about your human friend, Oniko?"

Sneezy rolled his eyes slowly. Oh, yes, he had had a million questions, but the thought that *maybe* there had been a real signal of emerging Assassins had driven all of them out of his mind. False alarm, all right, but how did any watcher know for certain that any alarm was false?

But those were the questions his father obviously did not want to discuss. Sneezy searched and came up with one of the things that had been troubling. "Father? It is not just the pod. Oniko has so much 'money.' Why are they so 'rich'?" He used the English words, although they had been speaking Heechee, since their own tongue had no such concepts.

Bremsstrahlung shrugged his wide, wiry shoulders—it was the Heechee equivalent of a frown. "Human beings," he said, as though it explained everything.

It did not. "Yes, Father," Sneezy said, "but not all human beings have so much 'wealth.'"

"No, of course they do not," his father said. "These particular humans chanced to acquire some Heechee devices. Some of our 'property,' Sterny. They didn't even seek it out. They simply discovered it by chance, and in human practice that gave them 'ownership,' which they then traded for 'money.'"

Femtowave said pacifyingly, "As far as they knew, the devices were abandoned, of course." She ticked her tongue to the cookthing, which removed the used utensils and served up their "dessert." It wasn't pie or ice cream; it was one of a variety of ropy vines the Heechee ate which both cleared their palates and lubricated their teeth antiseptically after a meal. "The concept of 'money' isn't without value," Femtowave added, "since it functions as a sort of rough servo-mechanism for social priority-setting."

Bremsstrahlung picked a fiber out of his teech and said indignantly, "Are you proposing that Heechee should take up the same system?"

"No, no, Bremmy! All the same, it is interesting."

"Interesting!" he groaned. "Foolish, I would say. What's

the use of 'money'? Don't we have everything we need without it?''

"Not as much as Oniko has," Sneezy put in wistfully.

Bremsstrahlung put down his eating knife and gazed at the boy in despair. When he spoke, it was not to his son but to his wife.

"Do you see?" he demanded. "Do you see what is happening to our son here? The next thing you know he'll be asking for an 'allowance.' And the 'crying shame,''' he said, unconsciously using the English expression, since Heechee didn't cry, "is that we are older and wiser than they! How did we get ourselves into a position where *we* accommodate our ways to *theirs*?''

Femtowave glanced from her husband to her son. Both were upset—in the boy's case, she was sure, mostly because Bremsstrahlung was; in her husband's case the reasons were graver.

"Bremmy dear," she said patiently, "what's the use of worrying about these things? We knew what exposing our son to human values meant; we talked it over before we left the core.''

"Yes, in five minutes altogether," said her husband moodily.

"Five minutes was all the time we had." Femtowave leaned down to whisper to her pod. Obediently it caused the housething to rearrange the wall images of their room. The pleasing monochrome traceries faded, and the nostalgic mural of Home, with its pavilions and terraces overlooking the bays and majestic hills, surrounded them. "Sneezy won't forget," she said reassuringly.

"Really I won't, Father," the boy said, his voice tremulous.

"No. No, of course," Bremsstrahlung said heavily.

They finished their dessert-weed in silence. Then, when the housething had cleared everything away, they communed with the Ancestors for a while, letting the weary old dead ones talk, complain, advise. It was a very Heechee thing to do. Slowly Bremsstrahlung calmed down. By Sneezy's bedtime he felt quite restored. "Sleep now, my son," he said affectionately.

"Yes, Father," said Sneezy. Then, "Father?"

"What is it?"

"Do I have to keep on sleeping in a cocoon? Can't I have a real bed, with blankets and pillows?"

His father looked at him with puzzlement, before he began to look at him with outrage. "A 'bed'?" he began, and Femtowave moved to cut off the explosion before it could get started.

"Now, please, Sternutator," she said, "not one more word. Go!"

Sneezy, injured, went off to his room to glower at the cocoon and its dense, soft litter. It was *embarrassing* to sleep in something like that when all the other boys had beds. He climbed in, pulled the cocoon closed over him, turned around ten or twelve times to mold the litter to his liking, and fell asleep.

His parents were unslinging the hammocks in the other room, preparing for their own sleep. Bremsstrahlung was silent, his belly tendons rippling in displeasure. Femtowave, seeing, changed the murals again. The lovely pastels disappeared. On every wall there was now blackness with a few objects visible. To one side, the great sprinkled sprawl of the Galaxy. To the other, the cluster of fuzzy, sulfur-colored objects that were their reason for being there.

"Don't you see, my dear?" she said. "None of this matters in comparison with the great purpose we serve. We must never forget why our people Removed to the core in the first place—and why we have come out again."

Bremsstrahlung gazed unhappily at the smoky, roiling mass. "Some things do matter," he answered stubbornly. "Fairness always matters!"

His wife said gently, "Yes, Bremmy, fairness always matters. But in comparison with the Assassins, it doesn't matter very much."

There's not a great deal more to say about the children just now. They had an interesting and happy life on the Wheel—for a while.

Being much of an age, the three of them spent much time together. They did interesting things. They explored the lungs of the Wheel, where tangles of leafy vines grew on the wastes from the sinks and toilets of the Wheel, and sopped up the carbon dioxide both human and Heechee bodies exhaled. They toured the workshops where anything at all could be fixed, from a toy to the Wheel's tiny fleet of spacecraft—Femtowave worked there, and fondly showed the children around. They poked into the spacecraft themselves, hanging in their docking teats like puppies nursing. They peered into the library, with its tens of millions of socketed and indexed data fans: There on those racks were all the stories humans had ever told, and all the memories of the Heechee Ancestors, and all the dictionaries and compilations and texts of either race—well, not really *all*, but enough to overwhelm Sneezy, Harold, and Oniko. They visited the zoo, where cats and cows and monkeys and Heechee pets and exotics grazed or hung from bars or rested, chin on paw, to stare back at the staring children. There were only a few dozen organisms represented, but for most of the children they were the only nonsentient beings they had ever seen.

They even visited the Dream Seats.

Children were rarely allowed there, but Sneezy's father guaranteed their behavior. So one day, on Bremsstrahlung's time off, they were permitted to gaze at the emplacements from a safe distance.

It was a thrilling experience. The Seats were sited in clusters of four, every three hundred meters or so around the external perimeter of the Wheel. Each cluster was in a little bubble of crystal, made of a substance that was transparent not only to light but to every other form of electromagnetic radiation. Was that necessary? No one could say for sure, but perhaps it would help—anything that could make the task of the watchers more sure was worth doing, even if there was only a remote chance it mattered.

As was normal when there was no Drill, only one seat in each group of four was occupied. "Hold hands," Bremsstrahlung instructed, "and you can come just a little closer."

Warily the children tiptoed within a meter of the on-duty watcher, a human female from another sector, her eyes closed, her ears stopped. She almost looked asleep as they peered at her through the interstices of the glittering web of antenna-metal that surrounded her. Through the crystal they could see below them—"below" by the geometry of the slowly spinning Wheel—space itself, including the distant muddy blob of the kugelblitz. Sneezy's hand tightened watchfully on Oniko's. He no longer was repelled by the touch of human flesh—so lardy, so springy, so *fat*. In fact, he rather enjoyed holding her hand. What surprised him was that she seemed rather to enjoy holding his, since Harold had not failed to let him know, long since, that to a human being the feel of hot, hard, writhing Heechee flesh was equally distasteful. Perhaps Oniko did not find it so. Or perhaps she was simply too polite to show it.

Bremsstrahlung escorted them back to the public parts of the Wheel when they had looked their fill. Then he returned to get ready for his own shift. On the way back to their home area the children gabbled excitedly about what they had seen, pausing only to be diverted by a class trip of tiny ones, going to the aquarium for the first time.

The aquarium wasn't just a sort of museum. Much of the Heechee diet was seafood, and so was some of the human. Many of the animals in the tanks were sooner or later going to wind up on a table. Sneezy, Harold, and Oniko followed the little kids, tolerant of their chatter, amused by their reactions to the weird, wide-mouthed seasnakes that Heechee loved, or the squid that were for human tables. One of the squid was near the tank wall, and as a three-year-old came close it flashed from white to mottled and ejected a plume of ink as it rocketed away. The child jumped and gasped. Harold laughed. Oniko laughed. And, after a moment, Sneezy laughed, too, although of course the Heechee laugh was not quite the same sound or rictus as the human.

"Silly little kid," Oniko said with maternal fondness. "I remember the first time I—"

She did not finish.

There was a sudden squeal of warning from all over, and the lights began to flash. "Drill! Drill!" cried the schoolthings.

As everyone dropped at once to the floor, Harold managed

a quick question. "Why do we have a Drill now? he demanded
of the nearest schoolthing.

"Lie still! Empty your mind!" it ordered, but then it relented
for just one second. "It is only a Class Two," it said. "An
unscheduled ship is approaching—now take your position!"

And so they did, all of them, even the tinies. But Sneezy
had trouble emptying his mind, because there was a question.
Yes, of course, when a ship came in there was always a Class
Two Drill, that was not very frightening . . . but never before
in his experience had a ship come in unscheduled.

And this ship was from JAWS.

By the time the Drill was over and Sneezy was back in his
parents' home, the unscheduled ship was secured and silent,
but it was still there. And the rumors had flown like fire.

Bremsstrahlung confirmed them. "Yes, Sternutator," he
said with worry, "you must leave. All children must. The
Wheel is being evacuated of everyone not an adult, because
we can't risk a child radiating at the wrong time."

"I am second in my class in satori, Father!"

"Of course you are! But the Joint Assassin Watch has ordered that you must go with the others. Please, my son. There
is nothing we can do about it."

"They'll take very good care of you," Femtowave put in,
but her voice was even hoarser with worry than his father's.

"But where will I go?" Sneezy begged.

His parents looked to each other. "To a good place," his
mother said at last. "We don't know where, yet. You children
all come from different places, and I don't think they will get
all of you to your proper homes at once. But truly, Sterny,
you will be taken care of. And it is only for a while, until this
false alarm is cleared up. You will be back with us soon."

"I hope that is true," said his father.

And there was no time, no time for any last visits to the zoo
or the coconut grove or anywhere, just one short session at
the schoolhall so that each could pick up possessions and say
good-bye to the schoolthing.

The schoolthing couldn't keep order that day. It didn't try. It only dealt with each student separately, bidding a farewell, making sure the lockers were emptied, while all the other children chattered excitedly in anticipation and fear. None of them knew where they were going yet. Harold, of course, was praying for his own home.

Sneezy listened wistfully. He wondered if he envied Harold. Was Peggys Planet really the way Harold pictured it? Summer all the time? and no school? and millions of hectares of wild fruits and berries to pick any time, any day?

"But it's a long way," Harold was saying. "I bet I'll have to change ships. That means I'll be a month getting home."

"It would take me nearly three months," Sneezy said wistfully.

"Oh, but that's because of your stupid Schwarzschild barrier," Harold explained, quite unnecessarily to a boy who had already penetrated it once. "You don't think you're going to go there, do you, Dopey? Good heavens, they're not going to run a whole ship for a couple of Heechee kids. That would be just *inefficient*. They wouldn't do that!"

In that, Harold was right. There were not that many children on the Wheel, and so the great Earth-built ship that received them was going to only one place. To Earth.

Harold was crushed. Oniko was fearful. Sneezy was—well, Sneezy did not know from one moment to the next what he was, because the excitement and the pangs of leaving his parents and the nagging worry about what this sudden and unprecedented move meant all fought for dominance in his mind. The result was only confusion.

They had less than twelve hours to board. That was a good thing. The less time for the excitement to melt away and the fears and miseries to grow, the better.

At last they trooped one by one into the great interstellar vehicle as soon as the hundred new Watchers and their gear had been taken off. Oniko's parents were there, hugging their daughter without words. So were Mr. and Mrs. Wroczek, and Sneezy politely looked away as Harold began to cry at the parting.

"Good-bye, Father. Good-bye, Mother," said Sneezy.

"Good-bye, dear Sternutator," said his father, trying to keep the emotion out of his voice. Sneezy's mother didn't even try.

"It will be a nice place, Sterny, dear," she promised, hugging him. "We won't be able to hear from you normally, because they've blacked out transmissions to the Wheel—but—oh, Sterny!" She hugged him hard. Heechee can't cry, but there is nothing in their physiology or minds that keeps them from feeling loss as keenly as any human.

Sneezy turned away.

It was not a Heechee custom to kiss on parting, but as Sneezy entered the ship he wished that, in this case, an exception had been made.

3
Albert Speaks

I'm Albert Einstein, or at least Robinette Broadhead calls me that, and I think I should clarify some matters.

With all his cutesy false starts, Robin has still failed to convey a good deal of data which I believe to be essential. Among others, who the Foe were. I will help out. That's what I do; I help Robinette Broadhead.

I should explain my own situation.

To begin with, I'm not the "real" Albert Einstein. He's dead. He died quite a good many years before it was possible, at least for human beings, to store a person as a database after the meat part wore out. As a result, we don't even have a real copy of that Albert Einstein around. I am at most a rough approximation of what he might have been if he had been me.

What I really am is something quite different from any sort of reconstruction of a human being. Basically I am a simple data-retrieval system, dressed up with some fancy touches for pretty's sake. (The way people used to conceal a bedside communications phone inside a teddy bear.) In order to make me more user-friendly, my user, Robinette, requested that I should look like and act like a person. So my programmer gave him me. She was glad to do it. She liked humoring Robinette, since she was not only his programmer but his wife, S. Ya. Lavorovna-Broadhead.

So the way I look and act is really only a whim of Robin's.

I think it is fair to say that Robin is a man of many whims, and many moods, too. I'm not disparaging him. He can't help it. Robin started out organic.

For that reason, he suffered the handicaps of all meat beings. His intelligence was only what could be produced by sloppy biochemical means. His mind was not precise, and certainly not mathematical. It was the product of a meat brain, bathed in constant floods of hormones, biased by sensory inputs like pain and pleasure, and quite capable of screwing itself up over programming elements beyond my personal experience, like "doubt" and "guilt" and "jealousy" and "fear." Imagine living like that! Actually, it's a wonder to me that he functions as well as he does. I don't see how I could, myself. But then I can't say I really understand these things, since I have never felt them, except in an analog sense.

That doesn't mean I can't deal with them. Essie Broadhead's programs can do damn near *anything*. "Understanding" is quite unnecessary—you don't have to understand how a spacecraft works to get into it and push the buttons. I can project how given stimuli will affect Robin's behavior at least as well as he can, and I don't have to "understand" to do it.

After all, I don't understand the square root of minus one, either, but that doesn't keep me from finding useful ways of employing it in equations. It works. e to the i times pi power equals -1. It does not in the least matter that all the quantities involved are irrational, transcendental, imaginary, or negative.

It doesn't matter that Robin himself is all these things, either.

He is. All of them. Especially he is negative a good part of the time, in ways that keep him from being that other irrational, not to say transcendental, state, "happy."

This is silly of him. By every objective standard, Robinette Broadhead has it made. He has everything human beings desire. He has vast wealth—well, it is true that he does not now *personally* have the wealth, since he is now machine-stored and there are fussy human legal problems over ownership by dead people; but the actual wealth is vested in his real wife (or "widow"), and there is so much of it that if Robin wants to spend a few hundred million here or there, he has but to say the word. He even uses the wealth wisely. Most of it he spends on the Robinette Broadhead Institute for Extra-Solar Research, with its facilities in places like London, Brasilia, Johore, Peggys Planet, and a dozen locations in the old United States, not to mention its fleet of exploration ships always busy poking around the Galaxy. Because of this his life has "purpose" and he has a lot of "power." What's left? "Health"? Of course he has that; if anything went wrong, it would simply be corrected at once. "Love"? Certainly! He has the best of all possible wives in S. Ya. Lavorovna-Broadhead—at least, he has the machine-stored simulation of her and the simulation is essentially perfect, since S. Ya. wrote her doppel's program herself.

In short, if ever a meat person, or anyway former meat person, had reason to be happy, Robin is that person.

This just shows that "reason" is not dominant in his psyche. All too often he isn't happy at all. His endless concerns and confusions about who he loved, and what he meant by "love," and whether he was being "fair" or "faithful" to his various love partners, are typical examples.

For instance:

Robin loved Gelle-Klara Moynlin, both being meat people at the time. They had a fight. They made up. Then, through an accident neither of them had any opportunity to prevent, he abandoned her in a black hole for thirty years.

Well, that was a bad thing, of course. But it wasn't his fault. Yet it took him endless hours of couch time with my colleague, the computer psychoanalyst Sigfrid von Shrink, to "relieve" his mind of the "guilt" that had caused him so much "pain."

Irrational? You bet. But there's more.

Meanwhile, while Klara was hopelessly out of reach—as far as he knew, forever—he met and fell "in love" with and married my basic creator, S. Ya. Lavorovna. By any figure of merit I can find to assess such matters, that was a fine thing. But then Klara reappeared. When Robin had to confront the fact that he "loved" both of them, he simply went into fugue.

What made it worse was that he happened to die around the same time. (At least, his meat body wore out and he had to be machine-stored in gigabit space.) One would think that would simplify things. It is obvious that these biological matters really should not have caused him any further concern. He didn't *have* any biology anymore. But no, not Robin Broadhead!

Robin is not hopelessly stupid, either. (I mean, for a former meat person.) He is as aware as I that, anthropologically speaking, questions of "fidelity" and "jealousy" and "sexual guilt" have only to do with the biological fact that "love" implies "intercourse" which implies "reproduction"—jealousy is at root only a question of ensuring that the child one raises is genetically one's own. He *knows* that. Unfortunately, he can't *feel* that. Even the fact that he never biologically fathered any children in the first place doesn't change anything.

What strange things meat people worry about!—and go on worrying about, even when they have been promoted to nonmaterial existence, like me.

But Robin did worry, a lot, and when Robin worried, I worried too. About him. Because that's one of the other things I was programmed to do.

I observe that I am becoming nearly as discursive as Robin.

Well, that can't be helped. "Like master, like man," as the old meat-person proverb says—even when the "man" is a purely synthetic artifact of subroutines and databases, like me.

We come now to the Foe.

They were the race of intelligent beings, nonmeat (in fact

nonmaterial) that the Heechee had learned of. The Foe (the Heechee called them "the Assassins" and so did many humans, but I never liked that term) had wiped out at least four civilizations and damaged a couple of others.

It was apparent that they didn't like meat people of any kind.

It even appeared that they didn't like *matter* of any kind. Somehow—even I did not know how—they had added so much mass to the universe that it was slowing its rate of expansion. At some time in the future it would collapse back on itself and rebound; the only logical inference was that then the Foe would somehow so tamper with it that the next universe would be more hospitable to them.

Viewed objectively, this was an impressive and elegant project. I was never able to make Robin see that, though; he remained matter-oriented because of his unfortunate background.

And the Foe were still around, locked away in their own black hole—that atypical black hole that contained no matter but was a sink of energy. (The energy that composed its mass was, of course, the Foe themselves.) There was a name for such a black hole. It was called a "kugelblitz."

When Robin and I first met the Heechee named Captain and his crew, it was traumatic for the Heechee.

Their way of dealing with the "Assassins" had been to run away and hide. They could not believe that human beings were so reckless as to choose any other course. They told us what was going on and were shocked when we refused to follow their example.

When Captain was at last convinced that humanity (including the likes of me in that category for the moment) was going to keep our Galaxy, he recognized the inevitable. He didn't like it. But he accepted it. He hightailed it back to the place where the Heechee had run to when they perceived what a threat the Foe were: the great black hole at the core of the Galaxy. His errand was to tell the rest of the Heechee that all their plans were ruined by this impudent race of human beings, and to get them to help us.

This was a pretty urgent matter. The Heechee possessed enormous resources. Even though we had spent decades learning their technology and adding it to our own, before ever living human laid eyes on living Heechee, there was bound to be much we didn't know about. So Captain promised to mobilize Heechee help for us—immediately—to help prepare for the day when the Foe might come out to destroy a few more races of meat people.

Unfortunately, what "immediately" meant to the Heechee was nothing like what "immediately" meant to us—even if we include the pitifully slow-motion meat human beings as part of "us." The clocks in black holes run slow. The time-dilation factor at the core made them slower than human, by a factor of about forty thousand to one.

Fortunately, "immediately" at least meant as soon as ever they possibly could, and in fact they responded astonishingly fast—everything considered. The first Heechee vessel to pop out of their ergosphere turned up practically instantly—that is, in only eighteen years! The second came along only nine years after that.

The reason they could be so prompt was that they had maintained a number of ships on permanent standby alert. And those first Heechee to reach us were invaluable. They were the ones who helped us build the Watch Wheel, to stand on sentry duty at the kugelblitz, and helped us locate all the caches and centers of mothballed Heechee apparatus all over the Galaxy . . . including, often enough, mothballed human Gateway prospectors who had got that far and couldn't get back.

I should, I think, tell you a little more about the annals of the Heechee, to explain just why they were so fearful.

As a matter of routine, hundreds of Heechee ships were constantly being deployed on voyages of exploration and discovery. The Heechee were as inquisitive as human beings, and as stubbornly determined to find out everything that could be found.

There were a good many theoretical problems in science that made them itch to learn the answers. What was the truth, they wanted to know, behind the "missing mass"—the fact that all the observable matter in the universe did not seem to weigh enough to account for the observed motion of galaxies? Did protons really decay? Was there something before the Big Bang, and if so, what?

Human scientists worried about all these questions, too, in the days before we met the Heechee. The Heechee had a big advantage over those early humans (my meat progenitor included). They could go out and take a look.

So they did. They sent out expeditions to study novae and supernovae and neutron stars and white dwarfs and pulsars. They measured the flow of matter between pairs of close binaries, and they metered the flux of radiation from the infall of gas around black holes. They even learned to look inside the Schwarzschild barrier around black holes, a trick which led to some useful technology later on; and I do not even speak of their equally great curiosity about the ways particles fit together to make atoms, atoms joined into molecules, and molecules became living things like themselves.

I can easily summarize exactly what it was that the Heechee wanted in the way of knowledge. They wanted it *all*.

But of all their quests none was more urgent, or more assiduously pursued, than the search for intelligent life in the universe other than their own.

Over time, the Heechee found a couple of examples—or almost did.

The first was a chance discovery that brought quick joy and almost instant disappointment. A small, icy planet, hardly worth a second look in the normal course of events, surprised them by showing some curious anomalies in its magnetic field. No one was greatly interested at first. Then, on a routine sweep, a Heechee-manned exploration ship checked out the reports from the instrument-only robot investigators. The planet was more than 200 AU from its parent not-very-bright K-3 star, certainly not the sort of place where you would expect life to develop. Its surface temperature was only about 200 K and nothing stirred on its glacial surface. But when the Heechee investigators sounded the ice, they found great masses of metal buried in it. Echoes showed the metal to be in regular shapes. When, excitedly, the crew called for thermal borers and sent them down to investigate, they found buildings! Factories! Machines!

And nothing living at all.

They faced the disheartening fact that once there had been intelligent life on that planet, well up to early industrial standards by the remnants they disinterred, but it was there no longer.

Dating the ice cores showed that they were half a million years too late to find anyone alive, and that wasn't the worst of it. The worst was a finding by the geologists and geochemists that said, inarguably, that that particular planet could not have evolved in that particular orbit; its composition was like that of Venus, the Earth, and Mars, the kind found only close to a primary.

Something had hurled it so far from its sun that it froze.

Of course, it could have been some astronomical accident like the (however statistically unlikely) near passage of another star. But none of the Heechee could believe that (though they wanted to).

Then they found the second heartbreak.

It wasn't a heartbreak at once. It was a bright hope that persisted for a long time—more than a century! It began when a Heechee vessel caught the scent of a radio transmission, tracked it down, and found a genuine, incontestable artifact of a highly technological civilization traveling through interstellar space.

It did not have a living crew. It couldn't have, except perhaps for microbes. The object was a vast, gossamer, metal spiderweb, a thousand kilometers across but so fairy-silk flimsy that the whole thing weighed less than a fingernail.

It did not take the Heechee long to realize what they had. Where the wires joined were transistor-like things and strips of piezoelectric materials. The object was a calculator. It was also a computer, a camera, a radio transmitter, all wonderfully crafted into a gauzy web you could crush into the palm of your hand.

It was a robot sailship, propelled by light.

The proof was certain: There was intelligent life in the universe like the Heechee themselves! Not just intelligent life; it was technological life, *starfaring* life. They understood at once that this was an ultralight interstellar probe, a starwisp, drifting out to explore the Galaxy by radiation pressure, surveying other stars and reporting back by radio to its makers on their home planet.

But where was the home planet?

The Heechee ship had unfortunately failed to measure the precise alignment of the web when they captured it. Though they knew within a few degrees of where it had pointed, those few degrees encompassed some hundred million stars, far and near.

So for the next century, every Heechee ship that went into space, wherever bound, carried a dedicated radio receiver. It was always on, and it did nothing but listen for the song of another of those starwisps.

And they found them.

The first one was damaged, its orientation no longer perfect—but even that limited the choices to only about a million stars, an improvement of two orders of magnitude. And then they found a fine new one, in perfect working order, zeroed in precisely.

Swarms of Heechee explorers pounced on that corner of the Galaxy. There were still a lot of stars to search, but now only hundreds instead of millions. They searched them all. This one had no planets. Those two were close binaries where no planets could possibly support life, even if planets had existed. These others were too new and bright, too young to have given life a chance to evolve—

And then there was this other one.

It wasn't prepossessing. It was a cinder, too small and dull to be even a neutron star. True, it was in the right place. True, it did have planets . . . but it had been a nova hundreds of thousands of years before. All its planets were scorched bare. There was nothing left that could be called a living thing.

But on the fourth planet . . . there was a line of rubble across a valley that had once been a dam, a tunnel buried inside the collapsed sides of a mountain—yes, this had been the place the starwisps had come from.

And once again the Heechee had got there too late.

It was almost as though, the Heechee thought, someone had been going around the Galaxy wiping out civilizations before the Heechee could get to them.

Or before those civilizations could get living representatives of themselves into interstellar space.

And then the Heechee made one final, terrifying discovery. They sent out an expedition under a wonderful Heechee female named Tangent, and the whole nightmare picture came together for them.

I won't tell you about Tangent.

The reason for that is that sooner or later Robin will. He doesn't know that yet. He doesn't know that he himself will hear it shortly from someone who knew it at first hand. He would know that if he would let me tell him about this person— or, indeed, about some other persons whose presence on Gateway will matter greatly to him. But Robin can be quite obstinate when I try to tell him things he really ought to know.

That is the story; I apologize for the discursions. Let me just add one thing. It is not, exactly, irrelevant.

I implied, a while ago, that although I "knew" that e to the i times pi power equaled -1, I didn't understand "why." I mean, there is no intuitive reason why (the base of the natural logarithms) raised to the power of ((the square root of minus one) times (the ratio between the circumference and the diameter of a circle)) should equal anything in particular at all, much less a simple negative integer like minus one.

I wasn't quite open about that.

I don't exactly *know* why that is, but I do have suspicions. Unfortunately they have to do with phenomena like the "missing mass" and the perplexing question of why we have only three perceptible dimensions in space instead of nine, and Robin simply won't listen to me when I talk about that, either.

4

Some Parties at the Party

There was one place on Gateway I absolutely had to see again.

After I got tired of brooding over all the things I had to brood over and hearing people say, "Hey, Robinette, you're looking great!" I went there. It was called Level Babe, Quadrant East, Tunnel 8, Room 51, and for several sick and scary months it had been my home.

I went there all by myself. I didn't want to take Essie away from her old Leningrad buddy, and anyway, the part of my life that was wrapped up in that dirty little hole was not a part she had shared. I stood gazing at it, taking it all in. I even actuated perceptors I don't usually bother with, because I didn't want to just see it. I wanted to smell and feel it.

It looked, smelled, and felt crummy, and I almost drowned in the huge, hot flood of nostalgia that washed over me.

Room 51 was the cubicle I had been assigned to when I first came to Gateway—Jesus! Decades and decades ago!

It had been cleaned out some, and redecorated a lot. It wasn't a hole for a scared Gateway prospector to hide himself and his funk in anymore. Now it belonged to some feeble old geriatric case who had come to Wrinkle Rock because that was where he had the best chance of clinging to his worn-out meat body a while longer. It looked different. They'd fixed it up with a real bed, if a narrow one, instead of my old hammock. There was a shiny new PV commset mounted on the wall, and a foldaway sink with actual running water, and about a million other luxuries I hadn't had. The geriatrics case had tottered off somewhere else to join the party, no doubt. Anyway, he wasn't there. I had it all to myself, all the closet-sized claustrophobic luxury of it.

I took a deep "breath."

That was another big difference. The smell was gone. They'd got rid of the old Gateway fug that soaked into your clothes and skin, the well-used air that everybody else had been breathing—and sweating into, and farting into—for years and years. Now it only smelled a little of green, growing things, no doubt from the plantings that helped the oxygen-replenishment system along. The walls still glimmered with the Heechee-metal shine—blue, only; Gateway had never had any of the other colors.

Changes? Sure there had been changes. But it was the same room. And what a world of misery and worriment I had crammed into it.

I'd lived the way every Gateway prospector lived—counting up the minutes until I would have to take a flight, any flight, or be kicked off the asteroid because my money was gone. Poring over the lists of expeditions that were seeking crew members, trying to guess which one might make me rich—or, really, trying to decide which one might at least not make me dead. I had bedded Gelle-Klara Moynlin in that room, when we weren't doing it in her own. I had cried myself crazy in it when I came back from the last mission I had shared with her . . . without her.

It seemed to me that I had lived a longer life right there, in those few lousy months I had spent on Gateway, than in all the decades since.

I don't know how many milliseconds I spent there, in maudlin nostalgia time, before I heard a voice behind me say, "Well, Robin! You know, I had an idea I might find you mooning around here."

Her name was Sheri Loffat.

I have to confess that, glad as I was to see Sheri again, I was also glad that Essie was busy hoisting a few with her old drinking buddy just then. Essie is not a jealous woman at all. But she might have made an exception for Sheri Loffat.

Sheri was peering in at me through the narrow doorway. She looked not a minute older than the last time I'd seen her, more than half a century back. She was looking a whole lot better than she had then, in fact, because then she was just out of the hospital after a mission that had gone sour in every way but financial. Now she was looking one other thing besides "good." She was looking extremely appetizing because what she was wearing, apart from a broad grin, was nothing but a knitted shirt and a pair of underwear panties.

I recognized the outfit immediately. "Like it?" she asked, leaning in to kiss me. "I put it on just for you. Remember?"

I answered indirectly. I said, "I'm a married man now." That was to set the record straight, but it didn't keep me from kissing her back as I said it.

"Well, who isn't married?" she asked reasonably. "I've got four kids, you know. Not to mention three grandchildren and a great-grand."

I said, "My God."

I leaned back to look at her. She wriggled her way in the doorway and hooked herself by the scruff of her tee shirt to a hook on the wall. That was just what we used to do sometimes, when we were still meat and Gateway was the doorway to the universe, because the asteroid's rotational "gravity" was so

light that hanging was more comfortable than sitting. I did like
the outfit. I was not likely to forget it. It was exactly what
Sheri had been wearing the first time she came into my bed.

"I didn't even know you were dead," I said, to welcome
her.

She looked uncomfortable with the subject, as though she
hadn't quite got used to it. "It only happened last year. Of
course, I didn't look quite this young then. So being dead isn't
a total loss." She put her fingers on her chin, studying me up
and down. She commented, "I keep seeing you on the news,
Robin. You've done well."

"So did you," I said, remembering. "You went home with
five or six million dollars, didn't you? From that Heechee tool-
box you found?"

"More like ten million, when you counted in the royalties."
She smiled.

"Rich lady!"

She shrugged. "I had a lot of fun with it. Bought myself a
couple of counties of ranchland on Peggys Planet, got married,
raised a family, died . . . it was pretty nice, all right. Not counting the last part. But I wasn't just talking about money, though
you've obviously got plenty of that. What do they say? 'The
richest man in the universe'? I should have hung on to you
while I had the chance."

I had realized she'd come down off the hook to get closer.
Now I discovered I was holding her hand. "Sorry," I said,
letting go.

"Sorry for what?"

The answer to that was that if she needed to ask the question
she wouldn't understand the answer, but I didn't have to say
so. She sighed. "I guess I'm not the lady you've got on your
mind right now."

"Well—"

"Oh, that's all right, Robin. Honest. It was just a kind of
for-old-time's-sake thought. Still," she went on, "honestly,
I'm a little surprised you aren't with her and that guy—what's
his name—"

"Sergei Borbosnoy?"

But she shook her head impatiently. "No, nothing like that. It's—wait a minute—yes, Eskladar. Harbin Eskladar."

I blinked at her, because I knew who Harbin Eskladar was. He'd been pretty famous once. Not that I'd ever met him. Certainly I hadn't wanted to, at least not at first, because Harbin Eskladar had been a terrorist, and what would my dear Portable-Essie be doing with an ex-terrorist?

But Sheri was going right on: "Of course, I guess you move in pretty high society these days. I know you knew Audee Walthers. And I guess you're tight with Glare and all those others—"

"Glare?" I was having trouble keeping up with Sheri, but that stopped me cold. Although she'd said it in English, it was a Heechee name.

She looked at me with surprise. "You didn't know? Gosh, Robin, maybe one time I'm ahead of you! Didn't you see the Heechee ship dock?"

And suddenly the party began to seem as though it might be fun again. I'd seen the Heechee ship, all right, but it had never occurred to me that there might be *Heechee* on it.

I don't think it was polite of me to duck out like that. By the look on her face Sheri didn't think so either, but I was glad of the excuse. I don't like to put too much of a strain on Essie's wonderful absence of jealousy; and, although I said, "See you soon," when I kissed Sheri good-bye, I didn't mean it.

In gigabit space and alone again I hollered for Albert. He was there before I knew it. "Yes?"

I said with annoyance, "You didn't tell me there were Heechee on the Rock. What are they doing here?"

He smiled placidly at me, scratching his ankle. "As to the second question, they have every right to be here, Robin. This party is a reunion for people who were on Gateway long ago, after all. All three of these Heechee have. *Very* long ago. As to the first part—" he let himself look put-upon "—I've been trying to tell you about some of the persons you would be interested in for quite some time, Robin. I didn't think it would be tactful of me to interrupt. If I may now—"

"You may now tell me about these Heechee! I already know about Eskladar."

"Oh?" For a moment Albert looked nonplussed. It is not an expression I often see on him. Then he said obediently, "The Heechee ship came direct from the core, and the three particular Heechee who I think would interest you are named Muon, Barrow, and Glare. It is especially Glare who is of interest, for she was a shipmate of Tangent on the expedition to the Sluggard planet."

That woke me right up. "Tangent!"

"Exactly yes, Robin." He beamed. "In addition—"

"I want to see them," I said, waving him quiet. "Where are they?"

"They're on Level Jane, Robin, in the old gymnasium; it's a recreation room now. But mayn't I also tell you about the others? Eskladar you know about, and I suppose you know about Dane Metchnikov, too, and—"

"First things first, Albert," I commanded. "Right now I want to see somebody who actually knew Tangent!"

He looked stricken. "Please? At least the message from Mrs. Broadhead?"

He hadn't mentioned a message before. "Well, sure," I said. "What are you waiting for?"

He looked indignant, but what he said—in exactly Essie's tone, with exactly Essie's inflections—was: "Tell old gloopy Robin is okay see old sweetheart but only look, don't touch."

I think I may have started to flush. I don't think Albert could have seen it, though, because I waved him away as he finished speaking, and I was on my way to Level Jane.

So conscience doth make cowards of us all . . . and make us deaf, too, even to things we really ought to hear.

I'll put a girdle round the Earth in forty milliseconds whenever I want to, so to get from Level Babe down to Level Jane took, basically, no time at all. Especially since (as I keep on reminding) I wasn't really on Level Babe in the first place, and wasn't on Level Jane when I got there.

But what seems like no time at all to a meat person can be

quite a stretch for somebody like me. I had time to wonder about a couple of things.

Had I heard right? Was my wife Essie actually with Harbin Eskladar? True, the time of terrorism was long over. All of those monstrous people who burned and bombed and destroyed were long irretrievably dead, or in prison, or reformed, and the reformed ones like Harbin Eskladar were, after all, back in the population. They'd paid their debt to society.

The thing was, I couldn't believe that Essie would have thought they had paid their debt to her. Never mind that their fooling around had very nearly killed her twice, and had had every intention of killing us both a third time but had missed. It wasn't a personal matter with Essie. It was (I thought) exactly the same as with me: The terrorists that had blighted the already miserable Earth, back in the days when there wasn't enough of anything to go around and thousands of twisted people tried to redress the situation by making sure there was less of everything for everybody, were not mere criminals. They were *filth*. It was true that Eskladar (I vaguely remembered) had finally come over to the side of the good guys in the white hats. Had even turned in some of the biggest and rottenest of the leaders, thus saving a lot more lives and property than he himself had ever damaged.

But still . . .

When I saw the three Heechee, I forgot about Eskladar. Fortunately they weren't meat (if those skeletal Heechee could ever be called "meat"). They were Ancient Ancestors, and that was good, because it meant I could talk to them.

I would not have known the place they were in if Albert hadn't mentioned that once it had been the Gateway gymnasium. It didn't look like a gymnasium anymore. It was a sunny little room (sunlight cooked out of electronic tubes, of course), with tables and chairs, and there were people all over it. The human people had drinks in their hands. The Heechee don't drink. They nibble things in the same manner, and for the same reasons; what they like are sort of mushroomy growths with a high intoxication index, and these Heechee had flat bowls of the nibble-stuff in front of them. "Hello," I said breezily, sliding up close. "I'm Robinette Broadhead."

I do get a certain amount of deference. The people around made room for me ungrudgingly, and the female of them flexed her wrists in courteous greeting. "We had hoped to meet you, of course," she said. "We know your name, for every Heechee does."

They had learned the custom of shaking hands, and we did it. These Ancient Ancestors were fresh out of the core—had started nearly eleven years ago, by our clocks, but only a matter of weeks by theirs. Most of that time had been spent crossing deep space from the core to Earth. I intimated my surprise at seeing Heechee on what I had always considered private property of the human race, and one of the machine-stored humans said: "Oh, but they've got every right to be here, Mr. Broadhead. Every person who ever served on Gateway was included in the invitation to this party, and each one of them did serve here, once."

Now, that was a creepy feeling. Because the last previous time a living (or even machine-stored) Heechee had been on Gateway was something like 400,000 years in the past.

"So you're the ones who left us the ships," I said, smiling as I lifted a glass to them. They responded by holding bits of mushrooms between fingertips, aimed generally in my direction, and the female said:

"Muon left what you call the Food Factory out in your what you call the Oort Cloud, yes. Barrow actually left the ship on your planet Venus that your Sylvester Macklen discovered. I left nothing; I only visited this system once."

"But you were with Tangent," I began, and felt a tap on my shoulder. I turned, and there was my dear Portable-Essie.

"Robin, dear?" she began.

"Tore yourself away from Harbin Eskladar, have you?" I said genially. "I'm glad you're here. This is Glare—"

She was shaking her head in puzzlement. "Have not been with this Harbin Eskladar. Is no matter. Wish to make sure you are aware—"

"You didn't understand," I said, all excited. "This is *Tan-*

gent we're talking about. Could you tell us about that trip, Glare?''

"If you wish—"

And Essie said, "But please, Robin, is certain matters to be considered in this matter. Dane Metchnikov has requested lawyer."

That halted me for a moment, because I had put Dane Metchnikov so far out of my mind that I hadn't thought of the reasons why he might want to talk to a lawyer. About me. It was a downer, but I shrugged. "Later, my darling, please."

Essie sighed, and I prepared myself for the story.

You can't blame me, really. The story of Tangent was *important*. If it hadn't been for her expedition, everything would have been very different. Not just Heechee history. *All* history. In fact, human history might have been so different that there might well never have been any. So I put everything aside to hear Glare's story of that famous voyage, and I didn't give another thought to whose presence on the asteroid the presence of Dane Metchnikov implied.

5
The Tide at Its Crest

The Heechee were great explorers, and in all the annals of the Heechee the most famous voyage of all was Tangent's.

It was a well-planned trip, and it had a wonderful leader. Tangent was very wise. It was her wisdom, as a matter of fact, that caused the Heechee to run away from the Gateway asteroid and nearly everything else.

It wasn't hard for Tangent to be wise. She had her own considerable knowledge and experience, plus those of the living members of her crew, like Glare. And best of all, she had twelve or thirteen dead people to contribute their smarts to her own. To all this she added an awful lot of courage, enterprise, and compassion. You would have liked her—not counting that she did look pretty funny to human eyes. She couldn't help that, of course, being a Heechee.

When I say Tangent was an explorer, I don't mean that she went hunting for new bits of geography, like Magellan or Captain Cook. Tangent's explorations didn't involve geography at all. Long before Tangent was born, the Heechee's huge spacegoing telescopes had done all the geography the Heechee would ever need. They had spied out every star, and nearly every planet, in all the Galaxy—several hundred billion pieces of geography in all, every one photographed and spectroscoped and catalogued in the central datastores.

So Tangent didn't have to trouble herself with maps and surveys. She had more interesting things to think about.

What Tangent explored was creatures. Living beings. Tangent's mission was to study the organic things that inhabited some of that geography.

The other thing to remember about Tangent is that, by Heechee standards, she was breathtakingly beautiful.

I don't personally happen to share Heechee standards. Heechee look like Heechee to me, and I wouldn't marry one on a bet. To me Tangent would have looked like something out of my childhood in the Food Mines in Wyoming. The way we celebrated Halloween in my childhood was with pumpkins and goblins; and one of the most popular figures, pulled out of the closet every October by every grade-school teacher, was a cardboard skeleton, arms and legs jointed, skull-faced, every bone articulated.

Tangent looked a lot like one of those figures, except that she was real. She actually lived. You couldn't see between her bones. Like all the Heechee, her bones were covered by a tough, dense, muscled skin about as voluptuous to the touch as an acorn squash. Because she was female, she was bald— males sometimes had a little fur on their scalps, females almost never. She had eyes that no popular songwriter would ever find rhymes for, because, basically, they looked terrible; the pupils were blotchy blue, and the overall color of the eyes was more or less pink. Her limbs were about as thick as a six-year-old famine victim's, though nowhere near that sexy—to a human being, anyway. Her pelvis was wide. Her legs came down off the ends of it, and between those pipestem legs she wore the typical Heechee survival kit. That was a pear-shaped pod that generated the microwave flux that they needed to stay healthy, as terrestrial plants need sunlight, and in addition contained all sorts of useful or merely enjoyable tools and sundries. Including the stored minds of dead ancestors, which the Heechee used instead of computers.

Sounds ravishing, doesn't it?

No, it doesn't. But beauty is in the eyes of the cultural norm. To Heechee eyes (those glittery, pink, reptilian things!), especially to male Heechee eyes, Tangent was a knockout.

To Heechee ears, even her name was kind of sexy. She had taken the name "Tangent," as all Heechee got their adult names, as soon as she was old enough to show an interest in any abstract thing. In her case the interest was in geometry. But the Heechee language provided many opportunities for puns and plays on words, and she was quickly called by a nickname, a word very much like "tangent" which can roughly (and politely) be translated as "that-which-causes-drooping-things-to-straighten."

None of this had anything to do with her qualifications as a leader of exploration parties, but those were equally impressive. She was a credit to the Heechee race.

This made the fact that she had a large part to play in their downfall even more traumatic.

On Tangent's historic trip, her command was a huge Heechee ship. It carried instruments and devices of a thousand kinds, and a crew of ninety-one. That included Glare, who was the penetration pilot. It wasn't just a very large ship, it was a very special one. Tangent's ship was purpose-designed, and its purpose was tailored to her special needs.

It could land on a planet.

Hardly any Heechee interstellar ships could do that, or ever needed to. They were designed to go into orbit around a planet and leave the problems of reentry and takeoff to specialized landing craft. Tangent's was an exception. It would not exactly "land," because the planet she was investigating hardly had a solid core to land on, apart from a lump of metallic hydrogen 2,000 kilometers inside its freezing, crushing, slushy atmosphere. But it had something more important to the Heechee:

It had life.

There was life on Tangent's ship, too. Every member of the crew of ninety-one was a specialist in one of the many varied kinds of operations that would be required. My new friend Glare, for instance, the penetration pilot, was the one who would guide the ship down into the frigid, sludgy, dense "atmosphere" of the Sluggard planet. It was a skill few Heechee had, and her training had been extensive. So there was a lot of life on that ship, and lusty, roaring life at that. The Heechee weren't emotionless machines. In their own peculiar Heechee way, they were as horny and as temperamental as human beings. This occasionally made problems for them, just as it does for humans.

The three male Heechee who constituted Tangent's particular problem in that respect were named Quark, Angstrom 3754, and Search-and-Say.

I don't mean you to believe that these were their precise names, even if you were to translate them literally from the Heechee. Those are just as close as I know how to come. Quark was named after a subatomic particle; Angstrom 3754 was named after a color of that wavelength; and Search-and-Say was a command given to their ancestral databases when they wanted to find out what was available.

Tangent thought they were a neat bunch of guys. Among the three of them they embodied all the Heechee manly virtues. Quark was brave, Angstrom was strong, and Search-and-Say was gentle. Any one of them would have made a fine mate. Since Tangent's mating time was coming up, it was good that a male was available who would make a perfect mate.

The Heechee race was at the crest of its flood tide. There is nothing in human history that approaches the vastness and majesty of the Heechee epic. Dutch merchants, Spanish dons, and English queens, centuries ago, sent adventurers out to capture slaves, collect spices, mine gold—to discover and to loot all of the unexplored world. But that was only one single world.

The Heechee conquered billions of worlds.

Now, that has a cruel sound. The Heechee were not cruel. They deprived no natives of anything they valued, not even clay tablets or cowrie shells.

For one thing, it wasn't necessary. The Heechee never had to enslave a native population to extract precious ores. It was much easier to locate an asteroid of the proper composition, then tow it to a factory that would swallow it whole and excrete finished products. They didn't even need to grow exotic foods, or rare spices, or pharmaceuticals. Heechee chemistry could sample any organic matter and duplicate it from its elements.

The other reason they weren't ruthless toward natives is that there almost never were any natives.

In all the Galaxy, the Heechee found fewer than 80,000 worlds with life anywhere above the prokaryote stage. And, of planets inhabited by civilized sentients comparable to themselves, none at all.

There were a few near misses.

One of the near misses was the good old planet Earth. They missed because the time was out of joint; they were about half a million years too early. On Earth, the closest thing to intelligence at that time was inside the hairy, sloped skull of a stooped and smelly little primate we now call Australopithecus. Too soon, the Heechee mused regretfully when they found them; so they took a few samples and went away. Another near miss was a handless, tubby creature that lived in a swill on the planet of an F-9 star not far from Canopus. If they weren't exactly intelligent, they had evolved, at least, as far as superstition. (And stayed there; when human beings found them, they christened them the "Voodoo Pigs.") There were vanished traces of extinct civilizations here and there, some of them puzzlingly fragmentary. There were a number of potentially interesting ones that might be expected to reach the point of social institutions some time in the next million years . . .

And then there were the ones Tangent was investigating now. They called them "the Sluggards."

The Sluggards were really quite intelligent. They had machines! They had governments. They had a language—they even had poetry. The Sluggards were not the only race the Heechee had found with some of such things, but they were by all odds the most promising.

If only one could talk to them!

So Tangent's ship settled itself in orbit, and the explorers gazed down at the turbulent planet below. Said Angstrom to Tangent, "Ugly-looking planet. It reminds me of the place where the Voodoo Pigs lived, remember?"

"I remember," Tangent said fondly. In fact, she remembered well enough that she let herself lean against Angstrom's exploring hand, which was delicately tweaking the ropy tendons of her back in the way she knew well.

Said Search-and-Say jealously, "It is not in the least like that planet! That one was hot; this one freezes gases. On this one we couldn't breathe even if it were warm enough, because the methane would poison us, while among the Voodoo Pigs we could walk about even without masks—except for the smell, anyway."

Tangent touched Angstrom affectionately. "But we didn't mind the smell, did we?" she asked. Then, considering, she stroked Search-and-Say as well. Although she was missing nothing of the view of the planet and was quite aware of the clicks and wheeps of the ship's sensors, which were busy drinking in data from the instruments that had been left on the planet many years before, she also missed nothing of the sexual innuendos.

Tangent said kindly, "Both of you have work to do—Quark too, and so do I. Let's do it."

Actually (Glare said, rubbing her abdomen nostalgically), the eighty-seven crew members not directly involved were rather touched by Tangent's romance. They liked her. They

wished her well. Besides, all the Heechee world loved lovers,
just like ours.

By the end of the second day of the voyage, Search-and-
Say reported peevishly that the Ancestors were not only ready
but positively clamorous to talk to Tangent. She sighed and
took her seat in the control cabin. What she was sitting on
mostly was her pod; her seat was so constructed that her pod
was plugged in directly to all the Ancestral pods on the ship.
It was a useful arrangement. It wasn't always a comfortable
one.

The Ancient Ancestors had neither sight nor hearing, being
only stored intelligences in a databank, just like me. But the
brightest and most experienced of them learned to read the
electron-flow of optics or instrumentation almost as well as
with ears and eyes. The most senior Ancestor aboard was a
long-dead male named Flocculence. Flocculence was a VIP.
He was the most valuable person aboard—perhaps even more
valuable than Tangent herself—because before his death Flocculence had actually visited this planet.

Tangent opened her ears to the Ancestors. There was an
immediate babble of voices. Every Ancestor in the ship's store
wanted to talk. The only one of them that had the right to talk
just then, though, was Flocculence. He quickly hushed the
others.

"I have been monitoring the recordings," he said at once.
"Nine of the recording channels we left in place have no data—
I don't yet know if they malfunctioned, or if the Sluggards
simply never visited those locations. The other fifty-one, however, are full; they average nearly three hundred thousand mor-
phemes each."

"But that's a lot!" cried Tangent, delighted. "That's almost
a whole book-equivalent for each channel!"

"More," Flocculence corrected her. "For the Sluggard language is extremely compact. Listen. I will replay a section of
one of the recordings—"

There was a faint, low hooting sound—Tangent did not so
much hear it as feel it in her bones—

"And now the same recording, speeded up and frequency-shifted to a normal bit-rate for us—"

The hooting became a quick, shrill twittering. Tangent listened with impatience. It hurt her ears. "Have you translated any of it?" she asked, less for information—she knew that if there had been any major breakthroughs she would have been notified at once—than to make the noise stop.

But surprisingly the Ancient Ancestor crowed, "Oh, yes! Much! In Listening Post Seventeen there was what I think you would call a political meeting. It has to do with the nature of the site itself; it is either theologically sacred or dangerously polluted, and the Sluggards were discussing what to do about it. The debate is still going on—"

"After sixty-one years?"

"Well, only about seven hours of their time, Tangent."

"Good, good," Tangent said happily. It was a major victory; there were few better ways of gaining insight into a culture than through studying its modes of settling public questions. "And you're sure that's what it is? Are your translations reliable?"

"Oh," said Flocculence doubtfully, "fairly reliable. I wish we had Binding Force here with us." Binding Force was Flocculence's former partner in many investigations. The two of them had made a wonderful team. Some day, no doubt, they would again. But for the moment Binding Force was far too ancient to go into space again, and too healthy to die.

"How reliable is 'fairly' reliable?"

"Well, at least half our Sluggard vocabulary is words deduced from context. I could be deducing wrong."

"Unlucky for you if you are," Tangent snapped, and then immediately caught herself. "I'm sure you're doing a fine job," she soothed. And hoped it was true.

Glare hadn't been on Flocculence's first trip, but before she shipped out with Tangent, she had learned quite a lot about the Sluggards. For that matter, everybody had. The Sluggards were, after all, really quite important to the Heechee. As important, say, as a diagnosis of cancer would have been to any human before Full Medical came along.

The Sluggards possessed an ancient civilization. In terms of years, it was far older even than the Heechee's own, but that didn't really signify, because nothing much had happened in it. What did happen happened very slowly. The Sluggard's planet was cold. The Sluggards themselves were both cold and sluggish—that was how they got their name. They swam slowly through a slush of gases; the chemistry of their bodies was as tedious as their movements, and so was their speech.

So was the propagation of impulses through their nervous systems—which is to say, their thoughts.

So when that first Heechee expedition could no longer doubt that these slushy, creepy creatures possessed intelligence, they were both delighted and ticked off. What was the use of discovering another intelligent race at last if so simple an exchange as—

"Take me to your leader."

"Which leader?"

—could take six months to complete?

That first Heechee discovery ship lingered in orbit around the Sluggard planet for a year. Flocculence and Binding Force dropped sondes into the sludgy atmosphere and painfully built up a slow recognition of discrete sounds that was the first step toward a vocabulary. It wasn't easy. It certainly wasn't simple. The sondes were dropped more or less at random, aiming only at spots where the deep-probe radars and sonars had identified clusters of beings. Often the clusters were gone by the time the sondes got there. The ones that were best aimed recorded slow, deep moans. Transmitters passed the sounds into orbit, recording experts speeded them up and transposed them down to the audible range, and after weeks each tape might produce a single word.

But Heechee semanticists had many resources. At the end of their year in orbit they had identified enough of a vocabulary to prepare a simple tape. Then they constructed a graven tablet with a picture of a Heechee, a picture of a Sluggard, a picture of a sound playback unit, and a picture of the tablet itself. All

the images were incised on flat surfaces of crystal, so that the
Sluggards could feel them—they were, after all, blind.

Then the Heechee duplicated the lot sixty times and dropped
a set into each of sixty Sluggard population centers.

The tapes read:

> Greetings.
> We are friends.
> Talk to this and we will hear.
> We will answer soon.

"Soon," in that context, meant a good long time. When that
was done, the Heechee ship left. The crew was somewhat
glum. There was no sense waiting around for an answer. The
best thing was to come back when the Sluggards had had time
to discover the messages, get over the initial shock, and respond. Even then there would be an inevitable longish period
of dumb questions and time-wasting answers; but they didn't
need a live Heechee for that. They chose their least valuable
Ancient Ancestor, explained to her what sorts of questions
might be asked and what sorts of answers—and urgings, and
counterquestions—should be returned, and left her in orbit to
spend a dismal few decades in solitude. Every Heechee in the
crew wished he could be there to get those answers, but few
could feel very confident of doing it—their best guess was that
to get any solid information from the Sluggards would take
more than half a century.

As indeed it did.

Twenty days after arrival in orbit around the Sluggard
planet, Tangent was as ready for the real work of the expedition
as she ever would be.

The Ancient Ancestor they had left behind was unfortunately no longer operational, but she had served her purpose.
Questions had been asked and answered, and the data was in
store. Radar, or the Heechee device that did for the Heechee
what radar had done for human beings, had located the present
positions of the physical clusters that marked Sluggard com-
munities, as well as other objects solid enough and large

enough to constitute navigation hazards. FTL radio contact had been made with the home planets and the data transmitted, and frail old Binding Force had sent a cheery message approving their translation attempts and urging them on. The special structures on Tangent's ship that would allow it to carry out its main mission had been checked and tested and reported ready.

There was one other Heechee device which they had hoped would serve them well, but it was a disappointment. That was a sort of communications instrument. What it transmitted and received was a special sort of data—well, what you might call "feelings." It neither transmitted nor received "information" in the classical sense—one could not use it to order another thousand kilotons of structural metal or to command a ship to change its course. But one Heechee wearing the appropriate metal-mesh helmet could "hear" the emotions of others, even at planetary distances.

It was what we came to call the "Dream Seat."

For the Heechee, the main domestic use of the device was for what passed among them as police work. The Heechee didn't detect crimes. They prevented them. The emanations from a mind so disordered as to be about to commit an antisocial act, a violent act in particular, could be detected in the early stages. A counseling-and-intervention team was then dispatched at once to apply corrective therapy.

The Dream Seats had also been very helpful in deciding that, for instance, the "Voodoo Pigs" were close enough to intelligent to bear watching, because their "feelings" were far more complex than those of the lower animals. So it was a standard Heechee resource instrument in that fundamental Heechee quest for interstellar companionship. It had been hoped that Tangent's orbiting spacecraft could simply listen in on the Sluggards and "hear" their moods and anxieties and joys.

The Dream Seat did work, as a matter of fact. It just didn't work in any very useful way. As with everything else the Sluggards did, their emotions were hopelessly slow. Said Quark glumly, pulling off the headset, "You might as well be listening to how a sedimentary rock feels about metamorphosis."

"Keep trying," Tangent instructed. "When at last we understand the Sluggards, it will all be worthwhile."

Later on she remembered saying that, and wondered how she could have been so wrong.

I've told you an awful lot about Tangent and her shipmates, and I haven't yet told you why it all matters. Trust me. It mattered a lot. Not only to Tangent, and to the whole Heechee race, but to humanity in general and, most especially, to me in particular.

But good old Albert tells me I talk too much, and so I'll try to keep to essentials. The essentials were that Tangent and her crew did what Heechee ships almost never did. They took their specially armored spacecraft and dived it down into the dense, frigid, damaging gases of the Sluggard planet in order to visit the Sluggards on their home turf.

"Turf" isn't the right word, either—I have a lot of trouble finding right words, because the vocabulary I learned as a meat person on Earth really doesn't apply anymore. The Sluggards didn't have turf, in the sense of plots of land to build on. They didn't have any land. Their specific gravity was so close to the specific gravity of the gases they lived in that they floated, along with all their household goods, their households, and their Sluggard equivalents of factories, farms, offices, and schools. And, of course, neither human nor Heechee could live in that environment unprotected. Although the Heechee were careful engineers (I know humans who would call them cowardly, in fact), there was at least a nagging worry that even their ship might fail in the crushing pressures where the Sluggards lived.

So before they entered the planet's atmosphere they checked and rechecked and double-checked everything there was to check. Flocculence and the other Ancient Ancestors had to do double duty, not only keeping up with their work of translation but storing and analyzing all the data about the ship's own systems.

"Are we ready?" Tangent asked at last, seated at the captain's stool in the control room, webbing herself in as did all the others. One by one the section chiefs reported readiness, and she took a deep breath. "I would commence descent now," she said to the penetration pilot, Glare.

Glare ordered the steerperson, "Commence descent."

The ship slowed its orbital speed and slipped down into the cold, thick, swirling poison gases the Sluggards swam in.

Entry was bouncy, but the ship had been built for that. Navigation was blind, at least optically speaking; but the ship had sonar and electronic eyes, and on the screens in the room they could see the shapes of clusters of Sluggard "homes" and other objects as they approached. "I would not go so fast," Tangent cautioned, "because of the risk of cavitation."

Glare agreed. "Slow down," she ordered, and the great ship inched toward the nearest Sluggard arcology.

The whole crew watched the screens with awe and delight. Sludgy objects began to appear. There were structures like clouds, and creatures like the soft-plastic toys, shaped like amoebae or jellyfish, that children play with. The Sluggards were almost as still as their "buildings." All of the females, and most of the males, moved so slowly that no Heechee eye could see a change; only a few of the males, going into what they called "high mode," now and then exhibited visible motion. And more and more of the males did that as the ship approached and their torpid senses let them know that something or other seemed to be happening.

That was when Tangent made her first mistake.

She assumed that the movement of the males was because they were startled at the sudden appearance of the Heechee ship. Heaven knows, that must have startled them—like a high-speed lander suddenly appearing over a primitive human village that had never seen a spacecraft, or even an airplane, before. But it wasn't startlement that sent the males lashing about so fast and destructively. It was pain. The high-frequency sound the Heechee ship steered by was agony to the Sluggards. It drove them out of their minds, and, before long, the weaker of them died of it.

Could the Heechee ever have really satisfied their yearning for interstellar friends with the Sluggards?

I don't see how. My own experience says no; it was as hard for Heechee to communicate with Sluggards as it is for us stored persons to get into any meaningful real-time relationship with meat people. It's not impossible. It's generally just more trouble than it's worth. And when I talk to meat people at close range, they don't usually die of it.

After that it wasn't a happy ship anymore (said Glare, morosely shrugging her belly muscles). The expectation had been so delicious; the letdown was mean.

It got worse.

The mission was teetering on the verge of failure. Though the sondes continued to trickle words into the recorders, the attempts to approach Sluggards in their homes were always both catastrophic and disappointing—disappointing for the Heechee, catastrophic for their new "friends."

And then, in orbit, there came the news from home.

It was a message from Binding Force, and what he said, with the testiness of age and the resentment of one who wishes he had been present, was, in free translation, "You've screwed it up. The important parts of the data were not customs and polity of the Sluggards. It is their poetry."

The shipboard Ancient Ancestors had recognized the poetry as poetry—as a sort of combination of the songs of the great whales and the old Norse eddas of Earth. Like the eddas, they sang of great battles of the past, and the battles were important.

The songs were of creatures who had appeared without bodies and had caused great destruction. The Sluggards called them the equivalent of "Assassins," and according to Binding Force they were in fact without bodies—were creatures of energy; had in fact really appeared and caused great destruction . . .

"What you thought were mere legends," scolded Binding Force in his message, "were not about gods and devils. They are straightforward accounts of an actual visit by creatures that seem totally hostile to all organic life. And there is every reason to believe they are still around."

That was the first time the Heechee had ever heard of the Foe.

6
Loves

By the time Glare finished her story there was quite a crowd gathered around. Every one of them had questions, but it took a moment for them to get the questions together. Glare sat silent, rubbing her rib cage. The movement made a faint grating noise, like someone running a finger across a washboard.

A short black man I didn't know said, "Excuse me, but I don't understand. How did Tangent know that was the Foe?" He was speaking in English, and I realized that someone had been translating Glare's story all along. The someone was Albert.

While he was translating the short man's question into Heechee for Glare, I gave him a look. He shrugged in response, meaning (I assumed), well, I wanted to hear the story, too.

Glare was shrugging, too, in response to the question—at least, she was giving her abdomen that quick contraction that is the Heechee equivalent. "We didn't know," she said. "That came later, after Binding Force had performed deep-structure analysis on the Sluggard eddas. Then it became clear that these intruding Assassins were not from that planet. Of course, there was much other data."

"Of course," Albert chimed in. "The missing mass, for one thing."

"Yes." said Glare. "The missing mass. This had been a great puzzle for our astrophysicists for some time, as I believe it had been for yours." She reached thoughtfully for another of the little fungus caps, while Albert explained to the others how the "missing mass" had turned out to be no natural cosmic phenomenon, but an artifact of the Foe; and at that point I stopped listening. I hear plenty of that kind of thing from Albert all the time. I stop listening a lot then, too. Hearing Glare tell us the story of Tangent's terrible trip was one thing. That was a story I could listen to with full attention. But when Albert gets into the *why* of things, my mind wanders. Next thing he would be getting into nine-dimensional space and Mach's Hypothesis.

He did. Glare seemed quite interested. I wasn't. I leaned back, waved to the waitress for another shot of "rocket juice"—the damn near lethal white whiskey that Gateway prospectors had drowned their worries in in the old days—and let him talk.

I wasn't listening. I was thinking about poor horny Tangent, all those hundreds of thousands of years ago, and her ill-fated trip.

I've always had a soft spot in my heart for Tangent—well, that's not exactly true, either. There are those words again. How inaccurately they convey meaning! I don't *have* a heart, so of course there are not any soft spots in it. (Essie says I can't be "soft" in any sense but "-ware," which is a cybernetic joke.) And "always" isn't exact, either, because I've only known about Tangent for about thirty, or perhaps I should say thirty million, years. But I do think of her often, and with sympathy, because I'd been shot down, too, and I knew how it felt.

I took a pull of my rocket juice, gazing benevolently at the group around the table. The rest of the audience was a lot more fascinated than I had been by the way Albert and Glare exchanged cosmological quips, but then they hadn't had Albert living in their pockets for the last fifty (or fifty million) years. In that time you get to know a program pretty well. I reflected that, generally speaking, I knew what Albert was going to say before he said it. I even knew the significance of the way he looked at me sidelong, now and then, as he talked. He was reproaching me, in a subliminal way, for not letting him tell me something he had wanted to tell me very much.

I gave him a tolerant smile to let him know I understood him . . . and, a little bit, to remind him that I was the one who decided who got told what when.

Then I felt a gentle hand on the back of my neck. It was Essie's hand. I leaned back against it pleasurably, just as Albert took another of those looks at me and said to Glare, "I suppose you had a chance to get to know Audee Walthers III on your trip here?"

That woke me up. I turned to Essie and whispered, "I didn't know Audee was here."

Said Essie in my ear, "Appear to be many things you are unwilling to know about meat persons present." Her tone made the back of my neck tingle; it was a mixture of love and severity. It is the tone Essie uses when she thinks I have been unusually gloopy, or silly, or obstinate.

"Oh, my God," I said, remembering. "Dane Metchnikov."

"Dane Metchnikov," she agreed. "Is also present here on Rock as meat. Along with person who rescued him."

"Oh, my God," I said again. Dane Metchnikov! He had been along on that black-hole expedition that had burdened my conscience for half a century. I had left him and the others there, and among the others had been—

"Gelle-Klara Moynlin, yes," whispered Essie. "Are presently in Central Park."

Central Park isn't much of a park. When Klara and I were

prospectors together, it was about a dozen mulberry and orange trees and not many more than that bushes.

It still wasn't much different. The little pond we called Lake Superior was still curving up around the shape of the asteroid. Now the park was much more densely grown, but I had no trouble at all spotting a dozen or more human beings in among the shrubbery. Eight or ten of them were the elderly veterans who lived on Wrinkle Rock, all meat, posed like statues under the trees. A few were partygoers like myself, only meat, and among them I had no difficulty in recognizing that other motionless meat-person statue who was Gelle-Klara Moynlin.

She hadn't changed a bit, at least physically.

In another way, she had changed almost terminally. She wasn't alone. She was, in fact, between two men; worse, she was holding hands with one of them, and the other had an arm draped around her shoulder.

That was a nasty blow all by itself, because the last I had known of Klara, the only person she was likely to be holding hands with or being held by was me.

It took me a moment to realize that the hand-holding man was Dane Metchnikov—it had, after all, been a *long* time since I had seen him last. The other one I didn't know at all. He was tall, slim, and good-looking, and, if those things hadn't been enough to damn him, he was resting his hand on Klara's shoulder in a fond and habitual way.

Sometimes, when I was young and enamored of some person or other, I had this burning desire to know her perfectly. Utterly. In every way; and one of the ways was a fantasy. The fantasy was that I would find her (whoever she was at the moment) so sound asleep that nothing I could do would wake her; and so I would steal up on the dear loved one, all asleep, and investigate all those secret things without her knowing. To see if there was stubble in her armpit. To check on how recently she had cleaned out the glop under her toenails. To peer up her nostrils, and into her ears—and to do all of this, see, when she didn't know I was doing it, because, although we conducted many a mutual exploration, it was a whole other thing when it was observed. As with most of my fantasies, it was the kind of thing that my former analyst program, Sigfrid von Shrink, looked on with toleration and not much approval; he read meanings into it that I didn't enjoy. And, as with most fantasies, it wasn't all that much fun when I had the chance to do it.

I could do it now. There was Klara, as though carved in eternal stone.

There was also Essie, right there with me, to dampen the urge to explore, but she would have gone away if I had asked her to. She didn't say a word, Essie didn't. She just hovered silently behind me as I stood there, invisible in gigabit space, staring at the woman I had mourned for most of my life.

Klara looked very good. It was hard to believe that she was actually older than I was—which is to say, about six months older than God. My birthday was almost the same as the discovery of Gateway, whose hundredth anniversary we were celebrating. Klara had been born some fifteen years earlier.

She didn't look it. She didn't look a day older.

Part of that, of course, was simply Full Medical. Klara was quite a rich woman, and she'd been able to afford all the tissue restoration and replacement around even before it became basically free for anyone. What's more, she had spent thirty years in the time trap of a black hole, where I had abandoned her to save myself—it had taken me all those thirty years to get over the guilt of that—and so in those long years she had aged only minutes, because of time dilation. In terms of elapsed time since her birth, she was well over a hundred. In terms of time counted by her own body clock, certainly in her sixties. In terms of the way she looked—

The way she looked was the way she had always looked to me. She looked really good.

She was standing there with her fingers interlaced with those of Dane Metchnikov. Her head was turned to the man who had his arm around her. Her eyebrows were dark and bold as ever, and her face was Klara's face, the one I had wept over for thirty years.

"Don't startle her, damn Robin," commanded Essie from behind me. Just in time. I had been about to display myself right in front of them, not thinking that this encounter would not be a whole lot easier for her than it was for me, and that she would need more time, an awful lot more time, to handle it.

"So then what?" I demanded, not taking my eyes off Klara.

"So then," said Essie, scowling, "you act like normal decent human being, you know? You give woman chance! You show up at edge of woods, maybe, and you walk toward her. Give her little chance to see you coming, get ready for quite traumatic encounter, before you speak."

"But that will take forever!"

"*Have* forever, dummy," said Essie firmly. "Anyway, have other thing to do. Aren't paying attention, right? Aren't aware doppel-Cassata is looking for you?"

"Hell with him," I said absently. I was so busy studying the face and form of my long-lost love that I had no patience for anything else—or brains for anything else, either; it took me a good many microseconds to remember that the longer I put off starting the conversation, the longer it would be before I could hear her voice.

"You're right," I said reluctantly. "Might as well see the bastard. Just let me get started here."

I calved off a doppel of me behind a drooping lime tree, rich with golden fruit, and started the doppel walking toward the pair. And then I followed Essie meekly enough back to the Spindle, where she said Cassata was waiting.

It would take a *long* time for my doppel to reach Klara, speak to her, wait for her to respond—many, many milliseconds. I wished desperately that I could shorten the time, because how could I wait?

And I also wished desperately that I could make it longer. Because what was I going to say?

Julio Cassata took my mind off these—what's Essie's word?—these gloopy maunderings. He's good at that. He's like the mosquito bite that takes your mind off the toothache for a moment. He's never a welcome distraction, but at least he is a distraction.

When we found him, he was in the Blue Hell. Essie squeezed my arm, grinning. Cassata was sitting at one of the little tables with a drink in front of him, reminiscently pawing a young woman I had never seen before.

I didn't see much of her then, either, because as soon as Cassata perceived we were there he changed it all. Partygoers, girl, and Blue Hell vanished; we were in his office on the JAWS satellite. His hair had got combed, his tunic collar had buttoned itself, and he was gazing at us frostily over his steel desk. He pointed to two metal chairs. "Sit down," he ordered.

Essie said dispassionately, "Cut crap, Julio. You want talk to us, fine, we talk. Not here. Is too ugly."

He gave her the kind of a look a major general gives a second lieutenant. Then he decided to be a good fellow. "Whatever you like, my dear. You pick."

Essie sniffed. She glanced at me, hesitated, then abolished the military office. Instead we were in our familiar *True Love*, complete with couches, bar, and gentle music playing.

"Yes." Cassata nodded agreeably, looking around appreciatively. "That's much better. Nice place you've got here. Mind if I help myself?" He didn't wait for permission but headed for the bar.

"Mind all this crap," said Essie. "Spit it out, Julio. Embargoed our ship, right? Why?"

"Only a temporary inconvenience, my dear." Cassata twinkled as he made himself a Chivas and nothing. "I only wanted to be sure I got a chance to talk to you."

Even a counterirritant can be too *damn* irritating. I said, "So talk." Essie gave me a quick, warning look, because she heard my tone. I was keeping myself under control. I wasn't in any good mood to talk to Julio Cassata.

Some people think that machine-stored people never get all wound up and flustered, because we're just bits of data arranged in a program. It isn't true. At least, it isn't true for me, and especially not just then. I'd been up and down in an emotional carnival ride—keyed up in the first place by the party; exalted and somber while I listened to the story of Tangent's terrible trip; torn with a hundred emotions by running into Klara. I wasn't about to enjoy talking to Cassata.

Of course, I seldom do enjoy talking to Cassata. I don't see why anyone would. His main conversational gambits are orders and insults; he doesn't talk, he issues statements. He hadn't changed. He took a long pull on his Scotch, looked me in the eye and said:

"You're a pest, Broadhead."

It wasn't a promising remark. Essie, halfway through making me a Mai Tai, twitched and almost spilled it. She looked at me worriedly. It's Essie's policy to do all the fighting herself when we're in a situation that calls for it. She thinks I get too excited when I'm the one that yells.

But I fooled her this time. I said politely, "I'm sorry if I've caused you any inconvenience, Julio. Would you be good enough to tell me why you say that?"

What remarkable self-control I displayed! It was a lot more than the lout deserved. A lot more than I would have given him if I hadn't, at the last moment, realized that I ought to feel sorry for him.

What I had realized was that, after all, he was under sentence of death.

Major General Julio Cassata and I go back a long way—there's no use adding up the years; arithmetic gets all mixed up when you're in gigabit time. We had had many contacts, and I hadn't enjoyed any of them.

He wasn't a stored personality himself, though. That is, usually he wasn't. Like many meat people who have to deal with us stored souls on an urgent basis, he makes a doppel of himself and sends it out to talk to us. It isn't quite the same as a face-to-face in real time, but the difference is only psychological. Well, *painfully* psychological. He inputs himself as a machine-stored intelligence and comes looking for us—whichever of us he wants to talk to, sometimes me. Then he says whatever he has to say, listens to what we have to say in return, carries on a conversation just as well, in the form of a disembodied bundle of bits in gigabit space, as he would if he and we were meat people around a table—no, not just as well; a hell of a lot better, at least in that we are that much faster. Then meat-Julio calls his doppelganger-Julio back and listens while it tells him what happened.

All that is straightforward, and certainly not painful at all. It is also very efficient. The pain comes later.

The doppel asks just what meat-Cassata would have asked, objects to what he would have objected to, says just what he would have said—as of course it must, *being* him. And it isn't like sending an ambassador out and waiting for a response, because even the best of ambassadors, assuming that any ambassador could do the job as well as a doppel does, would certainly take time to do it. The doppels take at most a matter of seconds, if the conference is to take place at planetary distances—longer, of course, if the person the meat man wants to talk to happens to be at the other end of the Galaxy. Before the meat person has a chance to wonder how the conference is going to go, the doppel is back and tells him.

That's the good part.

Then comes the only part that's not so good, because what do you do with the doppel after it's done its job?

You could just leave it in storage, of course. There's plenty of capacity in gigabit space, and one more stored personality wouldn't matter much. But it bothers some people to have duplicates of themselves around. It especially bothers someone like Cassata. Being military, he's got the military mind. A stored duplicate of him, knowing everything he knows, isn't just an annoying loose end. It's a security risk. Someone might find it and ask it questions! Threaten it! (With what?) Torture it! (How?) Hold its feet to the fire (if it had feet)—well, I don't know exactly what goes on in Julio Cassata's mind, and I thank God I don't every day.

All of that is quite foolish, of course, but the doppels are Cassata's own, and if he thinks some imaginary enemy might sometime find out from them the secrets of his service, no one else can interfere. He's a shift commander for JAWS, the Joint Assassin Watch. That means he's in charge of a large part of the defense programs against the eventual coming out of the

Assassins from their kugelblitz. So if he wants conferences with parties at a distance, which he does, he has to do this sort of thing almost daily, which means that if he left his doppels in storage, there would be hundreds and thousands of Major General Julio Cassatas around.

So he doesn't just store them. He kills them.

That's what it feels like to Cassata himself, anyway. When he terminates his doppel, it feels as though he's assassinated a twin.

And the other bad thing about that is that the doppel itself—*him*self, damn it—knows that's what's going to happen.

Sometimes it makes our conversations sort of gloomy.

That's why I didn't rip Julio Cassata to simulated bloody shreds for his impudence. He was as surprised as Essie. He unwrapped a fresh cigar, staring at me. "You all right?" he demanded.

"All right" wasn't anywhere near a correct diagnosis, because I was wondering just how close my doppel had got to Klara and how she would react when she saw it, but I had no intention of telling Julio Cassata any of that. So I just said:

"I'll be fine when you tell me what all this is about."

I was quite polite, but Cassata had never subscribed to the theory that politeness should go both ways. He worried off the end of the cigar with his teeth and spat the nasty little plug of tobacco on the floor, watching me carefully. Then he said: "You aren't as important as you think you are, Broadhead." I managed to keep the smile on my face, though the temperature was going up inside. "You think the embargo is just for you. Wrong. That Heechee ship came right here from the core, you know."

I hadn't known. I didn't see what difference it made, either, and said so.

"Classified material, Broadhead," Cassata rumbled. "Those Heechee Ancient Ancestors, they've been blabbing their heads off. They should've been debriefed at JAWS first!"

"Yes," I said, nodding. "That makes sense, because naturally things that happened half a million years ago or so are pretty important military secrets."

"Not just half a million years ago! They know all about the present state of readiness in the core! And there are meat Heechee there, plus this Walthers guy who's actually been there and seen it for himself."

I took a deep breath. What I wanted to do was to ask him all over again whom he possibly was trying to keep all these secrets *from*. But that would have meant prolonging an old argument, and I was tired of being with Cassata anyway. I just said, still politely, "You said I was a pest, and I don't see what the Heechee ship has to do with that."

He had the cigar well lit by then. He blew smoke at me and said, "Nothing. That's a separate thing. I came here because of the ship, but I also wanted to tell you to stay out of the way."

"Stay out of what way why?" I asked, and felt Essie stirring restlessly, because she had got tired of marveling at my self-control and was beginning to have trouble retaining her own.

"Because you're a civilian," he explained. "You mess around in JAWS affairs. You get in the way, and things are getting to a point where we can't afford civilian meddling anymore."

I began to get a glimmering of what was bugging him. I smiled at Essie to reassure her that I wasn't going to kill this impudent general. I really wasn't—at least, not yet. "The maneuvers didn't go well," I guessed.

Cassata choked and sputtered cigar smoke. "Who told you that?"

I shrugged. "It's obvious. If they'd been a success, your PR people would have had pictures on every newscast. You aren't bragging; therefore you've got nothing to brag about. So the people you want to keep secrets from are the ones who're paying your bills. Like me."

"Wise ass," he snarled. "If you say any of that, I'll take care of you personally."

"How are you going to do that?"

He was back in control now, all military, all brass, including the brain. "For openers," he said, "I'm withdrawing your JAWS clearance, effective immediately."

That was too much for Essie. "Julio," she rasped, "you gone crazy or what?"

I put a restraining hand on her arm. I said seriously, "Julio, I've got a lot of things on my mind right now and JAWS isn't one of them. Not right up top, anyway. I had no intention of bothering any of the people at JAWS anytime in the near future—until you came along with your arrogant orders. Now, of course, I'll make it my business to check up on everything JAWS does."

He bellowed, "I'll have you arrested!"

I was beginning to enjoy myself. I said, "No, you won't. You don't have the authority. And you don't have the clout. Because I've got the Institute."

That took him back for a moment. The Broadhead Institute for Extra-Solar Research was one of the best ideas I'd ever had. I'd endowed it a long, long time ago for quite different reasons—well, to tell the truth, about half of the reasons were *tax* reasons. But I'd endowed it well. I had given it a charter that let it do just about anything it wanted to outside of our solar system, and I'd taken the precaution of loading the board of directors with people who would do what I wanted them to.

Cassata recovered fast. "The hell I don't have the clout! That's an *order*."

I studied him thoughtfully. Then I called, "Albert?" He popped into existence, blinking at me over his pipe. "Transmit a message for me," I ordered. "Instruct all branches of the Institute that, effective at once, they are to cease cooperation with the Joint Assassin Watch Service and deny any JAWS personnel access to our premises or our data. Reason given: a direct order from Julio Cassata, Major General, JAWS."

Cassata's eyes began to pop. "Now, wait a minute, Broadhead!" he rumbled.

I turned back to him politely. "You have some comment to make about this?"

He was perspiring. "You wouldn't do that," he said. His

tone was funny, half wheedle and half snarl. "We're all in this together! The Foe is everybody's enemy!"

"Why, Julio," I said, "I'm glad to hear you say that. I thought you were under the impression they were your private property. Don't worry. I won't stop the Institute from functioning. It'll go on with its studies; the scout ships will keep on surveying; we'll go right on accumulating data about the Foe. We just won't bother sharing any of this with JAWS anymore. Now. Does Albert send the message or not?"

He tapped the ash off the end of his cigar for a moment, looking stricken. "No," he muttered.

"Sorry? I couldn't quite hear what you said."

"No!" Then he shook his head despairingly. "He'll blow his stack," he said.

But he said "he," and the only "he" he could have meant was the meat-General Cassata. Who was, of course, himself.

"He said 'he,'" I said to Essie when Cassata had gone glumly away.

She said soberly, "Is interesting, I agree. Doppel-Julio comes to consider meat-Julio separate individual."

"He's turning schizo?"

"Is turning scared," she corrected. "Realizes has only limited time to live. Sad little man." Then she said diffidently, "Dear Robin? Realize thoughts are elsewhere at this moment—"

I didn't agree, because it wouldn't have been polite; nor did I deny it, because it was true. Even while I was quarreling with Julio Cassata I was stealing peeks at the scene in Central Park. My doppel had finally reached Klara and said hello to her, and she was just beginning to say, "Robin! It's ni—"

"—but can I make suggestion?"

"Well, of course you can," I said, embarrassed. If I'd had blood vessels to redden my face (and a real face to be reddened), I probably would have blushed. Perhaps I did anyway.

"Suggestion," she said, "is, go easy."

"Of course," I said, nodding. I would have said "of course"

to almost anything she said. "Now, if you don't mind, I'd like to, uh—"

"Know what you would like to do. Only have problem with discrepancy in time scales, right? So really is no hurry at all for you, dear Robin. Can talk a little first?"

I sat still a moment. (Klara had just got out the "—ce to," and was parting her lips to begin, "see you again!") I was by then quite embarrassed. It isn't easy to be telling one woman that you want very much to talk to another, when you have as uneasy a conscience as I always seem to have about my wife, Essie, and my long-lost love, Gelle-Klara Moynlin.

On the other hand, Essie was absolutely right. There was no hurry at all. She was watching me with love and concern on her face. "Is tough situation for you, eh, dear Robin?" she put in.

The only useful thing I could think of to say was, "I love you a lot, Essie."

She didn't look loving in return, she looked exasperated. "Yes, of course." She shrugged. "Don't change subject. You love me, I love you, both have no doubt of this; is not relevant to present discussion. Discussion is how you feel about very nice lady whom you also love, Gelle-Klara Moynlin, and complications arising therefrom."

It sounded worse when she spelled it out. It did not make me any more comfortable. "We've had that discussion a million times!" I groaned.

"So why not one million times more? Get comfortable, dear Robin. Have at least fifteen, maybe eighteen hundred milliseconds before Klara finishes saying what nice surprise is to see you again. So we talk, you and I, unless you don't want?"

I thought it over and gave up. I said, "Why not?" And indeed there was no reason.

There was also no reason not to get comfortable. As Essie said, we had talked this out many times before, all one night and edging up on most of the next day once. That had been a long time ago—oh, billions of seconds—and I had been talking to the real Essie, the flesh-and-blood meat one. (Of course, I was flesh and blood at the time myself.) We were newly married at the time. We had been sitting on the veranda of our house, sipping iced tea and watching the sailboats on the Tappan Sea, and it had really been an easing, loving talk.

Obviously Essie remembered that long-ago meat-person conversation as well as I did, because when she got us comfortable, that was where she got us. Oh, not "really" in the sense that we were physically there—but, really, what does "really" mean? I could see the sailboats, and the evening summer breeze was warm.

"This is nice," I said appreciatively, feeling myself beginning to relax. "Being a disembodied datastring does have its advantages."

Essie grunted complacent agreement. She gazed affectionately around our old home and said: "Last time did this were drinking tea. Want something stronger this time, Robin?"

"Brandy and ginger," I said, and a moment later our faithful old maid, Marchesa, appeared with a tray. I took a long sip, thinking.

I thought too long for Essie's patience. She said, "So get on with it, dear Robin. What is frying your head? Afraid to talk to Klara?"

"No! I mean," I said, swallowing my quick indignation, "no. That's not it. We already did talk, back when she and Wan showed up with the Heechee ship."

"True," Essie agreed noncommittally.

"No, really! That part's all right. We got straightened out on the bad things. I'm not worrying that she'll blame me for dumping her in the hole, if that's what you mean."

Essie sat back and regarded me seriously. "What I mean, Robin," she said patiently, "is not important at all. Is what you mean that we wish to uncover. If not confrontation between Klara and you, what? Are worried she and I will scratch eyes out? Wouldn't happen, Robin!—apart from technical difficulties arising from fact that she is meat, I am only soul."

"No, of course not. I'm not worrying about her meeting you . . . exactly."

"Ah! And inexactly?"

"Well . . . what if real-Essie runs into her?"

Portable-Essie looked at me in silence for a moment, then took a thoughtful pull at her own drink. "Real-Essie, hah?"

"It was only a thought," I apologized.

"Understand that. Wish to understand more precisely. Are asking me if meat-me is likely to show up on Wrinkle Rock?" she inquired.

I thought that over. I wasn't sure exactly what I did mean. I hadn't meant to say anything at all about it . . . of course, as old Sigfrid von Shrink used to tell me, it's the things I say that I didn't mean to say that say the most.

And it was true that there was a real touchy, delicate bit here. Portable-Essie is only a doppelganger. Real-Essie, meat-Essie, is still alive and well.

She's also human. What with Full Medical and all, although she is getting along in years she is not just a woman, she is a really handsome, sexy, normal one.

She is also my wife. (Or was.)

She is also a wife whose husband is in no shape to provide her with, as they say, the benefits of consort.

All of that is already a nagging kind of worry that adds to all the other nagging worries Sigfrid (and Albert, and Portable-Essie, and just about everybody else I know) is always telling me I shouldn't beat my breast about. Their advice doesn't do much good; I guess I can't help it. But there's more. Meat-Essie is also an exact duplicate of Portable-Essie—or, to put it more accurately, she is the original of that exact duplicate who is Portable-Essie, my faithful wife, lover, advisor, friend, confidante, and co-construct in gigabit space.

So I know her very well. Worse than that, she knows me— even better—because she's not only all those things I just mentioned, she is also my, well, my creator.

Since Essie is better known in some circles as Dr. S. Ya. Lavorovna-Broadhead, one of the world's great authorities on data processing of any kind, she herself wrote most of our programs. When I say the copy is exact I mean *exact*. Essie even updates herself—I mean, meat-Essie revises Portable-Essie from time to time, to make sure the exactness is always up to the moment. So my Portable-Essie is in no way different, in any way that I can detect, from meat, or real, Essie . . .

But I never see meat-Essie. I couldn't handle it.

Call the reason for that whatever you like. Tact. Jealousy. Loopiness. Whatever it is, I am willing to accept as a fact of life that it is better that I don't see the meat original of my dear wife. I have a very clear idea of what I would learn if I did. Under the circumstances, either she takes a lover now and then or she is crazier than I believe possible.

I am willing to accept that this happens. I will even concede that it is fair. But I don't want to know about it.

So I said to Portable-Essie, "No. I don't think meat-Essie would be jealous enough to matter if she were here, and I don't think Klara would, and anyway I don't want to know where Essie is or what she's doing—not even negatively," I added swiftly as Portable-Essie opened her mouth, "so don't tell me what she is doing, even if it's something I would like to hear. It's not that at all."

Essie looked doubtful. She took another pull at her drink, with that look she gets when she is trying to work out the wiring architecture of the labyrinthine processes of my mind.

Then she shrugged. "Fine, accept what you say," she said decisively. "Is not that which is making you gloopy this time. So what then is reason? Is curiosity about Klara Moynlin, where has been all these years, why is Dane Metchnikov with her?"

I looked up. "Well, I did wonder—"

"No need to wonder! Is quite simple. After encounter with you, Klara wished to go away somewhere. Went very many places for long time. Ultimately went very far. Went back into black hole had just escaped from, rescued others in party— Metchnikov included."

I said, "Oh."

For some reason that didn't seem to satisfy Essie. She gave me an irritated look. Then she said slowly, "Think you are telling truth, Robin. Is not Klara is on your mind. Yet is clear you have been quite moody lately. Will say, if you can, what it is?"

"If you don't know, how can I?" I said, suddenly angry.

"Meaning," she sighed, "that as original writer I am in better position to overhaul your program, pick out bugs, make happy again?"

"No!"

"No," she agreed, "of course not. Have long agreed to leave old Robinette Broadhead program alone, bugginess and all. So then is only old-fashioned method of debugging. Talk. Talk it out, Robin. Say first word that comes into mind, just like for old Sigfrid von Shrink!"

And I took a deep breath and confronted the subject I had been spending a lot of time avoiding. I sighed:

"Mortality!"

Several thousand milliseconds later I was back in Central Park, watching Gelle-Klara Moynlin let go of her companions and move toward doppel-me, and wondering just why I had said that.

I hadn't intended to. I don't intend to describe the long, circular conversation I had with Essie after that, either, because although I do these things, I don't take much pleasure in talking about them. It got nowhere. It had nowhere to go. I had no reason to worry about mortality because, as Essie had wisely pointed out, how can you die when you're already dead?

Funnily, that didn't cheer me up at all.

Watching Klara didn't, either, so I sought other entertainment while I waited for either Klara or doppel-me to say something interesting in their glacier-slow way. It had been news to me that Audee Walthers III was on the Rock, and I sought him out.

That wasn't much better.

He was there, all right, or almost. Being meat, he was just getting there. He was in the process of disembarking, and it was not very entertaining to observe him slowly, g-r-a-d-u-a-l-l-y, pulling himself up out of the docking hatch onto the floor of the bay.

To make conversation, I said to Essie, "He doesn't look a

bit different." He didn't. Froggy faced, with solid, trustworthy eyes, he was exactly the same man he had been thirty and more years before when I saw him last.

"Has been in core, naturally," said Essie. She wasn't looking at him. She was looking at me—to see if I was going to do anything gloopy again, I supposed. So I wasn't sure, for a second, which of us she meant when she added, "Poor guy."

I gave her a noncommittal grunt. We weren't the only persons present; there were even meat people there, curious to see the ship that had been where few ships containing humans had ever boldly gone. Watching them, and Audee, was about as exciting as watching moss grow, and I began to fidget. Audee wasn't on my mind. Klara was on my mind. Essie was on my mind. Julio Cassata was on my mind and, most of all, my own slippery, uneasy internal worries were on my mind. What I wanted very badly was something to take my mind off all the things that were on my mind. Standing around among the statues wasn't doing the trick. "I wish," I said, "I could hear his story."

"Go ahead, then," Essie invited.

"What? Oh, you mean start a doppel so when he comes out—"

"No doppel, dummy," said Essie. "See? Audee is wearing pod. Pod contains Ancient Ancestor, no doubt. Ancient Ancestor is not meat but stored intelligence, almost as good as you and me. So ask Ancestor, why don't you?"

I gazed with love at my love. "What a highly intelligent person you are, Essie," I said fondly, "and adorable, too." And I reached out to the pod. Because I really did want to hear what had happened to Audee while he was gone. Almost as much as I wanted — wanted — wanted to know, really, just what it was that I did want.

7
Out of the Core

There was a real good reason why I wanted to hear about Audee's trip to the core right then.

Maybe from the strictly linear view of a meat person, it seems that, shoot, this is just one more damn digression. Linearly, maybe it is. I'm not linear. I do parallel processing, maybe a dozen things at a time in an average millisecond, and there was a really marked parallel going on here.

I'm sure Audee knew about the parallel when he volunteered to ride a Heechee ship back into the core. He probably hadn't thought it all out. He could have had only a tentative idea of what he was letting himself in for. But there's the parallel: Whatever it was going to turn out to be, he no doubt figured it would be better than trying to straighten out his life. Audee's life was as tangled, almost, as my own, for he had two loves, too.

So Audee took his chances, and his departure. He also took along with him our friend Janie Yee-xing, who was one of his loves. But that, as you will see, didn't last.

Audee was a pilot by profession. A *hot* pilot. Audee had flown airbodies on Venus, superlights on Earth, shuttles to the Gateway asteroid, private-party jet charters on Peggys Planet, and long-lines interstellar spacecraft to everywhere. In Audee's view, one Heechee ship was like any other Heechee ship, and he had no doubt he could fly anything. "Can I set course?" he asked the Heechee, Captain, because he wanted to start out on the right foot as a willing worker.

Captain wanted to start out on the right foot, too, so he obligingly waved the ship's pilot out of the way, and Audee took his seat.

Heechee seats are made for people wearing pods between their legs. Human beings don't usually do that, so most Heechee ships converted to human use have webbing stretched across the wings of the seat. This one, of course, had none.

Audee did not intend to start out by complaining. He made the best of it. He rested his bottom on the V-shaped seat, read off the course settings, and gave the control wheels the customary muscular shove into position. It took strength. It had been a while since Audee had had to do that; the new Earth-built ships were made easier to pilot. To make conversation, he panted, "A lot of the old-timers wondered about these wheels."

"Yes?" said Captain politely. "What about them, please?"

"Well, why are they so hard to turn?"

Captain glanced at his crewmates in puzzlement, then back at Audee. He reached out a negligent fingertip to touch the wheel. It moved easily. "What is hard?" he asked, hissing in the Heechee manner that expressed either annoyance or concern.

Audee looked at the slight, slim figure of the Heechee. He

coaxed the wheel back until the right-on vertical markers flashed shocking pink. It took as much muscle as ever.

As he reached for the starter-teat, he swallowed hard. It had become clear to him that the trip was going to be full of surprises.

The ship shuddered slightly, and the viewscreen blurred into the mottled gray that showed they were already going faster than light. No further action of the pilot would be necessary for some time, but Audee was reluctant to get up, for as long as he sat in the pilot's seat he felt some sense of being in control of what was going on. He tried making a little more conversation.

"We always wondered about those controls," he offered. "You know, because there are five of them? Some of the big brains thought you Heechee believed in five-dimensional space."

Captain hissed loudly for a moment, and the tendons that stood out from his flat chest writhed in the attempt to understand. His English had become quite good, but nuances of expression sometimes avoided him. "'Believe,' Audee Walthers? But there is no question of *belief*. There is no *faith* required, as in that concept you have of *religion*."

"Well, sure," said Audee grimly. "But *do* you believe that?"

"No, of course not," said Captain in surprise. "Space doesn't have five dimensions."

Audee grinned. "That's a relief, because I was having trouble trying to visualize—"

"It has nine," Captain explained.

They stopped, briefly, in their race to the core because Captain had left some of the stored Heechee craft in unstable orbits. That would not do, he explained. In the years they would be in the core the machines could drift to destruction, and Heechee did not like useful things destroyed. But Audee had stopped listening. "Years?" he said. "I thought this trip would be only a few months! How many years?"

"Quite a few, I think," said Captain. "To *us* it will be only months. But Home, you know, is in a black hole." And so when Captain left one of his crew to deal with the unmanned ships, Janie Yee-xing elected to go with him. She would, she said, fly one of them back to Earth, if Captain didn't mind; she really hadn't planned on *years*.

Captain didn't mind. Neither did Audee, oddly enough. He was quite confused enough about whom he loved to welcome a few months (or years) in which the question need not be faced.

A situation not unfamiliar to me.

It must have been a weird and wonderful trip for Audee, suddenly thrust into a Heechee ship with Heechee shipmates. For that matter, the Heechee didn't have any easy time of it, either, though at least they had previously had the experience of encountering bipeds that were markedly fat and hairy, while Audee had never before shared a ship with living skeletons.

But those problems were not unique to Audee or his hosts. We've all had them since, many times over, and that story is old. There's not much point in recounting Audee's difficulties with nine-dimensional space (no worse than my own with Albert Einstein) and with trying to make sense of Heechee arithmetic. Naturally everything in the ship was weird and strange to him—"chairs" designed to accommodate the Heechee pod, a "bed" that was a sack filled with dry, rustly stuff to burrow into . . . and we won't even mention the toilets.

It helped when, as time passed, he began to think of his shipmates as individual "persons," instead of as merely five examples of the category "Heechee."

Captain was the easiest to recognize. He was the darkest, the one with the fuzziest approximation of hair on his scalp, the one who spoke pretty good English. White-Noise was the little female, almost pale gold in color, approaching nubility and worried about it. Mongrel had great difficulty with the few English words he tried; Burst had a great sense of humor and loved trading dirty jokes with the others—even, now and then with Audee, through Captain as interpreter.

It helped still more when Captain had the bright idea of giving Audee a Heechee pod—a modified one, of course. As Captain told Audee, one part of the Heechee pod was useless to Audee, if not indeed dangerous to his health. That was the tiny microwave-radiation generator. The Heechee race had evolved on an otherwise pleasant planet of a star that happened to be near a large and active gas cloud; Bremsstrahlung radiation in the microwave frequencies had drenched that world from prebiotic times, and the Heechee had evolved to tolerate it—indeed, to need it, as human beings need the sun. So when they began venturing to places where the radiation could not follow, they had to bring their own source of microwave along.

Then, when a little later on in their history they discovered how to preserve the essentials of a deceased Heechee, they found another use for the pods. Each one contained the stored transcription of an Ancient Ancestor.

They even gave Audee an Ancient Ancestor of his own.

To his surprise, she wasn't really Ancient at all. She had been dead only a matter of weeks; she had been Captain's own lover, and her name was Twice.

That was the final step in Audee's assimilation of the notion that the Heechee were "people."

It's a small universe, isn't it?

As Audee began to get used to Captain, Captain got used to Audee—enough to open a discussion that had been very much on his mind. He got his chance when Audee asked about the Foe.

It was, after all, the central problem the universe posed to both Heechee and humans. The Foe. The Assassins. The race of inimical, death-dealing beings whose existence had caused the Heechee to pack up and flee to a safe hideout in the galactic core.

Audee made Captain go over and over the story, often with the other Heechee in the crew chiming in; it still wasn't easy to grasp. "I understand about Tangent's trip," he said, "and I understand that you knew a lot of civilized races had been wiped out, but how did you get from there to this idea of crumpling up the universe?"

The Heechee looked at each other. "I think first it was the deceleration parameter," said Shoe.

Captain writhed his biceps in agreement. "Yes, the deceleration parameter. Of course, it was only a question for theoretical astrophysicists at first, you understand."

"I would understand better if I knew what a deceleration parameter was," Audee groaned.

"It could also be called an anomalous braking effect," White-Noise offered from the other side of the room.

Captain flexed his twisty biceps in agreement. He went on: "It means only that our astronomers had observed that the universe was expanding less rapidly, by a power law, than it should have. Something was slowing it down."

"And you figured out it was the Foe?"

Captain said somberly, "In conjunction with the other evidence, and after ruling out every other possibility, it became clear that it could be nothing else but some artificial intervention on a cosmic scale. And there just were no other candidates."

"I can see that that would be disconcerting," said Audee.

"Disconcerting," Captain rasped. "It changed everything." He gazed thoughtfully at Audee out of those pink eyes with the blotch of pupil in the middle. He glanced at the other Heechee swiftly, then made the snuffling sound that was the Heechee equivalent of clearing one's throat to announce a change to a serious subject. "It is not too late," he announced.

Audee blinked. "Not too late for what?"

"It is not too late for your people to join ours in the core," Captain said precisely, speaking slowly to make sure that Audee understood. "It would be quite congenial for your human race inside the core if you were to come there."

"It sounds," said Audee politely, trying to lighten the conversation, "as though it might be a little crowded."

"Crowded? Why crowded?" asked Captain, cheek twitching—it was the equivalent of a frown. "We have mapped this Galaxy quite carefully, and when we retreated to the core, we chose the best planets to take there with us. There are not too many left outside that are congenial to your race—or to ours."

Audee saw a chance to do a little justified boasting on behalf of the human race. "Ah, but we *make* them congenial," he explained proudly. "There are six planets already mapped and explored, for example, that would be perfect for human beings except that the temperature range is a bit low. We can fix that. We're seeding those planets' atmospheres with chlorofluorocarbons. They trap heat—like carbon dioxide—which causes a greenhouse effect, which will—"

"I understand carbon dioxide," Captain gritted. "I also understand chlorofluorocarbons and, yes, it is true that certain of these compounds will in fact persist in an atmosphere for many centuries once put there. I agree that this may in certain cases raise the mean temperature of a planet by a few degrees."

"Well, a few degrees is all you need for some of them," Audee said reasonably. "And there's Venus. It's too hot by far. But before long we'll probably spread reflective dust particles in its upper atmosphere. This will cut down the insulation and make Venus habitable. Then we can do the same thing on other planets—there are two or three already identified. We can seed life where life never existed to make its own Gaea effect. We will move planets, if we must, to better orbits—"

Captain was growing testy. "But we have already done all of that inside the core," he urged. "Do you know how many habitable planets we already have in place? More than eight hundred fifty, most of them not yet occupied even by advance parties. As you see, we planned for a long stay."

"Yes," said Audee neutrally. "I see that."

Captain hissed faintly in puzzlement. He was aware that there was something in Audee's tone but couldn't tell what it was. He snuffled again and went on: "So you can join us! Some planets are prettier than others, to be sure, and I am certain you could have some of the very finest. Your entire race could fit on one of them!—two or three at the most," he corrected himself, thinking it over.

"And do what?" asked Audee.

Captain blinked at him. "Why—wait, of course," he said. "It is possible we would be safe there, Audee Walthers. Especially if we stop all transmissions at once and begin the trans-

fer of all human beings and energy-using devices into the core
as soon as possible."

"Energy-using devices?"

"Devices that radiate detectable energy. That would give
away our presence," Captain explained.

"Ah," said Audee, nodding, having spotted the flaw. "But
you people posted automatic sensors," he pointed out. "Why
wouldn't the Foe have done the same?"

"Perhaps they have," Captain said glumly. "I didn't say it
was certain we would be safe. I only said it was possible. And
if they have not in fact detected this—outbreak—then we can
stay inside there, for millions and billions of years, if necessary, waiting."

"But waiting for what, Captain?"

"Why—of course, waiting until some other race, perhaps,
evolves to challenge them!"

Audee studied the Heechee carefully, wonderingly. It was
clear that more than language differences lay between them.

"One has," he said gently. "Us."

For some time after that Audee worried that he might have
hurt Captain's feelings. He had, after all, implied against the
entire Heechee race an accusation of cowardice. What Audee
didn't know was that Captain took it as a compliment.

If there is one part of Audee's trip that I envy him more than
any other, it is his penetration of the black hole itself. Not that
Audee enjoyed it. No one would; it was scary.

As they approached that glowing, boiling, violently radiating
furnace of infalling gases that marked the approach to the Heechee hideout, Captain ordered everyone strapped into their
hammock sacks. White-Noise applied power to the crystal
helix the Heechee called a "disruptor of order." It glowed
diamond-bright. The temperature rose. The ship began to
shake.

Captain had learned to read human body language about as
well as Audee had learned Heechee—that is, not very well—
but he did not miss the whitening around Audee's jaw. "You
seem afraid," he commented.

By Heechee standards it was not an impolite remark. Audee took it without offense. "Yes," he said, gazing at the eye-wrenching surface of infalling gases, "I am terribly, terribly afraid of entering a black hole."

"That is curious," Captain said thoughtfully. "We have done this many times, and there is no peril to this ship. Tell me. Which are you more afraid of, this penetration or the Foe?"

Audee thought it over. The two kinds of fear were not at all the same. "I guess," he said slowly, "the Foe."

Captain's cheek muscles writhed approvingly. "That is not in any way nonrational," he said. "That is wise. Now we go in."

The diamond corkscrew erupted in showers of sparks; thousands of them struck Audee, and all the others aboard, but they did not burn; they did nothing at all, but seemed to pass right through the bodies and come out the other side. The lurching of the ship threw Audee violently against the harnesses of his safety cocoon; it had been built for Heechee mass, not that of the larger human body, and it creaked alarmingly.

The process went on for a long time. Audee had no way to measure it; many minutes, surely; perhaps an hour or more; and it didn't get less violent. He could hear the Heechee crew croaking comments and orders back and forth among themselves, and wondered dazedly how they were able to function when their gizzards were being jolted out of them . . . and wondered if Heechee had gizzards . . . and wondered if he were going to die . . .

And then, without warning it was over.

The Heechee began to unstrap themselves. Captain glanced curiously at Audee and called, "Would you like to see our core?" He waved a skinny arm at the viewscreen . . . and there it was.

What appeared on the ship's viewing plates was a dazzle of light.

The Heechee core was packed with suns—ten thousand suns—more suns than there are in a thousand light-years from

Earth, packed into a sphere of space only twenty light-years across. There were golden stars and dull crimson stars and blindingly blue-white stars. There was a whole rainbow Hertz-sprung-Russell spectrum of stars that made the night sky a flood of color on any planet in the core—that made the term "night" an exotic abstraction, in fact, because there was no place in the core that was ever dark.

I wish I could have seen it.

I don't envy very many people very many things, but I envied Audee Walthers that when I heard what he had seen. A *dense* compaction of stars—more than in any cluster—well, it would have to be, wouldn't it? Or else any globular cluster would itself have become a black hole. And constellations like Christmas trees! I mean, *colors*. Even from Earth the stars are different colors, everyone knows that, but hardly anyone ever sees what the colors are. They're all so far and so faint that the colors wash out, and mostly they look like various impure versions of white. But in the core—

In the core red is ruby and green is emerald and blue is sapphire and yellow is gleaming gold and white is, by God, *blinding*. And there isn't any gradation of first-magnitude down to faint or invisible. The bright ones are far brighter than first-magnitude. And there are hardly any stars on the borderline of visibility, because there aren't any faraway stars at all.

I did envy Audee for what he saw—

But, really, what he saw was only the viewscreen of the Heechee ship. He never set foot on a Heechee planet. He didn't have time.

First to last, Audee's elapsed time inside the core was about equal to the span of a normal night's sleep. He didn't do any sleeping, of course. He certainly didn't have time for that. He hardly had time to breathe, as a matter of fact, because there was so hopelessly much to see and do.

If it hadn't been for the Ancient Ancestors, things would have taken so ponderously long that it might hardly have mattered whether Audee got to the core or not. But Captain's messages had been received—only moments before, by Heechee standards. Their relay machines worked in machine-storage time, and the Ancient Ancestors nearly could, too.

With only minutes of warning, the Heechee had had time to do almost nothing but bleat and shake, but they rallied fast. They had always kept a full flotilla of standby crews and ships available for just this situation. They were dispatched at once. By the time Audee had been inside the core for four local hours, he had seen six large Heechee ships sent off with hastily drafted, often bewildered ship-handlers, historians, Dream-Seat sensitives, and diplomats—at least, what passed among the Heechee for diplomats. (Relations with foreign powers had never been much of a Heechee concern, since they hadn't been able to find any foreign powers to have relations with.)

Those first shiploads of Heechee specialists had been standing by, waiting for just that summons.

Probably none of them had actually expected to get it—"Not on *my* shift, anyway!" each one of them might have prayed, if Heechee had prayed, or a least asked of massed ancestral minds. Those crews had been standing by for a good long while—thousands of centuries, by galactic time. Even by the clocks in the core it had been a matter of decades.

No one crew stayed on standby for that long. They rotated at intervals of what local time measured as the equivalent of eight or nine months, then returned to their normal homes and habits. It was a lot like National Guard service in the old days in the United States. Like National Guardsmen, too, the surprise was ugly when the emergency they were standing by for turned out to be real, and immediate.

Half the Heechee had families. Half the ones with families had been allowed to bring mate and offspring with them, just as peacetime American soldiers had carried along wives and kids. The similarities ended there. Peacetime soldiers suddenly called on to fight usually had the chance to send their families out of the way. The Heechee didn't. The places they were stationed in were the ships they set out in, and so in those first half dozen ships the crews included pregnant females, infants, and a fair number of school-age Heechee children. Most of these were terrified. Few wanted to go on this mystery-bus excursion into the unknown . . . but then, much of the same was true of the crews themselves.

None of this Audee saw with his own eyes, only in the communications screens of Captain's spaceship. That was what he arrived in, and there he stayed.

By the beginning of the fifth hour of his visit to the core, another spaceship had had time to reach them.

The two ships docked. The second ship was much larger than Captain's. It had a complement of nearly thirty, and all of them slid as rapidly as they could through the mated hatches to observe this queer animal, this "human," at first hand.

The first thing that happened was that three of the new Heechee, gently and carefully, took Audee's pod away from him. So he was deprived at once of the comforting presence of Twice. He understood the necessity; none of the new Heechee spoke English, and anyway, they could get from the stored mind of the Ancient Ancestor all the information she had been getting from him over weeks, in far less time than he could say any of it. That was an explanation; it didn't make the loss less acute.

The second thing was that all his familiar Heechee shipmates were dragged away into the roil of newcomers, standing packed against each other in knots around each of the Heechee from the ship, talking and gesticulating and, yes, *smelling*. The typical, ammoniacal Heechee reek was overpowering, with so many of them squeezed into the ship. Audee had almost forgotten the smell existed, through custom; and besides, the Heechee who produced it were friends. The new ones were all strangers.

The third thing was that half a dozen of the new Heechee clustered around him, twittering and jabbering so fast that he could not make out the words. Finally he understood that they were asking him to hold still. He gave the best imitation he could of the Heechee upper-arm shrug of assent, wondering what he was being asked to hold still for.

It turned out to be a complete physical examination. They had his clothes off in no time, and in less time still they were

poking, prodding, peering. Slipping tiny, soft probes into ears
and nostrils and anus. Nicking off imperceptibly tiny specimens of skin and hair and toenails and mucus. None of it was
painful, but it was so damn *undignified*.

And already, Audee knew, a lot of time had passed back on
Earth. The clock that ticked so slowly in the core was spinning
away days and months at a click in the outside Galaxy.

The last thing that happened, or almost the last, was the
most surprising of all.

When they had finished giving him the most complete physical examination any human being had ever had in so short a
time, they allowed him to dress again. Then a short, pale female
Heechee touched his shoulder reassuringly. Speaking slowly
and carefully, as to a cat, she said, "We have finished with
your Ancient Ancestor. You may have it back now."

"Thank you," Audee growled, snatching the pod away from
her.

"Twice will tell you what you must do next." The female
Heechee smiled—the cheek-writhing that was the Heechee
smile, of course.

"I bet she will," Audee said bitterly, strapping on the pod
and bending down.

Twice sounded exhausted. She had been drained dry, and
it had been an ordeal for her; then she had been pumped full
of instructions, and that wasn't easy, either. "You are to make
a speech," she announced at once. "Don't try to speak our
tongue; you don't do it well enough—"

"Why not?" demanded Audee, surprised; actually, he
thought he had a pretty good accent by now, for a human.

"You only know the language of Do, not the language of
Feel," Twice explained, "and this is a matter of great emotional importance to all of us. So speak in English; I'll translate
for the audience."

Audee scowled. "What audience?"

"Why, all the Heechee, of course. You must tell them in
your own words that humans are going to help the Heechee
deal with the problem of the Foe."

"Oh, hell," Audee exploded, cursing his undignified position, bent double to be near the pod; cursing the Foe; cursing the stupid impulse that had made him volunteer in the first place. "I *hate* making speeches! Anyway, what can I tell them that you don't all already know?"

"Nothing, of course," Twice agreed. "But it will be good if they hear it from *you*."

So for the next ten minutes or so (while months and years were speeding by), Audee made his speech.

In a way it was a relief, because all the dozens of Heechee backed away from him to make a space; he saw several of them pointing objects at him and deduced that the objects were some sort of cameras. In another way, that time was worst of all, because as he was talking it occurred to him that Heechee were literal and when Twice said "all the Heechee" she undoubtedly meant *all* the Heechee. Billions of them! All looking with terror and fascination at, and making critical judgments on, this frightening alien, him!

They were indeed looking at him. All of them. All of the billions upon billions of them inside the core. Children in their schoolhalls and nurseries, workers stopped at their tasks, old ones, young ones—*dead* ones, too, for the massed minds of the Ancient Ancestors would not miss an experience like this. On the domed-in surface of planets, in the habitats in space, from the departing ships climbing up to their ordeal of passage through the Schwarzschild barrier . . . *all* of them were watching.

Audee had stage fright beyond belief.

He did it, though. He said, "I, uh, I—" And then he took a deep breath and started again. "I'm, ah, that is—I'm just one person, see, and I can't speak for everybody. But I know what people are like—human people, I mean. And we're not going to run away and hide like you guys. No offense. I mean, I know you can't help it—"

He shrugged and shook his head. "I'm sorry if I'm hurting your feelings," he said, forgetting the cameras, forgetting the billions and billions in the audience. "I just want to tell it like it is. We're used to struggling, you see. We thrive on it. We catch on quick—look at the way we've learned how to do everything you can do, a lot of the time better. Maybe we can't do anything about the Foe, but we're sure going to try. I don't mean I'm promising that—I don't have any right to promise anything for anybody but me. All I mean is, I *know* that. That's all, and," he finished, "thanks a lot for listening."

He stood there, obstinately smiling in silence, until the Heechee with the cameras at last, reluctantly, began to put them down.

A buzz of conversation broke out; Audee could not tell what they were saying, because none of them were saying it to him. But then the female Heechee who had given Twice back to him bent down to her pod for a moment and then approached. She said:

"I have this to say, Audee Walthers Third. I have consulted the Ancient Ancestors about the translation and I have it right, so I will say it in English."

She took a breath, moved her razor-thin lips silently for a second in rehearsal, and then, shaking her wrists at him as she spoke, she said:

"'Courage is not wisdom.

"'Wisdom is appropriate behavior.

"'Courage is sometimes suicide.'

"That is how the Ancestors told me to say to you what I want to say."

Audee waited for a second, but there didn't seem to be any more. So he said, "Thank you. Now, if you'll excuse me, I have to go to the bathroom."

Audee took his time about it, too. He had been a long time being poked and prodded and put on display, and besides the fact that his bladder was full, he wanted to be by himself for a minute. He took off his pod and left it outside the door, because he didn't even want Twice with him just then.

As he was filling the tulip-shaped toilet receptacle with urine, as he was washing his hands, as he was peering at his face in the rotating mirror, he was thinking. There was a current beating time in his head to a different tempo. It had taken him ten seconds to get inside and close the door—outside nearly half a million seconds had passed, at the ratio of something like forty thousand to one. Five seconds to open his fly. A minute, maybe, to urinate. Two more minutes to wash his hands and look at his face in the mirror.

He tried to calculate: What did all that add up to? The numbers eluded him; out of weeks of habit he kept trying to convert them into Heechee arithmetic and failing; but surely, he thought, something like eight or nine months on the outside had gone by just while he was having a pee.

It added a curious dimension to the act of relieving his bladder to reflect that, while he was doing it, a child could have been conceived and born in the outside world.

He opened the door and announced, "I want to go home."

Captain burrowed his way through the crowd to confront him. "Yes, Audee?" he asked, shaking his wrists in the negative; in this case it meant failure to understand, but Audee took it as refusal.

"No, I mean it," Audee said firmly. "I want to go back before everybody I know is a candidate for a retirement home."

"Yes, Audee?" said Captain again. Then he reflected. "Oh, I see," he said. "You have been thinking that we wanted you to remain here for an extended period. That won't be necessary. You have been seen. The information has been spread. Other human beings will be coming before long, prepared for a longer stay."

"You mean I can go?" Audee demanded.

"Of course you can go. There is a ship already en route to us here, part of a flotilla of supplies, personnel, and Ancient Ancestors, on their way outside. You can join them. By the time they transit the ergosphere, the elapsed time in the outside Galaxy will have been—" he ducked his head to communicate with his Ancient Ancestor "—in terms of the rotation of your planet around its primary, forty-four and one-half years."

8
Up in Central Park

And while I was listening, and speaking, and doing, and being in all those other places engaged in all those other things—hearing Audee's story, fretting about General Julio Cassata, wandering, partying—this was what was happening in slow time between Klara and me:

I marched up to Gelle-Klara Moynlin with a wide, fond smile on my (doppel's) face. "Hello, Klara," I said.

She looked up in astonishment. "Robin! How nice to see you again!" She disengaged herself from the men she was with and came toward me. As she reached up to kiss me, I had to back away. There are disadvantages to being a machine-stored person who is trying to be affectionate with a meat person,

128

and insubstantiality is one of them. You can love 'em. You can't kiss 'em.

"Sorry," I started to say, and at the same moment she looked repentant and said,

"Oh, hell, I forgot. We can't do that, can we? But you're looking really well, Robin."

I said, "I look any way I want to look. I'm dead, you know."

It took her a minute to grin back at my grin, but she did it. "Then you've got good taste. I hope I do that well when they can me." And up from behind her was coming Dane Metchnikov.

He said, "Hello, Robin." He said it neutrally. Not thrilled to see me again, not furious, either. He looked about the way Dane Metchnikov had always looked at everybody and everything—not very interested, or interested only to the extent that that person or thing might help or hinder whatever Dane was planning on.

I said, "Sorry we can't shake hands." "Sorry" seemed to be my favorite word, so I used it again: "Sorry you got stuck in the black hole. I'm glad you got out." And to set the record straight, because Metchnikov was always a guy who liked to keep the record straight, he said:

"I didn't get out. Klara came and rescued us."

It was only then that I recalled what Albert had said about Metchnikov seeking legal advice.

You have to remember that I wasn't actually saying any of this. My doppel was.

When you're speaking through a doppel, there are two ways to do it. One is to start the doppel off and let it carry on the conversation all by itself—it will do that as well as you can. The other way is when you're fidgety, nervous, and impatient and want to hear what's going on as soon as you can. That was the way I was, and what you do then is you prompt the doppel. That meant I was feeding lines to my doppel in a fraction of a millisecond or so, and the doppel was saying them at meat speed. You get the picture? It was something like a sing-

along, where the bunch doesn't know the words and somebody
has to line them out:

> "In a cavern, in a canyon—"
> "IN A CAVERN, IN A CANYON—"
> "—excavating for a mine—"
> "—EXCAVATING FOR A MINE—"
> "—lived a miner, forty-niner—"

and so on, only I wasn't leading a crowd of boozers around a
piano, I was feeding sentences to my doppel.

In between the sentences I had plenty of time to think and
observe.

What I mostly observed was Klara, but I spared attention
for the two men she was with, too.

Although their movements were slower than snails, I had
seen that Metchnikov was putting his hand out to be shaken.
That was a good sign, in itself. I would have taken it to mean
that he was not going to hold it against me that I had abandoned
him, as well as Klara and the others, in that black hole . . . if
it weren't for the fact that he had been talking to lawyers.

The other man with Klara was a total stranger. When I took
his measure, I didn't like the measurements much. The son of
a bitch was good-looking. He was tall. He was bronzed and
smiling and paunchless, and he was in the process of resting
a hand in a familiar way on Klara's shoulders again, even as
she was talking to me.

I explained to myself that that wasn't important. Klara had
been holding hands with Dane Metchnikov, too, and why not?
They'd been old friends—unfortunately, once a little more
than friends. It was only natural. This other guy put his hand
on her shoulder? Well, that didn't mean anything at all, really.
It was only a friendly gesture. He could have been a relative,
or even, I don't know, a psychoanalyst or something, there to
help her over the shock of encountering me again.

Looking at Klara's face didn't clear any of the questions up, although I did enjoy looking at it and remembering all the other times I'd looked at it, in love.

She hadn't changed. She still looked exactly like my eternal and deeply loved One (or at least one of not very many) True Love. The present Gelle-Klara Moynlin was indistinguishable from the Klara I had left in the space near the kugelblitz, just after I died—who in turn had been hardly a hair different from the one I had dumped in the black hole decades earlier.

It wasn't just Full Medical that accounted for the way she looked. Meat-Essie was an example of what Full Medical could do. She looked really youthful and adorable, too. But although they can do marvelous things with meat, the clock doesn't stop entirely. It just gets set back every once in a while. And, for most people, as long as you're getting restored, you might as well get improved a little at the same time—a perkier nose or a natural (natural!) wave in the hair; even Essie did that, a little.

Klara had not. The black eyebrows were still just a smidgen too thick, the figure stockier than (I remembered) she herself had wished it. She hadn't been kept young. She had *stayed* young, and there was only one way to do that.

She had been back in the black hole. She had voluntarily returned to the place where I had marooned her, where time slowed to a crawl, and all the decades that had passed for me had been only weeks or months for her.

I could hardly take my eyes off her. Although it had been the better part of a century since Klara and I had been lovers, I had no trouble at all in seeing—in memory only; I did nothing rude—the texture of Klara's skin, and the dimples at the base of her spine, and the touch and taste of her. It was a funny sensation. I wasn't exactly lusting for her bod. I wasn't on the point of ripping her clothes off and bedding her right there on the turf of Central Park, with the cherry tree in full blossom overhead and Metchnikov and the paunchless, good-looking other guy gazing on. It wasn't like that. I didn't really want to make love to her at all, at least not in any urgent or tangible sense. The reason wasn't just because it was (of course) impossible. Impossibility doesn't matter to horniness.

The thing was, whatever I myself wanted or didn't want to do with Klara, I certainly didn't want either Metchnikov or the other guy doing any of it.

I know what that is. The name for it is "jealousy," and I have to concede I've had a lot of it in my time.

Dane Metchnikov had managed to get a whole sentence out: "You look a lot different to *me*," he had said.

He wasn't smiling. That didn't mean much, because even in the old days on Gateway Metchnikov had never been a smiley sort of guy. And, of course, I looked different to him, because he hadn't seen me in a lot longer time than Klara— not since Gateway itself.

I could see that it was just about time to explore this question of lawyers, so I did what I always did when I needed advice and information fast. I yelled for it: "Albert!"

Of course, I didn't speak "out loud"—I mean, in any way Klara or the two men could hear. And when Albert showed up, he was no more visible to them than was the real, not doppel, me.

That was a good thing. Albert was obviously in a playful mood.

He was a rare old spectacle. He had one of those tacky, worn-out sweaters he affects wrapped around his head like a turban. He had been taking liberties with his physical specifications, too. His eyes were narrower, and they seemed to be rimmed with black makeup. His features were darker. His hair was jet black. "I hear and obey, O Master," he chanted in a reverent singsong. "Why have you summoned your genie out of his nice warm bottle?"

When you have a faithful data-retrieval program like Albert Einstein, you don't need a court jester. "Clown," I said, "I'll summon Essie to have you reprogrammed if you don't straighten out. What's the idea of the comedy?"

"O Master," he said, bowing his head, "your humble messenger fears the just wrath of your noble self when he hears evil tidings."

I said, "Shit." But I had to admit he had made me laugh, and that was one way of making evil tidings easier to bear. "All right," I said, nodding to show that I knew what the evil tidings were going to be. "Tell me about Metchnikov. He was on the mission to the black hole, and now he's back. I just figured out that that means he's entitled to a share of the science bonus I got for the mission, right?"

Albert looked at me curiously. Then he said, unwinding the sweater from his head, "That's right, Robin. It's not just him, either. When Klara went back to the black hole with Harbin Eskladar—"

"Hold it! Who?"

"That's Harbin Eskladar," he said, pointing to the other man. "You told me you knew about him."

"Albert," I sighed, rearranging the conjectures and misunderstandings inside my mind to fit the new pattern, "you should know by now that when I tell you I know *anything*, I'm lying."

He looked at me seriously. "So I feared," he said. "That's the bad news, I'm afraid."

He paused there, as though he hadn't quite made up his mind what to say next, so I prompted him. "You said the two of them went back to the black hole where I'd dumped them all."

He shook his head. "Oh, Robin," he sighed, but thankfully did not start telling me about my guilt trips again. He just said, "Yes, that's right. He and Klara went there together to rescue them, only they rescued the whole crew: the two Dannys, Susie Hereira, the girls from Sierra Leone—"

"I know who was on the mission," I interrupted. "My God! They're all back!"

"They all are, yes, Robin." He nodded. "And they are all, in some sense, entitled to full shares. That is what Dane Metchnikov saw a lawyer about. Now," he said thoughtfully, reaching into a pocket and pulling out his pipe—his complexion had unobtrusively returned to normal, his hair was white and unruly again—"there are certainly some unusual ethical and legal questions here. As you remember from previous litigaton, there is the principle that lawyers refer to as 'the calf follows the cow,' which means that all your subsequently accumulated fortune can be considered to be in some sense the consequence of that original Science Bonus from that mission. In which, of course, they would all have shared if they had returned with you.''

"So I have to give them money?''

"'Have to' is putting it too strongly, but that's the general idea, Robin. As you did with Klara when she first showed up; one hundred million dollars was the amount you settled on her for a quitclaim. Since I perceived this question would arise, I've taken the liberty of having your legal program contact Mr. Metchnikov's. That figure seemed acceptable. Some sort of settlement of the same order of magnitude would be appropriate for each of the others, I believe. Of course, they could ask for more. But I don't think they would get it; there is also a statute of limitations, naturally.''

"Oh,'' I said, relieved. I never have any real idea how "rich'' I am within several dozen billion dollars, but a billion one way or another wouldn't make much difference. "I thought you said you had bad news.''

He lit the pipe. "I haven't given you the bad news yet, Robin,'' he said.

I looked at him. He was puffing at the pipe, peering at me through the smoke. "Damn it, do it!''

He said, "That other man, Harbin Eskladar.''

"What about him, damn you?''

"Klara met him after leaving us on the *True Love*. He was a pilot too. The two of them decided to go back to the black hole, so Klara rented Juan Henriquette Santos-Schmitz's ship, which was capable of the mission. And before they left— well—the thing is, Robin, Klara and Eskladar were married.''

There are surprises that, as soon as you hear them, you know instinctively you should have been prepared for. This one came out of nowhere.

"Thank you, Albert,'' I said hollowly, dismissing him. He was sighing as he left, but he left.

I didn't have the heart to go on talking to Klara. I instructed my doppel on what to say next to her, and to Metchnikov, and even to this Harbin Eskladar person. But I didn't stay around while it happened. I retreated into gigabit space and wrapped it around me.

I know that Albert thinks I spend too much time in my own head. I won't deny any of the things he says. I don't mean I agree with them. I don't. I'm not any smarter than he thinks I am, but I'm not as weird, either. What I am, basically, is, I'm *human*. I may really be only the digital transcription of a human being, but when I was transcribed, all the human parts were transcribed, too, and I still feel all the things that go with being meat. Both the good and the bad.

I do the best I can—mostly—and that's about all I can do.

I know what's important. I understood as well as Albert did that the Foe were *scary*. I would have had nightmares if I had slept (I did have, when I pretended to, but that's another subject) about the universe crashing down on our ears, and I had a lot more fits of agitation and depression when I thought of the gang of them, out there in their kugelblitz, ready at any time to come out and do to us what they had done to the Sluggards and the starwisp people and the ones buried under the ice.

But there's important and there's also *important*. I am still human enough to think interpersonal relationships are *important*. Even when they're past tense, and all that's left is the need to make absolutely sure there are no longer any hard feelings.

After Albert had gone away to wherever Albert goes when I don't have a use for him, I floated in gigabit space for a long time, doing nothing. A *long* time. Long enough so that when I peeked once more at the scene in Central Park, Klara had just got as far as, "Robin, I'd like you to meet my—"

It was funny. I didn't want to hear the word "husband." So I ran away.

What I just said isn't exactly true. I didn't run *away*. I ran *to*, and the person I ran to was Essie. She was on the dance floor at the Blue Hell, wildly polkaing with somebody with a beard, and when I cut in she caroled, "Oh, good to see you, dear Robin! Have you heard news? Embargo is lifted!"

"That's nice," I said, stumbling over my own feet. She took a good look at my face, sighed, and led me off the dance floor.

"Went badly with Gelle-Klara Moynlin," she guessed.

I shrugged. "It's still going. I left my doppel there." I let her shove me into a seat and sit herself across from me, elbows on table, chin propped on elbows, looking me over with great care.

"Ah," she said, nodding as she completed her diagnosis. "Gloopy stuff again. Angst. Anomie. All that good stuff, right? And most of all Gelle-Klara Moynlin?"

I said judiciously, "Not most of all, no, because it would take forever to tell you all the things that bother me, but, yes, that's one of them. She's married, you know."

"Uh." She didn't add, *So are you*, so I had to do it myself.

"It's not just that she's married, because so am I, of course—and I wouldn't want it to be any other way, honestly, Essie—"

She scowled at me. "Oh, Robin! Never thought it would be possible to find hearing that a bore, but how often you do say it!"

"I only say it because it's true," I protested, my feelings having suffered a minor flesh wound.

"Already *know* is true."

"Well, I guess you do, at that," I admitted. I didn't know what to say next. I discovered a drink in my hand and took a pull at it.

Essie sighed. "Sure are one big party-pooper, Robin. Was feeling grand when you were not nearby."

"I'm sorry, but, honest, Essie, I don't feel like partying."

"Comes more gloopy business," she said, martyred. "Okay. Spit out what is now on poor, tortured mind. What is worst thing of all?"

I said promptly, "Everything." And when she didn't look as though that had explained it clearly enough for her, I added: "It's just one damn thing after another, isn't it?"

"Ah," she said, and thought for a while. Then she sighed.

"What gloomy creature you are, dear Robin. Should perhaps talk again with headshrinker program, Sigfrid von Shrink?"

"No!"

"Ah," she said again, and thought some more. Then she said, "Tell you what, dear old gloom person. How about we skip this party a while and look at some home movies, okay?"

I had not expected that from her. "What kind of home movies?" I demanded, surprised. But she didn't answer. She didn't wait for me to agree, either. She began showing them.

The sounds of the Spindle and the sights of the partying Gateway prospectors faded away. We weren't there anymore. We were in a different place, and we were looking at a bench with a child on it.

Now, they weren't real movies, of course, any more than anything else in gigabit space is "real." They were simply computer simulations. Like everything else either one of us chose to imagine, they were quite compellingly "real" in all appearances—sight, sound, even smell, even the chill of cold air and the congestion of sooty air to our (nonexistent) breathing.

It was all very familiar. We were looking at me—the child me—many, many decades ago.

I felt myself shivering, not relevant to the temperature of the air. The child Robinette Broadhead was sitting hunched up against the cold air on a park bench. It was called a park, anyway. Really, it was a pretty lousy excuse for one. If things had been different, it could have been quite spectacular, for the Wyoming hills were behind the child-me. Beautiful they were not. They were smoggy gray lumps in the dingy air. You could actually see hydrocarbon particulates floating in it, and the limbs of every scrawny tree were coated with soot and smear. I—the child who had been me—was dressed for the climate, which was vile: It took three sweaters, a scarf, gloves, and a knitted cap pulled down over my ears. My nose was running. I was reading a book. I was—what? Oh, maybe I was ten years old; and I was coughing as I read.

"Remember, dear Robin? Is good old days for you," said Essie from her invisible place beside me.

"Good old days," I snorted. "You've been snooping around in my memories again," I accused—without any real anger, because of course both of us had invaded all of each other's memory stores often and completely before that.

"But just look, dear Robin," she said. "Look how things were."

I didn't need to be ordered to look. I couldn't have stopped. I had no trouble in recognizing the scene, either. It was the Food Mines, where all of my childhood was spent: the shale mines of Wyoming, where rock was quarried and baked into keratogens, and then the oil was fed to yeasts and bacteria to make the single-cell protein that fed most of the too-numerous and too-hungry human race. In those mining towns you never got the smell of oil off you as long as you lived, and as long as you lived was generally not very long.

"Anyway," I added, "I never said the old days were any good."

"Correct, Robin!" Essie cried triumphantly. "Good old days were distinctly bad. Much worse than now, no? Are now no children compelled to grow up breathing nasty hydrocarbon air, dying because cannot afford proper medical treatment."

"Oh, sure, that's true enough," I said, "but still—"

"Wait to argue, Robin! Is more to see. What book do you read there? Is not *Huckly-berry Finn* or *Little Mermaid*, I think."

I looked closer to oblige Essie, and then, with a shock, I saw the title.

She was right. It was no children's book. It was *The User's Guide to Medical Insurance Programs*, and I remembered exactly when I had sneaked that copy out of the house when my mother wasn't looking, so that I might try to understand just what catastrophe we were facing.

"My mother was sick," I groaned. "We didn't have enough coverage for both of us, and she—she—"

"She put off her own surgery so that you might have therapy, Robin," Essie said softly. "Yes, but that was later. Not this time. This time was only that you needed better food and supplements, and could not afford them."

I was finding this pretty painful. "Look at my buck teeth," I said.

"No money fix them either, Robin. Was bad time for children, correct?"

"So you're playing the Ghost of Christmas Past," I snapped, trying to relieve the pressure by confusing her with a reference she wouldn't understand.

But when you have gigabit resources, you can understand a lot. "No, nor are you Scrooge," she said, "but consider. In these times, not so very far behind us, whole Earth was overpopulated. Hungry. Full of strife and anger. Terrorists, Robin. Remember violence and stupid murdering?"

"I remember all that."

"Of course. Now, what happened, Robin? I will tell. *You* happened. You and hundreds other crazy, desperate Heecheeship prospectors from Gateway. Found technology of Heechee and brought it back to Earth. Found fine new planets to live on—like discovery of America, only one thousand times greater—and found ways for people to move there. Are now no more overcrowded places on Earth, Robin. People have gone to newer places, built better cities. Have not even damaged Earth to do so! Air is not destroyed by gasoline engines or rocket exhausts; use loop to get into orbit, then anywhere! No one so poor cannot have medicine now, Robin. Even organ transplants—and make organs out of CHON material, so need not even wait for other person to die to snatch secondhand bits out of corpse. Correct, Robin? Heechee Food Factory makes organs now; developments you have played large part in bringing about. Have extended meat life, always in good health, many decades; then transcribe mind like us to live very much longer—in, again, development you have partly financed and I have partly helped develop, so that not even dying is fatal. You see no progress? Is not because no progress is there! Is because old gloomy Robinette Broadhead looks hard at delicious feast of everything now on plate of everyone alive and sees only what will later become, namely, shit."

"But," I said obstinately, "there are still the Foe."

Essie laughed. She seemed actually to find it funny. The

picture disappeared. We were back in the Spindle, and she leaned forward to kiss my cheek.

"Foe?" she said fondly. "Oh, yes, dear Robin. Foe are one more damn thing after another, as you say. But will deal with as have always dealt. Taking one damn thing at a time. And now get back to important earlier business; we dance!"

She is a wonderful woman, my Essie. Real or not.

She was also quite right, in every way that one could logically argue, so I succumbed to logic. I can't say that I really felt cheerful, but the novocaine had, at least, dulled the pain—whatever that real pain was—enough so that I could go through the motions of having a good time. I did. I danced. I partied. I went whooping from one cluster of old machine-stored friends to another, and I joined Essie and half a dozen others in the Blue Hell. A bunch of people were dancing slowly to music that the rest of us didn't hear—Julio Cassata was one of them, moving zombielike around the floor with a pretty little Oriental girl in his arms. It didn't seem to bother the dancers when we began singing old songs. I sang right along with the rest, even when they switched to ancient Russian ballads about trolleybuses and the road to Smolensk—it didn't matter that I hadn't known the words because, as I say, when you're operating in gigabit space you know just about anything you want to, at the moment you want to know about it . . . and if in my case I didn't, Albert Einstein would be sure to come and tell me.

I felt his tap on my shoulder as we were leaning on the old piano, and looked up to see his smiling face. "Very good voice, Robin," he complimented, "and your Russian language has become quite fluent."

"Join us," I invited.

"I think not," he said. "Robin? Something has happened. All of the main broadcasting circuits went off the air about fifteen hundred milliseconds ago."

"Oh?" It took me a moment to understand what he was telling me. Then I swallowed and said, "Oh! They've never done that before!"

"No, Robin. I came here because I thought General Cassata might know something about it." He glanced over at where Cassata and his lady were shuffling aimlessly around.

"Shall we ask him?"

Albert frowned thoughtfully at that, and before he could answer, Essie had abandoned the singing to come over. "What?" she said sharply, and when Albert had told her, said in shock, "Is not possible to break down! Many independent circuits, all multiply redundant!"

"I don't think it was a breakdown, Mrs. Broadhead," said Albert.

"Then what?" she demanded. "More silly JAWS nonsense?"

"It is certainly a JAWS order, of course, but what caused the order is, I think, something that happened on Earth. I cannot guess what it might have been."

9
On Moorea

The passengers on the refugee flight from the Watch Wheel were almost all children, and it was a weepy journey. They perked up a little when they reached Earth Orbit, but not very much. Loop shuttles swarmed up to meet them, attaching themselves to the transport ship like sucklings to a sow.

It was the children's hard luck that the first ship to reach them was from JAWS. It was full of intelligence analysts.

So the next hours were no fun for the children. The JAWS analysts "debriefed" them, stubbornly asking the same questions over and over in the hope of getting some new datum that might be somehow of use in determining just how false the "false alarm" had been.

Of course, none of the children had any such information to give. It took a long time before the JAWS agents were convinced of that, but ultimately, and reluctantly, they allowed kinder people and programs to take over.

The new shift was in charge of finding places for the children to stay on Earth. For some of the children it was easy, because they had families there. The remainder went to schools all over the planet.

Sneezy, Harold, and Oniko were almost the last to find places. They stuck together out of friendship, and even more because none of them spoke French or Russian, which ruled out the schools in Paris and Leningrad, and besides, none of them was quite ready to face the confusion of a big city. That ruled out Sydney, New York, and Chicago, and when the billeting program had found places for all the other children, they three were left.

"I wish it could be some warm place, not too far from Japan," said Oniko. Sneezy, having given up hope of finding a Heechee colony to take him, added his vote to the request.

The billeting program was a schoolmarmy woman, middle-aged, bright-eyed, soft-spoken. Although she was human in form, Sneezy felt kindness emanating from her. She peered at her screen—which did not exist, any more than she did—puzzled over the readout for a moment, then gave Sneezy a pleased smile.

"I've got three vacancies on Moorea, Sternutator. That's very near Tahiti."

"Thank you," said Sneezy politely, looking without recognition at the map she displayed. The name of the island meant nothing to him. One human place sounded very much like any other human place, for they were all equally, wildly exotic to a Heechee boy. But Harold, glumly reconciled to the fact that he wouldn't be taken to Peggys Planet right away, shouted from behind:

"Oh, boy! I'm with you on that one, okay? And if it's nice, maybe you can buy it like you said, Oniko!"

The shuttle took them down through the buffeting air to a

loop on New Guinea. Then came the longest leg of the trip, stratospheric jet to Faa-Faa-Faa Airport in Papeete. As a special treat for the newcomers, the human principal of the school met them and took them across to the neighbor island by boat. "Look there," she said, holding Oniko's hand as the children clung to the seats of the open inertial-drive whaler. "Just around the point, inside the lagoon, you see those white buildings on the beach? With the taro patch on one side, on the side of the mountain, and the papaya plantation on the other? That's your school."

She didn't mention the other, grimmer buildings farther up the side of the mountain. Harold was too busy being sick over the side of the boat to ask about them, and Sneezy too consumed with tearless homesickness for the distant core, and Oniko too bludgeoned by Earth's harsh gravity to respond to anything at all.

For Oniko it was all painful, if not indeed threatening to her health. She was *crushed*. On Earth her slim body did not weigh more than thirty kilos, but that was twenty-odd more than her unpracticed bones and muscles had ever been required to carry before.

All of the refugee children had needed preparation for Earth's gravity after spending time on the Watch Wheel. For the whole long flight to Earth they had been made to drink calcium-laden things like milk, and hot chocolate, and, weirdest of all, "cheese soup," as well as having to exercise three hours each day in the spinning treadmills and with the springy machines. For most of the children it was simply a wise precaution. For Oniko it was the only alternative to snapping bones. The doctor programs had special plans for her, and she had spent hours on end on a table while humming sonar coaxed her bones to grow stronger and electric pulses made each muscle twitch and jump. As they neared Earth orbit, the doctor-thing assured her that she had recalcified quite a lot. She should be safe against fractures if she exercised reasonable care, and used a walker, and did not jump from any height. But if the bones had been propped up for their ordeal, not nearly enough had been done for her muscles. Every step tired her. Every time she stood up she *ached*. So the exotic thing that gave her most pleasure in her first days at Western Polynesian Preparatory School was the lagoon.

The water was scary as well as joyous, to be sure. There were living *creatures* under those pretty green wavelets! But she accepted the schoolthing's promise that none of them could hurt her, and when she immersed herself in the tepid, briny lagoon, there was hardly any weight at all on her bones. She floated around in it blissfully every chance she got. In the morning before class, during recess, even after dark when the (also wondrous, also scary) "Moon" lit the ripples for her.

For Sneezy the sea was neither greatly exciting nor any fun at all. He had seen seas on his own planet, inside the core. Why not? They were not considered particularly recreational, because Heechee couldn't swim. Bone and muscle don't float well without a sizable wrapping of fat, and there were no fat Heechee. So, to keep Oniko company, he allowed himself to be tempted into a rubber boat sometimes. But only rarely would he let himself drift into waters deeper than his own height.

Harold, at first, found a home on Moorea.

Earth was very much like Peggys Planet, he explained to their classmates. No, said some of the classmates, he had it the wrong way around: Peggys Planet was very much like *Earth*. Indeed it was, actually. That was what had made human beings so anxious to colonize it in those early days when the fecundity of human bodies outran the carrying capacity of the planet. Well, maybe, said Harold reasonably, but any half-wit could see at once that Peggys Planet was *better*.

Harold found it disappointing, not to say outrageous, that other children showed so little interest in hearing that from him.

The three children from the Wheel shared one special handicap. They were outsiders. They were the newest kids in school, entered well after the beginning of the term. Friendships and alliances had long since formed. Of course, the human principal had invited every student in the school to show special courtesy and consideration to the waifs from intergalactic space. The students did, for a while. It didn't last. Once the questions had been asked ("Did you *see* any of the Foe? When are they going to come out?") and the lack of satisfying answers had been noted, the powerful lines of room-mateship and fellow-soccer-player status tightened up and squeezed them out. Not meanly or violently. But out.

It was worse for Sneezy and Oniko. Sneezy was the only Heechee in the school and Oniko the only child who had been raised in Heechee ways. They were simply too alien to easily be best friends with anyone else. Harold had no such problem at first. Harold had only the problem of himself. He gazed up at Moorea's startling central peak and said, "You call that a mountain? Why, on Peggys Planet there's a peak fourteen kilometers tall!" He watched scenes from New York City and Brasilia and said disdainfully that on Peggys Planet people kept their cities clean. After the antiquities class discussed Pompeii and the Great Wall of China, Harold was heard to say in recess that on Peggys Planet, thank heaven, people knew enough to throw old junk away. Since there were students in the school from Khatmandu, New York, Brasilia, Beijing, and Naples, Harold's disparagement of their local tourist attractions did nothing to endear him. The schoolthings pleaded benignly, but the students were under no obligation to respect their wishes.

In the long run, Harold was more of an outsider than either Oniko or Sneezy. Those two studied hard. When they had spare time, they used it at the datamachines, learning even things they were not required to learn. Both were quickly at the top of their classes, and Harold, straining to maintain a respectable C+ average, was jealous. Ultimately he was furious. When the schoolthing handed out test results one day, the light bulb went on over Harold's head, and he leaped from his seat and cried, "Schoolmaster! It isn't fair. Naturally those two get better marks, because they're cheating!"

"Now, Harold." The schoolthing smiled patiently—it was the end of the day's lessons, and all the students were getting restless, if not irritable. "Certainly Sternutator and Oniko do not *cheat*."

"Well, what do you call it? They've got those A.I. databases with them all the time, and they use them. I've seen them do it!"

The schoolthing said firmly, "Really, Harold, you know that Sternutator, like all Heechee, requires a constant source of low-level microwave for his health—"

"Oniko doesn't!"

The schoolthing shook its head. "There's no grounds for using words like 'cheating' simply because a student carries his own data-retrieval system on his person. You have your own desk console, don't you? Now, please go back to your seat so we can discuss this evening's conceptualization assignment."

And that afternoon, down at the lagoon, Harold sat rigidly on the shelly beach while Oniko splashed in the shallows and Sneezy dug for bits of coral. "I am sorry you don't like us," Sneezy said.

"What are you talking about? We're friends! Of course I like you," Harold lied.

"No, I think not," Oniko called from two meters away. "Why is that, Harold? Have I ever harmed you?"

"No, but you're a human being. Why do you act like a Heechee?"

"What's wrong with acting like a Heechee?" Sneezy asked, hissing in annoyance.

"Well," said Harold reasonably, "you can't *help* what you are, but you're such cowards, you know. You ran off and hid from the Foe. I don't *blame* you," he added, looking as though he blamed them very much, "because my father says it's natural for a Heechee to be yellow."

"I am actually rather tan," Sneezy said proudly; his color had been changing, a sign that he was growing up.

"I don't mean *color*. I mean *chicken*. It's because you're not as sexy as people."

Oniko splashed closer to hear better, squatting in the wavelets. "I have never heard such a strange thing!" she complained.

"It's a matter of biology," Harold explained. "My father told me all about it. Human beings are the sexiest creatures in the Galaxy, that's why they're so brave and smart. If you look at some lower animal, say a lion or a gorilla or a wolf—''

"I've never seen any of those."

"No, but you've seen pictures, haven't you? And Sneezy has, too? Well. Did you ever see a gorilla with boobs like a girl's?" He caught Sneezy's eye going to Oniko's flat chest and said irritably, "Oh, God, I don't mean *now*. I mean when she grows *up*. Human women have big breasts all the time, not just when they're feeding a baby like some dumb animal. Human women can do, you know, can do sex all the time, not just once a year or something. That explains it, do you see? It's evolution's way of making us better, because human women can get men to hang around them all the time. So that's how civilization started, like hundreds of thousands of years ago.''

Oniko painfully waded out of the water, frowning. Trying to follow Harold's line of reasoning, she asked, "What does that have to do with being brave?"

"That's how human beings worked out so well! My father told me the whole thing. The human fathers stayed around all the time because they wanted to, like, make love, you know? So they got the food and stuff, and the mothers could do a better job taking care of the kids. Heechee don't have that going for them.''

"My parents stay together," Sneezy said forcefully. He wasn't angry. He hadn't decided yet whether there was something to get angry with Harold about, but he found the argument confusing.

"They do because they copied us, probably," Harold said doubtfully, and Sneezy looked thoughtful, because he suspected that part might be almost true. In the core, he knew, Heechee lived in communes, not nuclear families. "Anyway, they don't, uh, do sex all the time, the way my mom and dad do, do they?"

"Certainly not!" cried Sneezy, scandalized. Heechee women made love only when it was the biologically right time for them to do so. His father had explained that to him long before. The woman's body told her when it was time, and then she told the man—somehow or other—it didn't seem to need words, but Bremsstrahlung had been vague about that part of it.

"So you see?" Harold cried in triumph. "That makes human men, like, show off for their girlfriends all the time! In the old days they maybe hunted, or fought some other tribe. Now they do different kinds of things, like they play football or make scientific discoveries—or go exploring, don't you see? It makes us *braver*."

Oniko, toweling herself, said doubtfully, "My father told me my grandfather was terribly frightened when he went out from Gateway."

Harold shrugged. "There are individual exceptions."

"And women went out, too. There were almost as many women as men on the artifact."

"Oh, Oniko," said Harold, exasperated, "I'm talking about a general *law*, not about *individuals*. See, you just don't know what it's like in a human world, because you never got to live on a good one, like Peggys Planet."

Oniko dragged herself erect on her walker. "I don't think it's really that way on Earth either, Harold."

"Sure it is. Didn't I just *tell* you?"

"No, I don't think so. I did some research after we came here. Sneezy? Hand me my pod; I think I have it in my diary."

She put her pod on and bent down to it. Then, laboriously straightening, she said, "Yes, that's it. Listen: 'The old-fashioned "nuclear family" is less frequent on Earth now. Childless couples are frequent. When couples have children it is usual for both parents to work; there is also a large proportion of single-parent families.' So it's not exactly the way you say, Harold."

Harold sniffed disdainfully. "Keeping a diary is a baby thing to do," he said. "When did you start it?"

She looked at him thoughtfully. "I don't remember exactly. When we were on the Wheel."

"Why, I keep one too," cried Sneezy. "I guess when you told me you were doing it, I decided it sounded like a good idea."

Oniko frowned. "I thought you were the one who told me," she said. Then she grimaced. "But right now I want to get back to my dorm so I can lie down for a while before dinner, please."

I feel a little apologetic, because I've jerked us around in time so much (though not by a long shot, I'm sorry to say, as much as I will a little later on). I think I should pin this time frame down a little more accurately. This didn't happen while Essie and I were on the Wheel, not by many millions of milliseconds. It happened earlier, at a time when Essie and I were just beginning to debate whether we were really going to go to the one hundredth reunion on Wrinkle Rock and my life, almost, seemed placid. I didn't know what was coming.

Of course, the kids didn't know what was coming either. They were going about their business, which was the business of being children. When, in the normal course of school practice, Sneezy went for his twice-monthly examination, the docthing was pleased to see him; it didn't often get a chance to examine a healthy Heechee, with his double heart, almost fatless internal organs, and ropy musculature. "Everything is normative," it said, scanning the test monitors approvingly. "Only you don't seem to be sleeping well, Sneezy."

Sneezy said reluctantly, "Sometimes I have trouble getting to sleep. Then I dream—"

"Oh?" The docthing had taken the form of a young human male; it smiled reassuringly and said, "Tell me about it."

Sneezy hesitated. Then, unwillingly, he said, "I do not have a cocoon, you know."

"Ah," said the program. Sneezy waited. He did not want to have to tell this mechanical program what it was like for a young Heechee to have to sleep on a bed, with nothing but sheets to pull over his head. Heechee slept *enclosed*, preferably with some sort of warm, soft clumps of material to burrow down into; that was the right and proper way to sleep, and blankets and sheets were no substitute. How right his father had been to forbid him a bed, he thought wistfully.

He did not have to elaborate; the docthing's databases provided the explanation. "I have ordered you a cocoon," said the program benignly. "Now. About those dreams . . ."

"Yes?" said Sneezy dismally. He did not want to talk about the dreams. He never had, not even to Oniko; he didn't even like to remember them when he was awake.

"Well? What do you dream?"

Sneezy hesitated. What did he dream? What did he not! "I dream about my parents," he began, "and about Home. I mean my real home, in the core—"

"Of course you do," said the docthing, smiling.

"And then there are the other dreams. They're—different." Sneezy paused for a moment, thinking. "They're scary. They're—well, sometimes there are these bugs. Clouds of them. Swarming, floating, flickering—" They swooped around him and crept into his clothing, into his mouth, into his skin, stinging without pain . . . "They're like fireflies," he finished, trembling.

"Have you ever seen a firefly?" the program asked patiently.

"No. Only in pictures, I mean."

"Fireflies do not sting, Sneezy," the docthing pointed out. "And the sort of insects which do sting cause itching and pain. Do you have any of that?"

"Oh, no. Nothing like that— At least, not exactly," Sneezy corrected himself. "But there is a kind of, I don't know how to say it, an itch in the head. I mean, it makes me—I don't know—it makes me want to learn things."

"What sort of things, Sneezy?"

"Things," the boy said unhappily. Sneezy knew that he was describing the dreams poorly. What else could you do when you tried to put a dream into words? Dreams were soft and fuzzy and shapeless. Words were hard and exact. The Heechee language of Feel would have been a little better for the purpose, but the program had chosen to speak in English, and Sneezy was too polite to complain.

But the program nodded understandingly. "Yes, yes, Sneezy," it said kindly, "such dreams are symbols. Perhaps they represent your perfectly normal child's interest in the sexuality of your parents. Perhaps they refer to the traumas you have experienced. You may not realize it, Sneezy, but you have gone through more stress in the past few weeks than most adults experience in years.''

"Oh,'' said Sneezy. He did actually realize it very well.

"And also,'' the program sighed, "there is the general apprehension everyone feels these days. Not just children. Adults of both races, and even machine intelligences; no one is exempt. You understand that I am referring to the Foe.''

"They are frightening,'' Sneezy agreed.

"And particularly for an impressionable child, who has even had some personal experience of the scare, apparently baseless though it was, on the Watch Wheel.'' The docthing cleared its throat, announcing a change of subject. "Now, what about these diaries of yours?'' It beamed.

Sneezy hissed faintly, then accommodated himself to the new course. "They keep me from being homesick,'' he said, not because that was true—they didn't—but because Sneezy had learned what every child learns, human or Heechee: When adults ask hard questions, you can satisfy them with the easy answers they expect.

"Very good therapy.'' The docthing nodded, "But such detail, Sneezy! So many pages of data! One would think you were trying to compile an encyclopedia. Don't you think you should spend less time on that sort of thing and more playing with your classmates?''

"I'll try,'' Sneezy promised, and when he was released at last, he rehearsed entries for his diary all the way back to his dormitory. They mostly began with a single observation: "Human programs don't know much about Heechee kids.''

But when he did begin writing in his diary again, that was not what he wrote at all.

I don't care what Albert says, I can't help feeling sorry for Sneezy. And for Oniko. And—oh, hell, yes, even for Harold Wroczek. Harold wasn't really bad. He simply hadn't had much practice at being nice.

The three of them continued to spend more time with each

other than with any of the three hundred-odd other students,
though Harold hated it when Sneezy and Oniko insisted on
spending hours on end with the databases. "My God," he
complained, "do you think you have to learn *everything* there
is to know?"

"We like it," Oniko said simply. Harold spread his hands
in resignation. But then he trailed after them to the study rooms
and, having nothing better to do, studied on his own. To everyone's astonishment his grades began to climb.

Apart from lonesomeness and the troublesome dreams,
Sneezy rather liked school. The beach was neat, once you got
used to being in water; the sportsthing contrived a sort of har-
ness of floats that Sneezy could wear, and before long he was
swimming with the best of them. The classes were interesting.
The other students were at least tolerable, if not warmly
friendly. And the island was beautiful, if filled with curious
and sometimes worrisome things. For example, there was the
meadow just above the school. Large horned ruminants grazed
there. When Sneezy looked them up in the databases, he discovered they were called "cattle," and when he found out
what cattle were generally raised for, he was appalled. Sneezy
had spent all four of his years on the Watch Wheel resolutely
not thinking about where his human schoolmates preferred to
get their protein. Now he was confronted with the mooing,
defecating source of roasts and hamburgers themselves. Disgusting! Ninety-five percent of Sneezy's diet, like that of any
proper Heechee, came from frozen cometary gases—or from
any other handy source of the four basic elements of human
nutrition, carbon, hydrogen, oxygen, and nitrogen. Add a few
trace elements, and CHON-food could be made into anything
you liked. It was cheap. It was maximally nutritious, being
manufactured for all dietary requirements. And it did not require murdering anything that could feel pain.

Half the school's meals were CHON, anyway. There was a
Food Factory afloat in the shallow seas off the neighbor island
of Tahiti, sucking its basic raw materials out of the sea and
the air. But human children, like human adults, seemed actually to relish the thought that the bloody "steaks" they ate

actually came from living animals—though not, to be sure, the ones on the pasture just above the school, because they were a prize herd devoted to special ends.

He didn't discuss those ends with his schoolmates. That was fortunate for Sneezy, for raising animals to eat (he would have discovered) was not after all the most repellent use that could be made of them.

In Sneezy's second month on the island of Moorea two good things happened.

The first was that his cocoon arrived and was installed in his dormitory cubicle, so that from then on he could snuggle down into soft, burrowable clumps of foam and pull a lid over his head to sleep, like any proper Heechee. It caused a fair amount of joking from his dormitory mates, but Sneezy tolerated that all right. It didn't seem to stop the dreams, either; but it was a vast improvement over the sterile and unwelcoming sheets and blankets the poor human kids had to put up with.

The second thing was that the principal of the school discovered how ill adjusted the regular medical program was for a Heechee child, and went to the trouble of acquiring a more suitable one. The new program took the form of a handsome young Heechee male, copper-skinned and deep-eyed. It had a centimeter of down atop its smooth skull, and its shoulder and neck tendons twitched amiably as it greeted Sneezy. He liked the new docthing very much on first encounter, and when it came time for the second he actually looked forward to it. Oniko was scheduled for her checkup at the same time. Sneezy helped her carefully through the narrow hall, though with her cane she was reasonably able to get along by herself by now, and greeted the nursething cheerfully.

To the surprise of both of them, the nurse conducted them into a single room. Sneezy's young Heechee and Oniko's middle-aged human female were seated together at a desk, and there were two chairs for the children.

"We thought we would talk to you together," said Oniko's

docthing—in Heechee!—"because you have a lot in common."

"You both have the same sort of dreams," the Heechee figure chimed in. "Tiny luminous creatures buzzing around you, even stinging you. But never really causing you pain."

"And they go on and on," said the female thing.

"That's true," said Sneezy, looking at Oniko. She nodded.

"And neither of you seems to take much interest in sports," the female added. "I can understand that about you, Oniko, since you are still not quite physically strong enough for much exertion. But you, Sternutator, are in excellent physical condition. And neither of you even watch them on the PV, do you? Not football, baseball, jai alai, anything at all."

"I think they are quite boring, yes," Sneezy admitted.

"Listen to yourself, Sternutator," said the Heechee docthing. "Do you sound like a ten-year old?"

"He sounds normal enough to me," sniffed Oniko. The female nodded.

"By your standards, yes," it said. "You both seem to have extremely adult interests. We've checked your data-retrieval logs. We can understand that each of you has spent many hours learning all you can about the Foe. To be sure, anyone might do that—they are certainly important to us all! Still, very few of your schoolmates seem so motivated in this area. But why do you have such an interest in a faster-than-light transportation, Oniko?"

She looked puzzled. "It's just *interesting*, I guess. Isn't everybody interested in that?"

"Not to the same extent, nor in such alien races as the Sluggards, the Quanices, and the Voodoo Pigs."

"But they're kind of funny," Oniko said defensively.

"Yes," said the Heechee docthing, taking over. "And the subjects that most interest you, Sternutator, are also both amusing and quite important, I would say. The locations of Heechee outposts and depots; the history of Heechee exploration; the principles involved in penetrating black holes. But you see, Sternutator, even a perfectly normal curiosity, when carried to extremes, can be— Excuse me," it said suddenly, glancing at the female beside it. And the female said, with an abrupt change of tone:

"Children, there is a very important news broadcast coming in. The principal wishes every student to see it, so we will terminate this interview to display it." And the two of them turned around in their chairs to gaze at the wall behind them. It lighted up with a shimmering silvery haze that cleared to display a male human face, expression serious, far larger than life. It was speaking as it appeared:

"—and here is another part of the decoded message."

The face paused, listening, as another voice, disembodied, spoke rapidly in a hurried, mechanical way. It said: "The total number of species presently existing in the Galaxy which are either already technologically capable or give indications of possible future development to that stage is eleven. Only three of these have mastered interstellar flight, and one of the three uses only Einstein-limited propulsion systems. Two of the remainder may achieve spaceflight within the next few centuries. The others are tool users in varying stages of development."

The voice died, and the face, eyes narrowed in concern, said: "The entire message, when slowed to normal speaking speed, is estimated to run more than nine hours. Only a few portions of it have as yet been rerecorded for real-time study. However, for the benefit of those who may just have joined us, the message was in the form of a burst transmission which lasted only one point oh oh eight three seconds. The origin of the transmission has not yet been established, except that it was fed into the Earth satellite transmission net and beamed in the direction of the kugelblitz, apparently from Tokyo Tower. All landlines feeding into the Tower are now being investigated." The face paused, gazing steely-eyed out at its audience. "Of course, no transmissions at FTL velocities in the direction of the Watch Wheel or the kugelblitz are permitted, under the emergency rules laid down by the Joint Assassin Watch more than ten weeks ago."

A movement beside Sneezy shook him out of the staring trance the broadcast had caused. He looked around. Oniko had got out of her chair and was hobbling out the door.

"Excuse me," Sneezy muttered, and followed. Outside, Oniko was leaning against the wall, sobbing.

"What's the matter?" he demanded in alarm. "It's—well, certainly it's scary, but it could be just some technical error, or a practical joker, or—"

"Oh, Sneezy," the girl wailed. "Don't you see?"

He opened his mouth to answer, but she rushed on: "That message, do you know what it was? It was part of my *diary*!"

10
In Deep Time

Cassata was doing his dreamy, draggy two-step with his eyes closed and the little Oriental woman's head on his shoulder. Incredible! She looked exactly like a normal human being with any human's common sense, and yet she was actually cuddling up to the man! I snarled, "Cassata, what the hell is going on?"

He gave me a peculiar look. I don't know how else to describe it. It wasn't apologetic, it wasn't arrogant. What it seemed to be was—I don't know—maybe the word is "doomed." To be sure, he was. What was waiting for him when he got back to his meat-time original was termination, but he'd known that for a long time and he hadn't looked that way. He seemed to be waiting for an ax to fall.

He courteously released his partner, kissed her forehead, and turned to me. "You want to talk to me," he said.

"Damn-eye right I—"

He headed me off. "I suppose we might as well," he sighed, "but not here. Not your ship, either. Something nice. Something I can enjoy."

I opened my mouth to tell him how little I cared what he enjoyed, but Albert was ahead of me. "The Rue de la Paix, perhaps, General Cassata? A little open-air café along the Left Bank?"

"Something like that would be fine," Cassata agreed . . . and there we were, seated around a metal table on a sunny boulevard, under a striped umbrella that advertised an aperitif, while a white-aproned waiter was taking our orders.

"Nice choice, Albert," Cassata said appreciatively, but I was having none of that.

"Cut the crap," I barked. "Why've you blacked out all Earthside radio?"

Cassata picked a Campari-soda off the waiter's tray and sniffed at it thoughtfully. "I don't know," he said, and added, "yet."

"But you know why you embargoed my ship!"

"Oh, yes, Robin. It was an order."

"And embargoing ship from core?" Essie put in, not waiting her turn—I was nowhere near through with Cassata. He shrugged. That was all Essie needed. She gave him a killing look, then turned one on me. "You believe this? Even Heechee Ancient Ancestors must report first to JAWS! Then will see if rest of us are grown-up enough to hear before releasing data!"

Cassata repeated, "Orders." Then he took a better look at Essie and said placatingly, "It's only a technicality, Mrs. Broadhead."

"*Stupid* technicality! Robin? Send order off to Institute; these uncultured clowns don't deserve cooperation."

"Well, now, wait a minute," he said hastily, doing his best to be agreeable. "This is just an emergency measure. Later on, I'm sure that if you and Robinette want to access any of the information there's not going to be any difficulty—I mean, *real* difficulty; but they have to be debriefed by the Joint Assassin Watch Service before any public disclosure, of course."

"*Not* 'of course'! No 'of course' involved!" She turned to me, eyes blazing. "Robin, tell this soldier man is not a question of personal favor for you and me, is information which belongs to all."

I said, "It's information which belongs to everybody, Cassata."

Essie wasn't letting it go at that. "*Tell* him, Robin!" she snapped, so fiercely that the passersby on the Rue de la Paix glanced at us curiously. They weren't real, of course, just part of the surround, but when Essie programs surrounds, she goes all the way. One pretty little dark woman seemed fascinated by us—more so than you would have expected from mere stage dressing. I took a second look, and it was the woman Cassata had been dancing with; evidently Cassata had left a trail of bread crumbs so she could sneak into our new surround.

I stepped up the voltage. I told him, "You don't have a choice. Look, Cassata, this isn't a question of classifying material so an enemy won't get it. There aren't any enemies on this matter except the Foe themselves. Do you think we're spying for them?"

"No, of course not," he said unhappily, trying to please. "But these are high-level orders."

"We're high-level people!"

He gave me one of those I-just-work-here shrugs. "Of course you are, only—" He paused, having caught a glimpse of the young woman in the fringe of the crowd. He shook his head at her; she grinned, blew him a kiss, and ducked away.

"Sorry," he said. "Friend of mine; I told her this was a private meeting. What were you saying?"

I snarled, "You know damn well what I was saying!" And I would have gone on, but Cassata's expression suddenly changed.

He wasn't listening to me anymore. His face froze. His eyes were vacant, as though hearing something none of the rest of us could hear.

And indeed he was, for I recognized the look. It was the way someone in machine storage looks when he is being told something on a private band. I even had a pretty good idea of what he was going to say. He frowned, shook himself, looked around vacantly for a moment, and then said it.

"Oh, *shit*," said General Julio Cassata.

I felt Essie's hand slip into mine. She knew something bad was coming, too. "Tell us!" I demanded.

He sighed a deep sigh. "I've got to get back to JAWS," he said. "Give me a lift, will you?"

That time he surprised me. The first thing I said was only a reflexive, "What?" And then I got better organized. "You change your mind pretty fast, Cassata! First you tell me to stay away entirely, then you freeze my ship—"

"Forget that," he said impatiently. "It's a new ball game. I have to get there right away, and you've got the fastest ship. Will you take me?"

"Well— Maybe, but— But what—"

He said, "I just got word. The blackout isn't an exercise. It's real. I think the Foe have a base on Earth."

To give a machine-stored intelligence like General Cassata (or, for that matter, me) a lift somewhere doesn't take much space. All you have to do is take the storage chip, fan, tape, or cube and put it in the ship, and away you go. Cassata was in a hurry. He had a workthing moving it even as he asked me for permission, and as it reached the hatch we buttoned down and went.

Total elapsed time for the transfer, less than three minutes.

Long enough.

I didn't waste the three minutes. While we were waiting the long, long time for the workthing to get from one bay to another, I was paying my last respects to a lost love.

It didn't take long. The word of the blackout had reached even the meat people by now, and those stone-statue folks were drifting toward the PV plate, where a news program was telling the asteroid that all radio communciation had been cut off.

My doppel was standing well back from the others, looking unhappy. I saw why at once. There was Klara, and there was her—her *husband*—and they were holding each other tighter than ever.

I wished . . .

I wished mostly (or at least, most reasonably) that I had had a chance to know Harbin Eskladar better. Strange that Klara should have married a former terrorist! Strange that she should ever have married anyone but me, I thought—

And then I thought, Robin, old sod, you'd better get out of this. And I zapped myself back to the *True Love* and zipped myself in, and we were gone.

"Robin! Come look!" cried Essie, and I swooped into the control room to do as I was ordered. Julio Cassata was looking hangdog and depressed under the viewscreen, and Essie was pointing at it with fury. "Warships!" she cried. "Look, Robin! Trigger-happy JAWS is getting ready to wipe out world!"

Cassata glowered at me. "Your wife's driving me crazy," he said. I didn't look at him. I was looking at the screen. In that first moment before we went into FTL drive the screens had picked up the JAWS satellite, a hundred thousand kilometers away; even in our far-out orbit it was almost hidden by the bulge of the Earth, but I could see that JAWS was not alone. Midges swarmed around it.

Ships. Essie was right. *Warships*.

Then we were moving into FTL. The screen clouded, and Cassata protested: "They're not going to *attack* anything. They're just a *precaution*."

"Precaution to send out whole fleet with weapons ready," Essie scolded. "Of such precautions are wars made!"

"Would you rather have us do nothing?" he demanded. "Anyway, you'll be there soon. You can complain right to him if you want to—I mean—"

He stopped, looking glum again; because of course the "him" was himself, in his meat version.

But he was right. "We right well will complain," I told him. "Starting with why this 'message' was kept secret from us."

Albert coughed politely. "It wasn't, Robin," he said.

Cassata chimed in belligerently, "You see! You're always going off half-cocked. The whole message was broadcast in burst transmission, just as it was received first time out. I'll bet Albert recorded it."

Albert said apologetically, "It was only a sort of synoptic report on everything about the Heechee and the human race, Robin. There's nothing in it that you couldn't find in the *Encyclopaedia Britannica* and so on."

"Hah," said Essie, still disgruntled, but she stopped there. She thought for a moment. Then she shrugged. "You fellows, you help yourself to drinks et cetera," she said, remembering her duties as a hostess. "Me, I go listen to this burst for self."

I started to follow, because Essie's company on the worst day of her life was still better than Julio Cassata's, but he stopped me. "Robin," he said, "I didn't want to say anything while she was here—"

I looked at him in astonishment. I could not believe there was anything he and I could ever share as a confidence. Then he said, "It's about that guy your old girlfriend is married to."

"Oh," I said. That didn't seem to satisfy Cassata, so I added, "I never met him before, but his name's Harbin Eskladar, I think."

"His name's Eskladar, all right," Cassata said savagely, "and I *know*. I hate his effing guts."

I can't deny that that perked me up right away. The topic of what a lousy person Klara's husband might be was quite congenial to me. "Have a drink," I said.

He looked hesitant, then shrugged. "Just a quick one," he said. "You don't remember him? Well, do you remember *me*? I mean, like thirty or forty years ago, when we first met? I was a brigadier at the time?"

"I remember that, sure," I said, producing drinks.

He took what I offered without looking to see what it was. "Did it ever occur to you to wonder why it took me all these years to be promoted a lousy two grades?"

Actually, I never had. I hadn't even thought about Cassata very much, far less about how he was doing in his job, because

he had been nothing but bad news even back in the High
Pentagon, when I was still meat and all the armed forces had
to worry about was human terrorists. My opinion of Cassata
at that time was that he was a wart on the face of the human
race. Nothing had changed it since, but I said politely, "I guess
I never knew why."

"Eskladar! Eskladar was why! He was my aide-de-camp,
and I damn near got thrown out of the service because of him!
The son of a bitch was moonlighting, and what he did for an
after-hours job was terrorism. He was part of General Beaupre
Heimat's old secret terrorist cell in the High Pentagon!"

After a moment, I said again, "Oh," and this time Cassata
nodded angrily, as though I had said it all.

In a sense I had, because anyone who had been through the
days of misery and terrorism needed no discussion of what
they were like. It was not something you forgot. For twenty
years and more the whole planet had been bombed, raped,
ravaged, and gouged by people whose fury had so exceeded
their judgment that the only thing they could think of to do to
express their discontent was to kill somebody. Not just *one*
somebody; hundreds of thousands had died, one way and another, in virus-poisoned water supplies or wrecked buildings
or bombed cities. And not even any particular somebody, because the terrorists had struck at anyone, the innocent as well
as the guilty—or the ones they considered guilty, anyway.

And the worst part of it was that trusted people, high-ranking
military officers and even heads of state, had been secret members of terrorist groups. A whole nest of them had been un-
covered in the High Pentagon itself.

"But Eskladar broke up the ring," I said, remembering.

Cassata tried to laugh. It came out more like a snarl. "He
turned over to save his own skin," he said—and then, reluctantly, "Well, maybe not just to save himself. He was an ide-
alist, I guess. But as far as I was concerned, it didn't matter.
He was my ADC, and he cost me promotion for twenty years."

He finished his drink. Brightening, he said, "Well, I don't
want to keep her waiting—" And then he stopped, but a little
too late.

"Keep *who* waiting?" I asked, and he winced at the way I said it.

"Well, Robin," he said abjectly, "I didn't think you'd mind if I, uh, if besides me there was—well—"

"A woman," I said, cleverly deducing. "We've got a stowaway on board."

He looked unrepentant. "She's just a canned deader, like you," he said—diplomacy had never been Cassata's strength. "I just had them put her store on along with mine. It won't take up much room, for God's sake, and I've only got . . . "

He stopped there without quite saying just what he'd only got a little of left. He was a little, just a very little, too proud to beg.

He didn't have to. "What's her name?" I asked.

"Alicia Lo. She's the one I was dancing with."

"Well," I said, "it's only for this one flight. All right. Go keep your friend company."

I didn't add, "Just stay out of my sight." I didn't have to. That was exactly what he was certain to do, and if I had been in his position I expect I would certainly have done exactly the same thing myself.

And then there was nothing to get through but the interminable trip itself.

In the *True Love*, it takes only twenty-three minutes for a faster-than-light trip from Wrinkle Rock to JAWS. That's actually real slow. In fact, it isn't even faster than light, because eleven and a half of those minutes go into getting up speed at one end, and eleven and a half to slowing down again at the other; the actual trip time is, oh, a wink and a half. Still, twenty-three minutes isn't much—by meat-person standards.

We were not on Meat Standard Time. But, oh, how many milliseconds a single minute holds.

By the time we were well free of the asteroid, and Albert was setting course for the satellite, I was (metaphorically) biting my metaphoric nails. We keep *True Love* pretty much in the Earth solar system, hardly ever very far from the Earth itself, and so I always have contact with all the many projects

I've got going on Earth to keep me amused—slow, yes, but only seconds slow, not eternities. Not this time. This time there was the radio blackout. I could have sent messages, all right (though Cassata forbade it furiously), but answers I could have none.

What I had to entertain me was Essie, and Albert, and my memories. Cassata wasn't much good. My memories are plentitudinous (they include, after all, everything we could fit into *True Love*'s datastores, which is a lot), but the memories on top were largely Klara and largely sad.

Essie, on the other hand, is always rewarding . . . or almost always. The only times she isn't rewarding is when I'm stuck in a tangle of irritation or worry or misery, and I'm afraid that's where I was just then. After she'd arranged our Johore surround, pretty palace overlooking the straits and Singapore, and I just sat glumly, ignoring the Malaysian meal she'd ordered up, she gave me one of her searching Oh-God-is-he-getting-gloopy-again looks. "Something is bothering you," she asserted. I shrugged. "Not hungry, I guess," she offered, spearing a ball of rice with some kind of black things in it and chewing lustily. I made the pretense of picking up something in a leaf and chewing it. "Robin," she said, "have two choices. Talk to me. Or talk to Albert-Sigfrid—any damn body, only talk. No sense twisting poor old head around alone."

"I guess I will," I said, because it was true. I was getting gloopy again.

Albert found me back on Wrinkle Rock, or anyway the simulation of it I had created to match my mood. I was on Level Tango, where the ships docked, wandering around and looking at the places where people I knew had departed from and never come back.

"You seemed a little depressed," he said apologetically. "I thought I'd just see if there was anything I could do."

"Not a thing." I said, but I didn't tell him to go away. Especially since, I was sure, Essie had sent him there.

He pulled out his pipe, lit it, puffed thoughtfully for a while, and then said, "Would you like to tell me what is on your mind right now?"

"Not a bit," I said.

"Is it because you think I'm tired of hearing the same old things, Robin?" he asked, and there was real affection in those make-believe eyes.

I hesitated, then took the plunge. I said, "What's on my mind is *everything*, Albert. Now, wait, I know what you're going to say. You're going to say which of all the things in everything is right on top. Okay. That's the Foe. They *scare* me."

He said peacefully, "There is a lot to be afraid of in that context, yes, Robin. The Foe certainly threaten us all."

"No, no," I said impatiently, "I don't mean the threat, exactly. I mean it's so hard to understand."

"Ah," he said, smoking his pipe and gazing at me.

"I mean, I just don't have any good idea of what's going on with the universe," I said.

"No, Robin," he agreed kindly. "You don't. You could, though. If you'd let me explain nine-dimensional space and a few of the other concepts—"

"Shut up about that," I ordered, knowing I was making a mistake. I have a right to be humanly capricious, everybody agrees to that, but sometimes I think I carry it too far.

You see, there's an infinity of knowledge reachable to me, because I've been vastened.

I don't like to speak of what happened to me as being "vastened" when I talk to meat people, because it makes them think I feel superior to them. I don't want them to think that, especially because, of course, I really am superior. That infinite resource of data is only one part of the difference between me and meat.

The available datastore wasn't truly infinite, of course. Albert doesn't let me use words like "infinite" for anything that can be counted, and as all of that knowledge existed in chip, fan, or track storage somewhere, certainly someone could have counted the stores. Someone. Not me. I wasn't about to try to count the quantum bits of data, and I wasn't about to try to absorb it all because I was scared.

Oh, God, I was scared! What of? Not just the Foe, though they were fearsome. I was frightened by my own vastness, which I dared not fully explore.

I feared, I *hugely* feared, that if I let myself expand to absorb all that knowledge I would no longer be Robinette Broadhead at all. I feared I would not then be human. I feared that the tiny parcel of data that was me would simply be drowned in all that accumulated information.

When you are only a machine-stored memory of a human being, you do your best to defend your humanity.

Albert has often got impatient with me about that. He says it is a failure of nerve. Even Essie chides me now and then. She says things like, "Dear dumb Robin, why not take what is yours?" And then she tells me little stories from her own childhood to buck me up. "When I was young girl at akademy, pounding brain over some damn nonsense reference volume on maybe Boolean algebra or chip architecture in Lenin Library, would often look around me in horror. Oh, real horror, dear Robin! Would see all ten million volumes surrounding me, and feel sick. I mean, Robin, *sick*. Almost physical sickness. Almost to point of throwing up at thought of swallowing all those gray and green and yellow books, to know all that *could* know. Was impossible for me!"

I said eagerly, "That's exactly it, Essie, I—"

"But is not impossible for you, Robin!" she cut in severely. "Chew, Robin! Open mouth! Swallow!"

But I couldn't.

At least, I wouldn't. I held tightly to my physical human shape (however imaginary), and to my meat-human limitations, however self-imposed.

Naturally I dipped into that vast store from time to time. Just dipped. I only nibbled at the feast. When I wanted, as you might say, one particular volume, I would access that file. I kept my eyes resolutely fixed on that single "volume" and ignored the endless shelves of "books" all around.

Or, better still, I would call on my retinue of savants.

Kings used to do that. I had all the prerogatives of any king. I did what kings did. When they wanted to know something about counterpoint, they would send for Handel or Salieri. If they had a moment's curiosity about the next eclipse, Tycho Brahe would come running. They kept on hand a lavish retinue of philosophers, alchemists, mathematicians, and theologians. The court of Frederick the Great, for instance, was almost a university turned upside down. There was a faculty of all the experts in all the disciplines he could afford to feed, and a student body of one. Him.

More kingly than any king who ever lived, I could afford better than that. I could afford *every* authority on *every* subject. They were cheap enough, because I didn't have to feed them or pay off their mistresses, and it wasn't even a "them." They were all subsumed into my one all-purpose data-retrieval program, Albert Einstein.

So when I complained to Essie, "I wish I understood what all this talk about shrinking the universe meant," she simply looked at me for a moment.

Then she said, "Ha."

"No, I mean it," I said, and I really did.

"Ask Albert," she said sunnily.

"Oh, hell! You know what that means. He'll tell me anything I want to know, but he'll go *on* telling me until it's a lot *more* than I want to know."

"Dear Robin," she said, "is it not possible that Albert knows better than you how much is enough?"

"Oh, hell," I said.

But, standing there with Albert in the gloomy metal tunnel of the (simulated) asteroid ship docks, it seemed to me that the time had come. There wasn't any help for it anymore.

I said, "Albert, okay. Open my head. Dump everything into it. I guess I can stand it if you can."

He gave me a sunny smile. "It won't be that bad, Robin," he promised, and then corrected himself. "It won't be *wonderful*, though. I admit it's going to be hard work. Maybe—"

He glanced around. "Maybe we should start out by getting a little more comfortable. With your permission?"

He didn't wait for the permission, of course. He just went ahead and surrounded us with the study in our house on the Tappan Sea. I began to relax a little. I clapped my hands for the butlerthing to bring me a tall drink, and I sat back in comfort. Albert was watching me quizzically, but he didn't say a word until I said to him, "I'm ready."

He sat down, puffing on his pipe as he regarded me. "For what, exactly?"

"For you to tell me all the things you've been wanting to tell me for the last million years."

"Ah, but Robin—" he smiled "—there are so many of them! Can you be specific? Which particular thing are you willing to let me explain now?"

"I want to know what the Foe have to gain from collapsing the universe."

Albert thought that over for a moment. Then he sighed. "Oh, Robin," he said sorrowfully.

"No," I said, "no, 'Oh, Robin,' no telling me I should have done this long ago, no explaining to me that I have to learn quantum mechanics or something before I can understand. I want to know *now*."

"What a hard taskmaster you are, Robin," he complained.

"Do it! Please."

He paused to reflect, tamping tobacco into his pipe. "I suppose I could just tell you the whole enchilada," he said, "as I have tried to do before, and you have refused to listen."

I braced myself. "You're going to start with your nine-dimensional space again, aren't you?"

"That and many other things, Robin," he said firmly. "They are all involved. The answer to your question is meaningless without them."

"Make it as easy on me as you can," I begged.

He looked at me in some surprise. "You're serious this time, aren't you? Of course I'll try to do that, my dear boy. Do you know what I think? I think the best way to start isn't to tell you anything at all. I'll just show you the pictures."

I blinked. "Pictures?"

"I will show you the birth and death of the universe," he said, pleased with himself. "That's what you asked for, you know."

"It is?"

"It is. The difficulty is that you simply refuse to grasp what a complicated question you are asking. It will take quite a while, several thousand milliseconds at least, even if you try not to interrupt—"

"I'll interrupt whenever I want to, Albert."

He nodded in acceptance. "Yes, you will. That's one of the reasons it will take so long. But if you are willing to take the time required—"

"Oh, do it, for heaven's sake!"

"But I already am doing it, Robin. Just a moment. It takes a little work to set up the display—there we are," he finished, beaming.

And then he disappeared. Beam and all.

The last thing I saw was Albert's smile. It lingered for a moment, and then there was nothing.

"You're playing Alice in Wonderland games with me," I accused—accused nothing and no one, because there was nothing to taste, see, feel, or smell.

But there was something to hear, because Albert's reassuring voice said: "Only a bit of fun to start off with, Robin, because it gets very serious from now on. Now. What do you see?"

"Nothing," I said.

"Quite right. That is what you *see*. But what you are *looking at* is everything. It is the entire universe, Robin. It is all the matter, energy, time, and space there ever was or will be. It is the primordial atom, Robin, the monobloc, the thing in the Big Bang that banged."

"I don't see a goddamn thing."

"Naturally not. You can't see without light, and light hasn't been invented yet."

"Albert," I said, "do me a favor. I hate this feeling of being nowhere at all. Can't you let me see a little something?"

Silence for a moment. Then Albert's beaming face came shadowily back. "I don't suppose it would do any real harm if we could at least see each other," he admitted. "Is that better?"

"*Worlds* better."

"Fine. Only please remember there's no real light yet. There is no light without photons, and all the photons are still in that single, invisible point. Not only that," he went on, enjoying himself, "but if you *could* see, there'd be no place to see it *from*, because there isn't any space to have a 'place' in. Space hasn't been invented yet, either—or, to put it a bit more precisely, all the space, and all the light, and all the everything else is still in that single point right there." ·

"In that case," I said, sulking, "what do you mean by 'there'?"

"Ah, Robin!" he cried in gratification. "You're not so dumb, after all! That's a *really* good question—unfortunately, like many of the best questions, it's meaningless. The answer is that the question is wrong. There isn't any 'there' there; there is only the appearance of a 'there' because I am trying to show you what by definition cannot be shown."

I was beginning to lose heart. "Albert," I said, "if that's the way this show is going to go—"

"Now, hang on," he ordered. "Don't quit now. The show hasn't started yet, Robin; I am only setting the stage. To understand the beginning of the universe you must throw off all your preconceptions of 'time' and 'space' and 'seeing.' None of them exist at this point, some eighteen billion years ago."

"If time doesn't exist yet," I said cleverly, "how do you know it was eighteen billion years ago?"

"Another fine question! And the same fine answer. It is true that before the Big Bang there was no such thing as time. So what you are looking at could be eighteen billion years ago. It could also be eighteen billion trillion quadrillion quintillion whatever-you-like years ago. The question does not apply. But this—object—did exist, Robin, and then it blew up."

I flinched back. It did blow up, right in front of my eyes! Nothing suddenly became something, a point of intolerably bright light, and the point exploded.

It was like an H-bomb going off in my lap. I could almost feel myself shriveled, vaporized, turned into plasma, and dispersed. Rolling thunders of sound battered my nonexistent ears and pounded my incorporeal body.

"My *God*," I yelled.

Albert said thoughtfully, "Possibly so." The idea seemed to please him. "Not in the sense of a personal deity, I mean— you know me too well for that. But there surely was a Creation, and this was it."

"What *happened?*"

"Why, the Big Bang just banged," said Albert in surprise. "That's what you saw. I thought you'd recognize it. The universe has started."

"It has also stopped," I said, beginning to recover, because the great burst had frozen.

"I've stopped it, yes, because I want you to see this point. The universe isn't very old yet—approximately ten-to-the-minus-thirty seconds later. I can't say much about anything earlier, because I don't know anything much. I can't even tell you how big the universe, or that what-do-you-call-it that existed before the universe, was. Bigger than a proton, probably. Smaller than a Ping-Pong ball, maybe. I can tell you—I think— that the dominant force in there was probably the strong nuclear force, or, possibly, gravity, maybe—because it was so compact, the gravity was of course high. *Very* high. So was the temperature. How high I don't know exactly. Probably as high as possible. There is some theoretical reason to believe that the highest possible temperature is something of the order of ten-to-the-twelfth Kelvin—I could give you the argument, if you like—"

"Only if absolutely necessary, please!"

He said reluctantly, "I don't suppose that particular point is *absolutely* necessary. All right. Let me tell you what else I can't say. I can't even say anything much about the stage you are looking at now, except to point out a few things that may not be apparent to you. For instance, that fireburst you are looking at contains *everything*. It contains the atoms and particles that now constitute you, and me, and the *True Love* and the Watch Wheel and the Earth and the Sun and the planet Jupiter and the Magellanic Clouds and all the galaxies in the Virgo clusters and—"

"And everything, right," I said, to stop him. "I get the picture. It's *big*."

"Ah," he said, in satisfaction, "but you see, you don't. It isn't *big*. I've taken a few liberties, you see. I've magnified it a lot, because the Big Bang wasn't very big at all. How big would you say that fireball was?"

"I have no way of telling. A thousand light-years across?"

He shook his head and said thoughtfully, "I don't think so. Smaller. Maybe before the Bang it had no size at all, because space hadn't been invented yet, and it's not far from that now. But it's definitely *small*. And yet it contained everything. Have you got that so far?"

I just looked at him, and he relented. "I know this is dreary for you, Robin, but I want to make sure you understand. Now, about the 'bang.' There wasn't any *sound*, of course. There wasn't any medium to carry sound. For that matter, there wasn't any place to carry it to; that was just another little liberty I took. More important, the Big Bang wasn't the kind of explosion that starts from a firecracker and spreads out into the air as the gases expand, because—"

"Because there wasn't any air, right? Or even space?"

"Very good, Robin! But there's another way in which that bang was different from all other bangs. It didn't expand like a balloon or a chemical or a nuclear explosion. It was something quite different. You've seen those Japanese paper flowers that you put into an aquarium? As they soak up water, they expand? It was more like that, Robin. But what crept in between the parts of the original—*thing*, whatever you want to call it, primordial atom or whatever—wasn't water. It was space. The universe didn't explode. It swelled. Very fast and very far, and it's still doing it."

I said, "Oh."

Albert looked at me searchingly for a moment. Then he sighed, and the burst began to go on bursting.

It surrounded us. I thought it would consume us. It didn't, but we were drenched in a sea of terrible light. From the middle of it came Albert's voice.

"I am going to back us away some light-years," he said. "I don't know how many, just enough so we can see it at a respectable distance." The great ball of fire contracted and fled from us until it was no larger than the full Moon.

"Now, the universe is pretty old," he said. "About a hundredth of a second. It's hot. The temperature is around ten-to-the-eleventh degrees Kelvin, and it's dense. I don't mean dense as matter is dense. There wasn't any matter. It was too dense for that. The universe was a mass of electrons, positrons, neutrons, and photons. Its density was about four times ten-to-the-ninth times as dense as water. Do you know what that means?"

"I think I know how dense dense is, but how hot is hot?"

Albert said reflectively, "There's no good way to tell you, because there isn't anything that hot to compare it with. Now I have to use one of those terms you hate. The whole thing was in 'thermal equilibrium.' "

"Well, Albert," I began.

"No, *listen* to me," he snapped. "That just means that all those particles were interacting and changing. Think of it like a billion trillion light switches, all going on and off at random. But at any time there are as many going on as there are going off, so the total balance is always preserved; that's equilibrium. It wasn't light switches, of course. It was electrons and positrons annihilating each other to produce neutrinos and photons, and so on; but as many events went one way as went the other. Result, equilibrium. Even though inside that state of equilibrium everything was constantly bouncing around like crazy."

I said, "I guess so, Albert, but you're taking a hell of a long time over the first hundredth of a second, if we're going to go eighteen billion years."

"Oh," he said, "we're going to go *much* farther than that.

Don't anticipate, please, Robin. Here we go.'' And the distant puff of flame expanded. "A tenth of a second—now the temperature's dropped to three times ten-to-the-tenth Kelvin. One second, it's dropped by another factor of three. Now—here, let me stop it for a moment. This is fourteen seconds after the Big Bang. It has cooled by another factor of three; it's only three times ten-to-the-ninth Kelvin now. This means that equilibrium is upset for a while, because the electrons and positrons now can annihilate each other faster than they're recreated in the opposite reaction. We'll come back to around this point, Robin, because that's where the answer to your question is.''

"Well," I said, as tactfully as I could, "actually, if it's all the same to you, why don't you just give me the answer now and we can skip the rest of the show?"

"It is not the same to me," he said severely, "and you won't understand. We'll speed up, though. Here we are a few minutes after the bang. The temperature's fallen by two-thirds again; it's only ten-to-the-ninth Kelvin. It's so cool, in fact, that actual protons and neutrons exist—they've even begun to combine in nuclei of hydrogen and helium. Actual matter!—or almost; they're only nuclei, not whole atoms. And all that so-called matter put together is only a tiny fraction of the mass of the universe. Most of it is light and neutrinos. There are a few electrons, but hardly any positrons.''

"How come?" I asked, surprised. "What happened to all the positrons?"

"There were more electrons than positrons in the first batch. So when they annihilated each other, there were electrons left over.''

"Why?"

"Ah, Robin," he said seriously, "that's the best question of all. I will give you an answer that I don't expect you to understand: Since electrons and positrons, and all the other particles for that matter, are only harmonics of closed strings, the numbers that were created are essentially random. Do you want to get into superstring theory? I didn't think so. Just remember the word 'random,' and let's get on with it.''

"Wait a minute, Albert," I said. "Where are we now?"

"About two hundred seconds after the Big Bang."

"Uh-huh," I said. "Albert? We've still got billions and billions of years to go—"

"More than that, Robin. *Much* more."

"Oh, wonderful. And it's taken us this long to go a couple of minutes, so, really—"

"Robin," he said, "you can call it off any time you like, but then how can I answer the questions you will certainly keep on asking? We can take a break if you want a little time to assimilate all this. Or, better still, I can just speed things up."

"Yeah," I said, staring without pleasure at that fuzzy, blinding glob of everything there was.

I didn't really want to take a break. What I wanted was for this to be over.

I admit that Albert always knows what's good for me. What he doesn't understand is that "good" is an abstract concept, and there are lots of times when what is good for me is something I really don't want. I was nearly sorry I'd brought the whole thing up, because I wasn't enjoying this.

So I knew exactly what I wanted of Albert's three alternatives. I would much have preferred the first, because I was getting really tired of heat and pressure and, most of all, of sitting nowhere in the middle of nothing. Second choice would have been to take a break and maybe relax a little with Essie.

So I picked the third. "Just speed it up a little, okay, Albert?"

"Sure thing, Robin. Here we go." The glob swelled menacingly. It still was really nothing but a glob. There weren't any stars or planets or even lumps in the pudding; it was just an unsorted mass of stuff, very bright. It did, however, seem a little less eye-destroyingly bright than it had been.

"Now we're a good long jump ahead," Albert said happily. "About half a million years have gone by. The temperature has gone *way* down. It's only about four thousand Kelvin now—there are plenty of stars hotter than that, but of course we're not talking about isolated points of heat here, we're talking about the average temperature of the whole thing. Notice that it's not quite as bright anymore? Up until now, Robin, the universe was 'radiation-dominated.' The dominant thing was photons. Now matter dominates radiation.''

"Because there aren't so many photons anymore, right?"

"Wrong, I'm afraid," Albert said apologetically. "There are still plenty of photons, but the overall temperature is lower which means the average energy per photon is lower. Therefore its mass is lower. From now on, matter outweighs radiation in the universe and—here we go—" The glob inflated and darkened. "Now we're a couple hundred thousand years later and the temperature has dropped another thousand degrees. This is according to Weinberg's Law: 'The time it takes for the universe to cool from one temperature to another is proportional to the difference in the inverse squares of the temperatures.' I don't suppose you really need to understand that, Robin," he added wistfully, "although there's a really neat demonstration in ten-dimensional supersymmetry—"

"Cut it out, Albert! Why's the damn thing so dark?"

"Ah," he said, gratified, "that's an interesting point. There are so *many* nuclear and electron-like particles now that they get in the way of the light. So the universe is opaque. But that will change. Up to now we've had electrons and we've had protons, but the universe was so hot that they just stayed that way. As free particles. They couldn't combine. Or, rather, they kept combining all the time to make atoms, but the heat just blew them apart again. Now we roll the cameras"—and the glob enlarged itself again, and suddenly brightened—"and all of a sudden, look, Robin! The mixture has cleared! Light shines through! The electrons and protons have combined to make atoms, and the photons can move freely again!"

He paused. His shadowy face was beaming in pure pleasure.

I thought hard for a moment, staring at the glob. It was beginning to show—oh, no real structure, but at least hints that maybe something was happening somewhere inside there, like the planet Uranus seen from afar. "Albert?" I said. "That's all fine, but, look, there are still plenty of photons, right? So why don't they collide and make more particles to make it all opaque again?"

"Oh, Robin," he said affectionately, "Sometimes I think you're not really stupid, after all. I'll give you the answer. Remember my famous e equals m-c-squared? The photons have energy, e. If two of them collide and their combined energy equals the mass of any particle, m, times the square of the speed of light, then they can create that particle in their collision. When the universe was young—the threshold temperature is somewhere around ten-to-the-ninth Kelvin—they had plenty of energy and they could create hellish big particles. But it has cooled down. Now they can't. They just don't have it anymore, Robin."

"Oh, wow," I said. "You know? I almost have the illusion that I nearly understand!"

"Don't put yourself down," he chided—meaning, I supposed, that I should leave that sort of thing to him. He was silent for a moment, then he fretted, "I haven't told you about the creation of quarks and hadrons. I haven't even said anything about acceleration, and that's important. You see, for the model to work, you have to account for the fact that at some point in the Big Bang the outward expansion got *faster*. I can give you an analogy. It's as though you had an explosion that *kept on* exploding for a time, so instead of slowing down it expanded faster. The actual explanation is more complicated, and—"

"Albert! Do I have to know this?"

"Not really, Robin," he said after a moment. His tone was wistful but not insistent.

"So why don't you just roll the camera some more?"

"Oh, very well."

I suppose every kid loves electric trains. Watching Albert's model of the universe grow was almost like having the most hellishly huge set of trains to play with that any boy could imagine.

I couldn't make them run, of course. But just watching was a lot of fun. The glob roiled and swirled and began to break up. Our "camera" zoomed in tight on one particular smudge in the swarm, and I saw that, too, breaking up into smaller blobs. Clusters and metagalaxies formed, and actual galaxies began to pinwheel into their familiar spiral forms. Individual points of light blew up and died; new ones formed in the center of clouds of gas.

"We have actual stars now, Robin," Albert announced from beside me. "This is the first generation. Clouds of hydrogen and helium fall together and contract and start nuclear fusion in their interiors. That's where they cook all the heavier elements, the ones your meat body was made of—carbon, nitrogen, oxygen, iron, all the elements higher than helium. Then, when they blow up as supernovae—" he pointed to one particular star, that obligingly exploded in a tiny torrent of light "—all those elements float around in space until they happen to contract into another star and its planets. And then they form other things. Like you, Robin."

I yelped, "You mean all the atoms that make me up used to be in the core of a star?"

"That made up your meat body," he corrected. "Yes, Robin. In fact, our own Galaxy is in there now. See if you can pick it out."

He froze the expanding cloud so I could peer around. "They all look alike," I complained.

"Most of them do, pretty much," he conceded. "But there's M-31, and there are the Magellanic Clouds. And that spiral there, that's us."

He was pointing to a glowing whirlpool of firefly light, surrounded by other firefly patches in a vast thinly sprinkled darkness. "I don't see you and me anywhere in there," I said, trying for a joke.

He took it seriously. He coughed. "I'm afraid I let it run a little past present time," he apologized. "All of human history, including the formation of the solar system and the expansion of the sun into a red giant, has already taken place. You missed it."

I turned to look at his shadowy face. "I don't know if I want to hear this," I said, and very nearly meant it.

He looked gently chiding. "But it's only reality, Robin," he said. "It's a truth, whether you want to know it or not. I suppose that, in a sense, it might shake your notions of your own personal importance in the universe—"

"Damn right it does!"

"Well," he said, "that's not a bad thing. But don't get too crushed. Remember, it is this—*all* of this—that the Foe are trying to change."

"Oh, fine! Is that supposed to make me feel better?"

He studied me for a moment. "Not better, exactly, no. But more in touch with reality. After all, remember that you, and I, and all the rest of the human race and the Heechee and the machine intelligences have only two choices. We can let the Foe do what they're doing. Or we can try to oppose them."

"And how, exactly, are we supposed to do that?"

He looked thoughtfully at the frozen model. "Shall I run it a little further?" he asked.

"You're changing the subject!"

"I know I am, Robin. I'm going to run the model. Perhaps if you understand what all this entails you may, in some way, contribute to the solution of this problem. Perhaps not. Perhaps it can't be solved; but in any case I don't see that we, or someone else sooner or later, have any choice but to *try*; and you can't effectively even try without knowledge."

"But I'm *scared*!"

"You'd be crazy if you weren't, Robin. Now, do you want to see what happens next or not?"

"I don't know if I do!"

I meant it. I was beginning to get really nervous. I gazed at that patchy glow that had once held me and Essie and Klara and all the pharaohs and kings and saviors and villains and Heechee explorers and Sluggard singers and dinosaurs and trilobites—all once there and now gone—all gone, *long* gone, as far behind us as the birth of the Sun itself.

I was scared, all right. It was all too *big*.

I felt tinier and more helpless and unreal than I had felt ever before in my life. In either of my lives. It was worse than dying, worse even than when I had been vastened. That had certainly been terrifying, but it had had a future.

Now the future was past. It was like looking at my own grave.

Albert said impatiently, "You do want to see. I'll go ahead."

The Galaxy spun like a top. I knew it was taking a quarter-billion years to the turn, but it whirled madly, and something else was happening. The surrounding satellite galaxies crept away. "They're spreading out," I cried.

"Yes," Albert agreed. "The universe is expanding. It can't make any more matter or energy, but it keeps on making more space. Everything gets farther apart from everything else."

"But the stars in the Galaxy aren't doing that."

"Not yet. Not exactly, anyway. Just watch; we're heading for a hundred billion years in the future."

The Galaxy spun faster still, so fast that I couldn't make out the actual motion, only a blur. What I did see was that even the Local Group was beginning to move almost out of sight.

"I'll stop it for a moment," Albert said. "There. Do you notice anything about our own Galaxy?"

"Somebody turned off a lot of stars."

"Exactly. It is dimmer, yes. What turned the stars off is time. They got old. They died. You will note that the Galaxy is reddish in color now, rather than white. The big white stars die first; the old red ones die slowly. Even the little F and G stars, the yellow dwarfs, no bigger than our own Sun, have already burned up all their nuclear fuel. The dim red ones will go soon, too. Watch."

Slowly, slowly, the Galaxy . . . went out.

There was nothing visible anywhere but the shadowy outlines of our imaginary bodies, and Albert's imaginary face. Gazing. Pondering.

Sad.

As to myself, the word "sad" does not begin to describe it. Everything else that had ever happened to me, every formless fear that had ever kept me awake at night—they were all nothing.

I was looking at *The End*.

Or so I thought, and so it felt, and all human concerns dwindled to nothingness by comparison; but when I said, "Is this the end of the universe, then?" Albert looked surprised.

"Oh, no, Robin," he said. "Whatever gave you that idea?"

"But there's nothing there!"

He shook his shadowy head. "Wrong. Everything is still there. It has grown old, and the stars have died, yes. But they're there. They even still have their planets, most of them. The planets are dead, of course. They're not much above absolute zero; there's no more *life*, if that's what you mean."

"That's exactly what I mean!"

"Yes, Robin," he said patiently, "but that's just your anthropomorphic view. The universe has kept right on cooling as it kept on making space to expand into. But it's *dead*. And it will keep on being dead, forever . . . unless . . . "

"Unless *what*?" I barked.

Albert sighed. "Let's get comfortable again," he said.

I blinked as I found myself again in the world.

That awesome blackness was gone from around us. I was sitting on the lanai of my house on the Tappan Sea, with my still cold drink still unfinished in my hand, and Albert was calmly stoking his pipe in the wicker armchair.

"My God," I said faintly.

He just nodded, deep in thought. I finished my drink in a single gulp and rang for another.

Albert said, out of his reverie, "That's how it would be if the universe kept on expanding."

"It's scary!"

"Yes," he agreed, "it is frightening even to me, Robin." He struck a wooden kitchen match on the sole of his scuffed shoe and puffed. "I should point out to you that this demonstration has taken quite a bit longer than I planned. We are almost ready to dock at the Joint Assassin Watch satellite. If you would like a closer look . . . "

"It can wait!" I snapped. "You took me this far, now what about the rest of it? What does all this stuff you've been showing me have to do with the Foe?"

"Ah, yes," he said reflectively. "The Foe."

He seemed lost in thought for a moment, sucking the pipe-stem, staring blankly into space. When he spoke, it sounded as though he were discussing something else entirely.

"You know," he said, "when I was—alive—there was considerable argument among cosmologists about whether the universe would go on expanding, as I have just displayed for you, or only expand to a certain point and then fall back on itself, like the water in a fountain. You understand that, basically, that depends on how dense the universe is?"

"I think so," I said, trying to keep up with what he was telling me.

"Please be sure so," he said sharply. "That's the cornerstone of the argument. If there is enough matter in the universe, its combined gravitation will stop the expansion, and then it will fall back on itself again. If there isn't, it won't. Then it will go on expanding forever, as you have seen."

"I sure have, Albert."

"Yes. Well, the critical density—that is, the total mass of everything in the universe, divided by the total volume of the universe—turns out to be about five times ten-to-the-minus-thirtieth power grams per cubic centimeter. In more familiar terms, that amounts to about one atom of hydrogen in a space equal to your body."

"That's not much, is it?"

"Unfortunately," he sighed, "that's an awful *lot*. The universe isn't that dense. There aren't that many atoms in an average volume. People have been looking for mass for a long time, but nobody has ever been able to find enough stars, dust clouds, planets, physical bodies of any kind, or photons of energy to add up to that much mass. There would have to be a least ten times as much as we can find to close the universe. Maybe a hundred times as much. More than that. We can't even find enough mass to account for the observed behavior of galaxies rotating around their own cores. That's the famous 'missing mass.' The Heechee worried about that a lot, and so did a lot of my own colleagues . . . But now," he said somberly, "I think we know the answer to that problem, Robin. The deceleration parameter measurements are right. The mass estimates are wrong. Left to itself, the universe would go on expanding forever, an open universe. But the Foe have closed it.''

I was floundering badly, still numb from the spectacle of that terrible history. The housething came with my next margarita, and I took a deep swallow before I asked, "How could they do that?''

He shrugged reprovingly. "I don't know. I could guess that somehow they've added mass, but that's only an idle speculation; in any case, that isn't relevant to your question. I mean your *original* question; do you remember what it was?''

"Of course I do!'' Then I qualified, "That is, it had something to do with— Oh, right! I wanted to know what the Foe had to gain by collapsing the universe again, and instead of answering you took me about a zillion years in the future.''

He looked faintly apologetic, but only faintly. "Perhaps I got carried away,'' he conceded, "but it was interesting, wasn't it? And it does have a bearing. Here, let's take another look at the universe at about the one-trillion-year mark—''

"Let me finish my damn drink, damn it!''

"Of course you can,'' he said, soothing me. "I'll just display it for you; you can stay right where you are, and I won't suppress the ambience. Now!''

A great frame of blackness spread itself across the view of the Tappan Sea. The windsailers and fishermen disappeared, along with the hills on the opposite shore, replaced by that hatefully familiar black void sprinkled with faint red dots.

"We're looking at a time about a million million years from now,'' he said comfortably, gesturing with the stem of his pipe.

"And what are those little pimply things? Let me guess— red dwarf stars?'' I said cleverly. "Because all the big ones are burned out? But why are we going into the future again, anyhow?''

He explained, "Because even for the Foe the universe has a lot of momentum. It can't stop on a dime and turn around. It has to go on expanding for a while until the extra drag of the 'missing mass' that they have—somehow—added can begin to draw it back. But now watch. We are at the limit of expansion, and I'm going to show what happens next. We will see the universe shrink, and I'll speed it up so we'll go back pretty rapidly. Watch what happens."

I nodded, sitting back comfortably and sipping my drink. Perhaps the unreal alcohol was having its soothing effect on my unreal metabolism, or perhaps it was only that I was sitting in a comfortable chair in pleasant surroundings. One way or another, it didn't seem as scary this time. I stretched out my bare feet and wriggled my toes in front of that vast black backdrop that blotted out the sea, marking the progression of the galaxies as they began to creep back together. They didn't seem very bright. "No more big stars?" I asked, somehow disappointed.

"No. How could there be? They're dead. But watch as I speed things up a little."

The black backdrop began to gray and brighten, though the galaxies themselves didn't. I yelped, "There's more light! What's happening? Are there stars I can't see?"

"No, no. It's the *radiation*, Robin. It's getting brighter because of the blue shift. Do you understand that? All the time the universe was expanding, the radiation from distant objects was shifted into the red—the old Doppler effect, remember? Because they are going away from us. But now they're coming toward us as the universe contracts. So what must then happen?"

"Light shifts toward the blue end of the spectrum?" I hazarded.

"Wonderful, Robin! Exactly. The light shifts in the direction of the blue—all of it, way beyond the visible range. That means that the photons become more energetic. The temperature of space—the average temperature of the universe—is already a good many degrees above absolute zero, and it's getting rapidly warmer. Do you see those little dark blobs floating together?"

"They look like raisins in Jell-O."

"Yes, all right, only what they really are is what's left of the galaxies. Really, they're mostly enormous black holes.

They're falling together, even beginning to coalesce. Do you
see that, Robin? They're eating each other up.''

"And the whole thing's getting a lot brighter," I said, shad-
ing my eyes. I couldn't even see the sailboats beyond the edges
of the picture now; the brightness blanked them out.

"Oh, much brighter. The background temperature's in the
thousands of degrees now, as hot as the surface of the Sun.
All those old, dead stars are getting a kind of new life again,
like zombies, because the external heat is warming them up.
Most of them will simply be vaporized, but others—there!"
A point of light rushed toward us and past. "That was a big
old one, big enough to have a little fusible matter left. The heat
started its nuclear fires again, a little."

I flinched from the—unreal—heat.

Albert shook his pipe at me, back in the lecture mode.
"What's left of all the stars and galaxies are racing together!
The black holes are merging, all the photons are now far into
the ultraviolet and past—the temperature is now in the millions
of degrees—Himmelgott!" he shouted, and I cried out too, as
the whole scene shrank and brightened to one intolerable ultimate flare of light.

Then it was gone.

The windsurfers were still on the Tappan Sea. The mild
breeze stirred the leaves on the azaleas. My sight began to
return.

Albert wiped his eyes. "I should have slowed it down a little
at the end, I think," he said reflectively. "I could do it over—
no, of course not. But you get the idea."

"I do indeed," I said shakily. "And now what?"

"And now it rebounds, Robin! The universe explodes and
starts up all over again, new—and different!" He looked
around at the pleasant scene wonderingly. Then he turned toward me. "Do you know," he said, "I think I would like a
little something myself. Perhaps some dark beer, Swiss or
German?"

I said seriously, "You never fail to astonish me, Albert." I
clapped my hand, of course quite unnecessarily, and in a mo-

ment the workthing appeared with a tall ceramic stein, golden froth humped over the top.

"And that's what the Foe want to do, make a new universe?"

"A *different* universe," Albert corrected, wiping foam off his lip. He looked at me repentantly. "Robin? I'm neglecting my other duties to you. We're approaching the JAWS satellite. Perhaps you wish to join your friends at the viewscreens?"

"What I wish," I said, "is to get this the hell over with. Finish up! What do you mean, a 'different' universe?"

He inclined his head. "That's where my old friend Ernst Mach comes in," he explained. "Do you remember what I told you about the positrons and electrons annihilating each other? Only electrons were left, because there had been more of them to start out? Well, suppose the universe started with an equal number so that, at the end of the process, there were *no* electrons left? And no protons or neutrons, either; what would we have?" I shook my head. "A universe without matter, Robin! Pure radiation! Nothing to perturb or upset the free flow of energy—or of energy beings!"

"And is that what the Foe want?" I asked.

"I don't know," he said. "It is one possibility, perhaps. But if Mach was correct there are other, more serious possibilities. At that same point in the history of the universe, when the balance of electrons and positrons was determined by random events—"

"What *sort* of random events?" I demanded.

"I don't know that, either. All particles are, really, only harmonics of closed strings, though. I suppose the properties of the strings can produce any kind of harmonics you like. Please be patient with me here, Robin, because as you know I have some difficulty with this concept of indeterminacy, or random events—it was always a difficulty for me in my meat life, you remember." He twinkled.

"Don't twinkle! Don't be cute at all!"

"Oh, very well. But if Mach is correct, such random fluctuations determined not only the balance of particles, but many other things, including the physical constants of the universe."

"How can that be, Albert? I mean, those are *laws*."

"They are laws arising from facts, and the facts themselves are what Mach says were generated at random. I'm not sure how many 'fundamental facts' are really fundamental in any universal sense—perhaps I should say, in any multiuniversal sense. Did it ever occur to you to ask yourself why, for example, Bolzmann's constant should equal zero point zero zero zero zero eight six one seven electron volts per degree Kelvin, and not some other number?"

I said truthfully, "The thought never crossed my mind."

He sighed. "But it has mine, Robin. There should be a *reason* why this number is what it is. Mach says sure, there is a reason, it is that at some early point things just happened to go that way. So indeed all of the physical constants might be different if those random fluctuations had fluctuated just a bit differently."

He took another pull at his beer, thinking. "This point where things can change—the Heechee call it the 'Phase Locus,' because it represents a phase change, like the transformation of water into ice. It is where random events became frozen, and all the 'gosh numbers' were established. I don't mean the trivial or man-made ones, I mean the ones that are fundamental to the laws we know, but that we cannot account for from basic principles. Pi. The base of the natural logarithms. The speed of light. The fine-structure constant. Planck's number—I don't know how many others, Robin. Perhaps in a different universe arithmetic would be noncommutative and there would be no law of inverse squares. I cannot believe this is likely—but then, none of this sounds so, does it?"

"And you think the Foe are just going to keep on remaking the universe until they get it right?"

"I don't know," he said. "Perhaps they have some hope of being there to *make* it right—right for them, I mean. Change the laws of the universe! Create new laws! Construct a universe which will be more congenial to life like theirs. . ."

I was silent for a long time, trying to grasp it all. Failing.

I said, "Well, what would that universe be like?"

Albert took a long pull of his stein and set it down carefully.

His eyes were on infinity. In his left hand was his pipe; he was scratching his wrinkled forehead slowly with the stem.

I blinked and shifted position. "Would it have nine-dimensional space?"

No answer. Nothing but that vacant look directed at nothing.

I was feeling alarm. I said, "Albert! I asked you a question! What sort of universe would the Foe want to create?"

He looked at me without recognition. Then he sighed. He reached down reflectively to scratch his bare ankle, and he said, very seriously:

"Robin, I don't have a clue."

11
Heimat

I've told you about some good people and some flawed people, and now it is time to tell about a really bad person. You won't like him, but you need to know him. I mentioned him briefly when I was talking about terrorists, but I didn't do him justice. I would certainly have liked to do him justice—plenty of justice, preferably at the end of a rope—but that hadn't happened. Unfortunately.

His name was Beaupre Heimat, and once he had been a two-star general on the High Pentagon.

It was Heimat who had persuaded Klara's new husband that the only way to achieve peace and justice was to blow a lot of people up. That was one of the least of his crimes.

Among other bad things, he once tried to kill me personally. It may have been twice, because not everything came out at his trial. With me he failed. With several hundred others, though—at least several hundred—he was more efficient. Heimat refused to plead guilty to murder at his trial. He wouldn't call it murder. He called it revolutionary justice, because he was a terrorist. The court, on the other hand, had no trouble calling it murder—calling each individual case of it murder—and they gave him a life sentence for each one of the deaths. And as Heimat had been not just any mixed-up moke but a trusted general in the American space forces, they made the sentences consecutive. Altogether, Heimat's sentences added up to an aggregate minimum stay in jail of 8,750 years, but time had passed and now Heimat had only 8,683 yet to serve.

He had every reason to believe that he would serve every day of those years, too, because even felons were entitled to machine storage. His prison term would not automatically end with his death.

Actually, I rather enjoy talking about General Beaupre Heimat now. It makes a welcome relief. After Albert's soul-numbing display of immensity and eternity, it is relaxing to think about a mere person, who is merely despicable.

One day for Heimat was much like every other. This is how he started his days:

When he woke up, the bedthing was still and curled beside him, but he knew she wasn't asleep. He also knew she was not a she but an it, but as Heimat had almost nothing but its for company anymore, he had stopped recognizing the difference.

As Heimat threw his legs over the side of the bed, she started to get up, too. He pushed her back down. Gently enough, after the violence of the night before. Not all that gently, because (disappointingly) she was very strong.

She watched him dress for a moment before she asked, "Where are you going?"

"Why," said Heimat, "I think I will walk down to the beach, then swim across the channel and catch a plane to Los Angeles,

where I propose to blow up a few buildings." He waited a
moment for a response, and got none. He hadn't expected any.
Typically, she had no sense of humor. It was a chronic disappointment. Heimat would have enjoyed his life a great deal
more if he could have made some of his bedthings laugh—
though not, of course, as much as if he had been able to make
them weep in pain. The authorities gave him female construc-
tions that looked and felt and smelled and tasted like humans,
why couldn't they be considerate enough to make them *feel*?

It did not occur to Heimat that he had not earned much
consideration from the authorities, or from anyone else.

Outside the door his guardthing winked and whispered,
"What do you say, Heimat? Was she all right?"

"Not really." Heimat kept walking and finished the conversation without turning his head: "I told you I like blondes.
Little young ones. Fragile."

The guard called after him, "I'll see what I can do tonight,"
but Heimat didn't answer. He was thinking of the word he had
just used—"fragile"—and the way it made him feel. Fragile.
A tiny fragile blonde. A live one! A real female human one,
with her fragile little limbs twisted and broken and her mouth
screaming and her face contorted in pain—

He stopped the thought at that point. He didn't stop because
what he was thinking shamed him, because Heimat was long
past shame. He stopped because he was enjoying it so much,
with such desperate yearning, that he was afraid his face might
give away something of what he was feeling; and the only
victory Heimat ever had anymore was to keep some secrets
to himself.

Heimat's island prison was very far from any continent or
any major city. It had been built to hold thirty-eight hundred
desperate convicts and keep them inside no matter what they
planned or did.

Now all that construction was overkill, because the only
active survivor in the prison was Heimat himself. There
weren't thirty-eight hundred desperate prisoners left in his
prison. There weren't that many in the whole world. Recruit-

ment had fallen off greatly since the bad old days of terrorism and famine. Oh, sociopaths turned up every now and then, of course, but what Albert (when he and I discussed such matters) called "the preconditions for opportunistic crime" were scarce.

The thing was, conditions had got a lot better. Nowhere in the human galaxy were there places where whole generations grew up to mug or murder or destroy because they had no easier way to ease their miseries. Most of the worst of the prisoners still somewhere jailed were veterans of the days of terrorism and mass crime, and there weren't many of those left. Many of the malcontents had long since let themselves be plea-bargained into a different kind of imprisonment in one of the hard-service colonies. Most of the others had finally become either sufficiently rehabilitated or sufficiently dead. Heimat himself was quite an old man—older than I, a hundred and thirty at least. Of course, he got Full Medical. He might go on another fifty years in the flesh, because the prisoners were repaired and reconditioned as often as necessary; it wasn't usually age, sickness, or accident that they died of when they died. It was almost always simple, terminal boredom. On one morning just like every other morning they would wake up and look around and decide that enough was at last enough and machine storage could be no worse. Then they would find the right chance and kill themselves.

But not Heimat.

The only other living meat inmate of the prison was a former Soviet marshal named Pernetsky. Like Heimat, he had been a mole for the terrorists, using his military position to help them kill and wreck. The two had been colleagues in the secret underground, then fellow prisoners for hell's own years. Not friends, exactly. Neither of them had any real friends. But close enough as inmates that Heimat had been really surprised when he heard one day that Pernetsky had eaten out his entire digestive system with cleaning fluids.

It was not an efficient suicide attempt. The guardthings had spotted it at once, and now Pernetsky was in intensive care in the prison hospital.

One destination is as good as any other for a man who has none, and Heimat decided to look in on Pernetsky.

The prison hospital was on the same scale as the great penitentiary complex itself. The hospital had a hundred and thirty beds, each one capable of being isolated with partitions of shatterproof glass and steel. Pernetsky was the only patient.

Heimat crossed the warm, wide lawn with its hibiscus and palm trees to the hospital, ignoring the workthings that picked the blossoms for his table and tidied up the fallen fronds. He could not ignore the medic in the reception room, though. As he entered she peered out at him and called, with a smile of professional cheer, "Good morning, General Heimat! You're looking a little flushed. Would you like me to check your blood pressure?"

"No chance," sneered Heimat, but he stopped within conversational range of her. He was always more courteous to the medics than to any other prison personnel—it was his theory, which he never chose to put to the test, that some of them, sometimes, were living humans. It was also his habit, because in the presence of the medical staff he could think of himself as hospital patient rather than jailbird. Role playing was important to Heimat. He had acted well in consecutive roles as West Point cadet, grunt lieutenant, company commander, division G-2, two-star general—secret soldier in the liberation forces!—convict. "I don't want you to take my blood pressure," he said, "because you already know perfectly well what it is and you just want to give me some medication I don't want. But I'll tell you. If you were about six centimeters shorter and ten years younger I'd let you raise it a little. Especially if you were blond." (*And fragile.*)

The nurse's professional smile stayed professional. "You want a lot from me," she murmured.

"You're supposed to give me everything I need," he said. The conversation had begun to bore him. He decided this one wasn't really human anyway, and moved on.

No one stopped him. What was the point? The shatterproof walls were not up around Pernetsky's bed, either. There was even less point in that, because Pernetsky's transplants were a long way from healed and he was tied to his life-support systems more firmly than by any chains.

Heimat looked down on his last living companion, trussed in his bed with the tubes in his nose and the tiny pumps whirring away. "Well, Pyotr," he said, "are you going to get up from there? Or is your next stop the Dead File?"

The Russian didn't respond. He hadn't responded to anything for weeks. It was only the traitorous CRT at the foot of his bed, with its telltale sine waves billowing and sometimes erupting, that showed he was not only alive but sometimes even awake. "I almost miss you," Heimat said meditatively, and lit a cigarette, heedless of the signs that warned of oxygen and risks of fire. A wardthing moved unobtrusively closer but did not interfere.

Once this had been the military ward of the prison. Beyond the glass doors of the wardrobes Heimat could see the racks of uniforms, American blue and khaki, Russian white and drab, that would never be worn again. "If you get up," Heimat wheedled, "I'll take off this stupid hospital robe and put on my Class As. You can too. We'll have a war game or something; remember how you used to nuke New York and Washington, and I'd wipe out your whole missile complex?"

There was no response from the patient. This was beginning to be boring, too, Heimat decided. "Ah, well," he said, blowing smoke in Pernetsky's face, "we knew all along that the winners always put the losers on trial. Foolish of us to lose."

As Heimat turned to leave, the Soviet marshal's head moved ever so slightly and one eye winked. "Ah, Pyotr!" cried Heimat. "You've been fooling them!"

The marshal's lips opened. "Last night," he whispered. "The hovertrucks. Find out why."

And then he closed lips and eyes and would not open either again.

Naturally none of the prisonthings would answer Heimat's questions. He had to go and find out what Pernetsky had been talking about for himself.

He roamed the prison compound, all the three square kilometers of it on the side of the mountain, with its heartbreaking view of the sea no prisoner could ever reach. Most of the cell blocks were empty and sealed. The engineering buildings— the power sources and the disposal units and the laundries— weren't empty because they had to keep on chugging away at their tasks. But they were sealed to Heimat anyway.

Everything else was open, but there wasn't much of everything else. The prison had a farm; it had been work for the inmates when there were enough inmates to matter, and it was kept going by the workthings even now because it produced a number of valuable, if sometimes peculiar, crops. But there was nothing there that hadn't always been there. Nor around the pool, nor in the gymnasium, nor in the vast, empty recreation hall, with its games and books and screens.

So what had Pernetsky meant about trucks?

Heimat wondered if it would be worth the trouble to look at the Dead File. It was trouble, because the building was off all by itself, upslope, near the outer barriers of the prison, and it was quite a climb. It had been some time since Heimat had made the effort.

When he realized this, he decided promptly to do it now. It was always a good idea to keep checking the prison perimeters. One day, just for a moment, someone might slip up, and then there would be a chance of—

Of what?

Heimat grinned sourly to himself as he climbed the flower-bordered walk to the Dead File. Of escape, of course. Even after all these years, that hope was what kept him going.

"Hope" was too strong a word. Heimat had no real hope of escaping, or at least not of staying escaped even if somehow he were able to get out of the prison itself. With all the wise and watching computer programs in the world, it would not be long before one or another of them penetrated any disguise.

On the other hand . . .

On the other hand, thought Heimat, careful not to show any expression on his face lest some nearby workthing catch a glimpse of it—on the other hand a man who was sufficiently courageous and daring, a natural leader gifted with charisma and power—a man like himself, in fact—might easily overturn the odds! Think of Napoleon back from Elba! The people flocking to him! Armies springing out of nowhere! Once free he would find followers, and then the hell with their machines and spies, the people would shield him. Of this Heimat had no doubt. He was certain in his heart that, whatever people pretended to themselves, most of the human race was as greedy and arrogant as himself, and what they really wanted most was a leader to tell them that greed and arrogance were permissible, even admirable, behavior.

But first one had to escape.

Heimat stopped at the fork in the walk, panting slightly. It was a hard climb for a man a hundred and some years old, even with so many new parts that he had long lost count, and the sun was hot. He surveyed the perimeter walls of the prison resignedly. They had not changed. They weren't even walls; there was a barrier of bushes, handsomely ornamental but filled with sensors, then a space and another barrier, equally beautiful to the eye but this time filled with paralyzing circuits—and, just to make sure, a third line behind them, and this one was lethal. The late Major Adrian Winterkoop had proven that for all of them, because that was the way he had chosen for his own suicide. The experiment had worked well. (Or as well as dying ever worked, when all that happened was that they put you into machine storage in the Dead File.)

And, in any case, those industrious gardenerthings that were never out of sight somewhere in the area could quickly become guardthings. Because you were never out of their sight, either.

Heimat sighed and took the left-hand fork, toward the Dead File.

Heimat didn't go there often. It was not a place a living prisoner enjoyed visiting, because a living prisoner knew that sooner or later he would be a dead one, and there he then would be. No well person enjoys looking at his own grave.

Of course, the five or six thousand true incorrigibles stored in the Dead File weren't really *dead*, they were only "dead." Major Winterkoop was still there, for instance, or at least the machine-stored analog of him was there, because the guard-

things had recovered his body in time. Not in time to revive
it, no. But before the quick processes of decay had made the
contents of that angry brain unrecoverable. Being dead had
not changed Winterkoop; he was still the same reckless, heedless person who had been Heimat's adjutant in the glory days,
when they used their position to bomb and kill and destroy for
the sake of the glorious new world to come.

And this, thought Heimat sourly, was the new world, and
neither he nor Major Winterkoop had any part in it.

As he walked toward the low pastel building that held the
Dead File, he thought briefly of accessing Winterkoop, or one
of the other Dead Men, just for the sake of a chat and a change.
But they were all so damned dull! Imprisonment didn't stop
with death. None of them would ever leave the Dead File, and
none of them had changed a bit since their deaths . . .

Heimat stopped short, gaping at the Dead File.

Around the corner, just out of sight from the path, was the
main cargo entrance that he had never once seen used. It was
being used now. Two huge trucks sat on their bellies outside
it, their fans silent, as a dozen workthings busily carried racks
of datafans and coils inside.

"Please, General Heimat," said a gardenerthing from behind
him, "don't go any closer. It is not allowed."

"They came in last night while I was asleep!" said Heimat,
staring. "But what is it?"

"Consolidation," the gardenerthing said apologetically.
"The Pensacola facility is being closed and all the inmates
moved here."

Heimat recovered himself. It was the first rule of his prison
existence that he never let any of the watchthings know what
he was thinking or feeling, so he simply said with a pleasant
· smile, "Not enough of us enemies of society left to keep you
all busy, I suppose. Do you fear for your job?"

"Oh, no, General Heimat," said the workthing seriously.
"We will simply be assigned to other tasks as needed, of
course. But it is only Pensacola that is being terminated. Here,
as you see, we are accepting their cases."

"Ah, yes, their *cases*," said Heimat, beaming at the workthing as he wondered if it would be worth the trouble to try to destroy it. It had been given the form of a young Polynesian male, even to the beads of sweat on the hairless chest. "So I suppose all of the Pensacola *cases* are now in our Dead File."

"Oh, no, General. There is one live one. According to your records you know him. Cyril Basingstoke."

Heimat lost his calm for a moment. "Basingstoke?" He gaped at the workthing. Cyril Basingstoke had been one of the major terrorist leaders, the only one, perhaps, who commanded a network as big as, and almost as deadly as, Heimat's own. "But Basingstoke was paroled a year ago," he said. "It was on the news."

"He was, General Heimat, yes." The workthing nodded. "But he is a recidivist. While he was on parole he killed thirty-five people."

To understand, they tell me, is to forgive, but I don't believe it.

I think I do pretty nearly understand people like Heimat and Basingstoke. Like every other terrorist from the Stone Age on, they killed and destroyed for a principle, and convinced themselves that the principle they killed for justified the bloodshed and agony they caused.

They never convinced me, though. I saw some of the casualties. Essie and I barely missed being two of them ourselves, when Heimat's hit squads blew up a Lofstrom loop they thought we were on. And, because we were witnesses to that one, we were there for Heimat's trial, and I heard all about the others. Most of all I heard Heimat, and saw him, erect and military in the prisoner's dock, looking the very model of a modern major general in his dress whites and strong, right-stuff face. He listened with polite attention as the witnesses detailed how, in his proper person as a major general in the United States Defense Forces, he had secretly organized the bands that blew up launch loops, struck down satellites, poisoned water supplies, and even managed to steal a Dream Couch to sicken the entire world with mad fantasies. Of course, he had been caught in the end. But he had fooled them all for nearly ten years, sitting straight-faced in staff meetings discussing antiterrorist measures, before people like Eskladar had come to their senses and through them the world's police forces at last succeeded in linking Heimat with the massacres and bombings. None of these were crimes to him. They were simple strategies.

Heimat's trial was a peculiar experience for me. I had died not long before, and that was the first time I had appeared in public in a holographic body, with my essential self stored in gigabit space. That was still a rather unusual situation, and Heimat's lawyers tried to keep me from testifying because I wasn't a "person." They failed, of course. It wouldn't have mattered if they had succeeded, because there were plenty of other witnesses.

Heimat obviously didn't care. His arrest and prosecution he regarded as an unfortunate misadventure. Cynically and confidently he resigned himself to the verdict of history, because he could have had no doubt what the verdict of the court would be. But when I was on the stand he insisted on taking the cross-examination himself, while his lawyers fumed. "You, Broadhead," he said. "You dare to accuse *me* of treason while you associate with the enemies of the human race! We shouldn't parley with the Heechee! Kill them, take them prisoner—surround that place in the core where they hide out, shoot them down—"

It was an incredible performance. When the court finally stopped it, Heimat bowed courteously to the bench, smiled, said, "I have no further questions of this contraption that calls itself Robinette Broadhead," and returned to look proud and confident for the rest of the trial.

That was Heimat. Cyril Basingstoke was, if anything, worse than he.

The meeting of the two retired monsters was wary on both sides. They knew each other.

Heimat hurried back to the recreation hall and found Basingstoke there already, idly glancing through the PV stores to see what entertainments this new place had to offer. They shook hands gravely, then stepped back to look at each other.

Cyril Basingstoke was a Curaçaon, a rich purple-black in color, as old as Heimat (or I), but fully cosseted by the medics so that he looked, maybe, forty-five. "It is good to see you, Beau," he said, voice deep and rich and friendly. Basingstoke had no accent—well, maybe a touch of what sounded German and was probably Dutch, from the good Frisian monks who had taught him English in the Catholic school. Basingstoke was Islands-born, but there was nothing "*Eye*lunds, mon!" about the way he talked. If you could not see him, you would not guess it was a black man speaking, although he said each word larger than an American would—vowels more resonant and rounded, intonation more marked.

Basingstoke glanced out the window, toward the distant lagoon. "This is no bad place, Beaupre," he said. "When they told me I was to be transferred, I thought it would be to some far worse one. That planet Aphrodite, perhaps—the one that goes around a flare star, so that one can live only in tunnels under the surface."

Heimat nodded, though in fact he did not much care where he was anymore. Remembering that he was, in a sense, the host, he ordered drinks from the waiterthing. "Unfortunately—" he smiled "—they don't allow alcohol."

"They did not in Pensacola, either," said Basingstoke. "That is why I was so pleased to be paroled, although if you remember, I was never a hard-drinking man."

Heimat nodded, studying him. "Cyril?" he ventured.

"Yes, Beau?"

"You were *out*. Then you violated parole. Why did you kill those people?"

"Ah, well," said Basingstoke, courteously accepting his ginger ale from the waiterthing, "they angered me, you see."

"I thought that was the case," Heimat said dryly. "But you must have known they'd just put you back here."

"Yes, but I have my pride. Or habit? I think it is a matter of habit."

Heimat said severely, "That's the kind of thing a prosecutor might say."

"Perhaps in some sense a prosecutor might be right for people like you and me, Beau. I didn't need to kill those people. I was not used to crowds, you see. There was pushing and shoving to board a bus. I fell. They all laughed. There was a policeman with a machine-pistol and he was laughing too. I got up and took it away from him—"

"And shot thirty-five people."

"Oh, no, Beau. I shot nearly ninety, but only thirty-five died. Or so they tell me." He smiled. "I did not count the corpses."

He nodded courteously to Heimat, who sat silent for a moment, sipping his own drink while Basingstoke idly summoned up pictures of Martinique and Curaçao and the Virgins. "What lovely places they are," he sighed. "I almost wish I had not killed those people."

Heimat laughed out loud, shaking his head. "Oh, Cyril! Is it true that we have the habit of killing?"

Basingstoke said politely, "For a matter of pride or principle, it is perhaps so."

"So we should never be released?"

"Ah, Beau," Basingstoke said fondly, "we never will, you know."

Heimat brushed the remark aside. "But do you think it is true, we are incorrigible?"

Basingstoke said reflectively, "I think— No. Let me show you." He whispered to the control, and the PV views flickered and returned to a scene of Curaçao. "You see, Beau," he said, settling himself down comfortably for a nice long chat, "in my case it is pride. We were very poor when I was a child, but we always had pride. We had nothing else. Seldom even enough to eat. We would open a snack shop for the tourists, but all the neighbors had snack shops, too, and so we never made money from it. We had only the things that were free— the beautiful sun, the sands, the lovely colibri hummingbirds, the palm trees. But we had no shoes. Do you know what it is like to have no shoes?"

"Well, actually—"

"You do not—" Basingstoke smiled "—because you were American and rich. Do you see that bridge?"

He pointed to the PV vista, a bay with two bridges across it. "Not that ugly high thing, the other one. The one on pontoons that floats. With the outboard motors that open and close it, there at the end."

"What about it?" asked Heimat, already beginning to wonder if having a companion would relieve boredom or add to it.

"That is a matter of pride without shoes, Beau. This I learned from my grandfather."

Heimat said, "Look, Basil, I'm glad to see you and all that, but do you really have to—"

"Patience, Beau! If you have pride you must also have patience; this is what my grandfather taught me. He too was *descamisado*—without shoes. So on this bridge when it was new they had a toll. Two cents to walk across it . . . but only for rich people, that is, the people who wore shoes. People who were barefoot, they crossed free. So the rich people who wore shoes were not stupid; they would take them off and hide them, and cross, and put them back on at the other side."

Heimat was beginning to get angry. "But your grandfather had no shoes!"

"No, but he had pride. Like you. Like me. So he would wait at the bridge until someone with shoes came along. Then he would borrow his shoes so he could pay his two cents and cross the bridge with his pride still safe. Do you see what I am saying, Beau? Pride is expensive. It has cost us both very much."

I didn't want to stop talking about the children because they were appealing; I can hardly stop talking about Heimat and Basingstoke, either, but for quite other reasons. If ever two persons were hateful to me, they are the ones. It is the attraction of the horrible.

When Cyril Basingstoke came to join Beaupre Heimat, the children on the Wheel were just getting the word that they were being evacuated. It made the news. Both Basingstoke and Heimat took an interest; probably they were rooting for the Foe, if anything, though it must have been a conflict for them both. (Pride in the human race? Resentment against that major fraction of it that had put them in prison?) But they had other conflicts, not least with each other. For neither Heimat nor Basingstoke cared much for the society of equals.

They bored each other, in fact. When Heimat found Basingstoke dreaming in front of the PV views of Curaçao or Sint Maarten or the coast of Venezuela, he would say, "Why do you let your mind rust out? I have made use of my prison time! Learn something. A language, as I have done."

Indeed he had, a new language, perfectly, every few years; with all the time he had had to do it he was now fluent in Mandarin, Heechee, Russian, Tamil, Classical Greek, and eight other languages. "And who will you speak them to?" Basingstoke would ask, not taking his eyes from the tropic scene before them.

"That isn't the point! The point is to keep sharp!"

And Basingstoke would look up at last and say, "For what?"

If Basingstoke was tired of Heimat's nagging, Heimat was tired of Basingstoke's interminable reminiscences. Every time the black man started a story, the general knew how to finish it. "When I was a boy," Basingstoke would begin, and Heimat would chime in:

"You were very poor."

"Yes, Heimat, very poor. We would sell snacks to the tourists—"

"But there was no money in it, because all your neighbors had snack shops, too."

"Precisely. None at all. So sometimes we boys would catch an iguana and try to find a tourist to buy that. None of them wanted an iguana, of course."

"But once in a while one would buy it, because he was sorry for you."

"He would, so then we would follow the tourist to see where he let it go, and then we'd catch it and sell it again."

"And after a while you'd eat it."

"Why, yes, Beau. Iguana is very good, like chicken. Have I told you this story before?"

It was not just the boredom. There was, each found, something about the other that really grated on the nerves. Basingstoke found Heimat's sexual habits revolting: "Why must you try to *hurt* the things, Beau? They are not alive anyway!"

"Because it gives me pleasure. The keepers have to take care of my needs; that is one of them. And it's none of your business, Basil. It does not affect you, while that filthy stuff you eat stinks up the whole prison."

"But that is one of *my* needs, Beau," said Basingstoke. He had given the cookthings exact instructions, and they had of course obliged. Heimat had to admit that some of the things weren't bad. There was an ugly-looking fruit that tasted splendid, and some kinds of shellfish that were divine. But some were awful. The worst was a sort of green pepper and onion stew made with salt dried codfish that tasted and smelled exactly like the garbage cans outside a seafood restaurant, after they have ripened all night. It was called a *chiki*, and when it wasn't made with the rotten fish, it was made with something only marginally less repulsive, like goat.

Heimat tried diluting Basingstoke's presence by introducing him to Pernetsky, but the Soviet marshal would not even open his eyes, much less speak to the newcomer. Outside the prison hospital Basingstoke asked, "But why is he doing this, Beaupre? He is certainly conscious, after all."

"I think he has some idea of escape. Maybe he thinks if he continues to pretend to be asleep, they will take him to another hospital somewhere, outside of the prison, and then he can make a try."

"They won't."

"I know," said Heimat, looking around. "Well, Cyril? Do you want to explore the grounds some more today?"

Basingstoke glanced down the hill toward the sparkling, distant lagoon and the broad Pacific beyond it, then back wistfully at the recreation hall. But Heimat had finally refused to look at any more pictures with him, and Heimat at least was an

audience. "Oh, I suppose so," he said. "What are those buildings down by the shore?"

"A school, I think. And there is a little port there, where
they have dredged out the lagoon so small ships can come in."

"Yes, I see the port," said Basingstoke. "We had such a
port in Curaçao, away from the big one. It was for slaves,
Beau. In the old days, when they brought a shipload of slaves
in, they would not parade them through the town; they would
bring them in a few kilometers away—"

"At the slave port," Heimat finished for him, "where the
auction block was. Yes. Let's walk down toward the baby
farm."

"I do not like such things!" Basingstoke sulked. But as Heimat started down the path without him, he added, "But I will
go with you."

The baby farm was within the outer perimeter of the prison,
but only just; it was a separate fenced-off enclave, green
meadow with a few handsome cows grazing, and the prisoners
were not allowed inside it.

Heimat was amused to find how much it offended Cyril. "It
is decadent, Beau," the old man muttered. "Oh, how I wish
we had not failed in our cause! We should have forced them
to forget such things. We should have made them *scream*."

"We did," said Heimat.

"We should have done more. I am revolted to think that a
human child should be in the womb of a cow. When I was a
tiny child—"

"Perhaps," Heimat cut in, to head off the reminiscence, "if
you were a woman, the idea of extra-uterine childbirth would
not be so revolting to you, Cyril. Pregnancy is not without
suffering."

"Of course, suffering! Why shouldn't they suffer? *We* suffered. When I was a boy—"

"Yes, I know what it was like when you were a boy," said
Heimat, but that didn't stop Cyril from telling him all over
again.

Heimat tuned the voice out. It was comfortably hot on the

island, but there was a breeze coming up the hill from the sea. He could smell the faint wisp of cattle aroma from the meadow, where the herdthings were moving about, checking the temperatures and conditions of their charges.

Actually, Heimat thought, surrogate childbearing was a good thing. Assuming childbearing was a good thing in the first place, anyway. His own sexual pleasures went in quite different lines but, for a couple who wanted to be a family, it made sense. They started the baby in the usual way, with frolicsome and slippery pokings; Heimat was broad-minded enough to accept that that was what turned most people on. So if that was their pleasure, why should the pleasure then turn to pain for one of them? It was so easy to take the fertilized ovum away. It had already received all it would ever need of ancestry. The DNA spirals had already danced apart and recombined; the heredity was established. The chef, as you might say, had assembled the soufflé that was his pièce-de-résistance. Now all it needed was a warm oven to rise in, and the oven did not have to be human. Anything that was vertebrate and mammalian, of human size or larger, would do. Cows were perfect.

There were not many cows in the baby farm, because there weren't very many human families left on the island to require them. But Heimat counted ten, twelve, fifteen—altogether eighteen surrogate mothers, placidly cropping grass while the herdthings poked thermometers into them and gazed into their ears.

"It is most *disgusting*," breathed Cyril Basingstoke.

"No, why?" Heimat argued. "They don't do drugs, or smoke, or do any of the other things human women might do to hurt the babies. No. If we had won, I would have instituted this system myself."

"I wouldn't," said Basingstoke pleasantly.

They grinned at each other, two old gladiators amused at the thought of the final conflict that would never have to take place. Old fool, Heimat thought comfortably; it would of course have been necessary to get rid of him, too—if the revolution had succeeded.

"Beau?" said Basingstoke. "Look."

One of the mothers was lowing in mild distress. Her temperature was being taken, but the herdthing was apparently holding the thermometer in an uncomfortable way. The cow shook its rear end free, trotted a few steps away, and began to graze again.

"It isn't moving," said Heimat, perplexed.

Basingstoke looked around at the four or five herders in the baby farm, then back up the hill toward the gardenerthings and the distant workthings on the paths. All were frozen motionless. Even the sounds of fans from the hoverbarrows had stopped.

Basingstoke said, "None of them are moving, Beau. They're all dead."

The pasture that was the baby farm was at the very lowermost edge of the prison compound. The slope steepened there, and Heimat looked at it with distaste. When you are an old man you are an old man, even with every possible replacement of tissue and recalcification of bone. "If we go down," he said, "we will just have to come up again."

"Will we, man?" said Basingstoke softly. "Have a look."

"Ah, some momentary power failure," muttered Heimat. "They'll be back on in a moment."

"Yes. And then the moment for us will be past."

"But, Basil," Heimat said reasonably, "all right, suppose the mobile units are out of service for a moment, the barriers are still there."

Basingstoke looked at him carefully. He didn't speak. He just turned away, lifted a strand of the wire that kept the cattle on their meadow, and ducked under it.

Heimat stared irritably after him. The guards would be back on in a moment, of course. And even if that moment lasted long enough for the two prisoners to, for example, cross the wide cow pasture, what he had said about the barriers was still true, perhaps. It wasn't the guards that kept the prisoners inside, but the sophisticated and unthwartable electronic pen. It came in three courses: pain, stun, death. It was difficult to get past the first and almost impossible to pass the second—also pointless, because there was the third. He told himself that Basingstoke simply didn't know, not having had the experience; for Heimat had, in fact, actually tried. He only once got past the terrible, heart-stopping pain line, and then only to be knocked out at the second and awaken in his own bed, with a guardthing grinning down at him.

The simple fact that the workthings were temporarily powered down meant nothing at all about the barriers, he told himself. What a fool Basingstoke was!

And while he was thinking all this, Beaupre Heimat was lifting the wire for himself and hurrying after the other man, fastidiously dodging the cowflops on the grass, pausing only to kick at a herdthing to make sure it would not respond.

It did not.

He caught up with Basingstoke, panting, at the very edge of the compound. The pain wires were quite visible here—for the sake of the cattle, not the prisoners—against a row of pretty hibiscus and torch flowers.

A gardenerthing was toppled motionless against a torch-flower shrub. Its hand was raised and frozen to a trowel. Heimat spat on it thoughtfully.

"The power is *off*, man," Basingstoke said softly.

Said Heimat, swallowing, "You go first, Cyril. I'll drag you back if you're caught."

Basingstoke laughed. "Oh, Beau, what a hero you are! Come along, we'll do it together!"

12
JAWS

What you must remember at all times is that all things end—
so Albert keeps telling me. I think he thinks it is some kind of
consolation.

It's true, though. Even the interminable trip from Wrinkle
Rock to JAWS ended at last.

JAWS lives in a geostationary satellite, or actually it's five
satellites tumbling around each other in parasitic orbits, a few
tens of thousands of kilometers over Conakry in Africa. It used
to be in a different place—just about over the Galapagos islands—but then it was for a different purpose. It was called
the High Pentagon then.

When we came out of orbit I wasn't looking at it. I was

looking down at the Earth, big and broad below us. Sunrise had passed the Gulf of Guinea, but the western bulge of Africa was still all dark. I took pleasure in the sight. It still think the Earth is about the prettiest planet there is. I could see sunlight hitting the tops of mountains off to the west, and that wonderfully blue Atlantic just below, and I was feeling quite affectionate toward the troublesome old place when I heard Essie cry, "Have *ruined* it!"

It took a moment to realize that she wasn't talking about the planet. "Sorry," I said, "I wasn't looking at the screen." She hadn't been, either, as a matter of fact. Generally we only use the screen out of habit. When we really want a good look at something, it's just as easy for us to use the *True Love*'s own external sensors direct. So I switched and saw what Essie saw.

There were a lot more than five objects in common orbit now, not even counting the flotilla of JAWS cruisers moving restlessly about in formation. People had been flocking to JAWS, and their spacecraft were in mooring orbits. There must have been a dozen of those shuttle ships, but the thing that Essie was talking about was a huge, crumpled mass of film. It took a moment to recognize it.

It had once been the main propulsive power for an interstellar photon-sailship. I had seen it once before, when it was in its glory, and then it had carried a crew of Sluggards on an exploration trip to some other star. "Why is it such a mess?" I demanded of Julio Cassata.

He gave me an irritated look. He was busy on the communications channels, and the person he was irritated with wasn't me. It was the Watch Officer on JAWS, and there wasn't much use in being irritated with him, or it, because it wasn't a him. He said, "I say again, this is Major General Julio Cassata's doppel, and I request immediate landing clearance. Effing machines," he snarled, looking at Albert before he looked at me. Then, "You mean the sailship? But it was your damn Institute that brought it here for study. What did you think we were going to do with the sail? Keep pulling it back when the sun was pushing it out of orbit? . . . Yes, *thank* you," he said to the commset, and nodded to Alicia Lo to take us in.

It wasn't that easy.

The particular section of JAWS we were headed for was Delta, a soup can that weighed forty thousand tons. You could tell it was the command satellite. For the convenience of the high brass, or anyway the meat portions of it, it rotated more rapidly than the others. That gave them a little better up-and-down orientation for their comfort, but it wasn't a convenience for Alicia Lo.

Still, she corkscrewed us neatly into the dock. It was a virtuoso performance, and she deserved a better audience than Essie and me. We weren't watching her. We were looking at that shark-ship fleet of JAWS cruisers, obviously ready for action—any kind of action. I murmured, "I hope they aren't going to do anything foolish."

"If do anything at all," Essie said soberly, "will be foolish. Is no nonfoolish thing to do."

And then we were aboard the JAWS satellite.

The way people like Essie and me come aboard a spacecraft or satellite is to bridge in to the internal communications facilities; after that, we can go anywhere the cables go, and maybe a little bit beyond. On Delta-JAWS we went as far as the hatch chamber and stopped. There *were* no comm facilities, or at least none we were allowed to use. The Watch Officer, a machine program in the form of a callow young lieutenant, said with military courtesy but no give, "General Cassata may proceed, sirs and madams, but the rest of you must remain in the secure lounge."

Of course, we didn't want to do that, not at all. It wasn't what I had come to JAWS for.

If Cassata had lingered a moment, I would have asked him to explain all this. As he hadn't, I explained it myself. The lieutenant listened politely and then took appropriate action. He bucked it to higher authority.

Higher authority was a short, stocky woman named Mohandan Dar Havandhi. When she appeared she stared at us silently for so long that I had the sudden conviction she was a meat person, but it was only her manner. When she opened her mouth she revealed herself to be as machine-stored as the rest of it, but all she opened her mouth to say was, "No."

"But, Commandant Havandhi," Essie purred soothingly, "is Mr. Robinette *Broadhead*."

"I am aware of that," said the commandant.

"Then must also be aware that Mr. Robinette Broadhead is executive of Broadhead Foundation, with full clearance for all extra-solar matters."

"That is true," the commandant said, "but we are under Condition Red. Peacetime clearances are suspended. Of course," she said, with a smile that showed gold teeth—how faithful some of us are to our meat originals!—"you need not be confined to the secure lounge if you prefer."

"Well," I said, smiling forgivingly, "in that case we'll just—"

"You may alternatively return to your ship," she said, and would not be budged.

Military minds! You can't reason with them. We tried, of course. We pointed out that "security" was a laughable anachronism, Condition Red or no Condition Red, because the only enemy who might need keeping out was fifty thousand light-years away, in the kugelblitz. She didn't bother telling us that wasn't true, since the message had come from much nearer. She just shook her head. We tried threatening to call marshals and heads of state. She just said we certainly could do that, all right, if we wanted to, as soon as the embargo on civilian radio messages was lifted. She did not offer any guess as to when that might be. We tried to be chummy with her. We asked what all those spaceships were doing at JAWS. She didn't answer at all; no, we weren't going to get any military secrets out of *her*.

It really wasn't as interminable as it seemed—a few thousand milliseconds at most—because Julio Cassata, or anyway his doppel, came back. Surprisingly, Cassata was looking faintly pleased. "My meat guy is in conference," he told us, "so it will be a little while before I can, uh, see him." He favored us with a smile—not favoring us all equally; the young woman named Alicia Lo got most of the smile. "So what would you like to do while we wait? Take a look around JAWS?"

"We can't," I said, pointing to the commandant.

"Of course you can," he said, secure in rank. He addressed her. "Commandant Havandhi, I relieve you of these guests. I will personally escort them around the base."

The five satellites of JAWS make up nearly two hundred thousand tons mass and are inhabited by something like thirty thousand people, meat and machine-stored. Two of the satellites are nothing but communications and data-processing centers. There's nothing to see there. Gamma is all hardware, *military* hardware; it's full of buster bombs and Heechee tunneling machines, converted to dig holes in ships or fortresses rather than rock. We didn't expect to be allowed there, either, apart from the fact that Albert already knew all about every last piece of ordnance anyway. Alpha is crew quarters and R&R facilities, and there wasn't any reason for us to go there— we didn't need any of their ideas of rest and recreation.

All the same, when the electronic barriers that kept unauthorized machine intelligences out of JAWS were let down for us, the fact that we were confined to Delta annoyed me. Cassata tried to soothe. "Forgive the old lady," he said, grinning. "She was an exchange officer here when this was the High Pentagon, and she thinks everything has gone downhill since." He glanced at his watch—as nonexistent as my own. "We've got at least ten thousand milliseconds and there's a lot of interesting stuff—Sluggards, Quancies, Voodoo Pigs, besides all the other stuff—I mean the parts of the other stuff I can let you into. What do you want to see?"

I said, "I don't want to *see* anything. I didn't come here to take the two-dollar tour. I want to talk to people! I want to find out what's going on—"

"And then," said Cassata, "you want to get in on the action yourself, right?"

I shrugged angrily. I had had plenty of time in the "secure lounge" to build up a head of steam, and Julio Cassata wasn't making it go away. There were a lot of things I wanted to say, but I held myself to one word:

"Yes."

Cassata was still edgy himself. He'd been given a reprieve from termination by his meat original, but that was all. He said, "You make trouble, Broadhead."

"I've got the power to make a lot of it," I agreed.

He looked at me narrowly, then shrugged. "It isn't up to me," he said. "It isn't even up to *me*. The Combined Chiefs make the rules around here. So what's it to be? The two-dollar tour? Or the secure lounge?"

Essie and I had seen JAWS before, back when the Combined Chiefs were a little more respectful to the guy who controlled the Broadhead Foundation. So had Albert. Alicia Lo was a lot more interested. To her it was one of those secret places that you hear about but never expect to see, like the inside of Fort Knox or the Mormon Temple in Salt Lake City.

You understand, we didn't actually "go" anywhere. We didn't have to. Cassata fed us into JAWS-Delta's communications system, and we saw what he wanted us to see. He was a polite host, so he did better than that; he created a sort of officer's club lounge for us to sit in, with a fire blazing at one end of the room and a table laid out with drinks and snacks. The other end of the room was—whatever we were being shown.

When Cassata offhandedly proposed a look at a nest of Sluggards, Alicia was thrilled—as, of course, he had intended she should be.

The Sluggards were a historic "first" for human beings, because they were the first alien intelligent race any member of the human race had ever seen. Or not "seen," exactly. *Felt.* Audee Walthers, fooling around with a Dream Couch, had detected their pathetic, huge, lumbering sailship in interstellar space decades before.

That was a most important event, but what it led to was more important by a whole lot, because the Slugs detected Audee, too. And that was what told the Heechee that people

like us were abroad in the Galaxy, and that was what brought
the Heechee, kicking and screaming, out of their hidey-hole
in the core.

"I thought the Heechee kidnaped this Sluggard ship back
to its own planet," Alicia offered.

"They did," Cassata agreed, "but old Broadhead here kidnaped them back here for study. Or his Institute did. The Slugs
don't mind. They were expecting another thousand years or
so on their trip. Their sail is still in orbit just outside
JAWS—"

"Saw. Looks seriously mashed," Essie said severely.

"Well, what else were we going to do? Spread out, the damn
thing's forty thousand kilometers long. Anyway, they won't
need it again. Do you want to see them or not?"

"Oh, yes," said Alicia Lo, cutting through the argument.
Cassata waved a hand, and there they were.

Sluggards aren't pretty. Some people say they sort of look
like some kind of tropical flower. Others think they look like
one of those deep-sea things with a lot of tentacles; it's hard
to say what they resemble, because they don't very much resemble anything on Earth. The males are considerably bigger
than the females, but that isn't the females' only problem. The
females have nothing but problems, because there's no such
thing as women's rights among Sluggards. A female Sluggard
may not worry about this much, though, since they are not
intellectual. Their lives are entirely taken up with birthing. One
infant comes out every cycle—the cycle runs a little less than
four months. If the lucky lady has been visited by a male at
the right time, the infant is male. If not, it's female. Sluggard
males do not seem to be particularly horny (considering the
Sluggard females, who can blame them?), and so usually the
female has not been sexually favored lately.

So there are endless numbers of female Sluggards being born
all the time.

They don't go to waste, though. From time to time one of
the males picks out a particularly fat and appealing female.
Then he eats her.

One supposes the females don't like that. No female Sluggard has ever complained, though. They can't. They don't talk at all.

Males, on the other hand, talk incessantly—or sing—or anyway make some sort of sounds continuously throughout their lives. You might not know that, though, if you happened to be sitting right next to a Sluggard in full cry—assuming you could, since what they live in is both cold and heavy and poisonous to meat people. You might be aware of a faint pulsing, like a heavy truck going by outside your house. The Slugs are *slow*. So are their voices; the shrillest coloratura soprano among the Slugs might get way up to twenty or twenty-five hertz. So you couldn't hear what they were singing.

There were several dozen of the creatures, male and female, floating around in the slush of their spaceship. One male was in a small compartment by himself. The rest were in a common tank, surrounded by all sorts of curious Slug devices that floated with them: the furnishings and gadgets, I supposed, that made up a comfortable Sluggard home, and the only way I could tell the people from the furniture was that I had seen pictures of Slugs before. I couldn't see anything move. They looked funny in another way, too. I didn't remember exactly what the natural hues of a Sluggard should be, but they looked as though they had been colored by someone who didn't remember even as well as I did.

"One is moving!" cried Essie.

It was clever of her to have noticed it. The one in the separate chamber was, barely, extending a tentacle. It was terribly slow even by meat-human standards (not to mention my own!). In the Slugs' own terms, however, he was writhing in great agitation and high speed; you could see little ripply lines in the sludge all around him, where he had made pressure waves.

"That's one of the new ones," said Cassata. "They finished debriefing the original crew, so they imported six more males from the Slug planet a few weeks ago."

"Why is he off by himself?" asked Alicia Lo.

"He's in high-speed mode so he can be interviewed. They thrash around so, you know? If he were in with the others in high mode, he'd mess up their living quarters."

Albert said professorially, "I observe we are not viewing them by visible light."

"No, right. It's tomography, because you couldn't see in visible light in that slush they live in. Want to hear what he's singing?"

He didn't wait for an answer, but cut in an audio feed. It wasn't the Sluggard we heard, but a machine translator. It declaimed:

> *Great blinding blistering brutes*
> *Thrashed and harmed with much cavitation*
> *And many deaths and highly painful injuries—*

"That's just the latest stanza," Cassata explained. "He's only been going for about an hour this time. We have to let them rest up between sessions. They can't stand high mode very long, and we can't deal with them at all when they're in normal. Want to keep on watching them for a while?"

I said, "What I want, General Cassata, is to talk to somebody in authority around here. How the hell much longer do we have to stall around?"

But Essie put her soft, sweet hand on my lips. "General will let us know soonest possible, is that not so, Julio? So have nothing better to do."

> *—also to females,*

the Sluggard's translation finished, and I began to think of causing some death and highly painful injuries myself.

See, there we were again, caught in the disparity between gigabit time and meat.

I don't think that I am basically a very patient man, but, oh, how much patience this machine-stored analog of me has had to learn! Especially in dealing with meat people. Not to mention with that particularly infuriating and exceptionally immovable section of the meat population, the military.

I stated my views on this matter for Julio Cassata's benefit. He only grinned some more. He was enjoying it. Of course, from his point of view, the longer we waited here, the longer he had left to "live"—that is to say, the longer his doppel had, and his doppel was obviously reluctant to get itself terminated. I was a little surprised that he didn't suggest that he take pretty Alicia Lo off for another little private sightseeing trip—I could well imagine what sights he had in mind—and perhaps he would have if Albert hadn't come up with an idea.

He coughed politely and said, "I believe, General Cassata, that the Sluggards are not the only aliens of whom specimens are present here."

Cassata raised his eyebrows. "You don't mean the Voodoo Pigs?"

"The Voodoo Pigs, yes. Also the Quancies. The Institute has provided colonies of both for study. Might we see them as well?"

If there is anything less interesting to look at than the Quancies, it is the Voodoo Pigs, but of course you don't know that until you try. "Oh, Julio," cried Alicia Lo, "*could* we?" And then of course it was certain that we would.

Cassata shrugged and changed the scene. We were looking at a rocky pool of gray-green water, where half a dozen fishy-looking creatures were basking under a pale orange light. We got sound, too, the honking of Quancies chatting among themselves.

Since I had seen all the Quancies I ever wanted to see, I turned to the table of snacks. It wasn't that I was hungry—or even "hungry." I just wished we would get on with it.

I called on all my long training in patience. I didn't like it, but I had no alternative that I could see. Real-Cassata was still in his meeting, and doppel-Cassata was just being a good host to us—if, I thought, mostly to his new girl. But the sky was falling, and it was no time for a trip to the zoo!

While the white-jacketed waiterthing was handing me a sandwich of chopped chicken liver and onion—all, of course, as simulated as the waiterthing itself—Albert wandered over to join me. "A good German bock, please," he said to the waiter, and smiled at me. "You don't care to hear what the Quancies are saying to each other, Rob?"

"Quancies never have anything to say." I took a sullen bite of my sandwich. It was delicious, but it wasn't what I wanted.

"It is probably futile to interview them," Albert agreed, accepting the stein of dark beer. You have to admit that Quancies are intelligent, more or less, because at least they have language. What they don't have is hands. They live in the sea, and their tiny flippers are no more use than a seal's. If they weren't air-breathing we probably never would have known they existed, because they don't have cities, or tools, or, what is most important, writing. Therefore they have no written history. Neither do the Sluggards; but their life span is so long (if so slow) that their bards remember eddas that are as trustworthy, at least, as Homer's songs. "I do have some news that may interest you," said Albert when he had finished his first deep swallow of the beer.

Good old Albert! "Finish that up and I'll buy you another," I cried. "And tell me!"

"It is nothing much," he said, "but of course I still have access to the datastore facilities on the *True Love*. There were a number of files that I thought might have some bearing on the present situation. It took quite a while to access them all, and there was very little useful data in the first few thousand. Then I checked out the immigration records for the past few months."

"You found something," I said to help him along. It isn't only meat people who have taught me patience.

"I did, yes," he said. "Most of the children who were evacuated from the Watch Wheel, you remember, were relocated on Earth. According to the immigration records, at least seven of them are presently in the area served by the western-Pacific communications net. Of course, it is from that net that the communication to the kugelblitz originated."

I gave him a shocked and unbelieving stare. "Why would human children work for the Assassins?" I demanded.

"I don't think they did," said Albert, thoughtfully accepting his second stein, "although the possibility cannot be ruled out. But we do know that they were present on the Wheel when the Watchers suspected they had detected something, and are now on Earth; it is at least possible that the Assassins have traveled with them.''

I felt myself shiver. ''We have to tell JAWS!''

''Yes, of course.'' Albert nodded. ''I have already done so. I fear, though, that this will have the result of prolonging the meeting the original General Cassata has been conducting.''

I said, ''Shit.''

''However—'' Albert smiled ''—I do not think it will be by very much, as I had already summed the data and presented it to Commandant Havandhi for transmittal to the meeting.''

''So what am I supposed to do now? Gape at the Quancies some more?''

''I think,'' said Albert, ''that the others are also losing interest in the Quancies and ready to go on to the Voodoo Pigs.''

''I've *seen* Voodoo Pigs!''

''There is nothing better to do, is there?'' He hesitated and then added, ''Also, I would like you to observe the carvings of the Voodoo Pigs. They are, I think, of some special interest.''

I could not tell, looking at the Voodoo Pigs, just what it was about them that Albert thought might be of interest. All I felt was disgust—I mean, not counting the impatience I worked so hard to quell. The Voodoo Pigs lived in slop. I had never understood why they didn't drown in their own filth, but they didn't seem to mind it.

That was the piggishness of the Voodoo Pigs. They didn't really look porcine. More than anything else, they looked like blue-skinned anteaters; they tapered to a point, fore and aft. They really were piggy, though. What they lived in couldn't be called a cage. It was a sty.

They lived in their own waste. The mud was not merely mud plus pigshit. It was stuck full of little garnishes, like raisins in a pudding of rotten fruit and excrement, and the garnishes were the carvings Albert had mentioned.

Since Albert had made a point of it, I took a careful look at the Voodoo Pig carvings. I didn't see what had interested him. The carvings weren't anything new. The museums all had them. I'd even once held one in my hand—gingerly, because the smell of the sty had survived even boiling and polishing. They were just carved bits of woody plant matter, or of tooth or bone. They ran about ten or twelve centimeters long, and when they were carved out of teeth, the teeth were not the Voodoo Pigs' own. The pigs didn't have any teeth. All they had were abrasive and very hard rasping surfaces at the skinny ends of their noses—or trunks, or mouths, depending on how you chose to describe them. The teeth came from their food animals, several dozen of which had been imported along with the pigs when the colony was established. The fact that they used the teeth of other animals for their carvings didn't prove any delicate sensibilities on the part of the pigs, though, because when they used bones, the bone was as likely as not to have come from their deceased nearest and dearest, once they had passed on and been eaten. "Carvings" isn't exactly the right word, either. The pigs *nibbled* the pieces into shape, because they didn't have tools to carve anything with. They didn't have any language, either.

In fact, take them all in all, they had about the IQ of a gopher—

Only they created, and obsessively went on creating, these works of art.

"Art," too, may be too strong a word, because they had only one subject. The carvings were like dolls. They resembled, as close as I can describe it, a six-limbed creature with the body of a lion and the head and torso of a gorilla, and there was nothing remotely resembling it anywhere on the planet they came from.

"So what's special about them?" I asked Albert.

He countered, "Why do you think the pigs carve them?"

The rest of the party got into the guessing game. "Religious objects," said Cassata.

"Dolls," said Alicia Lo. "They need something to cuddle."

And, "Visitors," said my dear Portable-Essie.

And Albert beamed at her approvingly.

As is so often the case between Albert and me, I had no idea what was on his mind. It would have been interesting to follow that up just then, but Cassata jerked upright. "Message," he said. "Excuse me," and vanished.

He didn't exactly come back. What happened was that we lost the sight and sound of the little nook he had created for us. We just heard a voice. Not his, at first. At first we got what I recognized as a pickup from the Sluggards' translator:

Huge they were and harmfully hot
And the people lashed each other in fear.

And then Cassata's voice, full of excitement:

"Come on! You can come into the staff meeting!" And then Cassata himself appeared, glowing with the happiness of a soldier who sees a chance to do some fighting. "They've done it, folks!" he cried. "They've tracked down the source of the message to the Assassins. They're shutting that whole sector down, and we'll be moving in!"

13
Kids in Captivity

The school's principal was not only human, she was good at dealing with children. She had four degrees and nineteen years of experience. In that time she had encountered nearly every problem kids could provide, which was roughly one problem per child per semester for all the thousands of children she had supervised over the years.

None of that helped now. She was out of her depth.

When she arrived in the waiting room of the counseling section she was breathless and unbelieving. "But that is fantastic, my dear," she told the sobbing Oniko. "How could they possibly— To be able to read your diary— But why in the world—" She flung herself into a chair, scowling at the incredibility of it all.

"Ma'am?" said Sneezy, and when he got a glance from the principal went on, "It's not just Oniko. I kept a diary, too, and that's part of the transmission."

The principal shook her head helplessly. She waved at the wall screen, which promptly displayed the school's private beach; workthings were tending barbecue fires, and students were beginning to assemble. She looked from the children to the screen and back again. "I should be there," she said fretfully. "It's luau night tonight, you know."

"Yes, ma'am," said Sneezy, and Harold nodded vigorously beside him.

"Roast pig," said Harold. "Dancing!"

The principal looked glum. She thought for a moment, then made her decision. "You'll have to tell the whole thing to the counselors," she said. "All three of you."

"I didn't keep any diary!" Harold wailed.

"But, you see, we can't be sure of that. No," the principal said firmly, "that's the way it will have to be. You'll all have to tell your stories. The machines will have questions, I'm sure. Just tell the truth, don't leave anything out—I'm afraid you'll miss the luau, but I'll instruct the cookthings to save you something." And she rose, waved the door open, and was gone.

Harold gazed stonily at his friends. "You two!" he snarled in condemnation.

"I'm sorry," Sneezy said politely.

"Sorry! Making me miss the luau! Listen," said Harold, thinking fast, "I'll tell you what. I'll go first. Then maybe I can get through and down to the beach before the dancing starts, anyway. I mean, that's the *least* you two can do, isn't it, after all this trouble?"

Of course, at this point none of the kids knew just how much trouble all this trouble was. They were kids. They were not used to being at the center of events that shook the entire universe.

There was, Sneezy supposed, a certain amount of justice in what Harold said, though there was a second level of unfairness that was not dealt with at all. Neither he nor Oniko had *done* anything! No one had told them they shouldn't spend their time investigating Earth conditions in every way possible. No one had even hinted that there was anything wrong with synopsizing and organizing the data in their diaries—which, to be sure, were not really "diaries" at all, in the sense of little gilt-edged books that you wrote your latest crushes and enmities in. They had simply played all the information they could gather into their pods, as any right-thinking Heechee (or Heechee-influenced human) would have done.

They had done nothing at all that was in any way reprehensible—but, oh, how terrifying it was that their innocent activities had somehow been converted into that most forbidden of all possible actions, a transmission to the Foe! It was too scary a thought for Sneezy to deal with. Oniko was nearer. Her fears were easier to handle. He said, "There's another booth, Oniko. Would you like to go in now?"

She shook her head. Her dark eyes were darker still with recent tears, but she had stopped sobbing. "You go, Sternutator."

He hesitated, then said, "All right, but I'll wait until you're through. We can go down to the beach together."

"No, please, Sternutator. You go ahead when you're done. I'm not hungry, anyway."

Sneezy hissed in thought. He did not like the idea of Oniko missing the beach party, and liked even less the thought of her trying to hobble her way, walker and all, down the sands by herself. It was difficult enough for Oniko to get around on a level surface, with her muscles still unhardened to the full crush of Earth.

Then it occurred to him that he need promise nothing; he could wait for her whether she asked him to or not. "Very well, Oniko," he started to say.

And then the whole question became moot.

The lights went out.

The lounge was in twilight, the only illumination coming from the picture window that looked out on the mountain; but the mountain was already hiding the setting sun.

From the counseling booth Harold's enraged roar came:

"*Now* what the devil!" The door to the cubicle shook, then gradually slid wide enough for a boy to squeeze through as Harold shoved it open manually. "What's going on?" he demanded, glaring at Sneezy and Oniko. "The stupid program just cut off in the middle of asking me a question!"

Sneezy said helpfully, "I would guess that the power has gone off."

"Oh, Dopey, what a fool you are! The power *never* goes off!"

Sneezy looked around at the wall screen, now blank; at the lounge lighting fixtures, all dark; at the door that would no longer open at anyone's approach.

"But it has, Harold," he said reasonably. "So what are we going to do now?"

When the power was off the lights were off, and the corridors of the school buildings were now dark and disturbing. When the lights were off the elevators were off, and so their only way down to the main buildings and thence to the beach was to climb down the never-used stairs.

That was not a practical choice for Oniko and her rubbery legs.

"We'll have to *walk*," said Harold accusingly, and Sneezy agreed.

"But it will be better to go outside and use the road," he pointed out. Harold scowled out the mountainside window, then at the smaller one that let them see down onto the beach. Although the school was dead, the students were not. Nearly all of them were there, tiny in the distance, milling about the beach. The scene on the beach didn't look frightening. It looked rather like fun, and Harold sighed.

"Oh, good lord, I suppose we have to go by the road to take care of Oniko. Well, let's get on with it." He didn't mention that with the school out of service, the alternative was to slip and slide down the hillside, which wouldn't be much easier for him than for the girl. He walked toward the door. Having had little experience with doors that did not open when desired, he nearly bumped his nose before he stopped short and angrily wrestled it open.

It was nearly full dark now, and of course even the street-lights were out. That didn't matter much. There would be a quarter of a moon before long, and even the Pacific starlight would be nearly enough to see by. What worried Sneezy more than the power blackout was Oniko. She had rarely cried on the Wheel, even when bigger children had teased her. Now she seemed unable to stop for long. The tears had begun again, slow drops forming in the corners of her eyes; as one rolled down her chin, another was ready to take its place. "Please, Oniko," Sneezy begged. "It is only a problem with the electricity. Nothing is serious."

"It's not the electricity," she sobbed. "It's my diary."

"How silly you are," said Sneezy dismally, wishing he could at least convince himself, if not Oniko. "That must be a co-incidence. Do you think the Foe would bother with a child's compositions?"

She shifted on her crutches to gaze at him. "But they did!" she wailed. "My exact words, and yours, too."

"Yes, Dopey," Harold cut in roughly. "Don't try to get out of it! It's all your fault—and hers, I mean."

"Including the power failure?" Sneezy inquired. But he got no satisfaction from the retort. In some sense, he acknowledged to himself, it was their fault. The odds against coincidence were frightful. The Heechee had no analogy of forty million monkeys typing out the complete works of William Shakespeare, but that wasn't necessary to convince Sneezy. Coincidence was, to all intents and purposes, impossible . . .

Just about as impossible as the only alternative he could see, namely that somehow the Foe had been watching over their shoulders as they completed their notes.

Confronted with two equally preposterous alternatives, Sneezy did what any sensible child, Heechee or human, would have done. He put it out of his mind.

He pointed along the road to the winding driveway used by the hovertrucks. "Let's go down to the beach that way," he suggested.

"But it's *kilometers*," Harold groaned.

"Very well," said Sneezy, "you take a shortcut if you like. Oniko and I will use the road."

"Oh, lord," sighed Harold, adding one more charge to the indictment against Sneezy and Oniko, "I guess we might as well all stick together. But it's going to take all *night*."

He turned and led the way, Sneezy and Oniko following. The girl was tragic-faced and silent, limping along and refusing Sneezy's help. After a dozen meters Harold looked around and scowled. He was already far ahead. "Can't you go any faster?" he called.

"You may go without us," said Sneezy, wishing he would not. For reasons he could not identify, Sneezy was ill at ease. When Harold irritably came back to walk with exaggerated patience next to them, he was glad of the company.

Was there, really, anything to be afraid of?

Sneezy could think of nothing real. It was true that it was dark and that they could easily be run over by some speeding vehicle—but it was also true that there weren't any vehicles on the road; their power, too, was off.

All the same, he was very nearly afraid.

Sneezy had never felt fear of the island before. Of course it was human and remote and therefore wholly strange to a Heechee boy, but it had not occurred to him that there was anything to be afraid of. Certainly not of the few Polynesian natives who remained. They were almost all old people who kept to their homes and ways while most of the young ones had gone off to more exciting places than Moorea. He had not even been afraid of the prison buildings, because it had been explained to the children that there were almost no living convicts still there. In any case, although the couple who remained had done terrible things, they were not only securely confined but very old. There was, Sneezy assured himself, absolutely nothing to be afraid of beyond the chance that they might be late for the luau.

As a rational Heechee, he allowed the logic to convince him. And thus he was only startled, but not really afraid, when he heard a sudden squawk from Harold and saw two old men step out of the uphill path to confront the children.

"You're a Heechee," said the smaller of the two men, with a pleased smile of recognition.

"Of course he's a Heechee," Harold blustered. "Who the dickens are you?" The old man beamed at him and reached out a hand to his arm. It looked like a pat of reassurance, but the man didn't let go.

He said, "I am General Beaupre Heimat, and this is my colleague, Cyril Basingstoke. What a pleasant surprise to meet you here. I suppose you are students at the school?"

"Yes," said Sneezy. "My name is Sternutator, but I'm generally called Sneezy." As he introduced his companions according to diligently mastered Earth protocol, he tried to make out the expressions on the men's faces. The general was a tall man, though not as tall as his companion, and he had a broad face that wore a not very reassuring grin. Sneezy was not particularly attuned to the subtle ethnic differences that distinguished one sort of human from another, but it was apparent that the second old man was noticeably dark-skinned. They did not seem especially threatening, although the expression on the black man's face was concerned. As the general moved toward Oniko, Basingstoke said worriedly, "Man, we are *so* lucky to be out, please don't do anything to start trouble."

Heimat shrugged. "What sort of trouble? I just wanted to tell this pretty young lady how glad I am to see her."

"Sooner or later they'll get the power on again!"

"Cyril," said Heimat mildly, "fuck off." There was no palpable threat in the look he gave his companion, but the black man's eyes narrowed.

Then he turned toward Sneezy and took him by the arm. Basingstoke's grip was strong; under those layers of human blubber and the dried, tough skin of age there was a good deal of strength. "You are also the first Heechee I have seen in person," he announced, the subject changed. "Are your parents here?"

Harold chose that moment to cut in. "His parents are important Watchers on the Wheel," he boasted. "So are mine and Oniko's, and besides hers are very wealthy. You better not try anything with any of us!''

''Certainly not,'' said Heimat virtuously, but he didn't let go of Harold's arm. He looked thoughtful for a moment. ''You do not need wealthy parents to make you attractive, my dear,'' he said to Oniko, ''but I won't deny that that is a big plus. I am delighted to know you. We are going down to the beach. Why don't we all walk down together?''

''No chance!'' snapped Harold. ''We don't need—ouch!'' Without releasing his grip, the old man had backhanded him across the side of the face.

''It's what we need that matters,'' he said conversationally, and that seemed to settle that. Heimat looked about, getting his bearings. ''Over toward the point, don't you think, Cyril?'' he asked. ''I remember there was a road there, toward the breadfruit plantation. Let's go—and while we're walking, my dear Oniko, why don't you tell us all about how rich your parents are?''

It seemed to Sneezy that, strong as the old man was, it might not be impossible to jerk free and run away.

Sneezy weighed the prospect carefully while Oniko answered leadenly to the probing, jovial questions of the old general. He decided against it. Although Basingstoke was old, he seemed quite quick, and Sneezy thought it likely he would react unpleasantly to an attempt at escape.

And anyway, even assuming that he himself might break away, how could he get Oniko free?

Although the party was walking slowly on the dark roads, the girl was having trouble keeping up. For her to run away was simply impossible. Nor was it likely that Harold could make it, either, because the human boy seemed crushed by the weight of the slap across his face. He moped forward, never turning his face, but from the way his shoulders moved, Sneezy suspected he was crying.

As they turned off the perimeter road to the downward trail, Sneezy could see the luau on the beach. The students had improvised torches stuck in the sand and, although they were now nearly a kilometer away, Sneezy could hear the sounds of singing. He envied them considerably. He wished they would stop singing, so that if he or one of the others had to scream for help they might be heard, but realistically he did not think any of them should dare that anyway.

Behind them the island's great central mountain blocked out the stars, though overhead the constellations were bright. Even so, walking was difficult. Without warning Oniko stumbled on the path, tripped over her walker, and almost fell headlong. What saved her was Cyril Basingstoke's hand, thrust out as quickly as a striking snake. He set her on her feet again, and General Heimat turned around to look.

"Ah, the young lady is having trouble," he said sympathetically. "Do you know, Cyril, I think that if you would take charge of Harold, I could carry Oniko down."

Basingstoke didn't answer directly. With a quick motion he hefted Oniko to set her on his shoulder, never releasing Sneezy in the process. "You take her crutches, boy," he ordered.

The general turned and regarded him without speaking. Sneezy hissed softly to himself in foreboding. There was something humanly nasty hovering around them in the warm tropic air. Evidently Oniko perceived it too, because she said, in a shaky attempt to make neutral conversation, "Oh, look across the water! Papeete's lights are on!"

It was true: On the other side of the strait the sprawling lights of Tahiti's principal city were bright gold. Moreover, whatever had been about to happen between the two men was at least postponed.

"Their power is on," said Basingstoke thoughtfully, and Heimat chimed in, "We could go there!"

"Yes, we could, if we had a plane or a boat. But what would we do then?"

"There's an airport, Cyril. Planes go to Auckland, Honolulu, Los Angeles—"

"Indeed they do, man," said Basingstoke, "for people who have money to pay for the tickets. Are you carrying a credit card?"

"Why, Cyril," Heimat said reprovingly, "you haven't been

listening. These children have credits. Especially"—he smiled—"young Oniko here is very rich. I am sure she will do something nice for an old man, one way or another."

Basingstoke stood silent for a moment. Sneezy could feel the tension in the man's grip and wondered just what peculiar Earth-human nuances he was missing. Then the man said, "Beaupre, what you do for your own pleasure is no business of mine. But if it interferes with getting off these islands for me, then it becomes a personal matter. Then, man, I will kill you." He paused, letting the words hang there. Then he said, "Now, let us see if there is a boat."

There were boats, all right. There were at least a dozen drawn up along the beach, where the school kept its small fleet, but four of them were kayaks and six were windsurfing boards, and the only big one nearby was the sailing yawl, which none of them were skilled enough to operate. "You can't do it," Harold said, boldness returning. "So just let us go! We won't say anything—"

Heimat looked at him without speaking. Then he turned to Cyril Basingstoke. "They must have something we can use," he said. Each of the children looked as blank and ignorant as possible, because of course the school did.

"There is a pier," said Basingstoke softly, pointing down toward the point of land, and all three children sighed at once in resignation. As they crunched over the shelly sand toward the school's dock, Sneezy hoped against hope that the entire little flotilla had been taken in for repairs, or drifted out to sea, or sunk. And then when they reached the dock and Heimat uttered a roar of rage, his hopes rose. "No power!" he snarled. "They're all dead!"

But Basingstoke raised his chin as though sniffing the wind. "Listen, man," he commanded. Over the sound of the breeze that came down from the mountain, there was a mild, insistent hum. He leaped to the end of the dock, where the school's glass-bottomed boat lay moored to the power takeoff. "Flywheel drive," he crowed. "They must've been revving it up overnight. Get in!"

There wasn't any help for it. The old terrorists shepherded the boys in first, then Basingstoke handed Oniko in to Heimat, who stroked her head promissorily before setting her down. With Basingstoke at the tiller, Heimat cast off the lines, and the little boat purred out into the mirror-calm lagoon.

Sneezy and Oniko, holding hands on the bench over the dark glass, gazed sadly back at the looming mountain and the dark buildings of the school. No, not entirely dark, Sneezy saw with a quick flicker of hope; but it died as quickly, as he saw that only a few windows had faint glows behind them. Someone had rediscovered candles. Most of the students were still on the beach; Sneezy could see the shapes moving around in the torchlight. But as the glass-bottomed boat angled out toward the passage through the reef, they maintained their distance from the beach.

Then, just at a time when he needed all the alertness and strength he could find, Sneezy felt his eyes growing heavy. How odd, he thought, shaking himself awake. It was no time to be falling asleep—and no reason for it, either! He made a great effort to wake up and put his thoughts in order.

The first question was, What were his options?

To begin with, he calculated, the boat was still only a few hundred meters from the beach. To swim that distance, in the warm, shallow lagoon, would have been child's play for almost any child—almost any other child, he thought regretfully, than either Oniko or himself. She lacked the strength, he the buoyancy. A pity. Probably if they had been able to swim for it, the old men wouldn't even follow, Sneezy thought wistfully, since all they really wanted was escape . . .

He hissed softly to himself as he confronted the fact that one of them seemed to want something more, at least from Oniko.

It was not a thought Sneezy could easily come to terms with. The concept of rape was strange to any Heechee, especially rape of an immature female. Ancestors, it was all but impossible! Not to mention thoroughly repugnant. He had heard theoretical discussions of such things—as related to human

conduct, to be sure. He hadn't believed any of them. Even
among humans, such queer perversities were surely unreal.

But then, he had never before been in a situation like this.

No, he told himself, the risk was too great. Such things might
after all be true! They would have to escape. Was it possible
that Harold could get away and somehow summon help? He,
at least, would have no difficulty swimming to shore—

But Harold was wedged firmly beside the huge old black
man at the tiller. Sneezy did not think it likely that Basingstoke
would ever let himself be taken off guard. Weariness and
depression settled in again, and once more Sneezy's eyes
began to droop.

The old black man was humming to himself as he skillfully
guided the boat toward the exit channel. "Do you know,
Beaupre," he called to the other man, "I think we almost can
succeed in this venture! Unfortunately I have no way of telling
how much energy is stored in the flywheel of this contraption.
It is possible we will run out of power before we reach Tahiti."

"In that case," said Heimat, "we'll just hang these kids over
the stern to be outboard motors and kick us in—two of them,
anyway," he added, patting Oniko's bowed head.

Basingstoke chuckled. The possibility of running out of
power didn't seem to worry him, nor, Sneezy perceived, did
he seem as concerned about Heimat's plans for Oniko as he
had been before. Sneezy felt his abdominal muscles writhe in
apprehension. If only he weren't so inexplicably fatigued! It
was almost as though he were breathing oxygen-depleted air
or had swallowed some enervating drug. In fact, it was almost
like that deprivaton that no Heechee ever voluntarily permitted, as though he had stupidly left his pod somewhere and was
lacking the life-giving radiation it provided—

Sneezy hissed loudly in alarm.

Heimat turned from gazing fondly at Oniko and snapped,
"What's the matter with you?"

But Sneezy could not answer. It was too frightening to talk
about.

His pod was emitting nothing.

Heechee could survive for days, even for weeks, without

the constant flow of microwave radiation from their pods. It was never a problem on their home worlds, for of course there was always a steady microwave flux in the environment they had evolved in: That was how they had come to evolve to need it, as humans needed sunlight and fish needed water. But survival was not all there was to life. After an hour or two without the microwave the lack began to be felt. It had now been more than that since the power went off and the pod stopped radiating. Sneezy was feeling the effects. It was a sensation like—what could you compare it to in human terms? Thirst? Exhaustion? A sensation of *need*, at least, as a human being on a desert might feel unmet needs after the same length of time. He could go on for quite a while without a drink of water . . .

But he could not go on forever.

As the shallow-draft boat passed through the gap in the reef, they struck the waves of the strait.

They were not huge waves, but the boat was now in the Pacific Ocean. Although it was not stormy, the swells that lifted the boat and set it down again had started as ripples five thousand kilometers away, and they had been growing as they traveled.

Oniko gasped and struggled to the gunwale, where she began to retch violently into the sea. After a short, hard struggle inside himself, Sneezy joined her. He was not subject to seasickness in the same way as a human boy would have been— the architecture of the Heechee inner ear was vastly different in design—but the motion, the stress, above all the draining of all energy with the loss of his pod's radiation combined to make him physically ill.

From forward in the rocking boat Heimat laughed tolerantly. "You poor kids! I promise when we get to shore I'll give you something to take your minds off it."

"She is only frightened, Beau," rumbled Basingstoke. "Throw it all up, Oniko; it will do you no harm." The old black man seemed positively jubilant as he steered the boat into the waves. "When I was a boy," he said, settling himself for a traveler's tale to make the time pass, "we had storms around the island that you would not believe, children. Yet we must go out in them for the fish, because we were very poor. My father was an old man—not in years, but from breathing the hydrocarbons in the air. Petrochemicals. They made us all sick, and then when we went out in the fishing boats . . ."

Sneezy, having exhausted everything in his digestive system that could exit by mouth, lowered himself to the bottom of the boat, hardly listening. He pressed his face against the glass bottom, cooled by the water just on the other side, and felt Oniko slump beside him. He took her hand apathetically. He knew he must think and plan, but it was so hard!

"—and in the water," Basingstoke rolled on, "there were great sharks—almost as huge and ferocious, yes, as the ones in the Pacific here—"

Even in his fatigue, Sneezy's hand tightened convulsively on Oniko's. *Sharks?* They were another nasty phenomenon of the human planet that he had heard of only in theory. He strained his huge eyes to peer into the black water, but of course there was nothing to see. Many times he had looked through that glass at glittering schools of tiny fish, wheeling in unison, and at creepy-crawly crustaceans on the shallow sand. Those things had been scary, too, but pleasingly scary, like one child jumping out of concealment to startle another.

But *sharks*!

Sneezy firmly stopped thinking about sharks. Instead he listened to the old black man going on with his interminable reminiscences: "—for fifty years they pumped the oil wells dry, stinking up the fresh, sweet air of our island. They said they needed it to grow protein so that no one would starve. But we did starve, you know. And it was that that made me turn to the struggle, for there was no other way to justice—"

Justice, Sneezy thought fuzzily. How strange for this terrorist, murderer, kidnaper, to speak of *justice*. How *human*.

As they neared the Tahiti side of the strait, Sneezy forced himself to sit up and look around.

There was a great black shape in the water ahead of them,

moored and lighted, the size of a football field. Although Sneezy had known it was there, it took him a moment to recognize it as the floating CHON-food factory. Day and night it sucked oxygen and nitrogen from the air, hydrogen from the seawater of the strait, and carbon from the strait's luckless inhabitants to feed the people of Tahiti and the neighbor islands. He wondered that old Basingstoke had dared pass so near it, and then realized that of course it was fully automated; no human being would be on it, and the workthings would be unlikely to pay attention to a small boat passing nearby.

And then Sneezy realized two other things.

The first was that the lighted Food Factory was *lighted*. There was power there! And the second was that spreading up from his loins was a warm, gentle wash of good feeling.

They were out of the power blackout zone, and his pod was operating once more.

As they skirted the shore the waves were choppier. There was no lagoon here, no reef to shelter them from the Pacific, and the glass-bottomed boat rolled worrisomely.

"Don't drown us now, you old fool," Heimat snarled at his partner, and Harold squawked in fear as water came in over the side. Sneezy understood the humans' fear. As his head cleared, he began to share it. The little boat was broadside to the waves, and the risk of capsizing it was real. But their concern did not dampen his mood. The pod radiation was as refreshing as a cold drink on a hot day—no, better than that! As refreshing as a rum toddy after being out in a blizzard; warmth and pleasing numbness stole volition from him. The dreamy lassitude would last only a short time, until his body had soaked up enough microwave to be content again. But while it lasted he was simply too relaxed to worry.

So he sat docilely while Cyril Basingstoke searched the shore for a refuge. He listened uncaring while the two old men argued over what to choose. He obediently tried to help scoop water out of the bottom of the boat with his skinny, bare Heechee hands—so ill adapted to such a task—as they settled on a beach house with its own floating dock, and Basingstoke ran the craft to a mooring next to it.

Out of the boat, up the beach to the dwelling, gathering before the screened porch of the beach house—there were a dozen times when Sneezy might have broken free and run. The old men were tiring now, because the night was well advanced and they had been taxing themselves a great deal. But Sneezy didn't take the chance. Neither did Harold, though perhaps the human boy's chances were worse; General Heimat never once let go of his arm. And of course Oniko had never had a chance to escape on her own, and so Sneezy docilely helped Oniko and waited patiently as the old men argued.

"There will be a watch system, man," Basingstoke warned.

Heimat smiled. All he said was, "Take this boy's arm," and turned to his work. The skills that a dozen times had been pitted against the prison's multiply redundant guard programs were not to be defeated by some householder's burglar alarm.

In two minutes they were inside the house. The door was locked behind them. The chances of escape were gone; and, tardily, Sneezy realized what opportunities he had let slip away.

"On your bellies, my dears," Heimat ordered cheerfully, "and put your hands behind your necks. If you move you are dead—except you, of course, sweet Oniko."

Obediently the children lowered themselves to the floor, and Sneezy heard the sounds of the old men ransacking the house, muttering to each other. The lassitude was wearing off, now that it was too late, but he was beginning to be aware of something else. He hardly heard what the kidnapers were saying or doing. He wanted something . . . He had a need to do something . . .

Without intending it in the least, he got up and moved toward the bungalow's PV communications set.

It happened to be Basingstoke who saw him first, which perhaps saved Sneezy's life. The old man was beside him in a second, swatting him away. Sneezy landed halfway across the room, blinking at him. "Boy, boy," rumbled the old man chidingly. "What in the world do you think you're doing?"

"I have to make a call," Sneezy explained, standing up again. Nothing was broken. He started toward the set once more.

Basingstoke grabbed him. The old man was stronger than Sneezy had thought; the boy struggled for a moment, then let himself go limp. "What you have to do," Basingstoke scolded, "is exactly what we tell you to do, boy, and nothing more. You will sit quietly, or— Heimat! Watch the girl!"

For Oniko, too, had struggled to her feet and was advancing doggedly toward the set, the expression on her face determined.

Heimat had an arm around her in the first step. "What's the matter with you two?" he snarled. "Didn't you think we were serious? Perhaps we should kill the Heechee brat to convince you?"

"We will just tie them up, Beaupre," Basingstoke corrected. Then, observing the look on Heimat's face and the way he was holding the girl, he sighed, "Oh, give it a *rest*, man! There is plenty of time for what you want later!"

The beach house was a treasure trove for the old terrorists. There was food, there was power, they even found weapons of a sort—a spring-wound shark gun for scuba-diving, and a flat, mean-looking stun gun apparently designed for the times when a sportfisher had brought aboard a large game fish that still had enough life left to thrash dangerously around in the boat. Sneezy's lassitude wore off, and he looked at the guns with astonishment and more than a little horror. They were *weapons*! They could *kill* someone! What typically *human* devices they were!

When they had located food, the two men ate first, muttering to each other over the table, but when they were finished they untied Oniko and allowed her to feed the others. She had to spoon soup into the boys' mouths as though they were babies. Once she rose awkwardly and started once more toward the PV commset, but Heimat was ahead of her. She didn't try it again. Sneezy's own uncontrollable urge to do the same thing departed, leaving him puzzling over just what it was he was so anxious to do. Call someone, of course. But whom? The police? Yes, certainly, that would have been logical; but he did not think that was what had been in his mind.

When everyone was fed and the children had even been allowed, one by one, to make escorted visits to the toilet, Heimat came over and draped his arm fondly over Oniko's shoulders. The girl shuddered without looking at him.

"Heimat, man," said Cyril Basingstoke warningly.

The general looked surprised. "What have I done?" he asked, carelessly toying with the girl's bobbed black hair. "We've eaten. We're in a nice, safe place. We've earned the right, surely, to rest for a moment and enjoy ourselves."

Basingstoke said patiently, "We are still on an island in the middle of the Pacific Ocean, man. We are not safe until we are off it. Sooner or later the people who own this house will come back, or some neighbor will see the lights and come to call, and what will we do then?"

Heimat sighed tolerantly and stood up, wandering about the room. "But we've got a long night ahead of us, and there won't be any flights until morning," he pointed out.

"Morning is not very far," Basingstoke countered. "And there is also the flywheel boat. If we leave it where it is, it will lead people to us. I think you and I, Beau, should go down and send it off to sea before it gets light."

"Oh?" said Heimat. "But why two of us, Cyril?" He sat down at a desk in the corner, watching the other man, and though no one's expression changed, Sneezy was suddenly aware of a new tension in the room.

Heimat went on thoughtfully, "Let me see if I can read your mind, old comrade. You are thinking that it will be harder for two to book passage than one. You are also thinking that if I, and these nice young people, were dead, our bodies could be left here in this house for maybe quite a long time."

"Oh, Beaupre, what an imagination you have," Basingstoke said tolerantly.

"Yes," Heimat agreed. "I imagine you are making a calculation, Cyril, of whether my help or my dead body would be of more use to you. I even think you are considering some plan in which all four of our bodies could be found in some way that would be helpful to you. Perhaps in the boat set adrift, so that people would think you had most likely drowned while crossing the strait. Am I very close to what you were thinking?''

Basingstoke gave his partner a tolerant smile. ''Oh, perhaps in general terms,'' he conceded. ''One has such idle thoughts now and then. But it was only a thought, man.''

''Then think of this.'' Heimat smiled, raising his hand from the desk to reveal the flat, mean fish-killing gun.

Oniko shrieked and collapsed against Sneezy. He wished he could pat her shoulder reassuringly, but the ropes did not allow that; he compromised by rubbing his leathery cheek against the top of her head. Basingstoke gazed at the children for a moment, then turned earnestly back to Heimat.

''Beaupre,'' he said, ''what I think is only what you yourself have surely been thinking, too; it is only sensible for each of us to consider alternatives. But I do not want your body found off the island. As far as anyone knows, we are still on Moorea. I hope no one will think otherwise until it is too late. So do not be a great fool, man. Let us get rid of the boat. Then let us arrange transportation away from here.''

Heimat studied him, scratching his chin with his thumbnail. He didn't speak.

''Also,'' said Basingstoke, ''there is something else to think of. No sensible person leaves a loaded gun in a drawer when he goes away. Do you think the owner of this house was so careless? How sure are you? You haven't checked to see if it was empty, or I would have seen you do it.''

Heimat gave him a respectful nod. He put his hands in his lap for a moment, looking down at the gun. What he saw was concealed from the others by the desk; there was a snick of metal opening and a snap as it closed. Heimat's expression didn't change as he looked up. ''Now I know whether it is loaded or not,'' he observed. ''But you don't.''

''Is it, then?'' Basingstoke inquired politely. He didn't wait for an answer. ''In any case, let us stop this nonsensical debate. We will both go and get rid of the boat; the children will be

safe enough here. Then we will come back and see about finding a way off this island. Then, Beaupre, while we wait until
it is time for our plane, you may entertain yourself in any
fashion you like.''

It had been General Beaupre Heimat who tied them up, and
Sneezy acknowledged that the old man knew what he was
doing. In the few minutes they were out of the house he
strained against the ropes uselessly. He was not helped by
Harold's complaining whine: ''What the dickens is the matter
with you, Dopey? You're so skinny, you should be able to
slide right out of those things! Then you could untie us and
then—''

Harold stopped there, because not even he could visualize
a good ''and then.'' In any case, the old men were back almost
at once, hovering over the PV commset.

They accessed the reservations clerk at Faa-Faa-Faa Airport
at once. It was—or looked to be—a pretty Polynesian girl in
a sarong, with flowers in her hair. She appeared both friendly
and real as she gazed out of the PV tank. For a moment Sneezy
thought of crying out for help, but the hope did not justify the
risk. She was undoubtedly only a simulation, and probably a
very rudimentary one.

''Display all flights nonstop for more than two thousand kilometers departing between now and noon,'' Heimat ordered.

''Oui, m'sieur.'' The girl smiled and disappeared. The PV
showed a list:

UA 495	Honolulu	06:40
JA 350	Tokyo	08:00
AF 781	Los Angeles	09:30
NZ 263	Auckland	11:10
QU 819	Sydney	11:40
UT 311	San Francisco	12:00

Heimat said at once, ''I want the Los Angeles flight.'' Basingstoke sighed. ''Yes, Beaupre, I suppose you do. So do I.''

Heimat looked displeased. ''You could take San Francisco,'' he argued. ''It's only a couple hours later, and it's

better if we're not on the same flight, isn't it? Or you could go to Honolulu, or Tokyo—"

"I do not want to be on another island, or in a place where I will not speak the language, and I don't want to wait a couple of hours. I will be on that plane to Los Angeles."

Heimat sighed and gave in. "Very well. We can be quit of each other there. Reservations!"

The girl reappeared, politely inquiring. *"M'sieur?"*

"We want space for two on Air France 781 this morning. Mr. J. Smith and Mr. R. Jones," Heimat improvised.

"First class or coach, sir?"

"Oh, by all means first class." Heimat smiled. "Our dear little niece has been good enough to fly us here for a little vacation and she is very generous. One moment," he said, signaling to Basingstoke to bring the little girl forward. Out of range of the PV pickup the old black man swiftly untied the girl's hands. Then he nodded to Heimat and lifted her to the commset. "Oniko, my dear," Heimat went on, "kindly give this nice young computer program your credit ID."

Sneezy held his breath. Would Oniko try to call for help? She did not. In a clear voice she gave the program her credit data and submitted her thumb to the pickup for verification. Sneezy felt a moment's disappointment. Where was this vaunted human courage when it was needed? And then he was ashamed of himself; certainly if Oniko had said the wrong word, it would have been very unpleasant for her as soon as the old terrorist could get her out of range of the PV.

That was all there was to it. There were no questions. The Polynesian-looking program verified the account in a second and announced, "You have confirmed space for two, Mr. J. Smith and Mr. R. Jones, nonstop from Faa-Faa-Faa Airport, departing at nine-thirty for Los Angeles Intercontinental. Will there be any continuing or return flights from there?"

"Not just now," Basingstoke said, and snapped off the commset.

"Wait a minute," Heimat protested. "What's the hurry? We will want to move on from Los Angeles, you know!"

"But not on her credit, man, It's too risky. You'll have to find your own way from there."

Heimat's eyes narrowed dangerously. "You take a lot on yourself, Cyril," he said softly. "Have you forgotten that I still have the gun?" And then, suddenly, he yelped, "What is she doing? Stop her, Cyril!" For Oniko, with Basingstoke's hand still on her, had reached out doggedly to the commset once more.

Basingstoke jerked her away. "Now, now," he chided. "This can get quite tiresome, child!" Oniko didn't respond. She only gazed at the commset, now out of reach.

"Tie her," Heimat ordered. Sneezy watched anxiously as Basingstoke did, setting her down again in the row of captives along the wall. As soon as Oniko was bound, she relaxed again, her body leaning against Sneezy's for comfort.

"I had to," she whispered to him, and he hissed agreement. She had to, just as he, too, had had to try to reach the commset as soon as they got into the house. Sneezy puzzled over that compulsive attempt; he could not remember just why it had seemed to be so important, only that it had. In the same way, he thought, he had wanted to find and record every bit of data he could get on Heechee history and activities for his diary. It seemed likely to him that the urges were related, but he could not understand them.

"They will be gone soon," he whispered to Oniko, offering the only reassurance he could find.

She looked at him without speaking. She didn't have to speak; what she would have said would have been only, "Not soon enough."

The old men were doing what they were always doing. They were arguing.

How strange humans were, to decide even the simplest questions only by fierce dispute. This time the argument was over whether or not they should sleep, and which should do it first. Heimat was saying, "We might as well rest, Cyril. An hour or two each, so we'll be alert when we go to the airport. Why

don't you go first? I'll stay awake to entertain our young
guests.''

"If you entertain that little one the way you want," snapped
Basingstoke, "she will probably die of it.''

Heimat shook his head sadly. "Old age has weakened you.
What do you care what happens to the little charmer?''

"Old age has made you a fool! There is a whole world of
little girls out there. Once we are off this island, you can do
what you like with all of them, for all I care, but this one has
credit we can use. Can she pay our bills dead?''

"What bills? We've already got plane tickets.''

"And how do we get to the airport?" Basingstoke inquired.
"Shall we walk?''

Heimat looked thoughtful, then glum. "Perhaps you are right
this time," he conceded grudgingly. Then he brightened. "So
let us order a limousine now, and there will be time for other
things while we are waiting for it to come!''

How much of this Oniko was following Sneezy couldn't tell.
Her body was limp as she slumped against him. She lay with
her eyes closed, but those slow tears were still trickling down
her cheeks, one after another, from her apparently inexhaust-
ible supply.

Sneezy closed his own eyes. It wasn't so much weariness,
although there was plenty of weariness, too, as an effort at
concentration. Was there any possibility at all of escape? Suppose he told the old men that he had to go to the toilet again.
Suppose they untied him for that; could he then break free,
catch Oniko up in his arms, and run out of the building with
her? Could Harold help? Was there any chance that such a
plan, or any other plan, could succeed?

Or would they simply solve the problem of Sneezy and Harold, who had neither credit nor sexual victimization to offer,
by terminating their lives at the first inconvenience?

For the first time in his young life, Sneezy contemplated the
real possibility that it would end within the next few hours at
most. It was quite frightening to a young Heechee. It was not
merely a question of death—death came to everyone sooner
or later. But death under these circumstances could well be

total death, since there was no one nearby to do what was
necessary to take the dead brain of Sneezy and empty it into
storage; it was not death he feared so much as the prospect of
his brain irretrievably decaying before he could be transformed
into an Ancestor . . .

He became aware that the old men were quarreling again,
this time more violently. "What is the matter with the damned
thing!" cried Basingstoke in exasperation, and Heimat chimed
in:

"You've done something wrong, you old fool. Here! Let me
try!"

"Try as much as you like," growled Basingstoke. "It simply
will not go on." He stood back, glowering as the paler old man
bent to the commset. Then Heimat sat back, his expression
bleak.

"What did you do?" he demanded.

"I did nothing! I simply turned it off. Then I tried to turn it
on again, and it will not work!"

For a quick moment Sneezy felt a rush of hope. If the communications set had really been somehow broken, then perhaps the old men's plans would have to change. Perhaps they
must walk to the airport! Sneezy had no idea how far it was,
or even in what direction, but probably the men didn't either.
They would not dare waste time, perhaps. They would need
to start immediately, for the sun was almost rising outside, the
sky in the windows brightening.

And if they left at once—and if, for some reason, they failed
to kill the possible witnesses they would leave behind—and if
they did not decide to take the children somehow with them—
and if—

There were too many ifs.

But then none of the ifs mattered. Sneezy saw the beginning
glow in the PV tank. So did Basingstoke, and he cried, "We
need not accuse each other any longer, Beau! Look, it is coming on at last."

So it was.

So it did; but the face that looked out of the PV at them was
not the smiling Polynesian girl with the hibiscus in her hair. It

was a man's face. A man of indeterminate age, rather handsome (or so I would like to think), smiling out at them in a friendly way. Sneezy didn't recognize it. One human looked much like another to any Heechee, except for the few they happened to have spent a fair amount of time with.

Cyril Basingstoke and Beaupre Heimat, however, knew the face at once. "Robinette Broadhead!" Basingstoke cried, and Heimat snarled, "What the hell is *that* son of a bitch doing here?"

Watching it all in gigabit space, Essie chuckled nervously. "Are quite famous, Robin," she said. "Even wicked old terrorists recognize you at once."

Albert said, "That is not astonishing, Mrs. Broadhead. General Heimat on at least two occasions tried to assassinate Robinette. And probably every terrorist on Earth would have done the same if they had the chance."

"Do not give them chance at anything bad now, Robin," Essie begged. "Go on. Do thing. And, dear Robin, be very careful! Wicked old terrorists are nothing compared to other dangers you insist on encountering now!"

14
Stowaways

I think I should review a little at this point.

When word of the transmission to the kugelblitz reached JAWS, they sprang into action. Programs and people in gigabit time tracked down the source of the message and located it on an island called Moorea in the Pacific Ocean, and that happened fast enough to suit even me.

Then they put the brakes on, because meat people had to make the next decision.

They did it as fast as meat people possibly could, I'll give them that, but meat people just aren't in the running when you want real speed. It took many, many milliseconds before they took the next step, and a lot longer than that before they could put it into effect. They isolated Moorea from the power grid. They cut off every kind of electromagnetic energy anywhere on the island. Moorea was in quarantine. No further messages could get out.

That was the right thing to do, and I agreed with them. But it took them so long! And then it took long, long, longer for the next step. Not to know what to do, because Albert and Essie and I figured that out for them in no time at all, but *interminably* long to convince the meat people we were right, and to get them to do the right thing about it.

It was clear from the beginning that there were Foe loose on Earth. Albert and I went round and round that for thousands of milliseconds, and there simply was no other explanation. Those "false alarms" on the Watch Wheel had not been false at all. We managed to spell that out, millisecond by millisecond, for the meat people. Damn their souls, they argued. "You don't *know* that," General Halverssen objected, and I yelled (as much as I can yell in meat-people time), "Of course we do!" and Albert put in reasonably (and oh! how slowly), "It is true, General Halverssen, that we do not know it for a certainty. But science is not built on certainties; it is only a question of probabilities, and the probability that this is an accurate statement of reality is overwhelming. Really, there is no more convincing competing hypothesis."

Can you image how much time just that kind of thing took?

And then we had to convince them of the next statement: That the Foe had human beings working for them. There we got into a long hassle because the generals of JAWS got bogged down on whether any human being, however vile or insane, would cooperate with the enemies of all organic life everywhere. It took forever to explain to them that we didn't mean *voluntary* cooperation. Well, what did we mean, then? Well, we didn't *know* what we meant, only that the fact that the transmission had been in the English language, however speeded up, was an unarguable bit of evidence that some human being somewhere had interfaced between the Foe and the transmission. And of course the contents of the transmission further supported the theory that it was Foe-generated and Foe-aimed. "If you were a scout for the Foe on Earth," Albert inquired politely, "what would you do? Your first mission would be to learn everything you could about what human beings, and Heechee, were like; about what sort of technology they had and where it was deployed; about everything that could be useful in the event of a conflict. That is precisely what the transmission contained, Generals. There can really be no doubt."

The arguments didn't just take milliseconds. They took *minutes*, and the minutes stretched into hours, because the meat generals were not spending all their time talking to us. They had other things on their minds. They were *acting*. Moorea was isolated so no message traffic could go in either direction; so their only way of establishing any sort of control there was to insert new warm bodies with instructions to take over. Take over what? we asked in vain. Take over the island, of course, was all the answer we got.

So long-range aircraft on Nandu and Oahu were loaded with parachute soldiers and launched for Moorea. They were brave men and women in those aircraft—a lot braver than I would have been, since their status as "soldiers" had been purely honorary for at least as long as most of them had been alive. But they flew over the island and dropped in in the darkness— onto the slopes of that great central mountain, some of them, others into the waters of the lagoon, a few lucky ones onto taro patches or beaches. Their mission was to arrest everybody they could find and, when that was done, to signal by mirror to the watch satellites overhead so that Moorea could be put back into the power grid and the serious investigators could land there.

Can you imagine how much time all *that* took?

Can you imagine how much *trouble* it was? Two hundred soldiers dropped on Moorea, and nearly seventy of them broke arms, legs, or heads when they came down. It was a miracle that none of them died of it, and all for nothing.

Because while that was going on, the faster ones among us, like Albert and me, were doing the homework that would have saved all the effort. It took a lot longer than it should have, because we couldn't go to the records on the island of Moorea itself, due to the blackout. We had to reconstitute the information from other sources. So we did. We accessed every datum we could find about traffic to and from the island of Moorea. We studied the census reports on everyone who lived there. We looked for some clue, some linkage to something somehow related to the Foe . . .

And the names of Oniko, Sneezy, and Harold popped out of the files.

As soon as we saw who they were and where they'd been, we knew it was the answer. Who else had been on the Watch Wheel during the latest "false alarm"?

When we had explained all that to the meatheads, they agreed it was important. It was also pretty useless, because they had no good way of communicating with the paratroops that were even then flopping down all over the island, to tell them where to concentrate their efforts. But they did the next best thing. They made the satellite watch records available to us, and when we played these tapes we saw the little glass-bottomed boat slipping out of the lagoon on its way across the strait.

Unfortunately, by the time we saw it, it was history. But there they were. The three children, scrambling up onto the floating dock of the beach house belonging to a Mr. and Mrs. Henri Becquerel, now visiting grandchildren on Peggys Planet. And when we took the next step, monitoring all communications that had gone in or out of the beach house, we had no trouble identifying the two old loonies who had been with the children on the boat.

Then we stored the images and thought it over. "Ah-ha," said Albert wisely, puffing on his pipe. "Look at the children."

"Two of them are wearing pods," Julio Cassata announced, a moment before I would have.

"Exactly." Albert beamed. "And what better place for an energy being like the Foe to hide away than in a pod?"

I said, "But could they? I mean, *how* could they?"

Puff, puff. "It might be difficult for them, yes, Robin," said Albert thoughtfully, "because surely the storage systems are not anything they would be used to. But neither were Heechee Ancestor-storage and our own gigabit net compatible at first. We simply had to devise ways of transcribing one to the other. Do you think the Foe are stupider than we, Robin?" And, before I could answer, "In any case, there is no better hypothesis. We dare not assume anything else. The Foe are in the pods."

"And pods are on children," said Essie, "and children are captives of two known murderers. Robin! Whatever do, must be absolutely sure children are not harmed!"

"Of course, my dear," I said, wondering just how to do that. The data file on Basingstoke and Heimat had not been comforting, even if we overlooked Heimat's known obsession with young and helpless girls. I made an effort. "The first thing to do," I said, "is to persuade JAWS to isolate the house. We don't want Foe getting into gigabit space and wandering around."

"They've had plenty of time to do that already," Albert pointed out.

"But perhaps they haven't. Maybe they can't leave the pods—or didn't think they needed to?" I shook my head. "Your trouble, Albert, is that you're a machine construct. You don't know how natural beings behave. If I were one of the Foe, in what is surely a strange and bewildering place, I would find a nice hole to hide in and stay there until I was sure I knew what was safe."

Albert sighed and rolled his eyes upward. "You have never been a natural energy creature, so you know nothing about their behavior," he reminded me.

"But if I'm wrong, nothing's lost, is it? So let's cut them out."

"Oh," he said, "I have already suggested this to the organic leaders of JAWS. The house will be totally isolated in a few thousand milliseconds. Then what?"

"Oh," I said easily, "then I pay them a call.

It took a lot of milliseconds, actually. I not only had to persuade the JAWS meatheads that I was the best person to negotiate, I had to satisfy them, and Albert, that I could negotiate in some way that wouldn't give either the old men or the Foe any chance to escape.

"Fine," Cassata's doppel said forcefully. "I agree." I braced myself for the next part. It came. "Somebody must do that, but not you, Broadhead. You're a civilian."

I yelled, "Now, listen, stupid—" But Albert raised a hand.

"General Cassata," he said patiently, "the situation in that house is unstable. We can't wait for some meat person to get there and negotiate."

"Of course not," he said tightly, "but that doesn't mean it has to be Broadhead!"

"Oh?" said Albert. "Then who? It must be someone like ourselves, must it not? Someone who is familiar with what is going on? Really, one of us here, wouldn't you say?"

"Not necessarily," said Cassata, stalling, but Albert wouldn't let him.

"I think it must be," he said gently, "because time is of the essence, and the only question is which. I don't think I should be the one; I'm only a rude mechanical, after all."

Essie cut in, "Certainly not *me!*"

"And you yourself, General," said Albert politely, "are simply not good enough for the job. Which leaves only Robinette, I'm afraid."

He was afraid!

Cassata gave in. "But not in his own person," he ordered. "Something expendable, and that's *final.*"

So it was not precisely "I" who was grinning out of the commset at the two old monsters and their captive kids. It was only a doppel of me, because that was all Albert and the JAWS people would allow, but they also had to allow me one tightly constrained channel of contact with my doppel. They had no choice about that, because otherwise none of us could either know or affect what happened in that little house by the beach on the island of Tahiti.

So I peered out of the PV at the old monsters. I said at once—or my duplicate did—"General Heimat, Mr. Basingstoke, you're caught again. Don't do anything ridiculous. We'll let you go free—under certain conditions—provided you co-operate. Start by untying the children.'' And at the same time the other I, safe a hundred thousand kilometers away on the *True Love*, was complaining bitterly, ''But it takes so *long!*''

Essie said, ''Can't be helped, dear Robin,'' and Albert cleared his throat and offered:

''Do be careful. General Heimat will try some violent act, no doubt, but Basingstoke is more subtle. Watch him closely, please.''

''Do I have a choice?'' I grumbled. I did not. They were meat people, and I was I. While my doppel was delivering that interminably long first speech—six thousand milliseconds it took!—I was observing and displaying every person, item of furniture, wall hanging, window, particle of sand, and fluff of dust in that pleasant little room. It took an eternity for me to activate my image and say my words of greeting, and then for Heimat to respond took *forever*.

See, I didn't have the zippy perceptors and actuators that were part of the real me, back on the *True Love*. I had a simple piezovision commset, the kind people put in their living rooms. They're designed to be used by meat people. Therefore they are meat-people slow. They don't have to be fast, because meat people aren't. The commset's scanning system takes a look at what is before it, point by point. One by one it examines each of those points and registers its properties—so much luminance, at such-and-such a wavelength—and then, one by one, it plots them in its memory store for transmission.

We were not about to let the set transmit, of course. The only transmissions from that room went from doppel-me to real-me 100,000 kilometers out in space.

The set's scanners were quick enough for the purpose, by meat-person standards. They looked at every point twenty-four times a second, and meat persistence of vision filled in the gaps. What meat people saw was the illusion of real-time presence.

I did not. What both doppel-me and real-me saw was this painful building-up of images, point by point. We were on gigabit time, orders of magnitude faster. We could see each individual data point come in. It looked as though someone were filling in a paint-by-number canvas in each one-twenty-fourth of a second, a dot of red here, a darker scarlet next to it, another scarlet, and so, painstakingly, point by point, we saw displayed a single line of Oniko's red skirt. Then there were a thousand points for the next line, and the next, and the next, while I and doppel-I sat fidgeting and metaphorically gnawing our metaphorical thumbnails, waiting for the whole picture to show.

Sound was no better. The median frequency of human speech, say the middle A, is 440 hertz. So what I "heard" (perceived as pressure pulses, actually) was a *putt . . . putt . . . putt* of sound, each individual *putt* coming a couple of milliseconds after the last. Whereupon I had to take note of the amplitude of each pulse and the elapsed time between them, less or more as the tone was raised or lowered, and identify them as frequencies, and constitute them as sound spectrograms, and translate them into syllables and finally words. Oh, I could interpret them, all right. But, my God, it was *tedious*.

It was frustrating in all the ways there were to be frustrating, because it was urgent.

The urgency was the Foe, to be sure, but I had some private urgencies of my own. Curiosity, for instance. This crazy old man named Heimat, I well knew, had tried very hard to murder both me and my wife. I really wanted to talk to him about that. Then there were the kids. They were a very special urgency, because I had a clear picture of what they had been through and how terrified, worn out, and demoralized they had to be. I wanted to rescue them from that ordeal within the next millisecond, no time for meat-person haggling and deal-making with the old killers; and I couldn't.

I also couldn't wait, so while Heimat and Basingstoke were still opening their mouths, expressions shattered in astonishment, I cut in to say directly to the kids: "Oniko, Sneezy, Harold: You're safe now. These two men can't hurt you."

And where we all sat in the control room of the *True Love*,

Albert sucked his pipe meditatively and said, "I don't blame you for that, Robin, but please don't forget that the Foe are the first order of business."

I didn't get a chance to answer. Essie was in there before me, crying indignantly, "Albert! Are just a machine, after all? These poor children are scared out of wits!"

"He's right, though," argued Cassata. "The children will be all right. The Papeete police are on their way—"

"And will arrive when?" demanded Essie. It was a rhetorical question; we all knew the answer. She furnished it: "About one million milliseconds, is not right? How much can happen, even in meat-person time?"

My doppel was just finishing saying, "—o-u-'-r-e s-a-f-e," so there was plenty of time for debate. I said to Albert: "What do you think Heimat will do?"

"He has that gun," said Albert judiciously. "He will think, perhaps, of using Oniko as a hostage."

"That we can take care of," Cassata said grimly.

"No way, Julio!" I said. "You crazy? If you go throwing beam weapons around in that little room somebody could get hurt."

"Only the somebody we aim at!"

Albert coughed deprecatingly. "The accuracy of your weapons is undoubted, General. However, there is also the question of the integrity of the Faraday cage. We have that space completely isolated except for the single channel between Mr. Broadhead and his doppel. If you puncture it, what will happen with the stowaways?"

Cassata hesitated. We all hesitated, because that was, really, where the ultimate worry was. The stowaways. The Foe!

Looking at three decent little kids held hostage by two ancient thugs, you almost forgot where the real terror lay. Heimat and Basingstoke were amateurs! Between the two of them they had murdered a few tens of thousands, maybe, of innocent men, women, and children, wrecked some billions of dollars worth of property, upset the lives of tens of millions of people . . . why, how *trivial* they were, when you compared them with the race that shifted stars, annihilated whole planets, dared disturb the immense universe itself! Terror? No human terrorist was more than a naughty pipsqueak brat compared with the Foe—not these two, no, nor Hitler, nor Jenghiz Khan, nor Assurbanipal.

And there were Foe there in that room, and I was proposing to try to confront them . . .

My doppel finally finished its reassurance to the children. Cyril Basingstoke opened his mouth to say something. Through my doppel I could see his expression. His eyes were on me, with curiosity and a kind a respect. It was the sort of respect one gladiator might give another when they met in the arena—a gladiator who recognized the difference in weapons between his opponent's and his own, but still thought there was a pretty good chance that his trident could prevail over the other guy's net.

It was not at all the kind of look you would expect from someone ready to concede defeat.

Measured by the slow tick of meat-person clocks, what happened next must have seemed to happen very fast. The two ancient outlaws were way past their prime, but there were a lot of new parts in their organs and musculature, and the wicked old brains were still alert. "Beaupre!" Basingstoke snapped. "Cover the girl!" And he himself made a dash for the table where the spring-loaded spear gun had been sitting all this while.

From the screen I called anxiously: "Hold everything! We can make a deal with you!"

Heimat, already with one hand wrapped in Oniko's hair and the other pressing the fish-killer gun against her temple, snarled triumphantly, "You damn well will! You want to hear our terms? *Freedom!* Complete freedom, transportation to a planet of our choice, and—and—a million dollars each!"

"And more guns, man," added Cyril Basingstoke practically. He was always the shrewder of the two, I thought with a certain amount of admiration. And I really admired the quick thinking and precise actions of the two old monsters. I mean, consider! They must have been startled considerably by my sudden appearance on the commset screen; it had taken them no more than ten seconds to answer, make a plan, and carry it out, so that now they had the children covered and their demands stated.

Ten seconds, however, are ten thousand milliseconds.

I said from the screen, "Freedom you can have, both of you. That is, you can be out of prison, and you can be set free on another planet—not Earth, not Peggys, but a rather nice one. The only thing is, you'll be the only two people there." It was a sound and fair offer. I even had a specific planet in mind, because Albert had found a good one. True, it was inside the core, one of the extras the Heechee had prudently included for expansion purposes, but it was certainly a livable place. They could do what they liked there—especially since, being in the core, they would be doing it forty thousand times slower than on the Earth.

"The hell you say!" snapped Heimat. "We'll pick the planet, and don't forget the money!"

"I'll give you the money," I said politely. "A million each; you can use it to buy programs for yourselves for company. Think it over, you guys. You know we really can't let you kill off any more cities." And then I saw Heimat's eyes narrow as he heard sounds from the other room, so I added quickly: "You don't have any other choice, because otherwise you'll both be dead. Look at what we have for you," I invited, and displayed on the screen some of Nash's orbital particle-beam weapons.

They looked. It took them only a second or two (but more than a thousand milliseconds!) to register what was on the screen, but by then it was too late. For Albert had found something else for me out of the contents of the house. The workthing he had located and I had taken over came through the door, its cleaner hoses elevated. A workthing isn't a weapon. When designed as a houseboy it can scrub and mend and tidy up, it can even do windows and take out the garbage, but it doesn't kill. It does, however, have jets that can blast detergent into cracks, and pumps that can put extra muscle behind the jets; and when it has pumped up its charge to maximum and slipped paring knives into the nozzles of the jets, as I had commanded this one to do while I was talking, it can then project the knives with great force and considerable accuracy.

I didn't kill the old men, or at least not permanently. But before they could look around Heimat had a knife in his throat and Basingstoke one in his heart, and they were no longer a problem for the children, just for the technicians who would pump what remained of their minds into storage for the Dead Files. "I wonder," I said, watching the second slow knife gradually bury itself in Basingstoke's chest, "if we shouldn't have done that in the first place, Albert. They'll be a lot less trouble as machine-stored intelligences, won't they?"

"Why should they be?" Albert smiled. "You aren't, you know. But now take care of the children, please."

"Children!" Cassata cried. "You've got Foe there! They're the ones you have to pay attention to!"

"But in this case," said Albert politely, "it is the same thing, you see."

I didn't need to be reminded of that. I was sufficiently scared already.

A workthing isn't any better at untying knots than at overcoming criminals, but it has its scrapers and cutters; it simply chewed through the ropes. It freed Oniko first, then Sneezy and Harold, and I talked to them while it was still doing it.

I said soothingly, "You're all right now, kids, except for one important thing. I want you two to take your pods off, without any argument or discussion, because it is very important. And I want you to do it *right away*."

They were good kids. It wasn't easy for them. Nothing would have been easy for them after what they'd been through—especially for Oniko, exhausted as she was and terrified as she had been—harder still for Sneezy, I guess, because a Heechee is almost never without his pod from the age of three up. They did it, all the same, and they did it without any argument or discussion. But, oh, how many milliseconds it took for them to do it, while I waited on tenterhooks for the next step. That was the one I feared!

But there was no choice.

I said, "Now, I want the two of you to bring the pods to the commset and plug them in to the data receptors."

It wasn't that easy; pod terminals weren't meant for any such use, but Albert had already been figuring out ways and means. So Sneezy saw how an adapter could fit, and Harold rummaged something that would do out of the beach house's junk drawers, and with the help of the workthing they manhandled and wrestled it into shape, stepping carefully around the two grisly things on the floor . . .

And all that time, millisecond after millisecond, I watched them doing the thing that would make it possible for me to do what I dreaded, and wanted, most of anything in the world:

To come face to face—however metaphorically, since I had no real face and didn't suppose the Foe had ever had any—with the creatures who had upset the tranquillity of the never very tranquil universe I lived in.

And then Oniko touched the terminals of her pod to the terminals of the commset, and there they were.

I can't really tell you what the Foe looked like. How do you describe in terms of physical attributes what has none?

I could not tell you how big the Foe were, or what color, or what shape; they didn't have any of those things. If they had gender, or anything at all that distinguished one of them from another, I wasn't aware of it. I was not even sure there were two of them. More than one, yes. Less than many, I suppose. My assumption was that there were two, because in the time (quite a long time, by my standards and theirs) between Oniko putting her pod against the terminals of the commset and Sneezy following with his, I thought there was only a single being sharing gigabit space with me, and after that I thought there were more.

I tried to speak to them.

It wasn't easy. I didn't know how to go about it.

First I tried a question:

Who are you?

That wasn't precisely what I said, because I didn't say anything in words. It was more like a vast, soundless, *Hmmm?*

There wasn't any answer.

I tried again, this time in pictures. I recalled a picture of the kugelblitz, the dozen turd-colored smears turning restlessly by themselves in intergalactic space.

Nothing came back.

I made a picture of the Wheel and put it in the frame with the kugelblitz. I wiped that, and showed Sneezy and Oniko, and then their pods.

Then I tried another *Hmmm?*

No answer. Nothing. Just the knowledge that somebody, somehow was sharing that space with me—

No! There was an answer! Because I had shown the pods as they were, opaque, dull, top-shaped metal things; and in my own picture they were luminous. They were radiating.

Although all my attention was focused tightly on my doppel, there was still the other me, half a second away, in the *True Love* with Essie and Albert and General Cassata. I was aware of stirrings there, even questions, even comment; but the "real" me was always a couple of seconds behind the doppel, and by the time Albert cried sharply, "They're telling you they were in the pods!" I had already been told.

It was, after all, an answer of sorts. Communication had begun.

I tried a hard picture. I tried to show the entire universe— from outside; from the place that had never existed, because there was no "outside" of what was, by definition, everywhere. The only picture that conveyed any of that to me was simply a great, glowing, featureless blob; whether it would mean anything to the Foe I could not say, but it was the best I could approximate of the things Albert had showed me in Deep Time. Then, as Albert had, I zoomed in on it. The blob approached and spread out and displayed one section of the universe, a few thousand galaxies, ellipticals and spirals and odd pairs crashing through each other and singles spewing out arms of starlets and gas.

Was that right? Something was nagging at me that said I was doing something wrong.

Right, I thought; I was. I had been making an assumption I

had no right to make. I was showing the universe as it appeared to human eyes, in the optical frequencies of light. Bad assumption! I had no reason to assume the Foe had eyes. Even if they did, in some sense, what right had I to assume that they saw only the familiar, human rainbow frequencies from violet to red?

So I added to the picture the halos and gas clouds that showed up only in infrared or microwave, and even the clouds of particles that, we supposed, were the Foe's own contribution to the universe we lived in.

Actually, that is to say, I showed my unseen (and, I had to fear, perhaps wholly uncaring) audience the pictures Albert had showed me in Deep Time. I let it hang there for a moment, and then I made it move.

In reverse. Just as Albert had done for me.

I shrank the picture. Galaxies came closer together. As they approached, they spread out, so that I was showing less structure and less, more and more tightly compacted together.

I shrank it still farther. Catastrophically. I crushed the universe down to a single terrible point of light.

And then I reenacted the Big Bang, and froze the whole scene at that moment in time when all options were open. And then I tried another of those wordless questioning feelings: *Hmmm?*

And then I had my answer.

Of course, the answer didn't come in words.

Of course, the answer seemed hardly like an answer at all. I had not expected that it would. I hadn't expected anything, really, or at least I had had no idea what to expect.

What I had was a picture, and of all the possible responses I might have thought likely, this was the least. The picture was me. Grinning at the other me. My own face, angular, ugly, but recognizable, perhaps as I had looked to Oniko and Sneezy as I peered out of the commset.

It did not seem an appropriate response to the burning question I had tried to ask.

Probably the reason for that, I told myself, was that I had

failed to ask a proper question. Perhaps my picture of what
the Foe were trying to do—at least, what we *thought* the Foe
were trying to do—lacked some essential feature in their eyes.
("Eyes!") I didn't know how to remedy that. All our assump-
tions about the Foe were based on the conjecture that, as pure
energy beings, they found our present universe less hospitable
than they liked, and so they had resolved to create enough
"missing mass" to cause it to fall back together into the pri-
meval atom . . . from which it would explode in a second or
a third or an *n*th Big Bang, to create a new one more to their
liking. Reshaping the universe. "Foeforming" it, as you might
say, in the same way that both the Heechee and ourselves had
terraformed planets.

That was the sense of what I wanted to convey, but I didn't
know how to picture it in their terms.

Except that, it seemed, I just had.

How long I hung in there, staring at the caricature of my
own face and wondering what to try next, I cannot guess.

It was a long time. Even by meat standards it was long
enough to matter, because I was aware that the glacial movements of the people in the room were actually making changes.
There were more people there now. There were other human
beings in the room, and a lot of machines. When I took time
to flash a question to Albert and Essie, through the other me
back on the *True Love*, Albert said reassuringly, "It's the police, Robin, and the physics people to make sure confinement
is still working, and the death-reversal teams for Basingstoke
and General Heimat; don't worry; you're doing fine."

Fine?

And yes, perhaps I was. Because the pictures changed.

I didn't know what I was seeing at first, an odd ball of nasty-
looking fire that opened up to show stars and planets crowded
close together, and zoomed in on one of the planets to show
stick figures bounding about that were recognizably meant to
be Heechee. Their hideaway in the core? Of course.

And as soon as I recognized that, there was another picture.
It was almost like a documentary, or a travelogue: *Life Among*

the Heechee. I saw Heechee world-ships hanging near the Schwarzschild barrier, and Heechee cities under their glassed-in domes; I saw Heechee factories producing Heechee consumer goods, and Heechee persons working and marrying and giving birth and growing; I saw more about the Heechee in that long gigabit-time display than I had known about them before in all my long life.

I will put it mildly: I was astonished, and I was horribly, hopelessly confused. I had no idea why I was seeing what I saw; and then the picture changed again.

It was another travelogue. It wasn't the Heechee anymore. It was us.

I don't know, perhaps I saw every human being there ever was in that eternal-brief display. Some of them I recognized. I saw Oniko being born on the Heechee artifact, and the death of her grandparents. I saw her rescued with all her little colony, and I saw her brought to the Watch Wheel. I saw the human race, maybe all the hundred billion members of it there were on all the twenty inhabited planets and in ships between. I even saw history. I saw armies, and space navies, and weapons practice, and ships being launched that were armed to kill a world if they chose to. I saw cities bombed and obliterated. I saw a Gateway prospector in a Five, stealthily slitting the throats of his four companions. I saw my dear wife, Essie, with the tubes in her throat and nose and the life-support machines chugging all around her—a picture I remembered, because once she had been just like that.

I saw Basingstoke in tights and air mask, swimming through lucid tropical waters to fix a limpet bomb to the hull of a cruise ship. I saw General Beaupre Heimat press a button that destroyed a spacecraft, and I saw him again doing—oh, doing vile and terrible things to a tiny female child—it was only a minuscule relief from the stomach-twisting sight to realize that the "child" was only a robot.

The flood of pictures went on forever.

And then they forever ended.

I saw nothing. I did not even see the room, or Oniko and the other children, or the newcomers who were going about

their business in it. I saw nothing at all; my senses had been
blacked out.

And then I realized that I was indeed getting answers to my
questions, only they were not the questions I had asked. I was
not being told "what." I was only being told "why."

The other "I" back on the *True Love* was watching it all,
but I couldn't see him (me). I couldn't see anything at all.

And then I saw everything, all at once. All the pictures I
had seen before, floating before me at once like a storm of
confetti. They danced around and blended; Heechee became
half human, humans began to look like Heechee, and they
blurred into computer constructs and Sluggards and Voodoo
Pigs and into things that bore no resemblance at all to anything
the universe had ever known . . . and then it all began to dissolve in a torrent of multicolored sparks, all of it.

Even me.

I *felt* myself dissolving. I felt my very own person melting
and coruscating into nothingness.

It took quite a long time for me to understand what was
happening. "I'm *dying*, for God's sake!" I shouted into empty
gigabit space—

Just as I did.

"I died!" I screamed in terror to Albert and my dear Portable-Essie and the officers of JAWS, gathered solicitously
around me in the *True Love*.

I felt Essie's warm (if only virtual) arms around me. "Oh,
shoo, shoo, dear Robin," she soothed. "Is all right now. Are
not dead anymore, not here."

Cassata cried exultantly, "But you did the job, Robin!
You *talked* to them! Now we can go out to the Watch Wheel
and—"

"General Cassata," said Albert politely, "please shut up.
How do you feel, Robin? It is true that in a sense, yes, you
did die. At least that copy of you is gone forever, and maybe
the Foe with it; I think they neutralized you, Robin, even

though it cost them themselves. I'm sorry it was so traumatic for you."

"Sorry!" I screamed. "Do you know what it's like to *die*? To know that you are disappearing, and there won't be any you ever again anywhere?"

Essie hugged me tighter than ever, murmuring comfort in my ear. "But is still a you, Robin. Is here with me. Was only duplicate that entered gigabit-isolate with Foe, you know?"

I wrenched myself free (metaphorically) and glared at my two nearest and dearest; I wasn't even aware of the JAWS officers. "It's fine for you to say," I said bitterly. "You didn't have to feel it. I *died*. And it's not the first time, I remind you both. I've had the experience before, and I am so *terribly* tired of dying. If there's one thing I want in all the world, it's to do it again!"

I stopped, because they were looking at me in a peculiar way.

"Oh," I said, managing to grin, "I mean I want *not* to do it again." But which I meant really was very unclear even to me.

15
Scared Rats Running

When a stored personality in gigabit space has had a terrible shock, you don't give him a stiff drink and a place to lie down, but sometimes it helps if you pretend you do.

"You should rest for a moment, Robin," said Albert.

"Let me make comfortable, dove-heart," murmured Essie, and a moment later I was comfortable indeed. Essie made it so. I was lying in a (metaphorical) hammock on the (unreal) lanai outside my (datastored) home overlooking the Tappan Sea, with dear Portable-Essie hovering over me and pressing a (nonexistent) drink in my hand. It was an icy margarita with just enough salt on the rim of the glass, and it tasted quite as good as if it had been real.

I was the center of attention.

Essie was sitting next to the hammock, stroking my hair lovingly and looking worried. Albert was seated on the edge of a chaise longue, scratching his ear meditatively with the stem of his pipe as he watched my face. That was all homely and familiar enough, but there were other people there. I wasn't surprised to see Julio Cassata, who was pacing up and down on the grass just below the steps, but stopping at the end of each patrol to look searchingly in my direction. Even Alicia Lo, sitting quietly on a rocker at the edge of the lanai, was no surprise; but there was someone else there.

The someone was a Heechee.

I was not ready for surprises. I sat up and said, "What the hell?" I didn't say it meanly. If anything, I think I said it beseechingly.

Essie took it in the right way. "I don't know if you remember Double-Bond," she said. She was right. I didn't. "He was a Heechee representative to JAWS," Essie added, and vaguely I did remember. There had been a Heechee or two there, and, yes, one of them had been an Ancient Ancestor, like this one, and had had the sparse head-fuzz and deep-set eyes of age, like this one.

"I'm pleased to see you again," I said. I gulped the last of the tequila and looked around. And then I said again, "What the *hell*?" But this time it was in a quite different tone, because I had looked past the simulated, friendly Tappan Sea surround. I expected to find that we were in the *True Love*, and we were.

But the screen was showing only mottled gray. When I looked through the *True Love*'s skin sensors, I saw we were in faster-than-light travel. When I peered at the retrolog, I saw the JAWS satellites dwindling behind us. JAWS looked different to me in some way. I wasn't sure what, and didn't take the time to figure it out. What was more important was what *True Love* was doing. We were en route somewhere, and I had not expected that at all.

"Where are we going?" I cried.

Albert coughed. "There were some developments while you were working through your doppel," he said.

"Didn't dare disturb your concentration," Essie said worriedly. "Sorry about that. But is all right, honest, dearest Robin, are safe and sound in *True Love*, as you see."

"You didn't answer my question!"

She laid the hand that had been stroking my hair alongside my cheek. It felt warm and caring. "We go to source," she said soberly. "To kugelblitz. To home of Foe, fast as we can."

I let myself return to the pleasant Tappan Sea surround, feeling very disoriented. Essie had another margarita ready, and I reached out for it automatically. I held it in my hand, trying to figure out what was happening. We had left JAWS—

Then I remembered what was different about the way the JAWS satellites had looked when we departed. "The fleet is gone!" I cried.

"Exactly," said Albert. "We are following them."

"Against orders," added Julio Cassata.

"Cannot give orders to us!" snapped Essie.

"They can give orders to me," said Cassata, "and we're going against them. The fleet movement is a military operation, after all."

"Military!" I stared at the man, wondering if it was at all possible that he meant what I thought he meant. He shrugged. I translated the shrug easily enough; it was, yes, that was indeed what he meant.

"This is *crazy*!" I shouted.

He shrugged again. "But—" I said. "But— But I wasn't *ready* to go on a long trip just now!"

Essie leaned over and kissed me. "Dear Robin," she said, "is no choice, after all. Is there? JAWS fleet is not to be trusted by itself. Who knows what idiocy they may try?"

"But— But back on Wrinkle Rock—"

She said lovingly, "Is nothing on Wrinkle Rock for you anymore, dear Robin. Farewells are said. After all, party is now over."

16

The Long Voyage

All the time I was messing around with the kids and their captors on the island of Tahiti was meat time. There had been time for meat people to do things. Meat people had.

The meat people who ran JAWS had decided the threat on Earth was nothing they needed a fleet there for, so they had sent the cruisers off to the Watch Wheel. Meat-Cassata hadn't bothered to terminate doppel-Cassata, whose datastore was still on *True Love* along with the store for Alicia Lo. Albert was the one who had insisted on taking along the "prayer fan" that was the store for the Heechee Ancient Ancestor, Double-Bond. It wasn't the only store he had put aboard, and he had his reasons; when I realized what they were, I could only approve.

And, of course, doppel-Cassata approved very much. He hadn't been terminated! Not only that, he *couldn't* be terminated as long as he was aboard *True Love* in transit, because there was no one there to terminate him. For Cassata it was not only a reprieve, it was practically an eternity—weeks and weeks of travel—the equivalent, for him, of decades and decades of added life!

That's what is was for Julio Cassata.

For me it was something quite different.

The first thing I had to do was get over the terrible shocks that had come from my mind mingling with the Foe and the Foe entering into my mind, as well as that other shock of feeling myself die yet once again.

One of the (many) advantages of being a stored intelligence is that you can edit the stores if you want to. If something hurts, you can just take it out, seal it up, put it on a shelf marked "Warning. Not to be opened unless necessary," and go about your business pain-free.

Like many of those many advantages, it carries a penalty with it.

I know this, because I'd tried it. Long and long ago—oh, something like ten-to-the-eleventh milliseconds ago—I was really, really screwed up. I had just died then, too, only that time it was my real meat body that had died, and Albert and Essie had just poured me into machine storage. *That* is a real jolt. There was more. I had just encountered Klara, the woman I loved before I loved the woman who was my wife, Essie, and there were the two of them in my life; not only that, but I had actually thought I had murdered that other woman, Gelle-Klara Moynlin; and, oh, yes, I had just met a live Heechee for the first time.

Put them all together, it was bloody *shattering*.

So to get me through the worst of it, Albert and Essie had restructured the program that was all that remained of me. They had isolated the datastores that had to do with Klara and the terrible crush of guilt that had cost me years of psycho-analysis to ease, and they had encapsulated them in a read-only file and given it back to me, with a seal on it so I wouldn't open it until I was ready.

I don't think I ever was ready, but after a while I opened it anyway.

See, the way you remember things is associative. I had lost some associations. I could remember that something else had been on my mind, but I couldn't remember what. I could say, "Gee, sure, at that time I was really shaken up because—"

But I couldn't remember what the "because" was.

And that, I finally decided, was worse than having the whole thing right in front of me all the time, because if I had to stew and fret and worry, at least I could know what I was worrying about.

To give you an idea of how I felt after my little adventure with the Foe on Moorea, I seriously considered asking Essie to put that one away for me in mothballs, too.

But I couldn't.

I had to face it and live with it, and, oh, my God, it was *scary*.

I kept going over and over that long wordless meeting of minds, and the more I thought about it, the huger and more terrifying it was. I, little Robinette Broadhead, had been in the presence of the things—the creatures, the monsters, maybe one might even say the people—who were busy turning the entire universe upside down for their own pleasure.

What was a feckless, fragile little kid like me doing in the same league as superstars like them?

I need to try to put something into perspective.

It isn't going to be easy. It isn't even going to be possible, in any real sense, because the perspective is too immense— Albert would probably say "incommensurable," meaning that you can't measure the things involved on the same scale. It's like—like—well, suppose you were talking to one of those early australopithecines of half a million years ago or so. You could probably find a way to explain to him that where you had come from (say, somewhere in Europe) was a hell of a long way from where he was born—say, somewhere in Africa.

You might even be able to tell him that Alaska and Australia were a hell of a lot farther still. That much he might understand.

But is there any conceivable way in which you could tell him how much *farther* away were, say, the core of the Galaxy of the Magellanic Clouds? Impossible! After a certain point—for australopithecine or modern-day human or even machine-stored intelligence like me—big is simply indistinguishably *big*.

For that reason, I don't know how to describe just how long it took for me to experience that long, tedious faster-than-light trip from JAWS to the Watch Wheel.

It was *forever*. I can put the numbers in. Measured by gigabit time, it was well over ten-to-the-ninth milliseconds, which is about as much time, by meat standards, as my whole meat life had been before I was vastened.

But that doesn't really convey the slow, draggy way the time passed. On the "long" trip from Wrinkle Rock to JAWS I had made Albert show me the entire history of the universe.

Now I had begun a trip that was a good thousand times longer, and what could he do for an encore?

I needed a whole lot of things to do to keep busy. I had no trouble finding the first one.

Albert had persuaded General Cassata to persuade JAWS to let us access every bit of data they had on the Foe. There was a hell of a lot of it. The trouble was that, as far as what was going on right *now* was concerned, it was all negative. It didn't answer the questions I really wanted answered, which were mostly questions I didn't have enough background knowledge to ask.

Optimistic old Albert denied that. "We have learned much, Robin," he lectured, chalk in hand before his blackboard. "For example, we now know that the Galaxy is a horse, the dog did not bark, and the cat is among the pigeons."

"Albert," said Essie levelly. She was speaking to him, but she was looking at me. I supposed I had been looking confused at Albert's undesired playfulness, but that was not odd. I *was* confused, not to mention stressed, worried, and generally unhappy.

Albert got his stubborn look. "Yes, Mrs. Broadhead?"

"Have thought for some time program may need routine overhaul, Albert. Is this now necessary?"

"I don't think so," he said, looking uncomfortable.

"Whimsy," she said, "is useful and even desirable in Albert Einstein program, for Robin wishes it so. However."

He said uncomfortably, "I take your meaning, Mrs. Broadhead. What you want is a simple and lucid synoptic report. Very well. The data is as follows. First, we have no evidence that any other bits, pieces, pseudopods, or extrusions of the Foe other than the ones Robin encountered on Tahiti exist anywhere else in the Galaxy. Second, we have no evidence that they still exist. Third, as to those units themselves, we have no evidence that they are in any significant way different from ourselves, which is to say patterned, organized, and stored electromagnetic charges in some suitable substrate, specifically in this case the pods of Oniko and Sneezy." He looked directly at me. "Are you following this, Robin?"

"Not a lot," I said, making an effort. "You mean they're just electrons, like you and me? Just some other kind of Dead Men? Not some subnuclear particles, like?"

Albert winced. "Robin," he complained, "I know you know better than that. Not only as to particle physics but as to grammar."

"You know what I mean," I flared, trying not to be on edge and making myself more so by the effort.

Albert sighed. "Indeed I do. Very well, I will spell it out. With all of the instrumentation we were able to bring to bear, which was probably all that would have been of use, we were able to detect no field, ray, energy emission, or other physical effect associated with the Foe which was not compatible with the assumption that they are, yes, composed of electromagnetic energy just like us."

"No gamma rays, even?"

"Definitely no gamma rays," he said, looking irritated. "Also no x-rays, cosmic rays, quark flows, or neutrinos; also, in another category, no poltergeists, N-rays, psychic auras,

fairies at the bottom of the garden, or indications of the ade-
ledicnander force.''

"Albert!" cried Essie.

"You're patronizing me, Albert," I complained.

He gazed at me for a long moment.

Then he stood up. His hair had turned woolly, and his complexion had darkened. Straw hat in hand (I could not remember
seeing him with the hat before), he strutted a few steps in a
cakewalk and chanted, "'Deedy Ah is, suh, yassuh, yassuh,
yuk, yuk, yuk."

"*Damn* it, Albert!" I shouted.

He resumed his normal appearance. "You have no sense of
fun in your heart anymore, Robin," he complained.

Essie opened her mouth to speak. Then she closed it again,
looking at me in an inquiring way. Then she shook her head,
and, to my surprise, said only, "Go on, Albert."

"Thank you," he said, as though it had been no more than
he expected, in spite of her earlier threats. "To put it all more
prosaically, since you are determined to be a wet blanket, let
me return to my previous points which, if you remember, I
put in semihumorous fashion to make them more palatable,
and as a mnemonic device. 'The Galaxy is a horse.' Yes. A
Trojan horse. Every external appearance indicates that it is
just as it always has been in our lifetimes, but I infer that it is
full of enemy troops. Or, to put it more simply, there are a
whole lot of those Foe emissaries around, Robin, and we can't
detect them."

"But there's been no evidence," I cried, and then, as he
gazed at me, "Well, yeah, I see what you're saying. If we
don't see them, it's because they're hiding. Right. I follow that.
But how do you *know* they are hiding? There has been only
one single transmission that we can blame on the Foe—what?"

He was shaking his head. "No, Robin. We have *detected*
one. The only reason we did is that the Foe used the standard
Earth communications facilities, and so that particular burst
transmission, which the children on Moorea originated, turned
up on the logs as an anomaly. But we don't monitor everything,
Robin. If there were Foe on, say, Peggys Planet, where things

are a lot looser, would anyone have noticed one more transmission? Or from a ship in space? Or, for that matter, from
the Watch Wheel itself, say a few months ago, before we tightened everything up? I don't think so, Robin. I think we have
to assume that all the 'false alarms' on the Wheel were not
false; that the Foe penetrated it some time ago; that they have
gone wherever they wanted to go in our space and seen everything they wanted to see, and no doubt reported back to the
kugelblitz. That," he said, smiling cheerfully, "is what I meant
by 'The cat is among the pigeons.' Why," he finished, looking
around in mild curiosity, "it would not surprise me a bit if
there were a few of them right here with us on the *True Love*."
   I jumped.
   I couldn't help it. I was still bruised and shaken from that
terrible, hurtful experience. I looked around wildly, and Albert
chided, "Oh, you wouldn't *see* them, Robin."
   "I don't expect to see them," I snarled. "But where could
they hide?"
   He shrugged. "If I were forced to speculate," he said, "why,
I would try to put myself in their place. Where could I hide if
I wanted to stow away on the *True Love* without being seen?
It would not be difficult. We have a great deal of stored data
here. There are thousands of files that we haven't opened. Any
one of them might have a couple of stowaways—or a thousand
of them. I mean, assuming the concept of 'number' of individuals has any meaning to what may well be a collective intelligence. Robin," he said seriously, "I do not think that creatures capable of reversing the expansion of the universe can
be discounted lightly. If I can think of one place to hide—in
the programs for penetrating black holes, for example, or in
some of the subroutines for translating, say, Polish into Heechee—believe me, they will no doubt be able to think of thousands. I would not even assume they were destroyed on Tahiti
simply because you—" He stopped and cleared his throat,
glancing apologetically at me.
   "Go on," I growled. "You don't have to worry about reminding me that I died. I haven't forgotten."
   He shrugged. "At any rate," he finished, "as to whether

some of them are watching us right now, we simply have no evidence at all.''

''So we search the ship!'' shouted General Cassata, who had been listening without talking for a long time. ''Mrs. Broadhead, most of these programs are yours, aren't they? Fine! You tell us what to do, and—''

She was looking at Albert as she said, ''Moment, please, General. Tricky weird program has not finished its fooling-around report, I think.''

''Thank you, Mrs. Broadhead.'' Albert beamed. ''Perhaps you have forgotten the other main heading in my brief synoptic report. 'The dog did not bark.' ''

I couldn't help laughing. ''Oh, hell, Albert,'' I said, ''you'll be the death of me, with your silly literary references. What's that, Sherlock Holmes? Meaning the important thing is that something did *not* happen? And what something is that?''

''Why, simply that we're still here, Robin,'' he said, smiling approvingly at me for my sagacity.

I stopped laughing. I did not think I understood him exactly, and was afraid that perhaps I did.

''That is to say,'' he amplified, comfortably sucking on his pipe, ''although we must assume that the Foe have been able to roam more or less at will around the Galaxy for some time, and although they certainly have the capacity to wipe out entire civilizations at will, since they have done so in the past, and although we have no effective way known to me of interfering with this if they should choose to do it—we have not been wiped out.''

I was sitting straight up by then, and laughter was nowhere in my feelings. ''Go on!'' I barked.

He looked mildly surprised. ''Why, Robin,'' he said peaceably, ''I think the conclusion follows rather inescapably from all of that.''

''Maybe they just haven't gotten around to it,'' I said—or whimpered; because, to be truthful, I was no longer feeling even as good as I had when the discussion began.

''Yes, that's possible,'' he said solemnly, sucking on his pipe.

"Then, for God's sake," I yelled, "what the hell have you got to look cheerful about?"

He said gently, "Robin, I know this is upsetting to you, but do try to think it out logically. If they have the intention of wiping us out and we have no way of preventing it, then what is there for us to do? Nothing at all; it is a fruitless hypothesis, because it does not lead to any useful course of action. I prefer the opposite assumption."

"Which is what?"

"That they have, at least, reserved decision," he said. "That at some future point we may be able to take some action we don't yet know about. Until then, I think we might as well just relax and enjoy ourselves, don't you, Mrs. Broadhead?"

"Wait a God-damned *minute*," I yelled. "What kind of future action are we talking about? Why are we going out to the kugelblitz, anyway? You don't for one moment think that one of *us* is going to try to get into the kugelblitz and *talk* to these—"

I stopped. They were all looking at me with an expression I recognized.

I had seen it a long, long time ago, on the Gateway asteroid. It was the kind of look the other prospectors gave you after you had signed up for a mission that might make you rich and was a lot more likely to kill you dead. But I didn't even remember volunteering.

We had at that point, I guess, been on the way for maybe an hour or so, meat time; and already it had been a long, long trip.

See, although all this was— was— I guess the only way I can say it is, was a great pain in the ass, it wasn't unique in human history.

Human beings had gotten out of the habit of long travel times, that's all. We had to learn about them all over again.

Our ancestors of a couple of centuries back wouldn't have had that problem. They knew all about the relationship between space and time long before Albert Einstein. Go a long space, take a long time. That was the rule. It wasn't until jet airplanes came in that people began to forget it. (And had to remember again when they started into space.) Think of Admiral Nelson playing one last game of bowls before getting into his ship to meet the Spanish Armada. Napoleon invading Russia like a package tour, with a dinner, a ball, and an entertainment at every night's stop—oh, that was the way to fight a war! Old ways were best. When Alexander the Great came out of Macedonia to conquer the world, it wasn't any blitzkrieg. He took his time. He stopped off here to sit out the winter, there to set up a puppet government, this other place to get some lovely local lady pregnant—often enough, hanging around until the baby was born. If you've been in a battle and then are sitting around your troop transport to dawdle toward the next one, you've got a weird, unreal time in between.

We weren't fighting a war, exactly. At least, we hoped we weren't. But we were on our way to something just as decisive and dangerous, and, oh!, did we have time! Do you know how long fifty days is? It is roughly 4,000,000,000 milliseconds, and we spent them the way our distinguished predecessors did. We feasted, feted, and fucked our way across the Galaxy.

We did it in all the style of any Napoleon or Alexander, too, because Albert Einstein has great resources. He provided us with some of the neatest surrounds I have ever seen. For hours Essie and I hid away from our traveling companions, sunbathing and snorkeling on the Great Barrier Reef. We dragged ourselves out of the soft, salt shallows onto a quarter-hectare sand island, where we made love in a shady silk tent with its skirts raised to let the breezes through. There was a bar and a picnic table and a hot freshwater Jacuzzi, and that's how we passed the first "day."

Then we could face our traveling companions and reality—for a while. And when that began to get stale, Albert came up with a grape arbor in an oasis in the Big Sandy of Peggys Planet. It was on the side of a fault escarpment. Ice-cold springs trickled down the rock face. White grapes, black grapes and red, plums and berries, melons and peaches grew all around. We lay talking and touching under the leafy shade of the vines overhead, Essie and I, and so passed another fine "day."

We hardly thought of where we were going at all . . . for moments at a time.

Albert's infinite variety kept turning up wonderful surrounds. A tree house in an African forest, with lions and elephants sliding silently among the trees below at night. A houseboat on an Indian lake, with turbaned servants bringing us flowery-fresh sherbets and spicy tidbits of lamb and pastry, among the water lilies. A penthouse a hundred stories over Chicago, looking out at thunderclouds strobing the wide lake with lightning. A night in Rio at Carnival time, and another in New Orleans for the Mardi Gras. A hoverplatform vibrating restlessly on the crater rim of the planet Persephone's Mount Hell, with boiling lava fountains reaching up almost to where we sat. Albert had a million of them, and they were all good.

What wasn't quite so good was me.

Said Essie, panting and regarding me critically as she hoisted herself up the last half-meter to sit on a ledge over the Grand Canyon, "Is all right everything, my Robin?"

"Everything is *fine*," I said, voice as firm as it was false.

"Ah," she said, nodding. "Ha," she added, studying me closely. "Is enough sightseeing for now, I think. All play, no work has made Robin dull boy. Albert! Where are you?"

"I'm right here, Mrs. Broadhead," said Albert, leaning over the lip of the canyon to look down on us.

Essie squinted up at his friendly face, outlined against the bright, simulated Arizona sky. "Do you think," she said, "can find us setting less, ah, epicene and, uh, sybaritic for dear husband who is capable of doing anything but nothing at all?"

"I certainly can," said Albert. "In fact, I was about to suggest that we give up the simulated surrounds for a while. I think it might be interesting to spend a little more time with our guests on the *True Love*. After all, I'm afraid they're getting a little bored by now, too."

Over all the millions of milliseconds I have experienced, I've spent time with a lot of people and some of them were Heechee. This time with Double-Bond was special.

What was special about this time was that there was so *much* of it. Soothed by all those long days of beachcombing (and mountain-climbing and scuba-diving and even dirt-car racing) with Essie, I was ready to get serious.

So was Double-Bond. "I hope," he said courteously, the muscles on the backs of his skinny hands rippling in apology, "that you will forgive me for stowing away on your ship, Robinette Broadhead. It was Thermocline's suggestion. He is very wise."

"I'm sure he is," I said, repaying courtesy with courtesy, "but who's Thermocline, exactly?"

"He is one of the other Heechee representatives on the Joint Assassin Watch System council," said Double-Bond, and Julio Cassata put in:

"And a royal pain in the ass he is, too." He was smiling as he said it, and I looked at him curiously. That had been a very Cassata thing to say, but he hadn't said it in a Cassata way. Not only that, but he wasn't even behaving in a Cassata fashion. He was sitting next to Alicia Lo, and they were holding hands.

Double-Bond took the remark in a friendly spirit. "We have had differences, yes. Very often with you, General Cassata, or at least with your organic original."

"Old Blood-and-Slaughter Cassata," said his copy, grinning. "You Heechee don't like it when we talk about blowing up the kugelblitz."

Indeed they didn't. Double-Bond's neck tendons tensed; it was the equivalent of a human shudder. Albert cleared his throat and said peaceably, "Double-Bond, there is something I have had on my mind for some time. Perhaps you can help clear it up."

"With great pleasure," said the Heechee.

"While you were still organic, you were one of the great authorities on the Sluggard planet. I wonder. Do you remember well enough to be able to show us some of the Sluggard material visually?"

"No, I do not remember," said Double-Bond, smiling (it was a Heechee smile, the cheek muscles squeezing up against the huge, pink eyeballs). "However, we have incorporated some of your own storage systems into our fans and, yes, I do have a selection of such material available."

"I thought you did," said Albert, meaning, of course, that he had known that was so all along. "Let me show you something first. When we were on the JAWS satellite, we visited the Voodoo Pigs. Mrs. Broadhead and I had a similar notion. Do you remember?" he asked, looking at me.

"Sure," I said, because Albert had displayed the Voodoo Pig muck before us, all but the smell. One of the pigs was nibbling away industriously at one of their voodoo dolls, or whatever they were, and in the foreground was one of the little figures itself, washed clean of filth and slop. "Essie said something funny. Alicia Lo said she thought they were dolls, just to play with, and then you said—what was it you said, Essie?"

She said, "Visitors."

She said it in a voice that was half argumentative, as though she thought she would be challenged, and half—well—*scared*. Albert nodded. "Exactly, Mrs. Broadhead. Visitors. Aliens to the planet. This was a logical deduction, since all the figures were the same, and quite detailed, and there was nothing like that ever on that planet to use as a model."

"They're probably extinct," I said offhandedly. "Maybe the Voodoo Pigs ate them all."

Albert gave me one of those tolerant fatherly looks. "It would be more likely, to judge from their appearance, that they would have eaten the Voodoo Pigs. Indeed, I suspect perhaps they may have, but that's not what I am driving at. Trust me, Robin, those creatures were never indigenous to the planet of the Voodoo Pigs. I believe Double-Bond will agree."

"That is true," said Double-Bond politely. "We made extensive paleontological investigations. They were not native."

"Therefore," Albert began.

Essie finished for him. "Therefore was right! Visitors! Creatures from another planet, left such an impression on pigs, have been carving voodoo dolls to keep them away ever since."

"Yes," said Albert, nodding, "something like that, I think. Now, Double-Bond—"

But the Heechee was ahead of him, too. "I believe you now wish to see the creatures that attacked the Sluggards." He waited politely for Albert to dismiss his own construct, then substituted a new one. It was a Sluggard arcology, and it was being destroyed. Creatures the size of great blue whales, but with squidlike tentacles that held weapons, were systematically blowing it apart.

"The simulation," said Double-Bond regretfully, "is only very approximate, but it is probably correct in its gross features. The weapons are quite well documented. The lack of limbs, other than the tentacles, is highly probable; the Sluggards would not have failed to note arms or legs, since their own anatomy has neither."

"And the size?" said Albert.

"Oh, yes," said Double-Bond, shaking his wrists affirmatively, "that is quite definite. The relative sizes of the Assassins and the Sluggards are well established."

"And they are much bigger than the Voodoo Pigs," said Albert. "Assuming the dolls they made are of creatures about their own size, they could not be the same creatures."

Alicia Lo stirred. "But I thought—" She hesitated. "I thought the Foe were the only other space-traveling race there was."

"Yes," said Albert, nodding.

I looked at him, waiting. He stopped there. I said, "Come on, Albert! Yes, they were, or yes, everybody thought so because everybody else was dumber than you are?"

He said, "I don't really know, Robin. I'll tell you what I think, though. I think neither the creatures that nearly destroyed the Sluggards nor the creatures that the Voodoo Pigs keep depicting were actually space travelers. I think they were brought there."

Said Double-Bond, "I also think that, Albert. I believe that the Assassins were not actually Assassins. That is, they themselves did not physically attack other races, though perhaps they transported the beings who did. For this reason I like better the name you call them by: the Foe. It is more accurate, I think," he said, looking at Albert.

But Albert did not respond.

————

Guests are no trouble at all when they don't have to be fed and their bed linen doesn't have to be changed. I discovered, to my surprise, that I actually liked having Alicia Lo around, besotted though she seemed to be with a man I had little use for. What was even more surprising was that Cassata himself seemed to be coming almost close to being nearly tolerable. For one thing, he hardly ever wore the uniform anymore. That is, I didn't think he did. Most of the time I had no idea what he wore, doubted actually that he was wearing much at all, because he and Alicia were off in some private surround of their own. But when we were all together he was generally wearing something casual, shorts and a tank top, a safari suit, once elegant in white tie and tails. (Alicia was wearing a shimmery, sequiny evening dress at the time, so I assumed it was some private joke between them—but, you know, that was a little surprising, too, because I'd never thought of Cassata as being the kind of man who bothered with tender, private jokes.)

But, as Albert might have said, thermal equilibrium was maintained. Because as Julio Cassata became more bearable, I became more restless, itchy, ill at ease . . . yes, gloopy.

I tried to hide it. Waste of time; who can hide anything from my dear Portable-Essie? Finally she confronted me. "You want to talk about it?" she demanded. I tried to give her a bright smile. It turned itself into a morose shrug. "Not to me, dammit. To Albert."

"Ah, honey," I objected, "what about?"

"*I* don't know what about. Maybe Albert will know what about. Have nothing to lose, you know."

"Nothing at all," I said, meaning to agree—meaning also to give a sort of sardonic agreement, maybe with a twitch of the eyebrows; but the look I got back discouraged me. I said hastily, "I'll do it. Albert!"

And when Albert appeared, I just sat and looked at him.

He patiently looked back, puffing on his pipe, waiting for me to speak. Essie had taken herself away out of courtesy— I *wanted* to think it was courtesy, and not contempt or boredom. So we just sat for a while, and then it occurred to me that, indeed, there was something I wanted to talk to him

about. "Albert," I said, pleased to have a topic of conversation, "what's it like?"

"What's what like, Robin?"

"To be where you were before you were here, I mean," I
said. "What's it like to, you know, dissolve? When I tell you
to go away for a while. When you're not doing anything. When
you go back to being part of the gigabit store. When you stop
being, well, *you*, and just be a bunch of distributed bits and
pieces floating around in the great electronic bin of building-
block parts."

Albert didn't groan. He only looked as though he wanted
to. He said with patience sticking out all over him, "I have
told you, I think, that when I am not actively programmed to
be your data-retrieval source, the various bits of memory that
the 'Albert Einstein' program employs exist in the common
store. Of course, the common store in the *True Love* is much
smaller than that in the world's gigabit net, though still quite
large and performing many functions. Is that what you're talking about?"

"That's it, Albert. What does it feel like?"

He pulled out his pipe, which was the sign that he was thinking it over. "I don't know if I can tell you that, Robin."

"Why not?"

"Because the question is wrongly put. You presuppose that
there is a 'me' who can 'feel' what it is like. There isn't a 'me'
when my parts are distributed to other tasks. For that matter,
there isn't a 'me' now."

"But I see you," I said.

"Oh, Robin," he sighed, "we've had these discussions so
many times before, haven't we? You're simply dodging around
some real issue that concerns you. If I were your psychoanalytic program, I would ask you to—"

"You're not," I said, smiling but feeling the smile grow tight,
"so don't. Let's do it over again. This time I'll try to stay with
you. You know. Go back to where I say, 'But I see you,' and
then you tell me about Niagara Falls again."

He gave me a look that was part exasperation and part concern. I understood both very clearly. I know Albert is often

exasperated with me, but I know even better that he cares a lot about me. He said, "Very well, we'll play your game again. You see 'me' in the sense that you see a waterfall. If you look at Niagara Falls today, and come back a week later and look at it again, you will think you're seeing the same waterfall. In fact, not one atom of the waterfall is the same. The waterfall exists only because it is constrained to do so by the laws of hydraulics, surface tension, and Newton's laws, as they bear on the fact that one body of water is at a higher elevation than another. I appear to you only because I am constrained to do so by the rules of the 'Albert Einstein' program written for you by your wife, S. Ya. Lavorovna-Broadhead. The water molecules are not Niagara Falls. They are only what Niagara Falls is made of. The bytes and bits that allow me to function when my program is activated are not me. Have you understood that? Because, if so, you will then see that it is pointless to ask how I feel when I am not 'me,' because then there is no 'me' to feel anything. Now," he said, leaning forward earnestly, "suppose you tell me what you yourself are feeling that brings this on, Robin."

I thought it over. Listening to him talk in that soft, sweet accent of his had been soothing, and so it took me a moment to remember what the answer was.

Then I remembered, and I was lulled no more. I said: "Scared."

He pursed his lips as he regarded me. "Scared. I see. Robin, can you tell me what frightens you?"

"Well, which of the four or five hundred—"

"No, no, Robin. The *top* thing."

I said, "I'm just a program, too."

"Ah," he said, "I see." He dumped his pipe, regarding me. "I think I understand," he qualified. "Because you too are machine-stored, you think whatever happens to me might happen to you."

"Or worse."

"Oh, Robin," he said, shaking his head, "you worry about so many things. You are afraid, I think, that somehow you will forget and turn yourself off. Is that it? And then you can never get yourself together again? But, Robin, that can't happen."

"I don't believe you," I said.

That stopped him, at least for a moment.

Methodically and slowly, Albert refilled his pipe, struck a match on the sole of his foot, lit it, and puffed thoughtfully, never taking his eyes off me. He didn't answer.

Then he shrugged.

Albert almost never leaves me until I let him know I want him to, but it looked to me as though he had that in mind. "Don't go away," I said.

"All right, Robin," he said, looking surprised.

"Talk to me some more. It's been a long trip, and I'm getting kind of irritable, I guess."

"Oh, are you?" he asked, arching his brows; it was as close to judgmental as Albert usually gets. Then he said, "You know, Robin, you don't have to remain awake for all of it. Would you like to power down until we get there?"

"No!"

"But Robin, it's nothing to worry about. When you're in standby mode it's just as though no time at all were passing. Ask your wife."

"No!" I said again. I didn't even want to discuss it; standby mode sounded very much like that other mode they call "dead." "No, I just want to talk for a while. I think—I really think," I said, full of the new idea that had just occurred to me, "that this would be a good time for me to let you tell me about nine-dimensional space."

For the second time in a few milliseconds Albert gave me that look—not astonished, exactly, but at least skeptical.

"You want me to explain nine-dimensional space to you," he repeated.

"You bet, Albert."

He studied me carefully through the pipe smoke. "Well," he said, "I can see that just the idea perks you up a little. Probably you figure you'll have some pleasure out of making fun of me—"

"Who, me, Albert?" I grinned.

"Oh, I don't mind if you do. I'm just trying to understand what the ground rules will be."

"The ground rules," I said, "is that you tell me all about it. If I get tired of it, I'll let you know. So start, please. 'Nine-dimensional space is—' and then you fill in the blanks."

He looked pleased, if still skeptical. "We should take these long trips more often," he commented. "Anyway, that's not the way to start. This is the way: First we consider normal three-dimensional space, the kind you grew up in, or thought you were growing up in, when you were still meat—what, already?"

I had my hand up. I said, "I thought that was four-dimensional. What about the dimension of time?"

"That's four-dimensional space-*time*, Robin. I'm trying to make it simple for you, so let's stick to three dimensions at first. I'll give you an illustration. Suppose, for instance, that when you were a young man sitting with your girlfriend watching a PV show, you just happened to put your arm around her. The first thing you do is stretch your arm across the back of the couch—that's the first dimension, call it breadth. Then you crook your elbow at a right angle, so your forearm is pointing forward and resting on her shoulder—that's the second dimension, which we will call length. Then you drop your hand onto her breast. That's depth. The third dimension."

"That's depth, all right, because I'm getting in pretty deep by then." I grinned.

He sighed and ignored the remark. "You comprehend the image. You have so far demonstrated the three spatial dimensions. There is also, as you pointed out, the dimension of time: Five minutes ago your hand was not there, now it is, at some time in the future it will be elsewhere again. So if you want to specify the coordinates of any familiar system, you must add that dimension in, too. The three-dimensional 'where' and the fourth-dimensional 'when'; that's space-time."

I said patiently, "I'm waiting for you to get to the part where it turns out that all this stuff that I already know is wrong."

"I will, Robin, but to get to the hard part I have to make

sure you have the easy part under control. Now we get to the hard part. It involves supersymmetry."

"Oh, good. Are my eyes beginning to glaze over?"

He peered inquiringly into my face, just as solemnly as though I really had eyes and he had something to peer at them with. He's a good sport, Albert is. "Not yet," he said, pleased. "I'll try not to glaze them. 'Supersymmetry' sounds terrible, I know, but it is just the name given to a mathematical model which fairly satisfactorily describes the main features of the universe. It includes or is related to things like 'supergravity' and 'string theory' and 'archeocosmology.'" He peered at me again. "Still not glazed? All right. Now we start to understand the implications of those words. The implications are easier than the words are. These are pretty good fields of study. Taken together, they explain the behavior of both matter and energy in all their manifestations. More than that. They don't just *explain* them. The laws of supersymmetry and the others actually *drive* the behavior of all things. By that I mean that, from these laws, the observed behavior of everything that makes up the universe follows logically. Even inevitably."

"But—"

He was in full course; he waved me down. "Stay with it," he commanded. "These are *basic*. If the early Greeks had understood supersymmetry and its related subjects, they could have *deduced* Newton's laws of motion and universal gravitation, and Planck and Heisenberg's quantum rules, and even—" he twinkled "—my own relativity theory, both special and general. They would not have had to experiment and observe. They could have known that all these other things *must* be true, because they *followed*, just as Euclid knew that his geometry must be true because everything followed from the general laws."

"But it didn't!" I cried, surprised. "Did it? I mean, you've told me about non-Euclidean geometry—"

He paused, looking thoughtful. "That's the catch," he admitted. He looked at his pipe and discovered that it was out, so methodically he began tapping it empty again while he talked. "Euclidean geometry is not untrue, it is simply true only in the special case of a flat, two-dimensional surface. There aren't any of those in the real world. There's a catch in supersymmetry, too. The catch there is that it, too, is untrue in the real world—or at least the world of three-dimensional space we perceive. For supersymmetry to work, nine dimensions are required, and we can only observe three. What happened to the other six?"

I said with pleasure, "I don't have the faintest idea, but you're doing this a lot better than usual. I'm not lost yet."

"I've had a lot a practice," he said dryly. "I've got good news for you, too. I could demonstrate to you mathematically why nine dimensions are necessary—"

"Oh, *no*."

"No, of course not," he agreed. "The good news is that I don't have to in order to let you understand the rest of it."

"I'm grateful."

"I'm sure." He lit his pipe again. "Now, about the missing six dimensions . . . " He puffed for a while, thoughtfully. "If nine spatial dimensions had to exist in order for the universe to be formed as it is in the first place, why can we find only three now?"

"Does it have something to do with entropy?" I hazarded.

Albert looked aghast. "Entropy? Certainly not. How could it?"

"Well, with Mach's Hypothesis, then? Or some of the other things you were talking about in Deep Time?"

He said reprovingly, "Don't guess, Robin. You're just making it harder than it is. What happened to the other dimensions? They just disappeared."

Albert gazed at me happily, puffing his pipe with as much satisfaction as though he had explained something significant.

I waited for him to go on. When he didn't, I began to feel nettled. "Albert, I know you like to tweak me every now and then just to keep my interest up, but what the hell is 'they just disappeared' supposed to mean?"

He chuckled. He was having a good time, I could see that. He said, "They disappeared from our perception, at least. That doesn't mean they were *extinguished*. It probably just means that they got very *small*. They shriveled up to where they just weren't visible anymore."

I looked at him with outrage. "Can you explain how a dimension can just shrivel up?"

He smiled at me. "Fortunately not," he said. "I say 'fortunately' because, if I could, it would probably get very mathematical, and then you'd be cutting me off right here. However, I can shed a little bit of light on what probably happened, anyway. By 'shrivel up,' I mean they just don't register anymore. Let me give you an illustration. Think of a point—say, the tip of your nose—"

"Oh, come on, Albert! We already did three-dimensional space!"

"The tip of your *nose*," he repeated. "Relate that point to some other point, say your Adam's apple. Your nose is so many millimeters *up*, and so many millimeters *out*, and so many millimeters *across*—that is to say, you specify its location on the *x, y,* and *z* axes. When we talk about nine-dimensional space instead of three, you can also say that it is at a specific point on the *p, d, q, r, w,* and *k* axes—or whatever letters you want to use to specify them—*but*." He took a deep breath. "*But* you don't have to specify those coordinates for any normal purpose, because the distances are so small they don't signify. That's it, Robin! Got it so far?"

I said happily, "I almost think so."

"Fine," he said, "because that's almost right. It isn't quite as simple as that. Those missing six dimensions—they're not only small, they're *curved*. They're like little circles. Like little coiled-up spirals. They don't go any*where*. They just go *around*."

He stopped there, sucking his pipe and gazing approvingly at me.

He was twinkling again. There was something about the look in those guileless eyes that made me ask, "Albert, one question. Is all this stuff you've been telling me true?"

He hesitated. Then he shrugged. "'Truth,'" he said weightily, "is a really heavy word. I'm not ready to talk about reality yet, and that's what you mean by 'true.' This is a model that explains things very, very well. It may as well be taken as 'true,' at least until a better model comes along. But, unfortunately, if you remember,'' he said, perking up the way he always does when he gets a chance to quote from himself, "as my meat original said long ago, mathematics is most 'true' when it is least 'real,' and vice versa. There are many elements I have not characterized here. We have not yet considered the implications of string theory, or of Heisenberg's uncertainty principle, or—''

"Give it a rest, please,'' I begged.

"I gladly will, Robin,'' he said, "because you've been very good about all this. I appreciate your listening. Now there is some hope of your understanding the Foe and, more important, the basic structure of the universe.''

"More important!'' I repeated.

He smiled. "In an objective sense, oh, yes, Robin. It is much more important to know than to do, and it doesn't much matter who does the knowing.''

I got up and walked around. It seemed we'd been talking for a very long time, and then it occurred to me that that was good, because that was exactly what I wanted. I said, "Albert? How long did this little lecture of yours take?''

"You mean in galactic time? Let me see, yes, a little under four minutes." And he saw my face and hurriedly added, "But we're nearly a third of the way, Robin! Only a couple more weeks and we'll be at the Watch Wheel!''

"A couple of *weeks*.''

He looked at me with concern. "There is still the option of powering down . . . No, of course not,'' he said, watching my face. He looked irresolute for a moment, then he made up his mind. In a different tone he said, "Robin? When we were talking about what it is like for 'me' when I am not in being as your program, you said you didn't believe me. I'm afraid you were justified. I have not been entirely truthful with you.''

Nothing he ever said shocked me more. "Albert!'' I yelped. "You haven't lied to me? You *can't*!''

He said apologetically, "That's correct, Robin, I have never lied to you. But there are truths I haven't said."

"You mean you do feel something when you're turned off?"

"No. I told you that. There's no 'me' to feel."

"Then what, for God's sake?"

"There are things I do—experience—that you never have, Robin. When I am merged into another program, I *am* that program. Or him. Or her." He twinkled. "Or they."

"But you're not the same you anymore?"

"No, that's true. Not the same. But . . . perhaps . . . something better."

17
At the Throne

And time passed, and time passed, and the endless voyage went on.

I did everything there was to do.

Then I did it twice. Then I did it some more. Then I even began to think seriously about Albert's notion of a few weeks in standby mode, and that scared me enough to make Essie take notice.

She wrote a prescription for me. "Will have," Essie announced, "a party," and when Essie tells you you're going to have a party, you might as well relax and enjoy it.

That doesn't mean that that is what I did. Not right away, anyhow. I was not in a party mood. I hadn't got over the shock of my "death" in the house on Tahiti. I hadn't quite nerved myself up to confront the prospect of meeting more of those Assassin creatures—*millions* more of them—and on their home ground, at that. Hell, I hadn't even got all the way over everything else that had ever happened to me in my life, from my nasty little mental breakdown when I was a kid, through my mother's death and Klara's wreck in the black hole right up to the present moment. Everybody's life is full of tragedies, disasters, and lousy breaks. You keep on living it because now and then there are good times that make up for it, or at least you hope they will, but, my God, the number of miseries we all go through! And when you live so much longer, not only longer but in my case *faster*, you just multiply the bad things. "Grizzly grouch," laughed Essie, planting a big kiss on my mouth, "cheer up, wake up, have a good time, what the hell, because tomorrow we die, right? Or maybe not, you know."

She is a living doll, my Essie is. All of her. The meat one that was the model and the portable one who shares my life, and let's not get into any tricky debates about what I mean by "living."

So I did my best to smile, and, to my astonishment, I made it. And then I looked around me.

Whatever Essie had said to Albert about the luxurious surrounds he had been providing for us, she didn't mean to let such strictures cramp her own style. Her ideas of a party have changed a lot since we've been machine-stored. In the old days we could do pretty much anything we liked, because we were filthy rich. Now it's even better. There is just about *nothing* that would give us pleasure that we can't do. Not after we've got on a plane or a spaceship to get there. Not after we've invited a bunch of people to join us and waited for them to arrive. What we want to do we do *right now*, and we don't even have to worry about hangovers, harm to others, or getting fat.

So, to start, Essie provided us with a party room.

It wasn't anything outrageous. Actually, if we'd wanted one like it when we were still meat people, we could easily have had it. Probably it wouldn't have cost more than a million dollars or so. Neither Essie nor I had ever had a ski lodge, but we'd been in a couple, at one time or another, and liked the combination of the huge ceiling-high fireplace at one end, and the bear- and moosehead trophies on the wall, and the dozen many-paned windows along the walls with the snowy mountains crisp in the sunlight outside, and the comfortable chairs and couches and tables with fresh flowers and— And, I realized, a lot of things neither she nor I had ever seen in any ski lodge. There was a wine fountain on a table by the windows, and it was bubbling champagne. (The only way you could tell that it wasn't "real" champagne was that it never lost its bubbles.) Next to the champagne fountain was a long buffet table with white-jacketed waiters standing by to fill our plates. I saw a carved turkey and a ham, and hollowed-out fresh pineapples filled with kiwi fruit and cherries. I looked at it, and I looked at Essie. "Smoked oysters?" I ventured.

"God, Robin," she said in disgust, "of *course* smoked oysters! Not to mention caviar for me and Albert, and ribs for old Julio and dim sum for his girl, and whole big bucket of crummy stuff you like so much, what is it, tuna-fish salad." She clapped her hands. The leader of the little band on the dais at the far end of the room nodded, and they began to play that gentle nostalgic stuff our grandparents went crazy over. "Eat first or dance?" asked Essie.

I made the effort. I played up to her. "What do you think?" I asked in my sexiest and most vibrant movie-star voice, looking deeply into her eyes, with my hand cupped firm and strong on her bare shoulder, because of course by then she was wearing a low-cut evening dress.

"Think eat, dear Robin," she sighed, "but don't forget, dance soon, and often!"

And, you know, it turned out not to be all that much of an effort. There was all the tuna-fish salad I could ever hope to eat, and the waiter piled it high on slices of rye bread and squashed it flat to make a sandwich, just the way I liked. The champagne was perfectly chilled, and the bubbles (nonexistent though they were) pleasingly tickled my (nonexistent) nose. While we were eating, Albert cavalierly waved the orchestra off the stand and pulled out a violin and entertained us with a little unaccompanied Bach, a little solo Kreisler, and then, as members of the band started to come back to join him, wound up with a couple of Beethoven string quartets.

Now, you know, none of the other players that made up his chamber-music group were "real"—I mean, not even as real as we were. They were only quite limited programs taken out of Albert's stock of surround furnishings, but for what they were, they did very well. The good food and the great champagne weren't real either. But they tasted just as good going down. The onions in the tuna fish satisfactorily reminded me of themselves every now and then afterward, and the unreal alcohol in the simulated champagne activated my motion and sensory centers just as much and in just the same way as the real things would have done to the real things—what I'm trying to tell you is, the drinking and dancing and eating were doing their work and I was getting horny. And when Essie and I were dreamily circling the floor (the unreal sun had "set" and the "stars" were bright above the dark "mountain") and her head was on my shoulder and my fingers were gently kneading her soft, sweet back, I could feel that she was in a real receptive mood.

As I led her off the floor in the general direction of where, I was sure, she would have provided a bedroom, Albert looked up to wave a fond good-bye. He and General Cassata were chatting by the fire, and I heard Albert say, "That little impromptu minstrel show of mine, General. I was only trying to cheer Robin up, you know. I hope I didn't offend you."

General Cassata looked puzzled. He scratched his chocolate-colored cheekbone, just next to his close-cropped woolly sideburn, and said, "I don't know what you're talking about, Albert. Why would I be offended?"

I don't have to have a real body or real food to eat, I don't have to have a real chair to sit. I don't have to have any of the things you generally require to make love, either, and we did what we did with finesse, devotion, and a whole lot of fun. Simulated? Well, sure it was simulated. But it felt just as good

as it ever had, which was *fine*, and when it was over my simulated heart was pounding a little faster and my breath was
coming in simulated pants and I wrapped my arm around my
love and pulled her close to soak in the simulated smell and
feel and warmth of her.

"Am so glad," said my simulated darling drowsily, "that I
made our programs interactive."

She tickled my ear with her breath. I turned my head enough
to tickle hers. "My dearest Essie," I whispered, "you write
one hell of a program."

"Could not have done it without you," she said, and yawned
sleepily into the satin pillow. (We do sleep sometimes, you
know. We don't have to. We don't have to eat or make love,
either, but there are a lot of pleasures that we don't have to
have but have anyway, and one that I have always cherished
is that last few minutes when your head is on the pillow and
you're just about to drift off, warm, secure, and worrying about
nothing in the universe at all.)

I was kind of sleepy, because that was part of the whole
subroutine. But I knew I could shake it off if I chose, because
that's part of the subroutine, too.

And I did choose. Just for a moment, anyway, I thought,
because there were, after all, a few things on my mind. I said,
"I recognize the bed, honey."

She giggled. "Nice bed," she commented. She didn't deny
what I knew, that it was an exact, or maybe even somewhat
improved, copy of the anisokinetic bed we'd had in Rotterdam
years and years ago.

But that wasn't exactly what I wanted to talk about, so I
tried again. "Honey? Do you think there were just two Foe
in there with me? In the room in Tahiti, I mean?"

Essie lay silent a moment. Then she gently pulled free of
my arm and got up on one elbow, looking down at me.

She studied me silently for a moment before she said, "Is
no real way for us to tell, is that not so? Albert says may be
collective intelligence; if so, what you saw in Tahiti was only
perhaps quite small detached packets of Foe stuff, numbers in
that case meaningless."

"Uh-huh."

Essie sighed and rolled over. Through the closed door we could hear the music from the other room; they were playing old-fashioned rock now, probably for General Cassata's benefit. She sat up, naked as the day we first made love, and clapped her fingertips together for light. Light came, gentle, amber lights from concealed fixtures in the ceiling, for Essie had spared nothing in furnishing our little haven.

"Are still upset, dear Robin," she commented neutrally.

I thought it over. "I guess so," I said, as a first approximation to what would be a much more emphatic description if I had chosen to give it.

"You want talk?"

"I want," I said, suddenly wide awake, "to be *happy*. Why the hell does it have to be so God-damned hard?"

Essie reached over and brushed my forehead with her lips. "I see," she said. She didn't say anything else.

"Well, what I mean," I went on after a moment, "is I don't know what's going to happen."

"Have never known that, have we?"

"And maybe that," I said, a lot louder than I had intended, and maybe a lot nastier, "is why I've never been *happy*."

To that I got a silence. When you're talking in the megabaud range, even a twentieth of a millisecond is a significant pause, and this was a lot longer than that. Then Essie got up, picked up a robe from beside the bed, and pulled it on.

"Dear Robin," she said, sitting on the edge of the bed and looking at me. "Think maybe this long trip is quite bad for you. Gives you too much time to be gloopy in."

"But we didn't have any choice, did we? And that's part of it: I never have any choice!"

"Ah," she said, nodding. "We get to heart of question. Fine. Open up. Tell me what is matter."

I didn't answer her. I gave her the electronic equivalent of a sniff of exasperation. She didn't deserve it, of course. She had been going far out of her way to be loving and kind, and there was no reason for me to be getting unpleasant.

But unpleasant was how I felt.

"Tell me, dammit!" she barked.

I barked back: "Oh, hell! You ask some dumb questions, you know that? I mean, you are the truest of true loves and I adore you and all, but—but—but, *Jesus*, Essie, how can you ask a question like that? What's the matter? You mean, outside of the fact that the whole universe is at risk, and I died a while ago—again!—and I might very likely die again pretty soon, only this time forever, because I have to go up against some people I don't even want to think about, and I've got two wives, and I don't really exist, and all that— You mean, outside of that, how did you like the play, Mrs. Lincoln?"

"Oh, Robin," she sighed dismally. "Cannot even add right!"

She took me by surprise. "What?"

"Point one," she said, all brisk and businesslike. "Have not got two wives—unless, of course, count meat original of me separate from me here who has just been most enjoyably making love with you."

"I mean—"

"Know very well what you mean, Robin," she said firmly. "Mean love me and also love Gelle-Klara Moynlin, who keeps showing up every once in while to remind you. Have discussed this before. Is no problem. Have exactly one wife that matters, Robinette Broadhead, namely me, Portable-Essie, S. Ya. Lavorovna-Broadhead, who is not in least jealous of feelings toward Moynlin lady."

"That's not the real—" I began, but she waved me to silence.

"Second," she said firmly, "taking in reverse order—no, taking actually first point as second in present discussion—"

"Essie! You're losing me."

"No," she said, "never lose you, or you me; that is subset of first point, which we will deal with third. Pay attention! As to threat to entire sidereal universe, yes, granted, is so. Is great problem. Is, however, problem with which we are dealing as best we can. Now. Leaves only remaining point, maybe fifth or sixth in original presentation, I forget—"

I had begun to catch the rhythm. "The fact that we don't really exist, you mean," I said helpfully.

"Exactly. Glad are on your toes, Robin. Are not dead, you know; keep making this point. Are merely in fact discorporated, quite something else. Are no longer meat, but are still very much alive. Have just demonstrated that, dammit!"

I said tactfully, "It was wonderful, and I know that what you say is true—"

"No! Don't know it!"

"Well, I know it logically, anyway. Cogito ergo sum, right?"

"Exactly right!"

"The difficulty," I said wretchedly, "is that I just don't seem able to internalize it."

"Ah!" she cried. "Oh! I see! 'Internalize,' is that it? To be sure, *internalize*. First we get Descartes, now get head-shrinker talk. Is blowing smoke, Robin, smokescreen behind which to hide real concerns."

"But don't you see—"

I didn't finish, because she placed her hand on my lips to cut me off.

Then she got up and went to the door. "Robin, dearest person, give you word, I do see." She picked another robe from a chair by the door and rolled it in her hands. "See that it is not me you should be talking to now, but him."

"Him? What him?"

"That psychoanalytic him, Robin. Here. Put this on."

She tossed me the robe, and while I was dazedly doing as I was told, she went out the door, leaving it open, and a moment later in through it came a gentle, sad-looking elderly man.

"Hello, Robin. It's been a long time," said my old head-doctor program, Sigfrid von Shrink.

"Sigfrid," I said, "I didn't ask for you."

He nodded, smiling, as he went around the room. He was drawing blinds, extinguishing lights, making the bedroom less a passion pit and more a reasonably close approximation to his old consulting room.

"I didn't even want you!" I yelled. "And besides, I liked this room just the way it was."

He sat down in a chair by the bed, looking at me. It was almost as though nothing had changed. The bed was no longer a playpen; it was the agony couch I had lain on for so many tormented hours. Sigfrid said comfortably, "Since you are obviously in need of some sort of easing of tensions, Robbie, I thought I might as well reduce the extraneous distractions. It's not important. I can put it back the way it was if you like— but, truly, Rob, it would be more productive if you would tell me about your feelings of unease or worry instead of discussing the way the room is decorated."

So I laughed.

I couldn't help myself. I laughed out loud, big belly-busting laughter that went on for a long time—many microseconds at least—and when I stopped laughing, I wiped my streaming eyes (the laugh was soundless, the tears were nonmaterial, but that didn't matter), and I said:

"You kill me, Sigfrid. You know? You haven't changed a bit."

He smiled and said, "You, on the other hand, have. You have changed very much from that insecure, guilt-ridden, self-doubting young man who did his best to manipulate our sessions like parlor games. You've come a long way, Robin. I'm very pleased with you."

"Aw, shecks," I said, grinning—warily.

"On the other hand," he went on, "in a lot of ways you haven't changed at all. Do you want to spend our time in idle conversation and parlor games? Or would you like to tell me about what's worrying you?"

"Talk about games! You're playing one right now. You know everything I've said already. You probably know everything I've even thought!"

He said seriously, "What I know or don't know doesn't matter. You know that. It's what you know, particularly the things you know but don't want to admit to yourself, that are important. You have to get them out in the open. Start by telling me why you're worried."

I said, "Because I'm a wimp."

He looked at me, and he was smiling. "You don't really believe that, do you?"

"Well, I'm certainly no hero!"

"How do you know that, Robin?" he asked.

"Don't jerk me around! Heroes don't sit and brood! Heroes don't worry about whether they're going to die! Heroes don't get all snarled up in guilt and worries and head-crap, isn't that true?"

"It is true that heroes don't do any of those things," Sigfrid agreed, "but you left one trait out. There's one other thing heroes don't do. Heroes don't exist. Do you really think all those people you call 'heroes' are any better than you are?"

"I don't know if I *believe* it. I sure as hell *hope* it."

"But Robin," he said reasonably, "you really haven't done that badly, have you? You've done what no one else has ever done, not even a Heechee. You've talked with two of the Foe."

"I fucked it up," I said bitterly.

"Do you think that?" Sigfrid sighed. "Robbie, you often simultaneously hold quite contradictory views of yourself. But, given a choice, in the long run you adopt the least flattering one. Why is that? Do you remember that for many sessions, when we first met, you kept telling me what a coward you were?"

"But I was! God, Sigfrid, I stalled around on Gateway for*ever* before I got up the guts to ship out."

"That could be described as cowardice, yes," said Sigfrid. "It is true that that was your behavior. Yet there were other times when you behaved in ways that can only be called extraordinarily brave. When you jumped into a spaceship and headed for the Heechee Heaven, you faced terrible odds. You endangered your life—in fact, you very nearly lost it."

"There was big money involved that time. It made me rich."

"You already were rich, Rob." He shook his head. Then he said thoughtfully, "It is interesting that when you do something praiseworthy, you ascribe venal motives to yourself, but when you do something that appears bad, you jump to agree that the appearances are correct. When do you win, Robin?"

I didn't answer. I didn't have an answer. Maybe I didn't want to look for one. Sigfrid sighed and changed position. "All right," he said. "Let's get back to basics. Tell me why you're worried."

"Why I'm worried?" I cried. "Don't you think I've got plenty to worry about? If you don't think the entire basic universe-wide situation is something to worry any sane person, then maybe you just haven't caught on to what's happening!"

He said, with visible patience, "The Foe certainly are a sufficient cause for worry, yes, but—"

"But if that isn't enough, consider my personal situation! I'm in love with two women—three, actually, I mean," I corrected myself, remembering Essie's arithmetic.

He pursed his lips. "Is that a worry, Robbie? In any practical sense, I mean? For example, do you have to do anything about it—choose among them, for instance? I think not. No reason for conflict exists, really."

And I burst out, "No, you're God-damned right, and do you know *why* no reason for conflict exists? Because *I* don't exist! I'm just a damned datastore in gigabit space. I'm no more real than you are!"

He said mildly, "Do you really think I don't exist?"

"Damn straight you don't! Some computer programmer made you up!"

Sigfrid studied his thumbnail. There was another of those long, multimicrosecond pauses, and then he said, "Tell me, Robinette, what do you mean by 'exist'?"

"You know effing well what it means to exist! It means to be real!"

"I see. Are the Foe real?"

"Of course they're real," I said in disgust. "They weren't ever anything else. They're not copies of something that was real once."

"Ah. All right. Is the law of inverse squares real, Robbie?"

"Call me Robinette, damn it!" I flared. He raised his eyebrows, but nodded. And just sat there, waiting for an answer. I collected my thoughts. "The law of inverse squares, yes, is real. Not in a material sense, but in its ability to describe material events. You can predict its functioning. You can see its effects.''

''But I can see your effects, Robin—Robinette,'' he corrected himself hastily.

''One illusion recognizes another illusion!'' I sneered.

''Yes,'' he conceded, ''one might say that. But others see your effects, too. Was General Beaupre Heimat an illusion? But the two of you certainly interacted, as he would not deny. Are your banks an illusion? They hold your money. The people who work in your employ, the corporations that pay you dividends—they're all quite real, are they not?''

He'd given me time to collect my thoughts. I smiled. ''I think you're the one who's playing games now, Sigfrid. Or else you just miss the point. You see, the trouble with you,'' I said patronizingly, ''is that you've never *been* real, so you don't know the difference. Real people have real problems. Physical problems. Little ones, at least; that's how they know they're real. I don't! In all the years I've been—discorporated—I've never once had to grunt and strain on the toilet because I was constipated. I've never had a hangover, or a runny nose, or a sunburn, or any other of the ills the flesh is heir to.''

He said in exasperation, ''You don't get sick? Is that what you're pissing and moaning about?''

I looked at him in shock. ''Sigfrid, you never used to talk to me like this in the old days.''

''You weren't as healthy as this in the old days! Robinette, I really wonder if this conversation is doing either of us any good. Perhaps I'm not the one you should be talking to.''

''Well,'' I said, beginning almost to enjoy myself, ''at least I've heard you say—oh, Jesus, now what?'' I finished, because I wasn't talking to Sigfrid von Shrink anymore. ''What the hell are you up to now?''

Albert Einstein fumbled with his pipe, leaned over to scratch his bare ankle, and said: ''You see, Robin, perhaps your problem isn't psychoanalytic after all. So perhaps I'd be a better person to handle it.''

I sank back on the bed and closed my eyes.

In those old days when Sigfrid and I went round and round every Wednesday afternoon at four, I sometimes came away thinking I'd scored points in the game I thought we were playing, but I'd never, ever had the experience of having him simply give up. That was a real victory, of a kind I had never expected—and of a kind that made me feel worse than ever. I still felt like hell. If my problem wasn't psychoanalytic, then it was real; and "real," I thought, translated to "insoluble."

I opened my eyes.

Albert had been busy. We weren't in the two-hour adultery special anymore, we were in Albert's plain old Princeton study, with the bottle of Skrip on the desk and the blackboard full of indecipherable mathematics behind him. "Nice place you've got here," I said sourly, "if we're back to playing games again."

"Games are real, too, Robin," he said earnestly. "I hope you don't mind my cutting in. If you were just going to talk about tears and traumas, Dr. von Shrink would have been your best program, but metaphysics is more my line."

"Metaphysics!"

"But that's what you've been talking about, Robin," he said, surprised. "Didn't you know? The nature of reality? The meaning of life? Such things are not my main line, or at least not the subjects for which my name became famous, but I think I can help you, if you don't mind."

"And if I do?"

"Why, then you can dismiss me whenever you like," he said mildly. "Let's at least try."

I got up off the bed—it had become a worn leather couch, with the stuffing sticking out of one cushion—and walked around the study, shrugging one small shrug that meant, all right, what the hell.

"You see," he said, "you can be as real as you want to be, Robin."

I lifted a stack of journals off the chair by his desk and sat down to face him. "Don't you mean I can be as good an imitation as I want to be?"

"We come to the Turing test, maybe? If you are such a good

imitation that you can fool even yourself, isn't that a kind of reality? For instance, if you really want to have things like constipation and the common cold, that's easy enough. Dr. Lavorovna and I can easily write into your program all the minor ills you like, and monte-carlo them so that they appear at random—hemorrhoids today, perhaps, and maybe tomorrow a wart on the side of your nose. I can't believe you'd really want that."

"They'd still be illusions!"

Albert considered the matter, then conceded, "In a certain sense, yes, I suppose they would. But remember the Turing test. Forgive my impertinence, but when you and Dr. Lavorovna are together, don't you sometimes, well, make love?"

"You know damn well we do! We just did!"

"Is it any less pleasurable because it, too, as you would say, is an illusion?"

"It is *extremely* pleasurable. Maybe that's what's wrong with it. Because, damn it, Essie *can't get pregnant.*"

"Ah," he said, just as Essie had done, "oh. Is that really what you want?"

I thought for a moment to be sure. "I don't exactly know. It's something I've thought of wanting, sometimes."

"But it isn't really impossible, you know, Robin. It would not even be very difficult to program. Dr. Lavorovna, if she wished, could surely write a program in which she would experience all the physical aspects of pregnancy, even coming to term. With an actual child, Robin—'actual,' that is, in the sense that you yourself are actual," he added hastily. "But in that same way it could be your and her child. Complete with a monte-carloed assortment of your hereditary traits, with a personality that would develop as you reared it—the product, like all human beings, of nature plus nurture, with a dash of happenstance thrown in."

"And when it grew up to be our age, we'd still be our age!"

"Ah." Albert nodded, satisfied. "We come now to growing old. Is that what you want? Because I should tell you," he went on seriously, "that you will age, Robin. Not because anyone programs you to, but because you must. There will be transcription errors. You will change, and probably you will deteriorate. Oh, you have a great deal of redundancy in your storage, so the errors will not cumulate very quickly, at least not in any large matters. But in infinite time—oh, yes, Robin. The Robinette Broadhead of ten-to-the-twentieth milliseconds from now will not be the same as the Robinette Broadhead of today."

"Oh, *wonderful*," I cried. "I can't die, but I can grow old and feeble and stupid!"

"Do you *want* to die?"

"I . . . don't . . . *know*!"

"I see," said Albert thoughtfully. I covered my face in my hands, as close to crying as I have been for a long time. Every bit of fear and depression and worry and self-doubt was flooding in on me then, and these stupid conversations were doing no good at all!

"I see," said the voice again, but this time it wasn't Albert Einstein's voice. It was deeper and huger, and even before I looked up I knew Whose voice it was.

"Oh, God," I whispered.

"Yes, exactly." God smiled.

If you have never happened to appear before the Throne of Judgment, you probably don't really know what it would be like.

I didn't. I only had hazy ideas of grandeur, but the grandeur all around me was far grander than I had dreamed. I had expected, oh, I don't know—awesome? Splendid? Frightening, even?

It wasn't frightening, but it was certainly all the other things. The immense throne was gold. I don't mean your tacky, everyday common gold. It was luminous, warm, even almost transparent gold; it wasn't drab metal but the essence of goldenness made real. The immense throne towered above me, surrounded by drapes of pearly marble that looked as though Phidias and Praxiteles had joined forces to carve them. The chair I sat in was warm carved ivory, and I was wearing a white penitential shift, staring straight up into the great and all-seeing eyes of the Almighty.

As I said, it wasn't frightening. I stood up and stretched. "Nice illusion," I complimented. "Tell me, God, which One are You? Jehovah? Allah? Thor? Whose God are You?"

"Yours, Robin," rolled the majestic voice.

I smiled up at Him. "But I don't actually have one, You see. I've always been an atheist. The idea of a personal god is a childish one, as was pointed out by my friend—and doubtless your friend, too—Albert Einstein."

"That does not matter, Robin. I'm enough of a god even for an atheist. You see, I judge. I have all the godly attributes. I am the Creator and the Redeemer. I am not merely good. I am the standard by which goodness is measured."

"You're judging me?"

"Isn't that what gods are for?"

For no real reason, I was beginning to feel tense. "Well, but—I mean, what am I supposed to do here? Should I confess my sins, examine every moment of my life?"

"Well, no, Robin," God said reasonably. "Actually, you've been confessing and examining for the last hundred years or so. There's no need to go through all that again."

"But what if I don't want to be judged?"

"That doesn't matter either, you see. I do it anyhow. This is my judgment."

He leaned forward, gazing down at me with those sorrowful, kind, majestic, loving eyes. I couldn't help it. I squirmed.

"I find that you, Robinette Broadhead," He said, "are stubborn, guilt-ridden, easily distracted, vain, incomplete, and often foolish, and I am well pleased in you. I wouldn't have you any other way. Against the Foe you may well fail disgracefully, because you often do. But I know that you will do what you always do."

"And—" I stammered "—and what's that?"

"Why, you will do the best you can, and what more can even I ask? So go forth, Robin, and with you goes My blessing." He raised His hands in a grand gesture of grace. Then His expression changed as He peered down at me. You cannot say that God is "annoyed," but at least He looked displeased. "*Now* what's the matter?" He demanded.

I said stubbornly, "I'm still discontented."

"Of course you are discontented," God thundered. "I made you discontented, because if you weren't discontented, why would you bother to try to become better?"

"Better than what?" I asked, trembling in spite of myself.

"Better than Me," cried God.

18
Journey's End

Even the loneliest river winds somewhen to the sea, and at last—at long last—at long, *long* last—Albert appeared on the deck of the cruise ship simulation where Essie and I were playing shuffleboard (missing even the easiest of shots, because the cliffs and the unexpected waterfalls from the glaciers and the ice floes in the water were so spectacular) and pulled his pipe out of his mouth to say: "One minute to arrival. I thought you'd like to know."

We did like to know. "Let's look at once!" Essie cried, and disappeared. I took a little longer, studying Albert. He was wearing a brass-buttoned blue blazer and a yachting cap, and he smiled at me.

313

"I still have a lot of questions, you know," I told him.

"And unfortunately I have not nearly that many answers, Robin," he said kindly. "That's good, though."

"What's good?"

"To have many questions. As long as you know there are questions, there is some hope of answering them." He nodded approval, in that way he has that would drive me right up the wall if it didn't make me feel so good. He paused for a moment to see if we were going to get into metaphysics again and then added, "Shall we join Mrs. Broadhead and the general and his lady and the others?"

"There's plenty of time!"

"There's no doubt of that, Robin. Indeed there is plenty of time." He smiled; and I shrugged permission, and the Alaskan fjord disappeared. We were back in the control cabin of the *True Love*. Albert's jaunty cap was gone, along with his natty blue blazer. His slicked-down hair was flying in all directions again, and he was back in his sweater and baggy pants, and we were alone.

"Where'd everybody go?" I demanded, and then answered for myself: "They couldn't wait? They're scanning through the ship's instruments? But there's nothing to see yet."

He shrugged amiable agreement, watching me as he puffed on his pipe.

Albert knows that I don't really like looking directly through the ship's skin sensors. The good old viewscreen over the controls is usually good enough for me. When you slide into the instrumentation of the *True Love* and look in all directions at once, it is a disorienting experience—especially for people who still cling to their meat-person habits, like me. So I don't do it often. What Albert says is that it's just one of my old meat-person hang-ups. That's true. I grew up as a meat person, and meat people can only see in one direction at a time, unless they're cross-eyed. Albert says I should get over it, but I usually don't want to.

This time I did, but not just yet. A minute is, after all, quite a long stretch in gigabit time . . . and there was still something I wanted to ask him.

Albert told me a story once.

The story was about one of his old meat-time buddies, a mathematician named Bertrand Russell, a lifelong atheist like Albert himself.

Of course, my Albert was not really *that* Albert, and so they weren't actual buddies, but Albert (my Albert) often talked as though they were. He said that once some religious person had cornered Russell at a party and said, "Professor Russell, don't you realize what a grave risk you are taking with your immortal soul? Suppose you have guessed wrong? What will you do if, when you die, you find there really is a God, and He really does call you to judgment? And when you arrive at the Throne of Judgment He looks down on you and asks, 'Bertrand Russell, why did you not believe in Me?' What will you say?"

According to Albert, Russell didn't turn a hair. He simply replied, "I would say, 'God, You should have given me better evidence.' "

So when I said to Albert, "Do you really think you've given me enough evidence?" he simply nodded, understanding the reference, and leaned down to scratch his ankle, and said, "I thought you'd come back to that, Robin. No. I haven't given you any evidence at all. The only evidence, one way or the other, is in the universe itself."

"Then you're not God?" I burst out, finally daring.

He said gravely, "I wondered when you were going to ask me that."

"And I wonder when you're going to answer!"

"Why, right now, Robin," he said patiently. "If you are asking if the display you interacted with came from the same datastores as the simulation I generally display, why, yes. In that limited sense. But if you are asking a larger question, that's harder. What's God? More specifically, what is your God, Robin?"

"No, no," I snarled. "I'm the one who's asking the questions here."

"Then I must try to answer for you, mustn't I? Very well." He pointed the pipestem at me. "I would take God, in your sense, to be a sort of vector sum of all the qualities you believe to be 'just' and 'moral' and 'loving.' And I suppose that among all sentient beings, humans and Heechee and machine intelligences and all, there is a sort of consensus of what these virtuous things are, and that a mutually shared 'God' would be a sum of all the vectors. Does that answer your question?''

"Not a bit!"

He smiled again, glancing at the viewscreen. All it showed was the usual pebbly gray nothing of a ship in faster-than-light travel. "I didn't think it would, Robin. It doesn't satisfy me, either, but then the universe is not necessarily in business to make us happy. Now."

I opened my mouth to ask him the next question, but it took me a moment to formulate it and by then he was ahead of me. "With your permission, Robin," he said. "We are really almost back into normal space now, and I am sure we would both like to look."

And he didn't wait for that permission. He was gone; but first he gave me one of those sweet, sad, compassionate smiles that, like so much else about my very dear friend Albert Einstein, drives me ape.

But of course he was right.

I showed him who was boss, though. I didn't follow right away. I took, oh, maybe eight or nine milliseconds to—well, to do what Essie would have called "be gloopy," but what I thought of as pondering what he had said.

There wasn't all that much to ponder. Or, more accurately, there was one hell of a huge lot to ponder, but not enough detail to make pondering on it satisfactory. Maddening old Albert! If he made up his mind to play God—even an admitted imitation God—he could at least have been *specific*. I mean, that was what the rules called for! When Jehovah spoke to Moses out of the burning bush, when the Angel Moroni handed over graven tablets—they *said* what they expected.

I had, I felt with aggravation, a *right* to specifics from my very own source of all wisdom.

But I obviously wasn't going to get any, so I sulkily followed . . . just about in time.

The pebbly gray nothing was splotching and curdling even as I slid into the ship's sensors, and in only another millisecond or two the splotches froze up into sharp detail.

I could feel Essie's hand steal into mine as we looked in all directions at once. The old vertigo hit me, but I put it behind me.

There was too much to see. More spectacular than the Alaskan fjords, more awe-inspiring than anything I had ever perceived.

We were well out beyond the good old Galaxy itself—not just the fried-egg galactic disk, with its pearly lump of yolk in the middle, but way out past even the tenuous halo. "Below" us was a thin scattering of halo stars, like sparse little bubbles popping out of the galactic wine. "Above" was black velvet that someone had spilled tiny, faint curls of luminous paint on. Very near to us were the bright lights of the Watch Wheel, and off to one side were the dozen sulfur-yellow blobs of the kugelblitz.

They didn't look dangerous. They just looked nasty, like some unattractive little mess left on a living-room floor that somebody should get busy and clean up.

I wished I knew how to do that.

Cried Essie triumphantly: "Look, dear Robin! No hooligan JAWS ships on Wheel! Have beat them here!"

And when I looked at the Wheel, it seemed she was right. The Wheel rolled silently in solitude, not a single ship in its dock, not a JAWS cruiser anywhere around it. But Albert sighed, "I'm afraid not, Mrs. Broadhead."

"What the hell are you talking about?" Cassata demanded. I couldn't see him—none of us were bothering with visual simulations—but I could feel him bristling.

"Only that we have not beat them here, General Cassata," said Albert. "We really could not, you know. The *True Love* is an admirable spacecraft, but it does not have the speed of a JAWS vessel. If they are not here, it is not that they have not yet arrived; it is that they have been here and left already."

"Left where?" I barked.

He was silent for a moment. Then the vista before us began to swell. Albert was readjusting the ship's sensors. The "below" grew shadowy. The "above"—the direction toward the kugelblitz itself—grew closer. "Tell me," said Albert thoughtfully, "have you ever formed a visual impression of what it might be like when the Foe came out? I don't mean a rational conjecture. I mean the sort of half-dozing fantasy a person might have, imagining that moment."

"Albert!"

He disregarded me. "I think," he said, "that somewhere in everybody lurks a kind of primitive notion that they might suddenly erupt from the kugelblitz in a fleet of immense, invulnerable space battleships, conquering everything before them. Irresistible. Rays blazing. Missiles pouring out—"

"Damn you, Albert!" I yelled.

He said somberly, "But Robin. See for yourself."

And as the magnification increased . . . we did.

19
The Last Spacefight

Even when you see for yourself, you don't always believe what you're seeing. I didn't. It was *insane*.

But it was there. The JAWS ships, in STL flight, hurtling toward the kugelblitz; and, from the kugelblitz, hurtling toward them, little bits of somethings that spurted out of the swirling, mustard-colored blurs. The little somethings were not blurred at all. They were bright metal.

They looked very much like spaceships.

There really could not be very much doubt of that. We were at extreme range for such tiny objects, but the *True Love* had first-rate instrumentation. What we saw we saw in optical and IR and X-ray and all the other photon frequencies there were, and we "saw" it as well through magnetometers and grav-detectors; and all confirmed unmistakably the terrible fact:

The kugelblitz had launched an armada.

I might have expected almost anything else, but not that. I mean, what use did the Foe have for *spaceships*? I could not answer that question, but ships they were. Big ones! Armored ones! A thousand and more of them, it looked like, and every one of them slipping into an immense cone formation and bearing directly down on the game, tiny, hopelessly outnumbered clutch of JAWS cruisers.

"Blow their goddamn rocks off," yelled General Julio Cassata, and, you know, I yelled along with him.

I couldn't help it. It was a fight, and I was rooting for my side. There was no doubt the fight had commenced. You can't see rays in space, not even the converted Heechee digger rays that were the JAWS fleet's main armament, but there were bright flashes of chemical explosions and worse, startlingly visible, as the JAWS ships launched their secondary missiles.

The myriad Foe vessels bored on. They were untouched.

Considered purely as spectacle, it was, my God, *tremendous*. Even though at the same time it was terrifying. Even if I didn't know exactly what was going on.

It was my very first space battle. For that matter, it was everybody else's first, too, because the last fight between ships in space had been between the Brazilians and the ships of the People's Republic of China, nearly a century before, in that last bloody and inconclusive struggle that led to the foundation of the multinational Gateway authority. So I was no expert on what should have happened next, but what did happen was a lot less than I could have expected. Ships should have exploded or something. Bits and pieces of wreckage should have flown all over.

There wasn't any of that.

What happened was that the cone of Foe ships opened up and surrounded the battling JAWS vessels. They englobed them; and then they . . . well . . . what they did, they *vanished*.

They just disappeared, leaving the JAWS cruisers huddled together in space.

And then the cruisers disappeared, too.

And then, just below us, the Watch Wheel itself flickered and was gone.

Space was empty around us. There was nothing to be seen except the pearly whirl of the Galaxy below, the distant external firefly galaxies, the smoky yellow blobs of the kugelblitz.

We became visible to each other; it was too lonesome otherwise. We looked at each other uncomprehendingly.

"I wondered if something like this might happen," said Albert Einstein, soberly sucking his pipe.

Cassata roared: "Damn you! If you know what's going on, tell us!"

Albert shrugged. "I think you'll see for yourself," he said, "because I imagine it will be our turn next."

And it was. We looked at each other, and then there was nothing else to see. Nothing outside the ship, I mean. Nothing but the pebbly gray of faster-than-light travel. It was like looking out of an airplane window into dense fog.

And then it wasn't.

Fog vanished. The ship's sensors could see clearly again.

And what we suddenly saw, without warning, was solid, familiar black space and stars . . . and even a planet and a moon . . . and, yes, I knew what they were. That planet and that moon were the ones human eyes (or nearly human eyes) had looked at for half a million years.

We were in orbit around the Earth; and so were a good many other artifacts I recognized as JAWS cruisers, and even the immense Watch Wheel itself.

It was more than I could handle.

I thought I knew what to do about that, though, because when things are too much for me there is always one thing I can do to get help. I did it. "Albert!" I cried.

But Albert just went on gazing out at the Earth and the Moon and the other objects outside the *True Love*, and smoking his pipe, and didn't answer.

20
Back Home

Albert Einstein was not the only appliance that seemed to have stopped functioning. The JAWS ships had problems of their own. Every control system for weaponry of any kind had been simply fried. They didn't work.

Everything else was fully operational. Communications were fine—and busy, with everyone asking everyone else just what the hell had happened. Nothing nondestructive was damaged. The lights on the Wheel still worked, and so did the airchangers. The workthings prepared meals and tidied up spills. The bunks in the commodore's cabin in the JAWS flagship continued to make themselves, and the trash receptacles emptied themselves into the recycling pools.

The *True Love*, which had never had any arms, was as good as new. We could have started it and flown right off to anywhere at all.

But where should we go?

We went nowhere. Alicia Lo took the controls and kept us in a safe orbit, but that was it. I didn't bother. I was focused one hundred percent on my faithful data-retrieval system and very dear friend. I said desperately, "Albert, *please*."

He took the pipe out of his mouth and looked at me absently. "Robin," he said, "I must ask you to be patient for a while."

"But Albert! I *beg* you! What's going to happen next?"

He gave me what is called an unfathomable look—at least, I certainly couldn't fathom it.

"Please! Are we in danger? Are the Foe going to come down and kill us all?"

He looked astonished. "Kill us? What an idea, Robin! After they met you and me and Mrs. Broadhead and Miss Lo and General Cassata? No, of course not, Robin, but I must excuse myself; I'm quite busy now."

And that was all he would say.

And after a while the shuttles began to come up from the launch loops, and we had our datastores taken back down to the good old Earth, and we tried—oh, for a *long* time we tried—to sort things out.

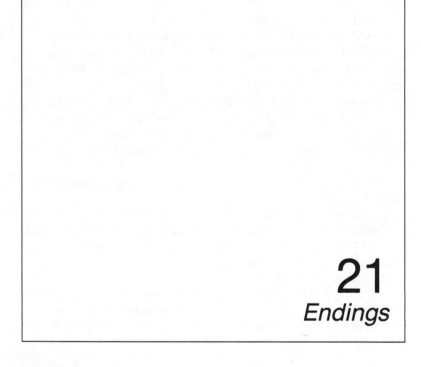

21
Endings

I didn't know how to begin this, and now I find I don't know how to end it, either.

You see, that was the ending. There's nothing else to tell except what happened.

I know that to linear meat ears that must sound odd (not to say revoltingly *cute*), just as so many of the other things I have said sounded odd (or worse). I can't help that. The odd cannot be expressed nonoddly, and I have to tell it like it is. What "happened" next didn't really matter, because what *happened* had done so already.

Of course, even vastened folks like myself are somewhat linear . . . and so it took us a while to find that out.

What Essie and I wanted more than anything else, we agreed, was breathing space—to rest up; to try to find out just what was going on; above all to collect our awry thoughts. We actually had our physical datastores taken to the old house on the Tappan Sea, the first time we had done that in a fairish number of years, and we settled down to get our heads straight.

Albert's datastore came with us.

Albert himself was another question. Albert no longer responded to my call. If Albert was still in the datastore, he did not show himself.

Essie was not about to admit defeat from one of her own programs. The first thing she did was to busy herself with program checks and debugging routines. Then Essie gave up.

"Can find nothing wrong with Albert Einstein program," she said, "except does not work." She looked angrily at the datafan that had held Albert Einstein. "Is only corpse!" she said fretfully. "Is body whence the life has died, you know?"

"What can we do?" I asked. It was a rhetorical question. I just was not used to having my machines fail me.

Essie shrugged. She offered a consolation prize: "Can write new Albert program for you," she said. I shook my head. I didn't want a new program. I wanted Albert. "Then," she said practically, "can rest and cultivate our gardens. How about nice swim and then scrumptious huge fattening lunch?"

"Who can eat? Essie, help me! I want to *know*," I complained. "I want to know what the hell he was talking about when he told us not to worry—what do you and Cassata and Alicia Lo have to do with it? What do the three of you have in common?"

She pursed her lips. Then she brightened. "How about ask them?"

"Ask them what?"

"Ask them all about selves. Invite them here—then can all have nice lunch!"

It didn't happen quite that fast.

In the first place, neither of them was physically (I mean, their datastores were physically) on Earth. Both were still in orbit. I didn't want to settle for doppels, because I didn't want even that infuriating quarter-second delay in the actual conversation, so they had to be shipped to the Tappan Sea, and that took a long time. It took longer than that, because for some reason Cassata couldn't get away at first.

I didn't waste the time.

Without Albert life was a little harder for me. That didn't make it really difficult because, after all, there was not much that Albert could do (other than answer the riddle that he himself proposed, I mean) that I couldn't do for myself if I had to. Now I had to. So it was I, not Albert, who roamed the world to see what was going on.

A lot was, though not much of it seemed helpful to me.

There had been a flurry of panic at first. JAWS issued alarming tight-lipped bulletins about the damage to its fleet, and then even more alarming urgent demands to build a new fleet, bigger and better than ever, on the principle that if you try something that doesn't work, you should keep on trying it forever.

But that in itself had a reassuringly normal sound. The populace at large, after that first shock of terror, realized that, after all, no one was dead. Foe spaceships did not appear in the skies over San Francisco and Beijing to blast them to cinders. Our planet was not hurled into the sun.

Nothing seemed to be happening at all, in fact, and slowly the panic trickled away. People went back to their lives, like any peasants on a volcano slope. The mountain had erupted; no one had been hurt. It would erupt again, to be sure—but not yet a while, pray God.

The Institute scheduled a hundred new workshops, pondering the events at the Watch Wheel. Half of them spent all their time analyzing and reanalyzing the "battle" between the Foe ships and JAWS. There was not much to analyze. What we had seen was what we knew. There wasn't anything else. There was nothing in any of the other sensory records to contradict, or even to embellish, what we had seen with our eyes. The Foe ships had come out and neutralized our cruisers; then the Foe had temperately picked us up and put us back in the playpen we belonged in. That was all.

The workshops on the Foe themselves argued and discussed, but added nothing new. Panels of eminent scientists agreed that what they had thought all along was probably what they should go on thinking: The Foe had been born shortly after the Big Bang. They had found the climate congenial. When the weather got worse—when matter intruded into their cosy soup of space and energy—they resolved to change it. They set the change in motion, then returned to their kugelblitzes to wait patiently for a nicer day.

As to the brief engagement around the Watch Wheel—well, if you woke a bear from hibernation, he would probably swat at you out of irritation. But then he would go back to hibernate; and the swat of this particular disturbed bear had been really quite gentle.

Oh, yes, there were plenty of speculations—God, were there *ever* speculations. Facts, no. There were not even any plausible theories, or at least none that offered any useful prospects for experiments to test them out or that suggested any worthwhile steps to be taken. Everyone (everyone outside of JAWS, anyway) agreed that JAWS's plan for building a huger and fiercer fleet was probably a silly idea, but, as no one had a better one, it looked as though that were likely to happen.

And, when Cassata and Alicia Lo were due to arrive, I went into the datastore files and put my hand (that is, my "hand") on Albert's store and said, "Please, Albert, as a personal favor to me, won't you tell me what's going on?"

Albert didn't answer.

But when I went into the drawing room to greet our guests there was a scrap of paper on my favorite chair. It said:

> Robin, I'm really sorry about all this, but I can't interrupt what I'm doing just now. You're doing the best you can, aren't you? Just carry on. With love, Albert

Julio Cassata was out of uniform again—shirt, shorts, sandals—and he looked positively pleased to see me. When I asked him about it, he said, "Oh, it's not *you*, Broadhead,"— he hadn't totally changed—"it's just that that bastard was finally getting around to terminating me. Which bastard? Me, naturally—the meat me. Doesn't like having copies of himself around. Would've done it long ago, but he was busy with the rebuilding program. Hated to let me come down here, because he was afraid you'd get the Institute to declare me essential or something."

I know a hint when I hear one, so I said, with some reservations, "Right, the Institute does." After all, the Institute could change its mind later on if it wanted to . . . but after I had said that, it did make him seem more human.

"Thanks," he said; and Essie said, "Let's go out on lanai, is beautiful," and I said, "What would you like to drink?" and, all in all, it was more like a little party than a workshop on just-what-the-hell-is-fundamentally-going-on.

Then I got down to it. "According to Albert Einstein, the reason the Foe aren't going to kill us is because they encountered the three of you, plus me and Albert Einstein. Not any other machine-stored person, just you three." Cassata and Lo looked surprised, then slightly flattered. "Any idea why?" I asked. Then they only looked blank.

Essie started out. "Have been thinking about this," she announced. "Question is, what do we three have in common? To begin with, are all machine-stored, but as Robin points out, so are umpteen zillion others not mentioned. Second thing. Am personally machine duplicate of still surving meat person. So is Julio."

"I'm not," said Alicia Lo.

"Yes," said Essie regretfully, "already know this. Checked first thing. Your meat body died of peritonitis eight years ago, so that's not it. Third thing. Are all quite bright by standard measurements; have all certain skills, pilotage, navigation, et cetera—but so here, too, have many many others. Have long since ruled out all obvious linkages, so must dig deeper. For instance. Am personally of Russian heritage."

"I'm American-Hispanic black," said Cassata, shaking his head, "and Alicia's Chinese; no good. And I'm male, but you two are female."

"Julio and I both used to play handball a lot," Alicia Lo offered, but it was Essie's turn to shake her head.

"Did not play such games in Leningrad. Don't think athletic prowess would be of interest to Foe, anyway."

I said, "The trouble is, we don't know what would interest them."

"You are as so often right, dear Robin," sighed Essie. "Hell. Wait. Can do this in less boring way, you know."

"I'm not in any real big hurry," said Cassata quickly, thinking of what he would be when he was no longer essential.

"Did not say faster, only less boring. You people? Have more drinks, maybe windsurf a little? I will run up quick cross-check program on all three stores, matching subroutines. Is easy enough and will not interfere with other activities." She grinned. "Might tickle a little," she added, and was gone to her programming office.

And left me to be the host.

That's a congenial enough occupation for me. I made them drinks. I offered them the facilities of the house for entertainment, which were considerable—including a private bedroom, which was what I had had at the back of my mind, but which they didn't seem to require just then. They were content just to sit and talk. It was pleasant to be there and do that, out on the lanai with the broad sea and the hills on the other shore in front of us, and that's what we did.

I verified the fact that Essie had once again made a shrewd character diagnosis. Doppel-Cassata was so much more tolerable than his meat original that I actually found myself listening with interest to his anecdotes and laughing at his jokes. Alicia Lo was a doll. I had not failed to notice that she was pretty, slim and small and quick, or that she had a naturally sweet personality. I discovered that she was very well informed, too. As one of the last of the Gateway prospectors, she had taken her chances on four hairy science missions, and after she was vastened she wandered all over the Galaxy. She had seen places I had explored only at second hand, and a few I hadn't even heard of. I was only beginning to have an idea of what she saw in Julio Cassata, but I could easily see why Cassata had fallen for her.

He was even beginning to be jealous. When she talked about

some of the shipmates she'd gone out with from Gateway, he paid particular attention to the talk about the men. "I bet you made a big hit with them," he said dourly.

Alicia laughed. "Didn't I wish!"

That surprised me. "Were they gays? Or maybe blind?"

She said, thanking me demurely for the implied compliment, "You don't know what I looked like then. Before my appendix burst I was tall and gawky and—well, what they called me was 'the Human Heechee.' What you see isn't what I was born with, Mr. Broadhead," she said, speaking to me, but looking at Cassata to see how he would take it.

He took it well. "You look grand," he said. "How come you died of appendicitis? No doctors around?"

"There was Full Medical around, and naturally they wanted to fix me up. They even wanted to do cosmetic work—take out some of the excess bone in the spine and the limbs, make some changes in the face—I didn't want it, Julio. I wanted to be really good-looking, not just the closest approximation they could manage. There was only one way. They had machine storage available. I took that."

And from the corner of the lanai, where it had been bending over to sniff at Essie's flowers, a figure rose up and beamed at us. "Now you know the reason," it said.

"Essie!" I yelled. "Come quick!" Because the figure was Albert Einstein.

"My God, Albert," I said, "where have you *been*?"

"Oh, Robin," he said pleasantly, "have we come to metaphysics again?"

"Not on purpose." I sank down in a chair, looking at him. He had not changed. The pipe was still unlit, the socks down around his ankles, the mop of hair flying in all directions.

And his manner was still oblique. He came sedately up to take a seat on the rocker facing us. "But, you see, Robin, there are metaphysical answers to that question. I was not any 'where.' And it is not merely 'I' who is here."

"I don't think I understand," I said. It wasn't entirely true. I just *hoped* I didn't understand.

He said patiently, "I have accessed the Foe, Robin. More accurately, they accessed me. More precisely still," he said apologetically, "the 'I' who is now speaking to you is not your data-retrieval program, Albert Einstein."

"Then who?" I demanded.

He smiled, and by the smile I knew that I had, after all, understood him very well.

22
And Not Endings

When I was a three-year-old child in Wyoming, I was not discouraged from believing in Santa Claus. My mother never said to me that Santa Claus was real, but she wouldn't tell me that he wasn't, either.

In all my long life since there has never been a question that I wanted answered more badly than I did that question then. I pondered it seriously, especially toward the last half of the month of December. I was *burning* to know. I could not wait to grow up—at least as far as, say, the teens—because when I was that old, I believed, I would be wise enough to know the answer to that question for sure.

When I was an adolescent sickie in the nut wards of the

hospital at the Food Mines, the doctors told me I would eventually get well. I would be able to deal with my fears and confusions. I would be self-confident, sure of myself—at least enough so, they promised, that I could hold a job, or anyway cross a street by myself. I couldn't wait for that, either.

When I was a shit-scared prospector on Gateway— When I was a horrified survivor of the mission to a black hole— When I was a sobbing mass of jelly on Sigfrid von Shrink's analysis couch— When I was all those things, I promised myself that, sooner or later, the time would come when I would be wiser and more sure. When I was thirty, I thought that might come at fifty. When I was fifty, I was positive it would happen by sixty-five or so. When I was seventy, I thought that, well, at least when I *died* there would be, anyway, some sort of final resolution of all the worries and uncertainties and doubts.

And then when I was older than I had ever thought possible (not to mention deader), with all the world's data available to me . . . why, I had the doubts and worries still.

Then Albert came back from the Foe, with all the knowledge they had given him, and offered to share it with me; and now what I want to know is how much older can I grow without feeling grown up at last? And how much more can I learn without being wise?

At least I know now why I have trouble with endings; it's because there isn't any end to endlessness. People like me don't have ends. We don't have to.

The Galaxy is our Wrinkle Rock, and the reunion party goes on forever. We have changes. We have interludes when we do something else for a while, maybe even a very long while. We have ends to conversations, but each end is a beginning of a new one, and the beginnings never stop, because that is what "eternity" means.

I can tell you about some of the ends (which were also beginnings), as, for example, Albert's conversation with Essie. "I apologize to you, Mrs. Broadhead," he said, "because I know it must have been upsetting for you to find a program of your own writing not responsive."

"Damn true," she said indignantly.

"But, you see, I'm no longer just your program. Part of me is now contributed by the others."

"Others?"

"What you've been calling the Foe," he explained. "What the Heechee called the Assassins. They are certainly not Assassins, or at least—"

"Oh?" Essie interrupted. "Can convince Sluggards of this? Not to mention any other races benign creatures who are not Assassins may have wiped out?"

"Mrs. Broadhead," he said gently, "what I was about to say was that they were not Assassins on *purpose*. The Sluggards were made of matter. It was not within the experience of we—of these *Others*, that is to say, to suspect that bound protons and electrons could possibly produce intelligence. Consider, please. Suppose your grandfather had discovered that one of his primitive computers was doing something that might, potentially, at some time in the future have interfered with his own plans. What would he have done?"

"Smash it up," Essie agreed. "Grandfather had one hellish short temper."

"He would not, I am sure—" Albert smiled "—have considered that a machine intelligence might have—what can I call it? Soul? At any rate, what we machine intelligences have. So—the others—'smashed them up,' as you put it. It was no problem for them; they observed that most matter creatures enjoyed destruction, so they simply encouraged them to do so to each other."

I put in, "Are you saying that the Assassins love us now?"

"That is not one of their terms," Albert said politely. "And, actually, you—myself included, I'm afraid—are rather rudimentary creatures by comparison. But when it was discovered, in a routine check, that there were machine-stored intelligences on the Watch Wheel, an investigation was ordered." He smiled again. "You passed the test. So they do not wish to be Foe to you, they only wish that no one do anything to interfere with their plan—and," he added seriously, "I do urge, Robin, that you do your best to see that no one does."

"You mean their plan to make the universe go back to where it started?"

"The plan to make a better one," Albert corrected.

"Ha," said Essie, shaking her head. "Better for *them*, you mean."

"I mean better for all of us." Albert smiled. "Because by the time the expansion stops and the fallback begins, we will all be like they are. We almost are already, you know—those of us who are machine-stored, at least. That's why they were able to communicate with me."

"Holy smoke," whispered my dear wife, Essie.

And I can tell you about his conversation with Julio Cassata:

"You know, of course," Albert said to him conversationally, "that weapons can never harm the others."

"The Foe! And that's what we're going to find out, Einstein!"

Albert puffed gravely on his pipe. He shook his head. "Don't you know why you must fail yet? Your very best hope is to find some way of destroying the kugelblitz that the Watch Wheel was set up to guard, just outside our own Galaxy. Tell me, General Cassata, do you have any reason at all to believe that our Galaxy is in any way special?"

"It's got us in it!" Cassata barked.

"Yes," Albert agreed, "it uniquely has us. But what makes you think it uniquely has the Foe? Do you suppose that our Galaxy is *special*?"

"Oh, Jesus, Albert," Cassata began, "if you're trying to tell me what I think you're trying to tell me—"

"That's exactly what I'm telling you, General Cassata. The others were not concerned about a single galaxy. It is the whole *universe* that they are planning to rebuild! A universe with hundreds of billions of galaxies, about almost all of which we know nothing at all."

"Yes, of course," he said desperately, "but we know they're here because we know they've intervened in this galaxy."

"That," said Albert somberly, "is how we can be certain

that they are not just here. You can't possibly believe that only our Galaxy is capable of evolving intelligent life. Any galaxy could! Perhaps even gas clouds in intergalactic space could! If the others were intent on keeping organic intelligence from interfering with their project, they would surely be wise enough to cover all the bases."

"So even if we could wipe the kugelblitz out—"

"You can't. But if you could," said Albert, "it would be like swatting one tsetse fly and thinking that encephalitis was wiped out forever."

He puffed smoke in silence for a while, looking at Julio Cassata. Then he smiled. "That's the bad news," he said. "The good news is that you're out of a job."

"Out of a—?"

"Unemployed, yes." Albert nodded. "There is of course no further need for the Joint Assassin Watch Service. Which implies that it can no longer give orders. Which implies that you need not return to be terminated. Which implies that you are quite at liberty to remain in your present state indefinitely, like the rest of us."

Cassata's eyes went wide. "Oh, *wow*," he said, looking at Alicia Lo.

And I can tell you about Albert's conversation with Alicia Lo:

"I'm sorry if I was cryptic, Ms. Lo," he began, "but when the others studied you on our flight to the Watch Wheel—"

"Dr. Einstein! I didn't know there were F— were others with us on that flight!"

He smiled. "Neither did I at the time, though of course I realize I should have presumed it. They were there. They're here now, in my program; they're anywhere they want to be, Ms. Lo, and I suppose they will be for the indefinite future, since we are very interesting to them. You more than the rest of us."

"Me? Why me?"

"Because you were a volunteer," Albert explained. "I had no choice; I was created as a computer program, and that's all I ever was. Robinette died. Machine storage was his only remaining option. Both General Cassata and Mrs. Broadhead were doppels of living persons—but you—why, you *chose* machine storage! You abandoned your material body deliberately.''

"Just because my material body was sick, and fairly ugly, and—''

"Because you perceived that machine storage was better,'' Albert said, nodding. "And the others found that quite reassuring, since it *is* better, and they have little doubt that long before the question becomes critical, all the rest of the human and Heechee races will follow your example.''

Alicia Lo looked at Julio Cassata. She said the same thing he had said: *"Wow!"*

And I can tell you about Albert's conversation with me— or at least about one last part of it. It was an ending that was also a beginning, because he had something for me. "I do regret that I couldn't attend to your questions when you wanted me to, Robin,'' he said, "but it wasn't possible while I was learning.''

I said forgivingly, "I suppose it took a long time to learn everything they know.''

"Everything! Oh, Robin, I learned next to *nothing*. Do you have any idea how old they are? And how much they've learned? No,'' he said, shaking his head, "I didn't learn the whole history of their race or how to go about causing a universe to fall back on itself. In fact, I didn't learn any of those practical things at all.''

"Hell,'' I said, "why not?''

"I didn't ask,'' he said simply.

I thought that over. I said, "Well, I suppose when the time is ripe, they'll have all sorts of things to tell us—''

"I doubt that very much,'' Albert said. "Why should they? Would you try to teach space navigation to a cat? Maybe some day, when everyone has progressed to the next stage of evolution—''

"You mean like you?''

"I mean like us, Robin," he said gently. "When all the humans and Heechee who are alive decide to be *more* alive, and *permanently* alive—as we are—then maybe there'll be a chance to carry on a real dialogue . . . But for the next few million years, I think they'll just leave us alone—if we leave them alone."

I shuddered. "That," I said, "I will certainly be happy to do."

"I'm glad," said Albert.

There was something about his voice that made me turn and look at him. It wasn't Albert's voice anymore. It was another voice, one that I had heard before. And it wasn't Albert speaking to me anymore.

It was Someone quite different. "After all," He added, smiling, "the others are My children, too."

So maybe I never will reach that wonderful time of wisdom and maturity when I know the answers to all the questions that continue to worry at me.

But maybe just to go on asking them is enough.

About the Author

Frederik Pohl has been everything one man can be in the world of science fiction: fan (a founder of the fabled Futurians), book and magazine editor, agent, and, above all, writer. As editor of *Galaxy* in the 1950s, he helped set the tone for a decade of sf—including his own memorable stories such as *The Space Merchants* (in collaboration with Cyril Kornbluth). *The Annals of the Heechee* is his latest novel. He has also written *The Way the Future Was*, a memoir of his first forty-five years in science fiction. Frederik Pohl was born in Brooklyn, New York, in 1919, and now lives in Palatine, Illinois.